BARN SONG

SONG SERIES
BOOK ONE

J.N. SMITH

To Sam, whose gentle nature has changed my life one bug at a time,
and to the barn that sang me this love song.

PROLOGUE

"W<small>AIT</small>!" M<small>AGGIE SHOUTED</small>. "S<small>TOP THE CAR</small>!"

Dean slammed on the brakes, and she threw her hands against the dashboard as the strap of the seat belt tightened across her chest.

"What the—" he grumbled.

Maggie cut him off, heart thumping at the sight of the beautiful old barn. "Pull over! There." She pointed. "I want to take a look."

Dean lifted his foot off the brake. They were on an empty dirt road in the middle of nowhere, but he signaled before pulling over. He was like that, always playing by the rules. Sometimes it bugged her, sometimes it didn't. Mostly it did.

"Jesus, Mags. What the hell? You scared the shit out of me," he complained, shifting the car into park. But she was already out the door with her sketchbook.

Despite her sunglasses, Maggie squinted in the bright July sun. Pushing her long auburn hair off her shoulders, she made her way through the ditch. It was full of wildflowers. Pausing, she picked daisies, purple clovers, and Queen Anne's Lace. There was something so beautiful and delicate about wildflowers. Although they'd been together for four months, and she'd told him a million times they were tacky, Dean still gave her roses for any occasion that warranted flora. *Red* ones.

"You're trespassing, you know!" he shouted from the car.

Maggie rolled her eyes and pulled on a stubborn stem of light purple chicory.

The place was abandoned. One look at the old orange brick

1

farmhouse and the nearly waist-high grass was enough to convince her that no one would be calling the police. She abandoned the chicory, and it slumped over sadly. Flipping to an empty page in her notebook and still holding the other flowers, she made a quick sketch of the house, then tucked her pencil behind her ear.

A cicada screamed at her from a gnarled oak that sat between the house and the barn. She looked past it, to the east and could just make out a sliver of Lake Huron pressed flat against the horizon. Most of that "thumb" area of the mitten that made up Michigan was flat, having been worn smooth by glaciers eons ago. But every once in a while, the land swelled and dipped. She knew about the topography, because although she was only nineteen, she was a junior in college and studying geology. This particular homestead sat up on the crest of a rise that sloped gently toward the lake, which was maybe three or four miles away.

Maggie shielded her eyes and looked beyond the patches of oaks, maples, and elms that lined the back of the house and barn, to the field of soybeans to the south. The nearest farm was more than a mile away.

Going back to her chicory, she wiggled the stem back and forth. It would not break. "Goddamn it," she grumbled. Dropping her bouquet and notebook, she grabbed the plant with both hands, dug her sneakers into the soft soil, and pulled. The chicory finally gave up its ghost and came up from the ground, roots and all, and Maggie fell on her butt.

Staring at the stem in her hand, she made an addition to her earlier thought. Wildflowers were delicate and *strong*. She smiled. Maybe that was why she liked them so much? Pressing the roots between her fingers, she rubbed the dirt from them. It was incredible how tightly nature gripped life. Almost a miracle, really. That was why she double majored in biology. Because she was just as fascinated by life as she was by the planet that had born it. If she was being honest, pretty much everything fascinated her. It was an exciting thing, being alive. And the best part? She had her whole future ahead of her.

Dean's laughter floated through the dry summer afternoon as she got to her feet, wiped her hands on the back of her jeans, and collected her bouquet and book. Ignoring him, she continued on up the shallow slope, across what was left of the driveway toward the barn, pausing beside a patch of thistles that had sprung up in the middle of the crumbly gravel.

It may have looked as most barns did in the Midwest, huge, plain, and topped with the familiar gambrel shaped lid, but it *felt* different. She'd sensed it the moment it came into view. It had pricked her skin and tugged at the hair on her arms, begging her to stop, to look. The sensation was even stronger now.

She tilted her head. Old, abandoned places often did that to her, and she wondered why. Was it the mystery of the lives that played out beneath their roofs that was so compelling? Or was it perhaps because, like mausoleums and grave markers, there was something about staring at the dead that made her feel *so* alive? Grabbing her pencil, she started another sketch.

Craning her neck, Maggie following the peak of the rusted tin roof to where it intersected a single lightning rod attached to its crest. A picture formed in her mind of a churning gray sky and a bolt of lightning pressing a fiery finger to it. It must have happened at least once. She glanced back toward the house. A large, deep covered porch faced the east and provided the perfect viewing point for storm watching. She imagined a woman, long ago, sitting on a chair smiling, peeling potatoes as the lightning struck and thunder rattled the windows.

Despite the heat, a small chill raced down Maggie's spine, and she shivered. Dragging her eyes back to the barn, she felt it again, the weird jolt, as if *she* was the rod, being struck by... something. Goosebumps spread across her arms, and she tapped them down.

A bumble bee buzzed and bumped into the leg of her jeans before landing on one of the fuzzy purple blossoms beside her. An odd sound like a sigh blew past her ears, as if the barn itself was quietly exhaling with her. She stared at it, unable to name the feeling it enticed.

If she were a believer in silly, romantic things, and maybe she was, she would have sworn it had whispered to her through the window of Dean's Acura, drawing her in, like the sirens of old, that tempted sailors with their songs.

Maggie rubbed her arms again and closed the gap between her and her bewitching prize.

From the road, the barn still held a red hue, but up close, the wood was rough, splintery, and gray. On the broad side facing the road, two large doors hung on gigantic rollers that looked like they hadn't moved in a century. There was a small rectangular opening off to the right toward the west end, at ground level, that looked like a missing tooth. Maggie could only imagine what kind of creatures had made their home inside.

Gently, she pressed her fingers to the frame of the small square window to the left of the massive doors. Specks of scarlet still clung to the wood in the deepest cracks of the weathered pine. Another small jolt bolted down her arm as she got on her tiptoes, pushed her sunglasses on top of her head, and pressed the side of her hand against the hot glass. Shading her wide hazel eyes from the blinding daylight, Maggie peered through the grimy pane.

All she could make out were points of light, tiny suns casting narrow horizontal beams that crisscrossed through the gritty darkness. It was beautiful, like spotlights on an empty stage. There were no actors. At least not anymore. But there had been. She could almost feel them there, lurking in the shadows. Another chill raced down her spine.

"Mags! Come on. I'm hungry, and I still have homework to do when we get home," Dean shouted from the car.

Maggie dropped back to her heels, having forgotten he was even there, and went to the giant doors. "I just want to take a quick…"

She yanked on the door, the wheels above her head screaming, as a seam of light cut the interior in half. "… look," she breathed.

A small voice somewhere inside told her she shouldn't go in there, but that was one of the nice things about being nineteen. It was easy to ignore those voices, *especially* when they sounded like her mom. Besides, doing questionable things was fun. It was exciting. Each time was an adventure into the unknown, and she was addicted to the thrill of fearlessly jumping into them.

Stepping into the musty coolness, her eyes slowly adjusted to the gloom. On the east side was a loft, a second floor, maybe for storing hay, and a square opening at the very top. But above her, and to the right, the ceiling soared overhead, arching over the darkness like a rusted rainbow.

Maggie took several steps along the path of light until she was fully inside. Everything else was in shadow.

Dean yelled at her again from the car, and she sighed. Just as she turned to go, a low, vibrating hum filled the barn, bringing her to a stop. Looking up, she listened as it changed octaves. It had to be the wind as it whistled through the hollowed-out knots in the pine, but it reminded her of the Om she practiced in yoga. It reverberated in her chest the same way. The tune itself, though, was more melodic, like the lullaby her mother used to sing to her when she was little. Maggie closed her eyes as it slowly filled her. Inspired, she sat down in the dirt, in the light, and crossed her legs, resting her flowers on one knee, and her notebook on the other.

"Mags!"

Ignoring him, she listened. As the wind outside blew, the vibration rushed through her body again, and she smiled. That was another nice thing about being nineteen. Ordinary moments were often infused with so much passion. Her mother said it was hormones, but her mom said weird things like that all the time, and Maggie didn't believe most of them.

The hum intensified as the sun warmed her closed eyelids through the open door.

She had read somewhere that some people think in images and others in words, but for her, it had always been both. Perhaps that was why she saw beauty in everything, because even if the scene or object was as forsaken as this place was, the words to describe it never were.

Squinting in the beam of sunlight that made the page almost glow, she jotted them down.

She set the notebook aside, picked up her bouquet and inhaled deeply. Lilies and musty earth. Yes, this place was—

Movement out of the corner of her eye caught her attention. There was something in the shadows, and it was... tall? Maggie's teenage brain finally registered the fear she should have felt all along, and she leaped to her feet.

A high-pitched chirp echoed off the walls and rattled the window beside the door. She jumped as a bird flew across it, dusting the glass with its wing.

"Shit," she breathed, rushing for the door as the rafters above erupted in chirps. A hundred tiny brown and blue barn sparrows exited through the narrow opening above her as she raced out the door. They hurled themselves skyward for a moment then took to the trees. Placing a hand over her heart to steady it, Maggie pulled the groaning door closed as Dean laughed at her from the car. Shaking her head with a smile, she turned back toward the driveway, glancing over her shoulder at the nervous birds. Poor things. She hadn't meant to startle them.

She made her way back down the ditch and up the other side to the car.

"I'm fucking starving," Dean complained, as she pulled the back side door open and grabbed her mom's old Nikon off the seat.

"Just one more second."

Pressing the bouquet between her thighs, she held the camera up and closed her left eye, allowing her right to see through the small rectangular opening. Maggie gazed at the top of the collapsing silo, noticing the way the Oriental Bittersweet, with its broad green leaves, seemed to crawl up the side of the decaying cylinder for a better view of the sapphire lake in the distance.

Her earlier musings returned. People always equated beauty with joy, perfection, completeness, but they were missing so much, she thought, because *really*, there was beauty in everything. And some of the most beautiful things were not cheerful and whole, but broken and lonely. She brought the barn into focus and snapped a handful of pictures.

"Mags."

"Fine. I'm coming," she sighed. Pulling her sunglasses over her eyes, she took one more sweeping look at the haunted scene, inhaling the earth, the sky, and all that surrounded it, then grabbed her flowers from between her legs and dumped her camera back on the seat.

Slamming the back door, she climbed into the front seat. Unscrewing the top to her bottle of water, she shoved the stems, and her chicory root in until they reached water and set the bottle in the cup holder between her and Dean. "Okay. I'm ready," she said, buckling her seatbelt.

Dean started the car. The tires spun on the gravel as he signaled *again* and made his way back onto the road.

Maggie turned as they drove past the old barn, and with her arm out the window, waved goodbye.

Dean cranked up the radio as she settled back into her seat.

CHAPTER ONE

MAGGIE'S VOICE WAVERED AS SHE TRIED DESPERATELY TO SUCK THE tears back into her eyeballs. "Call me once in a while. And if you go to parties, just please, please don't drink and—"

"Mom." Eric rolled his eyes.

She pulled him in for another hug, already missing the dirty socks he left on the bathroom floor and the empty bowls of cereal that seemed to continually litter the home they'd shared for the past eighteen years.

Maggie had promised herself she wouldn't cry, but who was she kidding? *What kind of mother doesn't cry when their baby heads off to college?* Her mom's voice asked inside her head. She'd been hearing it a lot lately, her mother's soft voice instead of her own demanding one, whispering inside her skull. It probably had to do with Eric leaving. Either way, it was nice.

He hugged her back, and she wondered when exactly her sweet little toothy boy had become this tall, handsome young man who shaved and smelled so... grown up. The transformation was as breathtaking as it was heartbreaking. And now he was leaving her to set out upon the world and forge his own path through it. A tear fell, and she swiped at it. She was both excited and terrified for him, knowing both sides of life's coin well.

"Tell your dad and Ann hi for me."

"I will." He tried to pull away, but she couldn't let go. "Mom."

The way he dragged out the 'o' and broke the word into two syllables *mo-om*, reminded her of a thousand days gone by, and

Maggie suddenly wanted them all back. Even the hard ones, like the day her mom dropped dead from a heart attack, or when she finally called it quits with Dean, knowing neither of them were happily married any longer. She wanted them all back, because through each of those struggles Eric had been within arm's reach, her joy, her anchor, there to hold, or at least peek at through the crack in his bedroom door as he slept soundly, and her world fell apart.

She sniffled, and he laughed, reminding her of a thousand more days, filled with first steps, baseball games, birthday parties, and trips to the water park. There was the time when she and Dean had taken him to Mackinac Island. He was seven. They'd rented a bicycle built for two while he insisted on riding his own bike. She had looked back to check on him, pulling her and Dean off balance. Dean had shouted a short string of obscenities, and the next thing she knew, they were sitting in water up to their waists, while Eric stood on the bike trail, staring at them wide-eyed, the beginning of a smile twitching at the corners of his mouth. Her phone had been ruined, but she had never heard a more beautiful sound than his laughter that day, as she and Dean splashed each other and dragged their mangled bike out of the lake.

"I'm literally going to be thirty minutes away," he argued.

She could tell from his tone he was trying to be patient. She could also tell he thought she was being ridiculous. Maybe she was.

Stepping back, she wiped her eyes. "I know. But you know," she shrugged. "I'm your mom."

"I know. And I love you. I also have to go. Are you going to be okay? Do I need to call Aunt Dee?" Tilting his head to his side, his blue eyes found hers. He looked so much like Dean when he did that. He pulled her in for another quick hug, and she pressed her cheek to his shoulder.

Once when he was five, he had wrapped his skinny little arms around her neck and said solemnly, 'Mom, I want to hug you forever. Even when we're old and dead. We'll be like two statues hugging each other *forever*.' Maggie huffed a laugh. Even now, it made her smile. Pushing back, she wiped her eyes.

"No. I'll survive."

"You sure?" Eric didn't look convinced.

Maggie looped her arm through his and led him down the walkway to his car. "I'll be fine. Really. This is the hardest part. After you're gone, I'll be fine." That was a lie, but if he called Dahlia, she'd never hear the end of it. Unlike her son, Maggie's best friend would have no qualms about telling her how completely ridiculous she was being. Dahlia would probably point out that Maggie's office was farther away than Eric's dorm was, and technically, they spent most of their time just as far apart as they would be now.

Eric gave her a quick peck on the cheek, then climbed into his car.

Maggie stepped back and hugged herself, trying her damnedest to smile as he backed down the driveway. She held her hand up and waved as he turned onto the street. He waved back, and his car disappeared behind the giant shrub that separated their yard from the next-door neighbors.

Then, for the first time in her life, at age thirty-eight and three months, Maggie Dubois was alone.

She stared out over the lawn, not quite knowing what to do with herself. Nothing had really changed, but somehow, everything had. Her entire life had evaporated in the time it took a Honda Civic to back down a driveway. And she most certainly was not okay.

Her mind peeled away from her body, as it did when her world fell apart, and empty, she turned and headed back into the house.

MAGGIE KICKED her shoes off at the door and closed it behind her. It was so quiet she could hear the ticking of the clock that hung over the table in the kitchen two rooms away. She turned and caught her reflection in the mirror that sat over the hall table and a bowl full of keys.

Her shoulder-length auburn hair hung in stylish waves, framing her bloodshot hazel eyes. She wiped at the black smudges beneath them and straightened her slumped shoulders, observing herself with a strange sort of detachment. She knew men found her attractive, even at her age, because she had been asked out by plenty of them since her divorce, single dads from Eric's school, clients, her landscaper even. And she'd accepted a few times. But as she sat across from their charming hopeful faces, she realized while they were hungry for companionship and looking for a fresh new start, all she wanted was to be left alone. She didn't want to begin again. She had Eric. He was enough. Until now. Her composure crumbled again, and she swiped at a tear.

She stared at her lips that had suddenly forgotten how to smile, her red nose, and sad, overflowing eyes. It reminded her of her mother's funeral. It had been such a shock. Her entire world had been turned upside-down, and for the first time in her life, she'd felt fear. And loss. It was a terrifying, lonely feeling, and instead of facing it, she'd thrown herself into motherhood, and clung to her marriage like the captain of a sinking ship, suddenly too afraid to even look in the water, much less jump in. The ever-dutiful wife, she had picked up Dean's dry cleaning, cooked his favorite meals, and did her best to make sure he never had a reason to leave her. She'd even opened her own business to supplement their income, so he could focus on his research at the university. She had given him everything except the one thing he wanted. Which was love. She *wanted* to be in love with him, she just *wasn't*. It had never been like that between them. Not for her, anyway.

The first night after Dean moved out had been like this too. But she still had Eric then. They had gone to the movies. As he ate his popcorn, she had sat beside him, no longer a wife, vowing to herself she would be the best mom the world had ever seen instead. And now, that was over too.

Maggie sighed. It was easy to keep up the facade of smiles and politeness when she was doing it for someone else. But doing it for *herself...* That was hard. Between her clients and social obligations, she spent eight to ten hours a *day* pretending to be someone she didn't even know. It was exhausting, and she was so tired of it. Meeting her eyes in the mirror again, she sighed, not recognizing the well-groomed, fairly composed woman staring back at her. But what choice did she have now? That was all that was left of her. Life went on, and there was nowhere to go but forward, empty or not.

Glancing into her office, she spied the stack of client folders waiting for her expertise. She had work to do. Instead, she turned to the pictures that hung on the wall. They lined the hall that led back to the kitchen and the table where Eric used to sit and do his homework while she cooked dinner.

The photos of Dean were right where they'd always been. Their wedding photo was there, and the old barn they'd passed on the first road trip they'd taken together in college. Below it was the 'premiere' picture of their little family when Eric was born. Her mother had taken it with tears in her eyes. Maggie had looked like shit after twelve hours of labor, but damn, she'd been happy.

Dee insisted it was weird to leave them, but Maggie disagreed. She didn't hate Dean, or the life they'd shared. For the most part, it had been amicable and fun. He'd just wanted more than she could give him. And she knew it was hurting him to stay. So, with the agreement that Eric would stay with her, she'd set him free to find 'more,' and he had.

Three months after the papers were signed, he was dating a woman named Ann. Six months later, they were engaged, and now, two years later, they had a baby girl named Sophia, who called her Aunt Maggie. They were friends now. Dean still taught at U of M and would only be three miles away from Eric if his son needed him. That brought her a great deal of comfort.

Maggie plopped on the bench that sat against the wall opposite the photos. How many times had she sat here and willed Eric to come home safely? From prom, or a party, or an out-of-town baseball game. How many times had she stared at these photos until wisps of memories swelled from them, smells, faces even, appeared out of nowhere and comforted her as she sat half asleep, waiting for the sound of his key in the lock? Maggie traced the familiar old barn with her eyes, the single lightning rod, the odd shadow in the small window beside the rolling doors. Then, they slid to the next photo, and she traced Eric's adorable first grade face, then his not-so-smiley fourth grade one.

A couple minutes later, her tour ended with his cocky, confident grin as her one-and-only son leaned against the tree out front in his letterman jacket, posing for his senior photo last spring. He had gone through many combinations of his parents before settling on Dean's eyes and profile, and her coloring and smile. He was a beautiful boy.

Maggie huffed. Kids were lucky they changed so much when they were little. It made it easy to accept their minds and opinions would change as they grew too. No one held an eleven-year-old to their word of wanting to be a ballerina or firefighter when they grew up. But with adults, it was different. Adults looked more or less the same for decades, and so people expected consistency. As soon as you hit twenty, the choices you made were expected to stick, to be permanent, lifelong, binding. How could a priest seriously ask you to promise to love and cherish till death do you part otherwise? Until death was a long time.

Maggie tucked her hair behind her ears and dropped her elbows onto her knees, staring at the scuffed bamboo floor.

And changing your mind about something like marriage, well it wasn't considered a simple mistake anymore, not like it would have been when you were a kid. Changing your mind equaled failure. It meant you were selfish and irresponsible. That was why twenty-year-old Maggie's life had ended before it had even begun. Because a poor decision had set her on a path she was too ashamed to admit had been a mistake, and she'd been too stupid and *proud* to say, 'I changed my mind,' when it still would have made a difference. Instead, she'd done the 'right' thing and stuck with it. She lifted her head. Now she was someone that girl wouldn't even recognize.

Just below and to the left of the barn picture hung her favorite photo of her and Eric. It had been taken at the lake maybe ten years ago. He was such a little boy then, big ears, big teeth, freckles, a goofy grin she could never seem to wipe off his face when someone had a camera around, while she had looked more or less the same as she did now. A few less wrinkles around her eyes, and smoother skin for sure, but otherwise, the same. That woman was who she'd become in lieu of the adventurer she'd planned to be. A doting mom, a business owner, a wife for a while. She had given one hundred percent to all of it while it lasted, and with the help of a strict schedule and a planner jam packed with baseball games, date nights, meetings, yoga classes, and vacations with her son circled in pink highlighter, she had done her best to take care of everything and everyone. *Everyone but yourself,* her mom's voice seemed to whisper in her head.

Maggie met her eyes in the glass. *Herself?* Who was that, exactly?

Tears filled her eyes again. The fact that she didn't know was as sad as it was terrifying. She pursed her lips, exhaling heavily. It had just all happened so fast. One minute, she was graduating high school, the next she was dropping out of college. One minute she was never getting married, then suddenly there she was, in a white dress, her dad walking her down the aisle. She smiled sadly at the photo through her tears. One minute she was at the beach with Eric with half his childhood still ahead of him, and in only the time it took to bend down and pick up a pretty piece of beach glass and stand back up, she was here. How had it gone by so quickly? And all that time being married to Dean, and when Eric was changing and growing into *him*self, who had *she* been? She knew *what* she was but not...

Her phone buzzed, and Maggie leaned forward pulling it out of her back pocket. It was Dahlia. She debated whether to answer. Not that she didn't love her friend, but she wasn't really in the mood—

The ringing stopped. A second later, she got a text.

Answer your fucking phone.

It immediately rang again as Maggie rolled her eyes and answered. "Hey."

"How'd it go?" Dahlia asked.

"How did what go?"

There was a pause and a sigh.

It took Maggie a moment. "Eric texted you."

"He did," Dahlia said slowly.

"It went fine. I'm fine." Getting up, she went into the kitchen.

"Are you sure?"

"Yes." Maggie pulled a coffee pod out of the drawer and popped it into the maker. Coffee made everything better.

Dahlia snorted. "Like hell you are. I'm picking you up at five, and I'm taking you out for dinner."

Maggie didn't feel like dinner or company. "No thanks. I'm just not feeling it tonight. How about a rain check?"

Dahlia didn't answer. Maggie pulled the phone away from her ear, and it was her turn to sigh. Her friend had already hung up.

Two hours later, Maggie was sitting at a small table across from Dahlia, whose full lips were pressed into a seam. An order of chips and salsa sat between them.

Her beautiful friend with a blonde-tipped Afro and flawless brown skin pointed a chip at her, as her meticulously sculpted brows came together over cider-colored eyes that bore into Maggie's. "Trust me. You need to get away. Even for a couple of days. Just get out of the fucking house. You get weird when you spend too much time alone."

Maggie sighed, sitting up straighter, wishing for the millionth time she had the elegant physique her best friend had. Dee was a lawyer, but she looked like a five-foot-ten ballerina, long arms, thin neck, graceful jaw, strong lean legs. Maggie was no slouch, but at five-foot-seven, she had a more average build, despite the tummy-tuck she'd gotten after she and Dean had split. Her breasts were bigger than Dee's, though, so she had at least that going for her, not that it had helped anything.

"Earth to Mags," Dahlia said, waving another chip in front of her nose. Or maybe it was the same one.

"What? Sorry. I was—"

"Yeah, I know where you were. In la-la land. You've been spending more and more time there lately. I don't like it."

"Sorry, I—"

Dahlia slapped the table, shaking Maggie's wine glass. "I know! Why don't you head up to Lakeside for the weekend? They opened a new hotel up there. It's right downtown. You'd be close enough to be on call if Eric needs you, but far enough from the house that you wouldn't be tempted to sneak back in the middle of the night and look through old baby albums and cry yourself to sleep."

Maggie rolled her eyes. "I wouldn't—"

Dahlia held her hand up. "*Don't*. Don't even *try* to lie to me. I'm a lawyer. I see right through that shit. And I've known you for thirty goddamn years. That's exactly what you'll do if you haven't already."

"Dee, I don't want to—"

"I already booked the room. It's for tomorrow and Saturday night."

Maggie choked on her glass of Chardonnay. "You what?"

"I booked a room. And it's nonrefundable. Two hundred bucks a night. You're going."

"What the hell, Dee? You didn't even ask me if I had plans or—"

Her friend shushed her again with a raised eyebrow and a stern look. It was the same face she made every time Maggie said something she thought was really stupid. She'd been making it a lot lately.

Maggie stared down into her glass and closed her mouth.

"You never have plans," Dahlia stated matter-of-factly. "Which is a shame because you're hot, and you're still young and—"

"What are we going to do in Lakeside for two days?" Maggie asked.

"You. Not me," Dahlia corrected. "Unlike you, I *do* have plans. And I don't know. Go shopping, take a walk on the beach. Sleep in."

"But—"

Dahlia placed a soft, manicured hand over hers and patted it. Their eyes met in the dim light of the restaurant. "You're lost, Mags. You have been for a while. And Eric leaving… I'm worried about it sending you over the edge."

Maggie rolled her eyes. "I'm fine."

"No, you're not. You need…" Dahlia's voice trailed off and tears unexpectedly filled Maggie's eyes. What did she need? Because she was desperate to know. Dahlia squeezed her hand. "You gotta find yourself, girl. As Gran would say, whoever you are, or want to be, you've got to go find her and let her fill you *now*, while you still have time to *be* her."

Gran was Dahlia's late grandmother, and Maggie had known her since she was seven. Gran had been graceful like Dahlia, but shorter, her soft brown eyes always smiling as if they had a funny secret they were dying to tell, and she *always* had a tin full of oatmeal chocolate chip cookies when the girls came to visit. Maggie felt like shaking her head, but refrained. You didn't shake your head at Gran, or her advice.

"You've got a lot of life ahead of you, and you can't go on like you've been," Dahlia said gently.

"How have I been?" Maggie asked, not sure she wanted to know.

"Pretending. Empty."

The server came with a tray and their food.

Maggie stared at the napkin in her lap, embarrassed by her tears. Dahlia was right. She'd come to the same conclusion earlier. But she hadn't realized it was obvious to anyone else.

"You've been a wonderful mother to Eric, and I know how much you love him, and love being a mom, but... You can't hide behind that role anymore, baby. You gotta find yourself. Find that crazy, happy-go-lucky girl I used to know, and set her free again."

The server left, and Maggie looked up. "What if she's not there to find, Dee? What if..." She shrugged. "What if there's no one there? Or what if there is, but you don't like her?"

Dahlia threw her head back and laughed. "Honey, I don't like you half the time right now, anyway." She leaned forward. "But I will *always* love you, no matter what. You can count on that."

Maggie picked up her fork. "I don't want to go on vacation."

Dahlia took a bite of her enchilada. "I don't fucking care. You're going."

CHAPTER TWO

MAGGIE CAUGHT GLIMPSES OF THE SPARKLING LAKE BETWEEN THE expensive houses that lined the coast as she made her way northward along M-25. She hadn't been up this way since college. For some reason, after she and Dean were married, they had always headed further north to explore the state. Skiing in Gaylord or camping up in St. Ignace.

As the road wove back and forth, following the outline of the coast, Maggie shook her head again, not quite believing she'd actually agreed to go. But Dee was like that, pushy but wise, like her Gran, and after her friend had splurged four-hundred bucks, how could she say no?

She looked down at the book she'd brought to occupy her afternoon at the beach. As soon as she checked in, she would change and head down to the public beach to soak up a few rays. Although...

Maggie leaned forward, frowning at the quickly graying sky. Rolling the window down a fraction, she stuck her fingers through the crack. The air was cool and humid, not a good sign for her lakeside plans. She rolled it back up and sighed. That was September in Michigan, though, sunny and eighty degrees one day, fifty and raining the next. Hopefully, the meteorologist was right, and it remained the former for just a little while longer.

On the floor of the passenger's seat was her overnight bag. She'd packed light, bringing only a swimsuit, sweatshirt, pajamas, and a toothbrush, figuring all she was going to do was sit at the beach and sleep. But now she had the sinking feeling she was going to have to come up with a Plan B.

FIFTEEN MINUTES LATER, she passed the sign that read *Entering the Village of Lakeside. Pop. 1,823.*

She was a little worried about finding the hotel, but sitting under the only stoplight in the entire town, she realized she could see literally every building it boasted from the intersection.

It was quaint, the way many were along the three thousand plus miles of Michigan coastline. For the most part, the buildings were old. Brick, two-stories, with apartments upstairs and souvenir shops below. They lined the aptly named Main Street that ran east-west and were dotted with old style lampposts, benches, and giant pots dripping with summer flowers. Where the road ended to the east, Maggie could just make out a sliver of blue water among the masts of sailboats that were moored in the harbor.

She immediately spotted the sign for the Lake House Hotel. It was attached to the building that took up the entire corner beside her. Kitty-corner was a modern-looking gas station. On the northwest corner was a gift shop, and the last corner held a small convenience store. The light turned green, and Maggie turned left twice, into the empty parking lot beside the hotel.

She hitched her overnight bag over her shoulder and followed the signs around the front across a broad covered porch that faced north and Main Street to the lobby.

As she pushed the door open, a long hallway and the smell of clean linens greeted her. To the left was a door that said Lounge, and a large window in the hall overlooked a nautical themed bar. To the right was a room with a giant fireplace and four tall stuffed chairs facing a coffee table in front of it. Like the rest of the town, it was quaint and charming. A woman with a blonde bob looked up

21

from behind an ornate wooden counter and smiled. Her name tag said Susan.

Maggie approached, admiring the dark custom trim that matched the furniture and mantle and the subtle nods to the hotel's lakeside location. A ship's wheel hung on the wall behind the receptionist. Above the mantle was a beautiful painting of a freighter on the lake at sunset.

"I have a reservation for two nights. Under Maggie Brad—" she paused. "Dubois. Maggie Dubois."

Every once in a while, Bradford still slipped out of her mouth, despite the fact that she'd changed her name back immediately after the divorce. She hadn't done it because she hated Dean's last name. It just seemed like the right thing to do. She wasn't keeping anything else of his. Why would she keep his name?

"Ah, yes. Congratulations. You are the first to arrive," Susan said, smiling.

Maggie frowned. Did she mean the first guest of the night? "Um, okay, thanks I guess."

Susan asked for her ID and a credit card. She signed a couple of papers and received the old-style key to her room. It was tied to a red velvet ribbon.

Maggie's brow went up.

"The key doesn't really work. It's got a chip in it, and you hold it up to the pad on the door," Susan explained.

Maggie turned to go, but Susan called. "Wait! You haven't picked up your packet yet."

She turned back around and set her bag at her feet. "Packet?"

Susan slid something across the counter. "Here's your name tag." She set a navy-blue folder beside it. The sticker on the front said, *End of Summer Singles Bash*.

The wheels in Maggie's head turned as she stared at her name on the glossy tag. It didn't take long for her to put two and Dahlia together. She groaned.

Susan's eyes widened. "Is there something wrong?"

Shaking her head, she sighed. *Damn it, Dee.* "No. It's fine."

Susan's smile returned. "Well, they have a tent set up in the park by the beach, if you want to head over there now while the weather is still good. There are snacks and music, I think. After, there's a mixer in the bar," she pointed to the hall, "just over there at five, light dinner at six, and karaoke until nine-thirty or so."

Maggie grabbed the folder and ground her teeth together. "Thanks," she managed, before storming out into the hallway.

She jerked the lobby door open and stepped back out onto the porch. Dropping her bags and the singles folder onto one of the white rocking chairs, she pulled her phone out of her purse and dialed Dahlia.

"Hey, baby. What's—"

"I can't believe you lied to me," Maggie hissed.

Instead of an apology, Dahlia laughed. "I didn't lie. I just didn't tell you."

"A singles weekend?" she cried.

Two women about her age glanced at her as they made their way inside, and she turned away.

"Have you lost your *mind*?" she asked, throwing her hand up and lowering her voice.

Dahlia laughed again. "It will do you good. Relax, get laid, just—"

"Get laid?" Maggie repeated. "Are you kidding me?" Placing an angry hand on her hip, she added, "They're doing *karaoke*. Did you know that? *Hu?*" Dahlia laughed as Maggie pressed the heel of her free hand into her forehead. "I hate you," she groaned.

Dahlia laughed again. "Worth it. Listen, I've got to go, but do me a favor, huh? Give it a chance. Try to enjoy yourself. Relax, be… I don't know. Wild, spontaneous. If you don't meet anyone you like, fine. You'll be home by Sunday, and everything will be as it's always been. But if you do… You got nothing to lose, girl. Not a damn thing. So, as Gran would say, get a little crazy, have a little fun."

"Gran would never say that, and you are definitely on my shit list," Maggie growled, pointing a finger at the empty space in front of her.

"Again, worth it."

Maggie massaged the bridge of her nose and the headache forming behind her eyes, as a rather good-looking man in his mid-thirties eyed her appreciatively on his way to the check in.

"Damn it, Dee." she said into the receiver, but as usual, Dahlia had already hung up.

Shoving her bags to the ground, she dropped into the rocking chair. Burying her head in her hands, she shook her head. "Damn it." What the hell was she going to do now? A hoard of hopeful singles was about to descend upon the entire town in one giant, sexually deprived, frustrated mob. Not that there was anything wrong with hopeful singles. She just wasn't one of them.

Staring at her feet, she sighed. Could the day possibly get any worse?

MORE and more people began to show up, and after being cornered by a chatty threesome of women her age for fifteen minutes, Maggie quickly grabbed her belongings and hurried upstairs to her room. It was on the third floor, and instead of facing east toward the lake, it looked out to the west, where the edge of town, only a block or so beyond the hotel, gave way to trees and the more open space of the countryside. She made out a saffron field in the distance, which was either goldenrod, ragweed, or soybeans drying in the sun.

Maggie dropped her things on the bed and sat down beside them studying the plain, but well-appointed room. Whoever the hotel had hired to do the rooms, they'd done a good job. She would know.

She may have studied science in school, but she had ended up a designer. It was a reoccurring theme in her life, starting out wanting one thing, ending up with something completely different. In the end, it had worked out though because it allowed her to be a stay-at-home mom for Eric, so she wasn't complaining. She did everything from interior design to branding, a sort of jack-of-all trades. The main thread that ran through her work, and the reason she was so successful, was her uncanny ability to find the beauty in *anything*. An old building, an antique wedding gown, radial tires. She took whatever her clients gave her, and she made it shine. At least, she used to. Lately, she'd been struggling. It wasn't really showing in her work, but the joy she'd once found in it had vanished. Her well, it seemed, had finally run dry.

A tinkling sound against her window brought her eyes up as fat drops of water smacked into the glass and slid down toward the sill, making beautiful patterns before they disappeared. The clouds, it appeared, had finally decided to rain.

Maggie threw herself back on the bed and closed her eyes. Maybe she could sleep for the next forty-eight hours.

There were definitely times over the past few years when she'd wished she could do just that. Disappear for a couple days and take a break from… everything. She'd never done it, of course, because of Eric, because she'd promised herself to always be there for him, but…

Her phone buzzed. Lifting her butt, she pulled it out of her pocket, smiling at the text that appeared on the screen.

Hey Mom. Just checking in. Everything here is good. My roommate is cool. Having dinner with Dad and Ann. Love you.

Apparently, her son was a mind reader. She rolled over and texted him back immediately.

Love you too. Have fun. Thanks for checking in.

Then she eyed the blue folder and opened it, scanning the handful of pages inside. She'd been right. They *were* taking over the town. There was nowhere to go that would be safe from unsolicited small-talk and potential one-night stands. *Get laid*, Dee had said so casually. But that was the last thing Maggie wanted to do. She had been very careful to keep it under wraps, because Dahlia would have a fit if she knew, but she hadn't actually slept with anyone since she split up with Dean. It wasn't because she was too shy or nervous. It was just because... Maggie sighed. It was because she didn't *want* to. She was capable of satisfying her own needs when they arose, which was almost never, and the rest of it, the touch of a man, compliments, romantic dinners. She just didn't care about any of those things anymore. If she was being honest, she didn't care about most things anymore. But that was a crisis for another day.

Sitting up, the yellow field caught her eye again through the drops sprinkled across the window. The rain had only lasted a moment, and the sun was already peeking out from behind the clouds. She got up and noticed the sign for the coffee shop across the street, and got an idea. Quickly, she grabbed her purse, phone, and her room key and hurried downstairs.

TWENTY MINUTES LATER, Maggie had a hot cup of coffee and was driving into the late afternoon sun. The field she'd seen was indeed goldenrod, beautiful and brilliant as it swayed in the light breeze. The earth climbed slowly away from the lake, and everything everywhere was covered in a fine mist. Steam rose from the road as she headed west down the highway. She passed a golf course, then an old farmhouse with a collapsing brown barn slumped behind it. If it hadn't been for the cars in the driveway, she might have stopped to photograph it. The splintered wood and gaping holes that hung over the bent frame reminded her of moth-eaten rags covering the bones of skeletons on Halloween.

She drove through one small farming community and another before the sun had fallen so low on the horizon that it hurt her eyes to see. Finishing the last sip of her cold coffee, she turned left onto a nondescript road and headed south a mile before turning left again down an unpaved country road that headed back east toward Lakeside.

The sun in the rearview was spectacular, and it set the whole countryside on fire. Fields of golden corn blazed by her window, pastures with cows, and a few fields already shorn and covered with bales of hay dotted the landscape. Rolling the window down, she sucked in the sweet, fresh, damp air. For the first time since Eric had pulled out of the drive, the knots in Maggie's stomach loosened.

She continued on, admiring the stands of birch and pine, the endless fields of crops, and the enormous clusters of metal silos that rose from the flat land like small cities. Every once in a while, the land swelled, and she caught a glimpse of the lake before it disappeared again beneath the horizon. The countryside was gorgeous.

Only a handful of miles away from town, she crossed over an old concrete bridge and a muddy creek that opened into a small pond that probably teemed with tadpoles in the spring.

She was watching a doe graze in the field to her left when the car bounced. It was followed by an ominous crack somewhere below her feet.

Clutching the steering wheel, she sat up and squinted in the rearview mirror as she released the gas. There was something on the road. Hopefully not a turtle. A rock maybe? It had sounded hard. Whatever it was, she'd hit it, but... She listened. Her car seemed to be making all its normal sounds. Maggie exhaled and relaxed against her seat. Still, she had better head back to the highway at the next intersection, just to be safe.

The sun had dipped even lower in the sky, and now, instead of being on fire, everything glowed, as if lit from within. The old barn just ahead looked almost holy as it stood beside a vine-covered house. Even the air—

Her car lurched, then rapidly began to decelerate. Maggie pressed the gas, but it wouldn't go down, as the steering wheel became almost impossible to turn. She managed to signal and wrestle the car to the side of the road before it came to a complete stop. Looking out over the long, lonely stretch of road in front of her, worry raced up her spine. "Shit."

Twisting the key, she turned the car off, then tried to restart it. The lights went on, but the engine refused to turn over. That was not good. Pressing her forehead to the steering wheel, she swore. "Damn it."

She was alone in the middle of nowhere. The blink of the gas light caught her eye, and where she'd had a half tank twenty minutes ago, the gauge now showed empty. Grabbing her phone, she checked to see if she had service and was thankful for the one bar it showed.

Turning off the car again, she got out.

"Damn it," she said again, raking her hands through her hair as she looked up and down the road. There wasn't a single vehicle in either direction. This was the last thing she needed. After checking the tires, which were fine, she bent down to inspect the underbelly of her car. The smell of gasoline was sharp. Slowly, she got to her feet, slapping the dirt from her knees as she leaned against the car. "Goddamn it!" she yelled at the field across the street. The deer she'd seen lifted its head and took off running in the opposite direction. She must have punctured the gas tank. She went around the passenger side of the car, crouched down and saw the dented tank. "Fuck!"

The tears came hard and fast. From where, and for what reason, she wasn't sure, but it was only seconds before they became an uncontrollable pressure behind her eyes. Maggie slumped against the muddy side of her car and slid onto the damp grass as great heaving sobs wracked her shoulders. Awful sounds poured from her mouth like vomit, and there was nothing she could do to keep them in, or stop them from wrenching themselves from her body as it shook.

She hugged her knees as the most horrible cries tore from her throat, scaring some nearby crows into flight. Even the crickets that had been singing only moments earlier in the tall grass fell silent.

What was wrong with her? It was only a car.

This isn't about the car, her mom's voice whispered. She wiped her eyes, and her breath stuttered as she inhaled. No, it wasn't. It was about... everything else.

Maggie stared across the grass-filled ditch, out into the swaying field of corn. She could see for a half mile down the long straight lines between the stalks.

That's what she thought her life would be like, when she imagined it growing up, an easy to follow, straightforward line. But when it actually happened, instead of staying on the straight path toward her goals, she had veered off, like most young people did. Then instead of finding her way back to where she wanted to be, she'd... given up, just let life have its way with her until she was... here.

Crossing her arms over her knees, she rested her forehead against them with a sigh. Lost, more in mind than body, really, sitting on her ass on the side of a road she didn't recognize, having no idea what she wanted or what to do with the rest of her life. God, she was a fucking—

"Look," a soft voice whispered, as something warm rushed across her cheek.

She gasped, and her head flew up, fully expecting to find someone standing in front of her. But no one was there. Touching her cheek, she scrambled to her feet. The road was empty too. She spun around, scanning the horizon. She was alone.

"What the..."

A light caught her eye, sparkling between the blades of grass in the ditch. The wind blew, and it flashed again. Wiping the tears away, she cautiously made her way toward it. As she stepped down into the ditch, she realized it was a spider web covered in droplets of water. In the late afternoon sun, it looked like a necklace made of orange pearls strung between the stalks of two milkweed plants. It was breathtaking.

Maggie wiped her eyes again, pulled out her phone, and took a photo. Then she saw another one, a few steps away.

Making her way over to it, she snapped another photo.

Then she saw them all, hundreds of webs hidden in the grass that lined the road.

"Oh my..." she exhaled, as a happy shiver raced down her spine. They were stunning. Each one was unique, and as fragile as spun glass. She was almost afraid to move for fear of destroying them as she picked her way through the waist-high weeds. Each web she came upon was more beautiful than the last, the patterns so perfectly imperfect it was mesmerizing. One web had been broken, its connection on one side severed. Draped loosely between two hearty stalks of grass, the broken threads dangled from it like a crystal chandelier over the archway into a castle. Maggie smiled.

How could that be? That the most broken was the most beautiful? Did that make sense?

She touched one of the threads, and a drop of water clung to her fingertip. *It did once,* her mother's voice said.

Yes, she almost remembered that feeling. *Almost.* Bending down, she spotted the spider, waiting patiently for its web to dry so it could rebuild. She took another photo. Like Dahlia's Gran, and her own mother, it seemed full of quiet wisdom.

Maggie stood up and stretched her aching back, as the wildflowers twinkled like Christmas lights in the breeze. The webs were everywhere. There were even some between the stalks of corn. Besides Eric, on the day he was born, they were possibly the most beautiful things she had ever seen, and they soothed her aching heart with their precious, lopsided beauty.

Maggie's skin prickled, and she rubbed her arms.

Glancing around, then down, she smiled at her wet jeans and sneakers. How long had it been since she'd done anything like this? Years? Decades?

She pocketed her phone and made her way back to her car, laughing at the sight of it alone against the backdrop of the endless field that lay across the street. She hadn't been exaggerating. If there was a middle of nowhere, this was it. She laughed again. It was kind of romantic that she should find herself in the same metaphorical and physical space at the same time. If she were her younger self, she might have even composed a shitty poem about it. Shaking her head, she wondered at the memories the countryside was stirring. God, she hadn't written in *years*. Those days were long gone, though. She was no longer a poet, shitty or otherwise.

Maggie took a couple of deep, calming breaths. Despite her earlier outburst, or maybe because of it, she felt better than she had in months, probably since Eric's senior year ended and the countdown to his departure had begun.

Pulling open the passenger's side door, she fished her wallet out of her purse.

"Thank god for AAA," she mumbled, pulling the card from her wallet.

The dispatcher answered almost immediately and asked for her location. Maggie squinted at the endless fields as she rested her elbows on the roof of her car. "I don't know where I am." It felt good to make that confession, even though it was lost on the woman on the other end of the line.

"Use the location tracker on your phone," the woman suggested.

Maggie felt like an idiot. "Of course." She opened her map and zoomed in on her location. "I'm on Morgan Line, between, um, Wilcox Road and North Road."

The woman thanked her and said someone would be out within the hour.

Maggie leaned against her car for a few more minutes before deciding to take a walk. She'd see the tow truck coming a mile away and would hurry back when it came. Grabbing her keys and phone, she locked her purse inside and started walking.

The gravel was wet, and there were tiny pools of water in the ruts that ran up and down the length of the road. Her sneakers ground against the stones at her feet as she made her way toward the homestead just up ahead. The wind picked up, pushing against her back, before rushing past her toward the lake. It whispered to her, urging her on.

Goosebumps sprang up across her arms as she pushed her hair back behind her ears and stopped in front of the house. It was an old two story with a steep pointed roof. It was so overgrown with vines she couldn't even see what color it was. The angled sun reflected off the glass that peeked out from between the wide leaves that covered the front of it. Somewhere under there were windows, Maggie thought.

As she walked farther, a porch came into view on the northeast corner of the house. The sunset bathed the part facing north while shadows darkened the east side. Maggie could see the lake from where she stood. The sunrises from that porch would be... Her thoughts were interrupted by movement in a darkened corner by the front door, but as her eyes adjusted, there was only empty space. It must have been her imagination. She rubbed her arms again as a white sign buried in knee-high grass caught her eye.

LakeView Realty, it read.

There was a phone number, and dangling beneath it by one severely frayed zip-tie was a plastic plaque that said Rebecca Santos.

The property was for sale, and from the look of it, had been for quite some time.

Maggie took several more steps, then glanced up at the house from the side. She could see it now, it was orange-red brick. Above the front porch was a little gable with a window. Again, she thought she saw something move behind it, but realized a moment later, it must have just been the reflection of the clouds in the glass.

Maggie chewed her lip, frowning. There was something familiar about the house. Or maybe not. After all, didn't most old farmhouses look like that?

She continued down the road toward the driveway and the giant oak that stood beside it.

Most of the summer flowers had dried up and died, but some of the more stubborn ones, the Queen Anne's lace and milkweed, still hung on, the latter releasing cotton fuzz into the sky every time the wind blew over it. She picked a few stems as she shooed the bees away.

The barn was aglow, as everything else was, a tangerine canvas streaked with woody brushstrokes. Her skin pricked again, and Maggie had the distinct feeling she was being watched. But not by a stranger. It was sweeter, gentler, like an old friend. The feeling tugged at her like a warm breeze.

It wasn't until she saw the hole, the missing tooth, that she recognized the barn.

She gasped. "No way…"

Could it be? She looked back toward the house, past the decay and the twenty years of weathering.

Chills raced down her spine. "Oh my god." This was the place.

Turning back to the barn, she traced the familiar lines of the doors and window. Yes. This was it, the very same barn she and Dean had stopped at all those years ago! Maggie looked down at the flowers in her hand, and was enveloped in a weird sense of déjà vu.

Shivering, she picked her way through the grass, climbed over the rusty chain and across the wide, overgrown gravel driveway that had once separated the house and barn, and headed toward the front steps of the house.

The place was overgrown, but upon closer inspection, it had actually held up pretty well. A board attached to the eave of the porch had come loose and hung at an odd angle, giving the place a dilapidated feel, but the structure itself was actually quite sturdy, she noted as she climbed the stairs. The banister was surprisingly solid under her hand.

Maggie peeked in the window beside the door and was surprised to find the house wasn't empty. There was an old tweed chair beside the fireplace and a bookshelf on the opposite wall filled with books. A lamp sat on the dusty wood floor and was plugged into an outlet beside the fireplace. An old rug, chipped veneer end table, and a pile of old papers rounded out the contents of the room.

She turned back to the barn, and for the first time, noticed the structure behind it. It was some sort of long roof over two narrow rows of fencing. The whole thing was covered in vines.

An old, red tractor sat amid the tall grass beside it, its mottled paint blending in with the dead flowers that surrounded it. Bathed in the sunset, it reminded her of a lion silently stalking its prey on the savannah. She smiled. Maybe that was what she had felt watching her.

A sound on the road brought her head around, and Maggie turned just in time to see the tow truck pass the house.

"Shit," she breathed, looking at her watch. She'd lost track of time.

Quickly, she ran down the stairs and back onto the road, waving at the man as he turned his truck around and hopped out.

Hopefully, she hadn't pierced the gas tank as she suspected, and her car could be fixed tomorrow. Maggie crossed her fingers as she jogged toward him.

AN HOUR LATER, Maggie was sitting smack dab in the middle of the dark stained oak bar. With her head hung over her glass of Pinot Noir, she tried desperately not to make eye contact with anyone that may or may not want to talk to her. She was sandwiched between a striking dark-haired woman with several 'suitors' that kept bumping her chair, and the chatty threesome she had met earlier on the porch who were not having as much luck, but seemed thankfully not to notice.

Why she was there, and not up in her room, was a bit of a

mystery. Maggie swirled her wine. If she had to guess, she would say it was because there was no alcohol upstairs. Sighing, she drained the glass. And after the news she had just received, wine was in order.

Her car was as she feared. The tow truck driver had dropped it off at the mechanic, which was two blocks away, and he'd confirmed her suspicion. Punctured gas tank. Then, he flipped the open sign in the window to closed, pushed her out the door, and told her he'd get started on it first thing Monday morning.

Monday. Fuck. Maggie dropped her head into her hands and groaned. She had things to do on Monday. She had—

Looking up, she met the eyes of the only person in the room she was even remotely interested in talking to, and pointed to her glass. The bartender, a pretty twenty-something girl with long curly blond hair, nodded and smiled.

Maggie quickly scanned the room, then went back to gazing into her glass, studying the crimson drops at the bottom as if they were tea leaves. What lay ahead for her? She wondered. But the drops revealed nothing but wine. She huffed a bitter laugh, remembering her earlier outburst on the side of the road. Maybe this *was* her future. Hiding, and copious amounts of mediocre wine. She ran her hands through her hair. It was a dire thought.

While Dahlia had been a complete ass to send her here for the weekend, she was right about one thing. The little roadside meltdown that afternoon proved it. Maggie found at her reflection in the window behind the bottles of booze that lined the back of the bar. She *was* lost. So lost, she didn't know where to begin to look for the woman she was supposed to be. Or what kind of woman she even *wanted* to be.

Her brows came together as she stared. She didn't want to do what she did at twenty anymore, but… She sighed. She longed to *feel* the way she did before her life had taken an unexpected left turn and she'd thrown herself into who she *thought* she should be. Dahlia was right about another thing. Without Eric, her identity was lost. If she didn't become someone else fast, she'd disappear. The problem was, she didn't want to see the Taj Mahal, or become a yoga instructor, or go back to school, or fall in fucking love. She just wanted...

Maggie waited, hoping the sentence would finish itself, but it didn't. The bartender swapped her empty glass for a *very* full one, and Maggie looked up in surprise.

The girl shrugged. "Don't take this the wrong way, but you look like you could use it."

Maggie laughed and thanked her, as the girl was called away.

Before she could disappear back into her thoughts, a very handsome man in his late-forties, early fifties expertly slid between her and the woman beside her.

"Are you from around here?" he asked, as he raised his hand and signaled the bartender.

To her horror, Maggie burst out laughing at the overused line. "I'm so sorry," she apologized in embarrassment. "Ah, no, I'm from down in the city, Birmingham."

Instead of being offended, he just shrugged and smiled. "No apology needed. That's a terrible line. Very sadly, it's also my best."

Maggie raised her brow, surprised by his frankness.

"This whole thing is turning out to be a nightmare," he admitted.

She nodded. "I couldn't agree more."

The man continued. "I'm so nervous... even *I* can't believe half the shit that is coming out of my mouth."

Maggie couldn't tell if it was a better crafted follow-up line or not, but it made her chuckle again.

The bartender came, and he ordered a Manhattan.

Maggie didn't want to get trapped in a conversation, so she pulled out her phone, texted Dahlia, and tried to look busy.

A moment later, the bartender reappeared and set his drink on the bar top. "Well, good luck tonight," the man said, raising his glass as he turned to go.

"I don't want to get lucky," she surprised herself by saying. "I just want…" Again, the answer wouldn't come. Something like empathy flashed through the man's eyes as he waited. "I don't know what I want," she confessed, shaking her head.

He leaned in conspiratorially. "I don't, either, but my advice? When you find it, don't hesitate. Grab on with both hands and never let it go." He stepped back, raised his glass again, and turned back to the crowd.

Maggie stared at his back as he walked away. The pain in his eyes had been obvious, and she realized how unfair she was being to the singles around her. These were people, just like she was, and while she wasn't interested in finding love, they were, and they were putting themselves out there, trying. All she was doing was wallowing in self-pity and alcohol. Shame on her for rolling eyes and ignoring their attempts at conversation. Especially since she was sitting in the middle of the damn bar. She might have no interest in getting 'laid,' but she didn't have to be a bitch about it. Imitating Dahlia's posture, Maggie sat up straight and tucked her hair behind her ears. "Best foot forward," she whispered before taking a healthy sip of wine.

She was kinder to the next man that came up to chat with her, and the next one after that. She declined to exchange numbers, but they didn't seem too hurt, especially after she lied and said she was there on business and not for the weekend.

She chatted with the ladies beside her for a while too. They were nice. Finishing her wine, and feeling pretty good about herself, she ordered *one* more glass. After all, she was single, and on vacation, and she had nowhere to be in the morning.

MAGGIE BLINKED. The ladies were gone. The crowd had thinned too, and—her eyes widened in surprise—she was talking to a man with a Magnum P.I. mustache covered in beer foam? That couldn't be good.

Swinging her head around, she gripped the bar rail. Where had everyone gone? A vague memory of the woman who was seated at the end of the bar, singing a truly terrifying rendition of Barry Manilow's "Copacabana," flashed in her head.

"You know what I mean?" Magnum asked with a laugh, as she turned back.

Maggie couldn't remember his name, if he'd even told her, and she had no idea what he was talking about.

Her fingers found the bridge of her nose and pinched it. Damn it. She was drunk.

She lifted her hand toward the bartender, who now looked like two bartenders overlapping in the middle. "Water?" she croaked. The girl nodded.

Magnum continued on, apparently unbothered by her silence, and Maggie's mind wandered again. She looked down at her hand. There was a red spot on her palm, and it hurt when she pressed on it. She must have gotten a splinter from the railing of the old house.

She smiled, still amazed by the strange coincidence. The picture of that very barn had been hanging in her hall for almost twenty years. She couldn't believe she'd found it again after all that time. The chances of that were... astronomical.

Magnum laughed again at his own joke.

She smiled and was about to say something that hopefully made her sound like she'd been paying attention when the conversation behind her grabbed her ear. She turned.

"I'm sorry, did you just say your name was Rebecca Santos?"

The older blond woman turned away from the very drunk man who was trying not to fall off his bar stool and smiled. "Yes, I am."

"The real estate agent?"

The woman laughed. "The one and only."

It could have been the gallon of wine she'd consumed, or the fact that she was just really desperate to get away from Magnum and his beer breath, but something told Maggie it was neither, and that *fate* that had brought this woman to her. She closed one eye and stared at her glass that was suddenly full again. Or maybe it was the wine… She shrugged. *Oh well, either way.*

She looked down, rubbed the splinter in her palm, and found the answer to the question she'd been asking herself all night. It had been right there, literally *in* her hand the whole time. Laughing, she hiccupped, then covered her mouth in embarrassment.

"Do I know you?" Ms. Santos asked, but Maggie wasn't listening.

The house. The barn. *That* was what she wanted.

Sure, it was falling apart, but so was she. So that was perfect. And yes, it looked lonely and empty and abandoned, but that was exactly the way she felt, and there wasn't a person in the world who could bear that part of her the way she was sure that land could. They would fix each other. It was a brilliant idea. The best idea she'd had in at least a decade.

"Are you okay?"

That was where Maggie would find herself again. Among the wildflowers and lightning storms. *It was always meant to be yours,* that weird inner voice that sounded like her mom said, and in her wine-soaked heart of hearts, she knew it was true.

She grinned and pushed aside her fourth, or was it fifth, glass of wine. The clouds in her head parted, and she found herself staring up at the brilliantly clear sky of possibility.

"I'd like to make an offer on one of your properties," she heard herself say.

Ms. Santos cast her a beaming smile as she dragged Maggie off her stool and away from the bar. "Come, let's sit over here where it's a little quieter."

Maggie followed her, leaning on the backs of the stools—she smiled at Mr. Manhattan as she passed his seat—then the wall for support, as they made their way out of the lounge and into the lobby.

"Which house are you interested in?" Ms. Santos asked with a cheerfully tipsy slur.

Maggie sat down, and for the first time in years, real excitement coursed through her veins. Her grin widened. "There's an old farmhouse and barn a couple miles out of town—"

Ms. Santos's smile faded, and her eyes widened. "The old Morgan homestead?"

'Homestead' made it sound like it had been built by the pioneers. It wasn't *that* old. "It's on Morgan Road. So, maybe. Do you happen to know offhand how much they are asking for it?"

"It's Morgan Line, and yes. It's bank owned, and they are asking fifty thousand for it. That includes the buildings and five acres on either side of the house and a ten-acre parcel—"

"Fifty thousand *dollars*?" Maggie interrupted.

"Yeah…"

"Are you serious?" It was too good to be true. Had she heard her wrong? Her car cost more than that!

"I'm sure you could get it for forty. It's been on the market for years. Hell, at this point, they might even just *give* it to you for what they owe in taxes."

Maggie's jaw dropped as she stared at Ms. Santos. Forty thousand dollars? That was it? And it would be hers? The tractor and everything?

Another grin plastered itself on Maggie's face, replacing her shock, and her brief conversation with Mr. Manhattan resurfaced. Maybe she was wrong. Maybe she would get lucky tonight after all.

CHAPTER THREE

WILL CAREFULLY SET THE LAST PAGE IN ITS HIDING PLACE. USING all his strength, he dropped the board back into its spot, then collapsed onto the steps. He sat silently as the light made its way in through the side windows of the house, illuminating the bookshelf, then slowly drawing itself over his chair and the living room that had once held a lot more furniture than it did now.

When his energy returned, he got up, went to the window beside the front door, and looked out. It overlooked the porch, the barn and silo, the east field, and the lake.

Will's six-foot-one frame flickered in and out of focus, casting human-shaped shadows on the floor behind him.

He could just make out the flecks of gold as the sun skipped off the waves like a stone, then raced across the countryside to flood his windows and blind him.

Will focused on his reflection in the glass. It was the same one that had stared back at him for the past seventy years, but somehow, it still managed to surprise him every now and then. Most often, he looked like his father, same strong but narrow jaw, same shock of brown hair, same cowlick that always parted his hair to the right, making it look styled even though it never was. He had his father's physique too, a lean body and wide shoulders. But there were times, like now, when his face and thoughts were softer, that he saw his mother. Her happy, brown eyes that crinkled at the corners. Her smile that always said she knew more than she was letting on.

It was the smile, maybe, that was surprising him now. Will

41

couldn't remember the last time he'd seen himself smile. It had been a while. Not that he'd *never* done it before, because of course he had. He'd smiled once or twice when he was alive. Maybe.

But after he'd died... The smiles had definitely been harder to come by. For the first few decades he was stranded in the 'in-between,' every time he glimpsed his reflection, which he tried to avoid at all costs, his lips had been drawn in a thin, angry line, and the eyes, staring back at him, had glowed with madness, and frightened him.

Will pressed his fingers to the glass as a fuzzy bumblebee, *Bombus terricola,* tapped on the other side.

Until *she* came.

After that, everything changed. He'd been reborn into someone new, and everything that had been in front of him from the very start finally came into focus.

The flock of *Hirundo rustica* exited the barn right on schedule and took to the sky as one, to explore the fields and find breakfast. Will had never even noticed the barn swallows when he was alive, and now, watching them was the highlight of his day.

His conversion reminded him of an illusion he'd seen once in a newspaper. On the front page, they had printed a picture of an old woman that was also a young woman depending on how you looked at it.

Will had spent his life seeing the old woman. He'd spent half of his death thinking she was a witch. Then, one day, out of the blue, the old crone had been split in half by a beautiful girl with wide, curious eyes. She emerged from the shadows on a beam of light like an angel, and he'd been unable to do anything but stare in wonder. She'd only stayed a moment, but she left him a gift, more precious than any he had received in life. *Wonder.* She reminded him there was beauty in all things and then she taught him how to see it. Now, when Will thought about that picture, he didn't see an old woman or a young one. All he saw was *her*.

Will passed through the door and down the steps. Going around the front of the house, he noted the towering pine that had only been up to his chest when he was killed. He crossed the tall grass and stepped out into the field, moving easily through the rows of corn until he reached the place where he'd found her.

"Mags," he said aloud, as the insects in the brush quieted.

He'd known it as soon as he saw her hair—the color of dried staghorn sumac flowers in late fall, and the swipe of her hand as she pushed her sunglasses on top of her head—she had returned.

By the time his shock had worn off and he'd made his way over to her, she'd been slumped in the grass crying.

For a brief moment, he had doubted her identity, not because she was older, but because, in his mind, she was always happy and smiling. Not once in the intervening years had he imagined tears in her eyes. Watching them run down her freckled cheeks was almost as shocking as seeing *her* there, sitting on the side of the road.

Will rubbed his eyes.

The image of Mags standing in the middle of the barn always reminded him of an angel, or since he'd never been a faithful Christian, perhaps more of a fairy, like she'd been rustled up from the grass, along with the insects, by a hare as it hopped quietly along. Half goddess shedding wisdom into dark places, half curious girl. She had been so youthful and bright, like his sisters when they were young.

The sun climbed the sky as the world turned, and Will shielded his eyes.

Over the years, her memory had become a friend, a cheerful companion that accompanied him as he stomped the fields, trying his best to appreciate the land and forget about why he could not leave.

He wouldn't have dreamed of touching her before.

But she had changed a lot in twenty years, and the person he saw last night was no longer a girl, but a woman. A beautiful woman with sad eyes, and she had stirred something in him, *places* in him he hadn't even known were there.

Her body seemed suddenly very touchable, and he'd been filled with an almost painful longing to wrap his arms around her, push the strands of hair back off her cheek, and wipe the tears from her eyes. Whether his desire had been to ease her suffering or his own, he wasn't sure. He still didn't know what possessed him to even try to touch her, and then when his fingers brushed her cheek instead of going through it... He didn't know which of them had been more surprised.

Will looked down at his hand. He'd figured out how to move objects a long time ago. With enough concentration, he could shove his sitting chair a couple of inches a day or carry a sheet of paper across the yard. But touching another human being had always been out of the question. His hand always passed through its target as if it were made of smoke.

Until now.

Until Mags.

Will looked down the empty road. Loneliness had thankfully abandoned him years ago. Otherwise, he'd be feeling... He rubbed at the sudden lump in his chest, shaking his head. Maybe it wasn't as gone as he'd hoped.

Sighing, he turned and headed back toward the green rows, back to his life... or death, as it were.

It had been good to see her anyway, even if only for a few moments. And he was grateful that he'd had the opportunity to share the dewy webs with her. Over the years, he'd always known they would be among her favorites. It brought him joy to know he was right, to see the magic sparkle in her eyes again, even if they were full of tears.

Will brushed his palms over the tops of the flowers as he made his way back into the field. They swayed as if caught in a summer breeze.

He needed a walk.

That always made him feel better.

CHAPTER FOUR

THE BUZZ OF HER PHONE BROUGHT MAGGIE TO EXCRUCIATING consciousness. It took a moment to remember where she was, and her head pounded like a drum as she stared at the white ceiling, fairly certain she was going to throw up. Closing her eyes again with a groan, she covered them with her arm as the evening before came back in fits and starts.

Her hand flew to her chest, grabbing at the fabric as she flung her eyes open again and looked down. Her shirt came into focus, followed by her jeans. She was still dressed. The breath she was holding escaped in one hard whoosh.

"Thank god."

Turning her head, she squinted at the still-made other side of the bed. It was empty except for an empty water bottle and a phone number written on a bar napkin. Thank god, again.

Her phone buzzed again. She dragged it off the nightstand she stared until the unfamiliar number came into focus.

"Nope." She dropped it onto the bed beside her and tried to sit up.

"Ugh." She was definitely going to throw up. "What the hell?" she demanded, rubbing her eyes. The last time she'd been this drunk was before Eric was born. It was the *reason* he was born. Damn tequila shots.

She hadn't bothered to close the curtains, and daylight seared straight through her eyeballs into her brain. Maggie could almost hear the plasma, or eyeball juice, or whatever it was sizzling.

She buried her face in her hands and tried to swallow the bile that had lurched up her throat. *Nope, again.*

Leaping from the bed, she made it to the bathroom just in time.

By the time her stomach was empty, it looked like she'd murdered someone in the toilet. She flushed it and scooted across the floor, pressing her back against the cool tile wall.

"Jesus." Maggie pressed her elbows to her knees, cradling her head in her hands. She sat against the wall until the room stopped spinning, then dragged herself back to the bed, and fell onto it.

SHE WOKE A WHILE LATER, feeling slightly better. But that wasn't saying much, considering earlier she'd felt like she was dying. She checked her purse for ibuprofen, and there was none. She groaned. "Damn it." Eric was constantly "borrowing" her bottle and forgetting to put it back.

Maggie pulled her hair into a ponytail and dragged herself down the stairs, feeling a bit like the thing in the *Grudge*, as she made her way to the reception counter. The same woman, Susan, from the day before, smiled at her. "What can I do for you this afternoon?"

Afternoon? Maggie looked out the window, then down at her phone. Twelve-eighteen p.m. *Shit.* "Do you happen to have any ibuprofen or any kind of pain reliever back there?"

Susan's smile faded. "No, unfortunately I don't, but the gas station across the street, just over there, does."

Maggie squinted through the window. It was too far. She'd never make it. "Okay, thanks."

"I've got some," a man's voice offered from behind one of the high-backed chairs.

Maggie looked around the side and sitting in it was the Manhattan guy from the night before, the one she'd been so rude to.

He pulled out a small bottle and popped two orange pills into her outstretched hand. Gratefully, she swallowed them sans water.

"Thanks," she said, feeling compelled to add, "I'm sorry if I was rude to you last night. I didn't mean to be, it's just… my best friend sent me up here for the weekend and forgot to mention she'd signed me up for this." She waved her hands around.

He laughed. "That's a much better excuse than mine."

Maggie sat down. "What's yours?"

"My wife left me a year ago for a minor league hockey player, and I have trust issues. That's according to my therapist, not me."

Maggie laughed. "Ouch. I'm sorry about your wife."

"I signed myself up for this, but clearly… I'm not ready."

"Me either."

Her phone rang again. It was the same number, and this was the fifth call. "If you'll excuse me," she said, getting up.

She pressed the green button and held the phone to her ear. "Hello?"

"Maggie?" a vaguely familiar woman's voice asked.

"Yes?"

"Ah! Finally, I thought maybe I'd copied down your number wrong. Great news! So, the bank accepted your offer, and they are willing to close immediately, just as you requested."

Maggie's eyes widened as she pulled the phone away from her ear and looked at the number. What in the hell was this woman talking about? Who the *hell* was she, even? She pressed the phone back to her ear. "Wh-what?"

"You said your car won't be ready till Monday, so I scheduled the closing for eight a.m. I thought you could do the walk-through this afternoon if you're free. Although really, it's just a formality, since as I told you last night, it's bank owned, so you are buying it as-is."

Maggie stumbled and fell into the nearest chair, pressing a hand to her forehead as more foggy memories from the night before surfaced. "Oh... I... I..." She pulled the phone away from her mouth. "Shit. Shit. Shit—"

A chuckle brought her head up. Mr. Manhattan, who was sitting kitty-corner to her now, was eyeing her, trying to hide a rather amused-looking smile.

Frowning at him, she pulled the phone back to her lips. "I can't today I–I have no transportation as you know."

"I'd take you, but I've got a showing at one-thirty," the woman said.

Maggie pulled the phone away from her ear again and looked at the number. It was the same one written on the napkin up in her room. More memories surfaced. Her stomach dropped. "Oh no."

"I can give you a lift if you need one," Mr. Manhattan said.

Maggie tried to signal him to hush, but it was too late.

"Oh! Is that your friend from last night?" Ms. Santos asked. It took Maggie that long to remember her name, as more of the previous night came back.

Her eyes widened as she met Mr. Manhattan's. "Wh-what friend?"

"The one you were talking to about the property. Didn't—didn't you two go upstairs together?"

Maggie's jaw dropped as Mr. Manhattan winked at her and burst out laughing.

"Oh my god. I have to go," Maggie said into the receiver, her eyes narrowing on the man across from her.

"Okay, no problem, just make sure you do the walk through before Monday morning, if you want to. Because once you sign the papers, there's no—"

Maggie hung up the phone.

Mr. Manhattan was still grinning at her.

"Who are you, and what in the hell happened last night?" she demanded.

He tried unsuccessfully to stop smiling. "My name is Connor, and as you told me several times, in between your very vivid description of the property you wisely decided to purchase after a bottle and a half of wine, 'you got lucky.'"

She wanted to call him a liar, but something about that last bit rang true. She might have said that… more than once. She met his eyes in horror.

"Oh my god. I am so sorry! Jesus. Was I…" she glanced around the mostly empty reception area, and lowered her voice, "was I inappropriate in any way?"

Connor's brow went up.

Maggie hesitated, not sure how to word her question. "Ms. Santos said we went upstairs…" She couldn't get the rest out.

"Ah." He shook his head. "No. You were fine. Just very drunk and *very* happy. Nothing happened. Like I said, I don't think I'm ready to…"

Maggie exhaled in relief. "Thank god."

They stared at each other. A long, awkward moment later, she gasped. "Not that I don't find you attractive. You're a very handsome man. What I mean to say is I—" What did she mean to say? Maggie buried her head in her hands for the third time and rubbed what she was sure were her very bloodshot eyes. She was too hung over to be having this conversation. "I don't know what I'm trying to say. I'm sorry to have bothered you."

"It was no bother."

Maggie got up. "Well, thanks for the ibuprofen—"

"You don't remember then?" Connor asked, interrupting her.

"Remember?" Maggie sighed. *This* was why she didn't drink.

"You invited me out to look at the place with you. We were supposed to meet at noon here, that's why I was—"

Maggie stared at his handsome face. He seemed nice, both last night and this morning, while she had… "Fuck," Maggie said, and Connor laughed again.

"It's okay. We can… take a raincheck if you like. Although the way you spoke about it, I'm kinda tempted now to drive by it myself, anyway."

Maggie sighed, wishing she could crawl under the table and hide. A man with a giant mustache walked in and smiled at her as more memories came. She jumped up. "No. Um, actually, that would be great. A ride, I mean. If you don't mind waiting, give me five minutes and I'll be right back down."

"How about we meet back here in fifteen?" Connor suggested.

She nodded gratefully. "Perfect. Thanks."

CHAPTER FIVE

WILL COULDN'T BELIEVE SHE WAS BACK. THE MAN WITH HER MUST have been her husband, although he looked different than he remembered. But then, it had been a couple of decades.

They pulled up in a Range Rover, stopping just in front of the chain that still hung across the driveway.

What were they doing here?

Her husband got out first. He was in good shape, handsome, a little older than Will, graying at the temples. He wore jeans and a thin pullover sweater, despite the warm afternoon.

He let out a low whistle as Mags climbed out the other side. Will noticed she was wearing the same clothes as she had the day before. Her hair was flipped up into a messy bun on top of her head.

"Are you sure this is the place?" her husband asked.

Mags sighed heavily and nodded.

"The same one you were talking about last night? The one filled with perfect light and dying magic that filled your soul and all that—"

"Yep," she said, sounding oddly embarrassed.

Dying magic? What did that mean? Will wondered. Had she sensed him? *If she had, she would have said dead magic.* But she was correct about the light. Precious few had noticed it over the years, the subtle way in which the house and barn had been built askew from the road. Instead of each wall facing north, south, east, or west, as they almost all did for a hundred miles, the front of his house faced north-east, and at that angle, sunrise and sunset always entered the windows in a way that sliced through every room of the house.

"How much are you paying for it?" her husband asked.

Will froze. He must have heard the other man wrong. There was no way *Mags* had bought his place. In the hundred plus years he'd been around, one thing he knew for sure was that Will Morgan was not a lucky man.

"Forty-three thousand."

Will's eyes widened, and he nearly fell off the porch.

Mags pushed her sunglasses on the top of her head and stared at the spot where he stood, then drew her eyes warily toward the barn.

Will pressed his palms against the rail of the porch. The splintering wood dug into his palms, like it used to when he was alive.

She'd bought the farm? His heart almost leaped out of his chest at the thought. It was a very unfamiliar feeling for him, even in life. He pressed a hand to his ribs, and tried to rein it in, but it took off like the swallows from the barn and fluttered restlessly about him. Will shook his head. No. No. It couldn't be.

"I think that field over there," she pointed to the east, "and that one," she pointed to the west field, "and..." she waved her hand around unsure, toward the south, behind the house and trees, "maybe some of that land back there is included."

Why? How? "What in the goddamn hell?" Will muttered. Of all the people on Earth that could have bought the place, the one that finally had was *her*? It didn't make a lick of sense.

"Oh," was all her husband said.

Will shook his head. Had he made it to heaven after all?

"Oh my god," she said, staring at the roof of the barn, where a panel of tin had blown off in a wild storm they'd had in mid-July.

He didn't quite understand the disbelief in her voice. She sounded as surprised as he felt by the whole thing.

"Wow. This is not at all what I was—not that it's unsalvageable, but—" Her husband tripped over his words.

Was it supposed to be a surprise? Will crossed the lawn. The tall grass swayed imperceptibly as he approached the couple. Had she purchased it maybe as a weekend get-away? Folks did that now, especially in this area, close to the city but far enough to still feel like somewhere else. He gleaned his news from the occasional newspaper that was accidentally delivered to the mailbox, and from the talk of the local farmers as they stopped in front of his house in their pickup trucks to chat a moment and complain about the 'weekenders' as they called them. If so, her husband didn't look too impressed.

Mags laughed. "Just say it."

Her husband shook his head. "This is a fucking disaster, Maggie."

Will's eyebrow went up. Maggie? Was that her name? He liked it better than Mags. It suited her better. Especially now.

"Well, come Monday, it's apparently going to be *my* fucking disaster."

Will stumbled. Partly because he'd never heard a woman swear before, but mostly because of what her words meant. *Her* disaster? He took another step, and his leg hit the chain link in front of him instead of going through it. It creaked as it swung gently between the posts. Maggie turned. For a moment, he thought she'd spotted him, but her gaze fell to the swinging chain and continued on. He could smell her perfume. She smelled like wildflowers and sugar cookies. She smelled like heaven. The swallows inside him fluttered again.

"And you plan to live here?" her husband asked.

Will finally realized the man couldn't possibly be her husband, and he was surprised to feel his heart soften toward the stranger. He hadn't even realized how jealous he'd been until the weight of it was gone. He shook his head and almost laughed. Jealousy? How long had it been since he'd felt that? And how ridiculous of him to feel it now. The ship that gave him the right to those kinds of emotions had sailed off long ago.

"I-I have no idea," Maggie said, sounding dazed. "I need to talk to my son first, and..." She crossed the grass to the steps of the house, climbed them, and sat on the top one in the shade.

Her friend laughed. "I have seen some strange things in my life, but you are the first person I have ever met who got drunk and bought a farm."

Both of Will's brows went up at that. *She what?*

Maggie laughed. "Yeah, just so we're clear, I don't do things like this normally. I just—"

"I know," her friend interrupted, as he sat beside her. "You told me twenty times last night."

Will's jealousy surged again. Last night? So, they *were* together? What else did Maggie do exactly besides get drunk enough to buy his home?

"I did?" Maggie asked. Will understood her embarrassment now. He crossed the lawn again and stood over them as they talked.

"Yep," her friend said with a laugh.

Maggie dropped her head into her hands. "Oh god. What did I say?"

"That you are just trying to find yourself, and you were pretty sure 'she' was hiding here."

Will sucked in a hard breath, and Maggie's eyes shot up. She frowned briefly, then her face relaxed, and she kicked the dirt at her feet. "Well, you'll be glad to know I'm an honest drunk. Because, as crazy as it sounds—" She rubbed her arms, and Will felt it too, something like... static crackled in the air between them. "It's true. Something about this place... I think it needs me as much as I need it."

"Well, congratulations then, I guess," her friend said.

"Thanks."

They sat in silence for a moment. "Should we go check out the rest of the place, or do you want to head out?" her friend asked.

"Do you mind taking a quick walk around with me? I want to

check out the barn, but I'm afraid I'll disrupt a family of raccoons or snakes and—"

Will hurried to the barn to frighten away the fox that lived behind the old water trough.

The animal, sensitive to his presence, jumped up and escaped through the hole it had dug under the small door on the south side of the barn.

Will turned just as the wheels above the main doors began to screech in protest. He smiled. It had been a long time since he'd heard that sound.

Light shot through the narrow crack that opened between them. And he had a moment of déjà vu as Maggie squeezed through the opening. Her friend followed.

They both pulled out... some kind of electronic device, a cellular phone perhaps, or a tiny television with a flashlight on it, and shined the light around. He was momentarily blinded.

"Connor! Look at these!"

Will blinked. She had shined her light on the dozen milk jugs that sat in a neat row against the west wall. It had taken him weeks to put them there, but the effort had been worth it, just to see the admiration on her face. She ran her fingers along their lids as she passed each one. They left a trail through the dust.

"It isn't nearly as bad as I expected," she said breathlessly.

Finally, there was some excitement in her voice, and it matched the feeling that was bubbling up in his chest.

"Hey, check this out." Her friend, Connor, had spotted his workbench. Only a couple of the tools were his originally. The rest were pilfered from the few occupants that had lived on his land before he frightened them away.

Will knew now that had not been a kind thing to do, scare people, but it happened back in the early days, when he was still angry and territorial. Now, he was neither of those things. Now he was...

Maggie caressed the pitted wood of his workbench, trailed her middle finger over the vice that was still bolted to it, and picked up his hammer. His longing returned, as she ran her thumb over the initials his father had soldered into the side of the metal head, W.M., and he ached to be the hammer beneath her thumb. It had been so long since anyone had touched him, like that or in any way at all. Hell, it had been forty years since anyone had even *seen* him.

"Everything is in such good condition," Maggie said, placing the hammer back exactly where he'd set it.

Connor glanced up at the missing planks of wood that had blown off the barn since the last inhabitants had run off.

"Well, not everything," she corrected.

Will wanted to fix those, but he didn't have a ladder, and the truth was his strength was... limited. Carrying pine boards up a twenty-foot ladder was far beyond his ability.

"But still," Maggie went on. "I don't know. I thought this place would be covered in spider webs and... filled with ghosts or something."

"Last night you told me it was," Connor said.

That seemed to surprise Maggie, and again, Will wondered exactly how drunk she'd been, and why.

"I did?"

"Yeah. You said your real estate agent told you it was haunted, at least according to the previous owners. And then you told me you already knew."

Both her and Will's brows went up at the same time.

"I did?"

"Yep."

Maggie rubbed her temples. "I am never drinking red wine again."

Connor laughed. "I think if you just avoid consuming whole bottles at singles events from now on, you'll probably be fine."

The puzzle was quickly coming together now. So, she was in Lakeside for some kind of singles... meeting, and she'd gotten drunk and met Connor, which meant Connor was single too and...

Were they on a date? "Damn it." He kicked at the dirt, and to his surprise, it billowed up around his feet. Maggie and Connor spun around in his direction.

"Let's get out of here," Connor suggested, heading for the door.

Maggie was quick on his heels.

Will followed them both out.

"Are you really going to go through with it?" Connor asked as they headed back to his vehicle. "Are you really going to buy this dump and move out here to the middle of nowhere?"

Will's heart sank. Connor was right. It made very little sense that she would. For a moment, he'd allowed himself to believe that, but it was just a drunken mistake. There was no way—

Maggie stopped and turned so abruptly, he almost walked through her. She pulled her sunglasses back over her eyes, and he held his breath. He was so close he could see them through the darkened lenses, count the freckles that dotted her cheeks. The corners of her mouth twitched as a shiver raced down her spine, arced off her, then struck him in the chest. "I don't know. Maybe."

He exhaled as they got into the Rover. A second later, they took off down the road.

Will stood as close as he could to the road and watched them go. He knew it was a fool's errand to pray that she'd be back, but he did anyway. There was something about her. He'd felt it twenty years ago, he felt it yesterday, and he felt it now.

The road fell silent, and the normal sounds resumed. Crickets, the desperate cry of late season cicadas, the wind through the papery oak leaves as they continued to dry in the sun.

She was right about one thing: there was a piece of her here. Will looked back at the house. He'd been holding onto it for almost two decades. And if she'd just give him and the land a chance, he'd give back to her everything she'd given him.

He rested his elbow on the old mailbox, and to his surprise, it fell over.

Will stared at it.

Normally, it would take him days to knock something like that over. He bent down and gripped the box, expecting the enormous weight that corporal things seemed to possess since he died. Instead, it felt light in his grasp, and it was only a moment before he'd stuffed it back in its hole beside the road.

Will stumbled back, staring at his hands. "What in the hell?"

He looked back at the chain and remembered hitting it, and the railing... Odd.

Heading back to the house, he kept glancing over his shoulder every few seconds to make sure the mailbox was still there. It was.

He stood on the porch and looked out in the direction of Lakeside. He couldn't see Maggie anymore, but he felt her. At least, he thought he did. And somehow, he knew she'd be back. He was sure of it. He pulled his fingers through his hair. "What in the hell?" he asked again, and for the first time in seventy years, William Morgan wondered if he was dreaming.

CHAPTER SIX

MAGGIE TAPPED HER FINGERS ON THE EDGE OF THE BATHROOM SINK as she stared at herself in the mirror. It was four-thirty, and she was only just feeling human again.

Connor had left her at the second-floor landing, after she'd agreed to be his "date" for the evening meal and following trivia activity some moron had planned. He'd promised it wasn't a real date, just a faux one to keep the others at bay. Hopefully, that was the truth, but she didn't have time to worry about that right now. She had bigger problems. Like *barn*-sized ones.

Her visit out to the farm earlier had left her feeling totally confused. While she clearly had made a mistake signing the purchase agreement, as soon as she'd stepped out of Connor's car, the *feeling* that she had, had... evaporated.

And now, she had spent the last hour trying to convince herself that the right thing to do was call Ms. Santos, apologize for her behavior the night before, and have her tear up the papers. Maggie reminded herself that she had a home in the city, a career, and a life there, and that while she wasn't quite sure where she belonged, she was pretty goddamn sure it wasn't out *here* in the middle of nowhere. She wanted to be close to Eric.

But as she'd sat on the steps of that old house and watched the wind rustle the grass, stirring the birds into flight, she had felt something. And it was like the spider webs, beautiful and comforting, a warm balm over the gaping wound that had sprung up in her chest, and it made her pause.

Maggie looked down at the papers that sat next to her nervous fingers, her stomach full of grasshoppers. *Walk away now,* a voice said. That one didn't sound like her mother. It was cynical and cautious and sounded like her.

Meeting her eyes in the mirror, she chewed on her lip. And she was *mightily* tempted to do as it said, but... That was the voice she'd been listening to for the last twenty years. *That* was the voice that had led her to where she was now.

Maggie searched her soul, wondering if she even still had one, for a second opinion, for a sign or her mother's voice, or even...

Look.

She glanced at the papers again.

"Look," she repeated, recalling a conversation with her mother. She and Dean had already been married for a year by then and she'd dropped out of school and had been home with Eric for six months.

Her mom had sat her down at the very same kitchen table Maggie had eaten her first birthday cake at, and said, *'Look, I know you don't think so honey, but you still have choices. Thinking you don't is the biggest mistake you can make right now. And the second biggest is taking forever to make them, because deciding to do nothing is a choice too. One that will eventually leave you powerless.'* Tucking Maggie's hair behind her ear, she'd gone on. *'You want to know a secret I've learned?'* Maggie had wiped her eyes and nodded. *'It's not what you decide that matters. You can always change that. And the truth is, most of the time there is no right or wrong anyway, just different.* Taking Maggie's hand, she had said, *'What matters is that you remain the driver of your own destiny. Life is too precious and too short to give it over to chance. Don't let indecision paralyze you. Don't let one... bump in the road turn you into a passenger in someone else's life. Not in Dean's, not even in my beautiful little grandson's. Chase what you love. Choose your path, don't let it choose you. If you do, one day, you'll wake up and...'*

"Find you have no idea where you are," Maggie whispered.

She glanced down at the papers again. She had forgotten that conversation. She'd only been twenty when they had it, and at the time she really didn't understand what her mom meant, but she had been encouraged enough to reapply to school.

Two days after Maggie got her acceptance letter, her mom dropped dead, and life became too complicated for the simple advice she'd been given. Happiness? Control? Those were gone the moment her mom was. In her grief, she did exactly what her mom begged her not to. She took her hands off the wheel and never got back in the driver's seat. Maggie met her eyes in the reflection of the window. She didn't understand *then*, but she sure as hell did now.

Squaring her shoulders, she snatched the papers off the counter. Then she went into the bedroom and grabbed her phone off the nightstand. "Better late than never."

Or you're still drunk, her cynical voice commented dryly.

Or that. Either way, she had a call to make.

CONNOR ALMOST SPIT his beer all over the small table they shared. "You *what*?"

"I called Ms. Santos, Rebecca, and said I needed to close today or the deal was off. So, she tracked down the bank manager, and I issued the transfer for the funds and…" Maggie unfolded the closing documents and slid them across the table. "It's mine."

Connor coughed into his napkin and picked up the papers.

Maggie smiled. The grasshoppers were still there, but her mother was right. She was at peace. Her smile widened. Because for the first time in forever, Maggie was in control. And she may have made a huge mistake, but *she* had made it, not life, not fear, not indecision, *her*. And damn, that felt good.

AFTER A ROUSING game of trivia that she and Connor actually won, they sat with coffees out on the porch, rocking in the chairs.

"I'm glad I came this weekend," Connor admitted. "At first, I thought it was a mistake, but… It's been an adventure meeting you, Maggie Dubois."

She laughed, liking the sound of that. *Adventurous* Maggie Dubois had a certain ring to it. "I feel the same way. Thanks for joining me." She laughed again. "My best friend, the one that set me up for this, is going to have a heart attack when I tell her I met a handsome doctor."

Connor laughed. "Well, thank you for the compliment."

Maggie took a sip, then placed the mug on her lap. "Really, I know maybe you were looking for something else this weekend, but I'm glad we're…"

"Friends?"

"Yeah. It's been a while."

Connor sipped his coffee. "Me too."

THE NEXT MORNING, they said their goodbyes over another cup of coffee, and Maggie gave Connor her number. "If you're ever up this way, give me a call."

He laughed.

"What?"

"Well, the next time you're sitting at the bar and a stranger asks you if you're from around here, your answer will be yes."

Maggie laughed and gave him an affectionate hug. "Oh, god," she said, and he laughed harder.

After he'd gone, she'd sat on her bed for about two minutes

before picking up her phone and ordering a taxi. An hour later, she was stepping over the chain onto her new property. At least, it would be at midnight once the transfer went through.

The taxi drove away, and it was just her and the birds and the bugs. Butterflies danced in her stomach and beat against her ribs as she inhaled heavily and stood in the middle of the drive, or at least what would be the driveway once she had the weeds mowed down.

Maggie's eyes went from the house, *her* house, to *her* barn, which were about an equal distance away from where she stood. She glanced up at the towering oak that grew midway between her and the road. It had to be the only thing on the property older than the house itself. She reached in her pocket and felt the sharp edge of the key. She would go inside, but... not yet.

Inhaling again, she tilted her head up toward the sun. The sky was a vault of blue, with a handful of clouds to the west. A moment later, she was lying on the ground, in the middle of the weeds, staring up at it. The gravel poked at her back, but she barely noticed it through the serenity that had enveloped her. A fly buzzed above her and landed on the seeded tip of a blade of grass. She lifted her hand, scaring it away, and tried to imagine the distance between her fingers and the edge of the sky. A cloud drifted into view, followed by several more. When she was younger, it had seemed so close, probably because she'd had her sights set on other worlds back then, Astrobiology, it was called. That had been her goal when she started college, to search for life on other planets. But now... now, those clouds seemed awfully far away.

She smiled and dropped her hand onto her stomach, shoving the other under her head. It had been years since she'd looked up at the sky. She hadn't realized how much she missed it until now.

Pushing her hair back off her forehead, she smiled. "Hello, old friend."

Maggie knew she would probably panic as soon as she got home and the reality of what she'd done to her simple, comfortable, *boring* life sunk in, but it was today. And today, she was going to be positive and optimistic. The butterflies in her belly begged to be set free, and she was determined to let whatever feeling this was fill her. Closing her eyes, she released them into the air to join the sparrows as they swooped in and out of the barn.

MAGGIE STARED AT THE SKY, watching the clouds slowly crawl by until her phone buzzed in the dirt beside her. She picked it up, shielding her eyes. It was a text from Eric, checking in.

Got my books. Am ready for classes tomorrow. Love you.

She sat up and texted him back.

Love you too. Thanks for checking in.

Out of all the worries she had about what she'd done, he was by far the biggest. What would Eric say when she told him she'd bought this place? What would he say when she told him she was thinking of selling the house? Would he be angry? Upset?

Maggie got up, dusted off her jeans, and felt the key in her pocket again. Taking a deep breath, she turned toward the house, then exhaled in one hard whoosh. It was time to see *exactly* what she had purchased.

Climbing the steps, she noticed again what good condition the porch was in. With only *slightly* shaking hands, she pulled the key from her pocket and pushed it into the lock. It took a moment of wiggling before it finally turned, and the knob twisted.

The door groaned as it swung open, and Maggie made her first mental note. WD-40. She pulled her sunglasses off and hung them on the neck of her sweatshirt as she stood for a moment in the entryway, which was also the living room, and her eyes adjusted to the dim interior. The house smelled musty, and there was just the faintest hint of wood smoke, but thankfully, it didn't smell like anything had died in there recently.

The chair and bookshelf were still there, where she'd seen them last, but strangely, the papers were gone. Maybe the bank had sent someone over to tidy up?

Maggie closed the door and noticed a closet behind it. Hesitantly, she opened it, feeling like a voyeur even though it was hers. It was empty. A bulb hung inside with a chain attached. She pulled it, but nothing happened. *The power is off.* Of course, as was the water and probably everything else. For the first time, it occurred to her that there was more to the house than the walls and floors, which seemed to be in okay shape. What if all the pipes had burst, or the furnace didn't work?

She pressed her hand against the cool plaster wall to steady herself. *One thing at a time,* her mom's voice soothed. "Breathe," she reminded herself, resting her forehead against it and gulping deep breaths of stale air. After her heart resumed its normal ticking, she stepped back.

Quietly, she made her way along the wall to where it ended. A stairwell leading to the second floor occupied the back side and divided the living room from the kitchen. A small window hung above the landing at the top.

Maggie caught her first glimpse of the bathroom, through the door on her right, directly across from the stairs, and the kitchen, which occupied the back of the house, simultaneously as she crossed the transition from the weathered wood floors onto the most hideous lime-green and orange linoleum she had ever seen. It ran from the base of the stairs through the two rooms, curling at the edges where it encountered the wall.

She entered the bathroom first. It was just as she'd imagined it would be. An old clawfoot tub sat across from the door. Beside it was the toilet. Above that, a small opaque window allowed the daylight in. Next to the door, opposite the toilet, was an ancient-looking vanity and sink. A small mirror hung off to the side, and Maggie caught her terrified reflection in it. For some reason, that made her laugh, and she jumped as her voice echoed through the empty house.

She looked down. Iron and lime deposits from the well water stained the bowl of the sink, but again, it was remarkably clean after being abandoned for so long.

Maggie added shower curtain, toilet brush, trash can, and bath tissue to her list before moving on to the kitchen.

The refrigerator was right next to the bathroom door and stuck out. A design flaw for sure. She practically had to walk around it to get into the room. Then she realized why it was there. There wasn't anywhere else to put it.

Once she got past it, though, the space opened up. There were two windows. One faced the barn. A small oval table with no chairs sat beneath it, serving as the dining area. Just to the right of the window was the stove. Based on its shade of dried mustard, Maggie guessed it was purchased around the same time the floor had been done. The other window faced the narrow backyard, where a row of trees separated it from the gigantic field behind.

The counter ran the length of the wall under it, and the sink was positioned in front of the window, so she could look out while she did dishes. The thought made her smile. There were more than enough cabinets on either side of the window to hold her kitchen supplies.

Maggie looked for a pantry and saw a small door behind the table that led to a small closet under the stairs. She opened it. There was a narrow row of shelves, but the majority of the space was taken up with the furnace and hot water heater. She was no expert, but they both seemed old, though in good shape. She glanced at the floor beneath the window and saw a vent. She had forced air at least, assuming it worked.

She closed the door and turned. All things considered, it wasn't too bad.

A door to the right of the counter and sink opened to the outside and led out back. Crossing the kitchen, she peeked through the window. To her surprise, there was another covered porch. It was much smaller than the one on the other side of the house, but... She unlocked the door, pulling hard before it opened. Maggie stepped out and gasped at the view. From there, she couldn't see the barn or the lake, but this was the spot to catch the sunset. And the trees were beautiful as they lined the south and west edge of the third field. *Her* third field. The road ran along the north side and headed off in a straight line as far as she could see.

Maggie caught the glimmer of running water between the thick underbrush that had overgrown the space between the trees. Was there a creek on her property? Really? It made her smile. Eric used to love to play in creeks when he was little.

Shaking her head, she realized she hadn't even walked around the back of the house before purchasing it, which was incredibly stupid of her, but... It was looking like luck had been on her side.

She shrugged. "Oh, well." Either way, it was too late now.

Maggie stepped off the porch and took a quick tour of the back, as the feeling of everything being just a *little* too good to be true grew.

A small creek did, in fact, gurgle behind the house. It followed the path of the trees that ran from the west side of her property, behind the house and barn, all the way to the south where her field ended and another began. *The trees follow the creek,* the biology student she'd once been corrected.

Maggie couldn't quite get to it through the mess of brambles, but what she could make out was gorgeous. It was two or three feet wide, filled with rounded stones that the water rushed over. If she cleared out all the dead brush, she could hang a hammock beside it and wile away hot summer afternoons.

With a smile, she headed back inside and up the narrow stairs to check out the second floor. There was a small landing at the top, and two doors on either side. Both bedrooms were about the same size, and empty. Their footprints were huge, but the way the roof peaked, only half of the space in the middle was tall enough to stand in. The sides that sloped were walled off and lined with doors. Maggie peeked inside the bedroom that faced the backyard first. The wood floors creaked, but not too bad for a creepy old farmhouse. She opened one of the closet doors. A wood bar hung the length of it. The opposite wall held more closet space. Glancing out the two windows at the back and down at the backyard, Maggie realized she was standing just above where the kitchen sink sat below. Turning, she imagined the room with a fresh coat of paint and a ceiling fan. This would be her room.

Eric could have the one that faced the road when he came up to visit, and the rest of the time, it would be her office. Crossing the landing, she went into the second room. It was almost a mirror image of the first and faced the road. Maggie headed back downstairs.

She wasn't sure she liked the closets, but otherwise, the rooms were... pleasant. Charming. The whole house was. There wasn't much to it, that was for certain, but what there was, was... *Enough.*

Maggie's cheeks ached, and she rubbed them, realizing it was from smiling. She went back into the living room and inspected the fireplace. It was brick and solid, with a beautiful, but plain wood mantle bolted into it. There were two windows on either side, both covered in vines, facing the road. For the first time, she noticed that the house sat at a slight angle to the road. She frowned. That was odd. Houses were almost exclusively built parallel to the road. In some places, the law even required it. Her eyes traced the massive field across the street. But this countryside was certainly not one of those places.

Remembering her new address 5557 Morgan Line, and the fact that this was the "Morgan homestead," Maggie wondered if maybe the house had been built before the road had.

She finished her tour at the window next to the front door, the one she'd peeked in only two days ago, and stared at her beloved barn. Again, she smiled. Or maybe she hadn't stopped. Yes, she'd only owned the house for thirty seconds, but that was what it was. *Her* barn. She was beginning to suspect it had been from the first moment she saw it and it sang to her, all those years ago.

"Beloved," she whispered, staring at it as she rubbed at a fingerprint on the glass with the sleeve of her sweatshirt. "You are mine, and I am yours now. What do you say we heal each other?"

There was a loud creak, and she spun around.

The room was empty. Placing a hand over her racing heart, she listened. *It's just an old house.* It was going to do that from time to time. The hair on the back of her neck prickled, and Maggie scratched at it.

"Enough for one day," she said nervously, reaching for the doorknob. She had several phone calls to make anyway, and the one she dreaded most was the one she needed to make first. Maggie locked the door and put her sunglasses back on. Plopping on the top step of the porch, she stretched out her legs as Dahlia's phone rang and she activated the video chat.

Dahlia appeared. "Hey, baby!" she said with a wide smile. "I was just about to..." Her smile faded as she squinted at her screen. "Where in the hell are you? That's not the hotel, I hope? If it is, we ought to sue them for false—"

"No. I'm not at the hotel," Maggie said, as the butterflies turned back into grasshoppers, then into raging bulls stampeding through her stomach. She needed to just get it out. *Just say it.*

"Then, where in the fuck—"

"I bought a house."

Dahlia stared at her for a moment. Then she made her face. The one that said—

"Please tell me you are joking."

Maggie shook her head. Her lips came together, and she braced herself, knowing she was about to get her ass handed to her on a—

"Are you fucking kidding me? You bought a *house*? *Where?*"

"It's—"

Dahlia didn't wait for the answer. "When I said go crazy, I meant get *laid*! Not—what the—" Dahlia paused abruptly and broke into another gorgeous smile. "You're messing with me, aren't you?"

Maggie shook her head.

"Yes. Yes, you are. Oh shit, girl. You scared—"

"No, Dee. I really did."

Dahlia shook her head. "Nope. You can't. Banks aren't open on the weekend."

Maggie unfolded the papers from her pocket and held them in front of her phone, trying to get the screen to focus on the text.

Dahlia's features hardened once more as she leaned closer to her phone to inspect them. "Margret Olivia Dubois, you better be lying to me, or I am going to fucking kill you."

"I'm not—"

"What in the hell—let me see it," she demanded.

"The house?"

"Yeah, the fucking—" Maggie turned the volume down as she got up and headed out into the driveway. She swiped at the button that turned the view around as Dahlia's shrill voice sliced through the quiet afternoon. "Is that a goddamn *barn?*" she shouted through the speaker.

The view flipped, and Maggie pointed her phone back toward the house.

"Oh, my lord. Oh, my dear, sweet Jesus." Dahlia moaned from the phone in her hands.

Maggie switched the view back to herself quickly. As soon as 'lord' entered Dahlia's vocabulary, she knew to brace herself. It was the calm before the storm.

"It's not as bad as it—" Maggie quickly turned the volume down even more as a slew of curse words spilled from her best friend's mouth faster than water over the mighty Niagara.

It was a full five minutes before there was room in the conversation for Maggie to speak again.

"I know you don't understand, Dee, but—"

"But *what?* What could you possibly say that would make any of this make sense? Jesus, Maggie."

"If you would just listen—"

"So, you're just gonna abandon your life, and me, and move to

—to a fucking *farm* in the middle of goddamn nowhere? And do what, exactly? Milk *fucking* cows?"

"I don't know!" Maggie shouted. "I haven't figured that out yet. And what do you mean, abandon my life? *What* life? Wasn't that the whole point of this weekend? To find—"

"A dick!" Dahlia shouted back. "I wanted you to find a *penis,* Maggie, one that would hopefully satisfy you and get you out of this funk you've been in. I know you haven't slept with anyone since Dean. I was just trying to... Shit. Shit, shit—"

"How do you know—"

"Please. I know you better than I know my own brother. You think you can keep something like that from me? And don't try to change the subject."

"I'm not—"

"What about Eric? Huh? Yesterday you were crying that he was moving thirty minutes away, and now you're just going to run off to god knows where and live in a haunted fucking house?"

"It's not haunted." As Maggie said that, the hair on her arms stood on end.

"You fucking know what I mean." Dahlia hissed. "You know what? We need to do this in person. I'll be at your house in an hour. You better—"

"I can't. My car is in the shop. I cracked the gas pan—"

Dahlia got up from wherever she was sitting, and Maggie heard the jangle of her keys. "Then I am coming to get you. Right *now.* And you better be ready to go *home* when I get there. The faster we put this nonsense—"

"You're not my mother—" Maggie began, finally finding a bit of the anger she knew she should feel for being treated like a five-year-old.

"No. I'm your best friend, and you are scaring the shit out of me right now. I'll see you in an hour."

Before Maggie could say anything else, the screen went dark. Her hand shook as she stared at it. "Shit," she breathed, leaning back against the barn, feeling lightheaded. It was warm through her shirt. Her hands continued to bounce as she pressed the back of her jittery hand to her forehead. She didn't know why. Her conversation with Dee had gone exactly as she'd expected it would. And Dee was right, except—

She tried to inhale, but there was something blocking her throat. Bracing herself on her knees, she doubled over as her phone fell into the dirt, gasping as her heart did a flip-flop in her chest and the edge of her vision darkened. Just as she was on the verge of passing out, the firm pressure of a hand settled against the middle of her back, and her throat opened abruptly. Electricity shot from her spine to her fingertips as she lunged away from the wall. Spinning around, she shoved the hair off her face, trying to see, certain that someone had touched her. But once again, there was no one there.

Maggie licked her lips and pressed her hand to her chest to steady her breath and her racing heart as she looked out over the fields. The wind blew over the tops of the corn in waves.

"You cannot lose it now," she whispered to herself, rubbing her arms. Lifting her head to the sky, she shouted, "I *am* doing the right thing!"

The universe didn't respond.

She was doing the right thing. It didn't feel that way *right* now —Maggie looked back at the porch, where she was going to put a comfortable wicker chair and a small table so she could sit and watch the sunrise over the lake every morning—but it would. The thumping in her chest slowed.

She was scared, yes. But that didn't make it wrong. It just made it... new. Unknown. And the unknown didn't have to be bad. It *could* be good. She used to love it. Maggie reminded herself of all the good things that had already happened over the last few days because Dahlia had forced her out of her comfort zone, into the unknown. She'd found her beloved barn. She'd met Connor. Maggie glanced at the road. She'd seen the most amazing spider webs and discovered memories of her mother she had forgotten, and most importantly, she felt *alive.*

The butterflies stirred in her stomach again as her spine tingled with awareness. Tears filled her eyes. She hadn't felt this alive in eons. She hadn't been this bold, or afraid, or excited, or on the verge of passing out since she was a teenager. *This* was the feeling she missed! And *that* meant this was *right.* Besides, *living* was better than just *surviving,* wasn't it?

Maggie wiped her eyes, and looked around again. *This* was better than the future she was facing a week ago, because all that one held was getting by, existing, surviving, coping, settling…

Look, the voice on the wind had whispered, and she had.

And what she'd found was hope.

CHAPTER SEVEN

FROM THE MOMENT SHE STOOD IN THE YARD AND CONFESSED TO HER best friend that she had in fact bought his house and intended to live in it, Maggie had turned Will's simple life upside-down. Half of September and the whole month of October went by in a blur.

He 'met' Dahlia that same day, when she came to get Maggie. Will had not seen many people of her coloring in his lifetime, or his deathtime for that matter. She was striking, both tall and slim, with intelligent brown eyes that Will could tell didn't miss much. Her hair was enormous, and her skin was a breathtaking shade that fell somewhere between the shimmery brown mica-sand at the bottom of the creek bed and the tawny stripe that outlined the wings of the *Hyalophora cecropia*, giant silk moths that emerged for a short time in mid-June and mesmerized him as they fluttered in the dark. In short, Dahlia was beautiful.

What he didn't care for was her vocabulary. But despite that, Will could tell immediately how closely her inside matched her outside and how much she loved Maggie, so he forgave her for the insults she spread rather generously about his home.

The following day, the power came on. Two days later, an unidentified man appeared with a key to the house. Will had been about to run him off when he noticed his t-shirt. ***Greg's Heating and Cooling.*** The man had gone straight to the furnace and began tinkering with it.

Then came the plumber and electrician. Will watched over their shoulders with interest as they worked. A lot had changed since the last time men had worked on the house. He was a quick study and paid close attention, should he need to make a repair himself in the future. He shook his head in amazement when the plumber used plastic pipes instead of copper. What was the world coming to?

A week later, Will was in the barn when he heard a strange sound coming from outside. When he peeked out the window, there was a landscaping truck in front of the house and several men with mowers and weed trimmers had descended upon the yard in a frenzy, battling the grass around the house, barn, and silo down to a civilized height. It almost brought tears to his eyes to see it so neat and cared for after so long.

The tractor that had killed him emerged from its hiding place among the weeds and sat like a monument to his death behind the barn. As crazy as it was, he missed that old thing. They'd spent a lot of time together when he was alive, and he hoped Maggie would keep it.

He 'met' Eric two days later. The boy was handsome and tall. He had Maggie's coloring and smile, but not her eyes. Will recalled Maggie's husband, Dean, she had called him. Those were his eyes. Eric was affectionate and supportive of his mother, but Will sensed his worry about her living out there all alone. He wished he could reassure the boy that he would look after her.

A week after that, she brought up a carload of cleaning supplies and sanitized the house from top to bottom. That was a relief, because his feet had begun to make prints in the dust. It was something they had never done before, and it would have been only a matter of time before she noticed it, so he had been staying out in the barn when she was there. It killed him to stay away, but he was afraid to come in, certain that if she discovered he was there, she'd leave and never come back. Once the floors were polished, though, he was free to resume roaming the house as she worked. Will stayed out of her way and made a point of giving her privacy when and where it was polite to do so.

A week after that, an enormous truck came, and two men carried about a hundred boxes into the house. Maggie stood by the door, directing them where to put each one. It took all afternoon, and by the time she and the movers were gone, it was dark out. He had wandered the house curiously, examining her things. He didn't open any of the boxes, but he read the labels and admired her furniture and paintings. Strangely, there was no television among her wares. The boxes in his old bedroom said 'master bed,' and he realized she'd claimed it as her own. It was a good choice. The light was better. He looked out the windows one last time, over a view he never *once* appreciated when he was alive, and vowed never to step foot in it again.

That was yesterday, and now, *now* they were here.

Will leaned against the wall by the foot of the stairs, arms crossed, watching her. The sky had grown dark, and only the soft light above the sink lit the kitchen. She was standing with her back against the counter, staring at the floor. She'd been like that for a while.

He'd been trying to guess what she was feeling before getting distracted by his own thoughts.

Maybe she was tired?

She had come early that morning, smelling like lilies—not the intoxicating *Lilium orientalis,* but the more subtle *lancifolium* that grew in the ditch—and coffee. He'd spent all day watching her wander from box to box. She emptied several in the kitchen, set up a machine he had never seen before on the counter, then made the bed upstairs. She tried and failed to hang an oval-shaped shower rod above the bathtub, putting a handful of holes in the ceiling before giving up, and set several photos of Eric on the mantle.

The machine, he learned, made coffee. Maggie made several cups throughout the day. He watched in fascination as she put a little white cup in it and a moment later, coffee came out in exactly the right amount to fill the mug beneath it.

To his surprise, the first photo she hung on the wall was the one she'd taken of the barn all those years ago. He could just barely make out his silhouette in the window and wondered if she'd ever noticed he had been watching her when she snapped it.

Maggie shifted her weight from one hip to the other. Was she regretting her decision to move out there? Or maybe she was feeling down about something else?

Her eyes closed and whispered something to herself that ended with 'freak out.' Was she nervous, then? Will pushed back from the wall. Could she sense him watching her? Or was it just the normal jitters of her first night in the house alone? He knew she was staying because she had set her toothbrush on the sink.

Her phone rang, and they both jumped.

Maggie's eyes flew up as she pulled the phone from her pocket, and Will ducked into the stairwell, even though she couldn't see him. Quietly, he sat down on the steps and listened. The house was so quiet he could hear Dahlia on the other end of the line, even though Maggie hadn't put her on the loudspeaker.

"How you holding up?" Dahlia asked.

Maggie sighed before answering. "Fine, you know, just..."

"Just what?"

"No big deal. Just wondering if I've lost my mind and made the biggest mistake of my life."

Will smiled. Her sense of humor was quickly becoming one of his favorite things about her. He heard Dahlia laugh. "It's too late for that, baby," her friend said.

Maggie snorted.

"You want me to come up? I told you I would. I can be there in an—"

"No. You have work, and I'm fine. Really. I'm probably going to head to bed soon anyway."

Will looked at the clock she'd hung over the refrigerator. It was only seven-thirty.

"Okay, but if you need me, promise you'll call?" Dahlia asked.

"Yeah. We'll talk tomorrow, okay?"

"Okay."

"I love you, Dee. Thanks for supporting me, even though you think I'm crazy."

"I love you too, you crazy bitch."

Silence followed.

Will peeked around the corner as Maggie 'texted' Eric. Why she would take the time to type words to him instead of using the phone was a mystery, but she seemed to prefer it. He knew it was Eric and not anyone else because of the way her face softened and her mouth curled into a gentle, motherly smile as she tapped on the screen.

Then she set her phone on the counter and went back to staring at the patterns on the hideous floor. Will had been so angry when Harvey Wilson's old lady had laid that ghastly linoleum over his beautiful floors. He'd tried to peel it up, but they'd used some kind of glue that bound it to the wood for all eternity.

"What am I doing?" Maggie whispered again, so quietly he almost didn't hear her.

That was an interesting question. Will pressed himself back from the wall, went to the front window, and looked out into the darkness. Why was she there? He thought he knew, but did she? The field across the street was a black smudge on the horizon. That meant there was no moon. He looked up at the stars sparkling through the branches of the vines that still blocked the window and got an idea.

Maybe she just needed to be reminded. He looked toward the kitchen. But how to get her outside?

Maggie turned around and pressed her hands to the edge of the sink. Her reflection in the window was like a mirror, and he recognized the struggle in her eyes.

It had taken a while, but over the last six weeks, he'd been able to piece most of her story together. She was divorced from Dean, and her son had gone off to college, leaving her alone for the first time. She was feeling lost and was bravely trying to start over, only… she didn't know where to begin. It was not an unfamiliar feeling. It had hit him in just the same way. Almost.

She didn't seem to know what she wanted. The only thing that seemed to bring her joy was... He blinked, remembering his plan.

Will hurried onto the porch. He needed to be quick before she gave up and headed upstairs. He looked around for something that he could use to draw her attention. It had to be loud enough that she could hear it, but he didn't want to scare her to death, either. But the porch was empty. He thought about gently rapping on the door, but ruled that out immediately. That was exactly the kind of thing that would send her packing. Feeling like a complete imbecile, he implemented the only other thing that came to mind.

"Meeeooowww," he called, frowning as soon as the sound escaped his lips. That didn't sound like a cat at all. At least not like one that wasn't on the verge of death. He cleared his throat and tried again. "Meeeooowww?" He pressed the palm of his hand to his forehead. Now it sounded like a question, and the cats he'd known didn't ask questions. They made goddamn statements. He needed to sound confident. Will squared his shoulders. "Meeeoow!" he bellowed.

That was better, but not quite... feline enough. "This is ridiculous," he muttered. But something made him try again. "Meeeooowww!" He smiled and stepped off the porch into the yard, finally liking what he was hearing. Yes. That was it! "Meeeeeeeoooooo—"

The front door opened, and he clamped his mouth shut. *Jackpot.* Now he just had to get her in the yard.

Shooting lightly across the driveway toward the barn, he passed inside. "Meeeooowww!" His voice bounced off the walls, while the swallows shifted nervously in their nests in the eaves. He was killing it now. "Eewoww!"

He hurried back outside.

Maggie was standing at the bottom of the steps looking toward the barn, hugging herself against the cool air. He quickly closed the distance between them, and then as quietly as he could, did as he had before, and whispered in her ear.

"Look."

A spark leaped from her body to his, and Will jumped back as it flashed in the darkness and vanished.

Shivering, Maggie looked up and her lips parted. The air around her prickled, washing over him, sending a shiver down his own spine. He couldn't remember the last time that had happened.

"Oh my god," she breathed.

Will smiled and followed her gaze.

Above them, the sky was *filled* with stars.

Back when he was a kid, the Milky Way shone like a ribbon across the sky. He and his brothers would use it like a compass when they went out exploring at night and got lost in the woods. Now it looked more like clouds, but the recognition in her eyes made him certain she knew what she was looking—

The grinding of her feet on the gravel brought his head down, and by the time his eyes got to where she had been, she was gone. He turned just as she ran up the stairs, into the house, and slammed the door.

Will stood, frozen in the darkness. Why had she run off? He looked down at his hands. Had he accidentally made himself visible to her? Or was she afraid of the—

The door opened again a moment later, and Maggie hurried back out. She wore a coat and a knitted winter hat with a ball on the top. She was carrying something in her arms. Rushing past him, to the small patch of grass between the driveway and the barn, she spread out the blanket, then laid down.

Will's smile returned as he quietly made his way over to where she lay. He lowered himself into the grass beside her and looked up.

How many times had he done this very thing over the last several decades? A million times? Once for every star he could see? It was possible. How many times in his actual life had he done this? Not once. Not after he was grown, anyway. That was why he was here now.

Fate, or God, or whatever the hell it was that had denied him entrance into heaven, had chained him here, to his land, because he had failed at living, failed the ones he loved most, and ignored every beautiful thing that had all been there, all the time, everywhere around him. It had bound him here because he'd never bothered to look up once. Instead, he had just... worked. Worked himself to death, as it were.

He hadn't enjoyed a single moment of his adult life. He hadn't loved enough when he should have. He hadn't appreciated a damn thing. Those were his crimes, and now he was paying for them. All of that sacrifice, and for what? To make a buck? He'd squandered every meaningful thing in his life for nineteen-cent bushels of corn. What a goddamn idiot.

He knew better now, of course. He made the most of things. But now, it was too late. He'd already been sentenced. *Now* all he had was the land he'd traded his life for.

He turned as Maggie lifted her hand toward the stars. Their reflection sparkled in her eyes. Will smiled at the freckles that still dotted her nose and cheeks. He'd noticed them when she came with Connor too. For the first time, he allowed himself to admit how attractive she'd become. Not just something beautiful. But someone *desirable*.

As if to prove his point, her mouth bowed into a smile as she gazed skyward. He longed to touch her again, but he refrained. The first time, he hadn't even known he could. The second time, he'd been so worried she'd pass out, he hadn't had time to think. But now that he had thought, he knew there could be no third time. Because of what he was. Because if he did, she would go, and he would lose the single miracle his lousy existence had ever afforded him, and the only company he'd had in fifty years.

Will hated to admit it, but having Maggie there made it incredibly clear to him how lonely he'd been, and he was frightened by how quickly he was becoming attached to her, and how afraid he already was of losing her.

He constantly had to remind himself that she didn't even know he was there, that the reason she bought the farm was not because of him, but because of the land and the house and the sky.

How he envied her. The life she still had in front of her. *Real* life. Even if she didn't know what to do with it. She didn't have to hide. She didn't have to remain silent when she wanted to speak. If she had a question, she could ask it. If she wanted to touch someone, she just had to reach out her hand like she was now, and they wouldn't run away. If she wanted to laugh or to be cheered up, she just activated her phone and called someone. He thought about her 'friend' Connor. Did she like him? He'd overheard Dahlia's comments about the state of Maggie's love life. Did she miss that kind of companionship the way he suddenly did?

She sighed and dropped her hand, shoving it into her pocket for warmth. A little cloud escaped her lips and evaporated in the night air.

She started to speak, her voice low and soft, and a spark arced between them again. As he listened, he realized she was quoting a poem by Walt Whitman. He knew it because it was in one of the two dozen books on the shelf inside. They had been his only reading material for fifty years, and he knew every line on every single page by heart, even the field guides.

He whispered the words silently with her and smiled when she was done. Perfect silence of the stars, indeed.

To his surprise, she fell asleep. He watched her for a while, but then, afraid she'd freeze to death; he did his second most ridiculous thing of the evening. Plucking a blade of grass, he tickled her nose until she woke up.

Sleepily, she gathered her things and headed inside. Without bothering to even remove her coat, she climbed the stairs and disappeared into her bedroom, leaving him standing at the bottom of the stairs in awe of the life that was suddenly his.

CHAPTER EIGHT

MAGGIE PULLED THE SWEATER OVER HER SHOULDERS AND WRAPPED the scarf around her neck twice. Then she yanked her hat over her unkempt hair, grabbed her sunglasses, coffee, and journal, and pulled the front door open.

Dropping the items on the small glass tabletop, she plopped into her oversized wicker rocker that sat under the porch light. Yesterday had been gray and dreary, but today, there was a bank of clouds hanging low over the lake, and some fluffy cottony ones up high. She was hopeful for a colorful sunrise.

It would be a while, though, before it appeared. So, she settled in, pulled the warm wool throw off the arm of the chair, and snuggled under it before retrieving her coffee. Steam rose from her mug, the wisps ghostly against the black silhouette of the barn and silo as they sat quietly beneath the ethereal blue sky. Goosebumps spread across her arms, as they often had since she'd moved in. At first, it had kind of freaked her out, but four weeks later, and after happening at least a hundred times, she was used to it. It was the beauty of the place that caused it. Just as it touched her mind, it touched her body as well, sometimes rolling across it like the breath of a whisper, sometimes pricking her like a little jolt of lightning. Or maybe it was just static electricity, she thought, as she tucked her hair under her cap. It was constantly frizzing out since she'd stopped using styling products in it every day.

Maggie looked at her chipped nails, then turned her hands over and admired the blisters on her palm. Her hair wasn't the only thing that was looking a little worse for the wear. *But* the house was looking better by the day.

She still had clients and contracts to fulfill, so she worked on those each Monday. Tuesdays she spent down in the city overseeing the projects, checking on their progress, and meeting with clients, and from Wednesday to Sunday, she worked on the house. And work she had.

The very first thing she had done was rip out the abomination someone had laid over the beautiful oak floors in the kitchen and bathroom. It had taken her five days to remove it all, and the chips had come up in maddening tiny pieces, most no larger than a quarter, but that was okay. After her night under the stars, it had rained for almost a week straight, and the work kept her from going stir crazy. After the last piece of floor was up and in a trash can beside the road, she'd spent hours on the internet trying to figure out the best way to get the glue off the floor. Then, she'd made her first of a thousand trips to the local hardware store and rented a sanding machine.

After the floor was smooth and the house covered in dust, she'd gotten on her hands and knees and stained and sealed the whole thing.

She could have just hired someone, and she probably should have because her body ached in a way it never had in all the years she'd gone to the gym. Maggie rubbed the back of her neck. But now that it was done, she was glad she'd done it herself. She'd brushed her hand over every nick. Her eyes had registered every imperfection. For as well as a person could *know* a floor, Maggie knew hers. It was nice to feel such an intimate connection to the house. It made it feel a little more like home, like a new friend.

Everything she'd done since had magnified that feeling. She'd felt the house's approval when she'd carried in the straight-backed Amish dining chairs for the kitchen table. It had smiled when she repainted the whole house, from floor to ceiling. It had nodded in agreement when she got and installed three ceiling fans herself. It had been in awe of the shiny new stainless-steel appliances for the kitchen.

On days when the weather was clear, and the sun returned, she worked outside. She felt it even out there; the house watching her, observing her work.

Maggie looked up at the thick beam she'd nailed back into place above the railing on the front porch, convinced the house had helped her. It had been almost impossible to lift, and she had been about to give up, when it suddenly became weightless and miraculously slid back up where it belonged. She'd had just enough energy left to pound one nail through it before collapsing on the porch exhausted.

She'd removed the vines from the front of the house, and as she pulled them down, memories of it, from when she was young, resurfaced along with the red-orange brick and the decorative arches above the four windows that sat on either side of the chimney.

Maggie bought a chainsaw, something she never thought she'd do. And learned how to use it, another thing she never thought she'd do. Channeling her inner mountain woman, she'd cut all the fallen trees into movable pieces. It was time-consuming work, but rewarding. In the same way she'd gotten to know her floor, she was getting to know her land, and something about that, and the brisk autumn air, and her cold, runny nose, was replacing the emptiness in her heart.

Slowly, she was making her way from the west side of her property, that she'd finally had surveyed, toward the east. She'd been surprised to find a small swampy pond hidden in the brush, between where the creek turned north and where it passed under the road. Beside it stood a friendly looking, but gnarled, old willow.

She bought a wheelbarrow and hauled all the wood she could lift to the house and stacked it in a beautiful pile beside the back porch.

Her hands had suffered until she was in the barn one day and found an old rotten leather glove just lying on the floor. How it got there, she couldn't imagine. She'd never noticed it before. She'd gone straight to the hardware store after breakfast, bought four pairs, and now her hands, though rough, were finally healing. Why she hadn't thought to buy gloves, she had no idea.

The only thing she hadn't done herself was replace the missing piece of roof that had blown off the barn. She'd found it on one of her walks, half buried on the edge of the east field, and dragged it back to the house. But she knew returning it to where it belonged was beyond her ability. So, she'd ended up calling a tree service, who came out with a cherry picker and replaced the tin and a few of the boards on the barn that were too high for her ladder to reach. She could just make out the light patches of new wood amidst the ancient gray planks that dominated her beloved.

There was an ache in her heart to paint it, but after talking to the owner of the hardware store, she had decided to wait until spring. The paint would not dry in the cold, he informed her, and the rains that so often came in the fall would wash all her hard work away.

Maggie smiled, looking from her hands to the barn. They were a perfect pair, patchy and a little rough around the edges, but slowly, the cracks were filling in and…

A fiery smear appeared on the horizon, and Maggie jumped up and ran inside. Quickly, she brewed another cup of coffee and raced back out. By the time she flung the door back open, the sky had turned from ghostly to magical. Glowing rose clouds hung in an orchid sky, and Maggie stared unblinking from her chair until the first ray of sun pierced the clouds.

The ground was covered in a thin white film of frost, and as the light grew, the fields began to sparkle. Golden rays raced across the earth as the lavender sky dulled and turned pale and blue.

Maggie was reminded of one of her favorite poems by Robert Frost.

"Nothing gold can stay," she whispered.

The pink clouds grayed for a breath, then turned pearly white as the sun cleared the horizon, and the day was born.

She smiled. Breathtaking. As usual.

A jolt shot through her as the wind tugged at a piece of hair that had blown across her eyes.

Blinking in the rapidly brightening sun, she traded her coffee for the journal she'd purchased in town. It had been a long time since she'd held a notebook like this in her hands. She flipped through the empty pages, waiting to be filled with thoughts and sketches. It had brought her so much joy when she was younger. Hopefully, it would do the same now, if she could stick with it long enough to get back in the habit. She'd been at it for five days, but it still felt unnatural. Still, she was determined to revive that part of herself, that inner voice that saw and felt beautiful things.

She looked for her pen, but it wasn't there..Hurrying inside, she found it on the end table and hurried back out. Curling back up under the blanket, she flexed her fingers, wrote the date at the top of the page, and tapped the pen against her lips.

How to begin?

The sunrise was so beautiful this morning, she wrote.

Maggie tapped her pen again, unable to think of what to write next. It wasn't for lack of something to write about. Every day was an adventure—Two days ago, she'd captured her first mouse, a cute little brown and white thing that had practically scared her to death before she cornered it, coaxed it into a cardboard box, and toss it outside. Unfortunately, she hadn't tossed him far enough because she'd seen him again last night during dinner. How it got back inside, she hadn't a clue—No; she was constantly discovering new experiences, and that was wonderful. It was just that none of that was on her mind right now. What was actually on her mind was...

I don't regret buying the farm, at least not yet. And I don't regret moving here, either. It's been an adventure, and it has certainly awakened my senses, but... I don't know. I am beginning to wonder if the isolation is getting to me. I don't feel like it is. I feel great. But... I don't know how to explain it. I've been getting these weird feelings. I've had them from the start, but they are getting stronger. I thought it was just the land, the history, speaking to me through my imagination. But now it feels different. Now, it feels like something more, and I don't know what to make of it. These sensations feel like hints now, real... deliberate hints, and they always lead me to something beautiful, like the spider webs that first day, or a reminder to look up once in a while when I work. Sometimes it feels like an actual voice in my head. Sometimes it feels like...

She paused.

... a physical touch. I've found myself staring at the old bookshelf, perusing the odd mix of poetry and fiction and field guides, or sitting in the chair that the previous owner left and wondering who lived here before me. Why he chose these books. Wondering what his life was like. I don't even know if he was a he, but then I'm sure he was. And I've created this fantasy...

Maggie stared at the page. She had been thinking it for a week, but for some reason, seeing in writing made it more real than it felt in her head, and it scared her a little. *He* didn't scare her. It was her, *believing* he was somehow still there, that did.

She wasn't exactly sure when it had started, the feeling that she wasn't alone. All she knew was the longer she was there, the clearer he was becoming in her mind, and the more her thoughts revolved around him.

Who?

The man whose home she now occupied. It was his approval she felt, not the houses, and she felt him everywhere. Every time she stepped foot in the barn, on her walks, when she sat at the kitchen table eating her dinner. Even when she went to retrieve the mail and straightened the mailbox, she found herself wondering if maybe they had taken the exact same path from the house to the road.

Something about the idea of her footsteps intertwining with his, crisscrossing their land, constantly meeting, and parting and coming together, thrilled her. It started as a spark, and each time it happened, she imagined they were crossing paths through time. But over the last few weeks, it had grown stronger, and now it was more like a little fire blazing in her chest that she couldn't extinguish, even if she wanted to, which she didn't. It was there now, and she was almost certain so was *he*.

That was the truth, but as she looked down at her unfinished sentence, she knew she wasn't ready to admit it. With a sigh, she tried to pull her head and heart out of the clouds.

Anyway, I don't know if it's my subconscious telling me I'm lonely or what. Dee sent me up here hoping I'd meet a man, and at the time, that was honestly the last thing I wanted to do. I still sort of feel that way or I think I do but then... Why am I thinking about the man who lived here? Why am I thinking about men at all? Am I falling into my old ways? I don't know. I don't know what I'm trying to say. Even now, months later, I don't. But the good news is I am feeling. A lot. All the time. So, sometimes I cry for no reason, and sometimes I scare myself, catching shadows out of the corner of my eye that aren't really there. Sometimes I feel this incredible stillness come over me, and I know I am exactly where I am meant to be, and other times, I am overcome with this ache for something I cannot even name, and it fills me until I can't breathe. I'm trying to just let it all happen. To be okay with whatever I feel. I think about all the times I've told Eric, when he was struggling with loss or heartbreak, that sometimes the only way out is through. I do believe that. I do. And hopefully, I am almost through the other side.

Maggie pulled her sunglasses over her eyes and reached for her rapidly cooling mug, wrapping her frozen fingers around it. She inhaled the crisp, clear air and exhaled slowly a moment later.

"Breath, life, out, in," she quoted from memory.

"Over and over, until it ends,
and when it's gone, when nothing is left,
You will see
Right and wrong never existed
and the miracle is
not what you did
but how you lived."

Maggie shivered and felt his quiet presence beside her again. She smiled, feeling her mother too. She had inspired that poem and Maggie had written it three days before she died, while waiting on hold to talk to the chair of the biology department, and breastfeeding Eric. Both ghosts warmed her heart. Maybe neither was really there, but the feeling was. And it was good.

Swallowing the last of her lukewarm coffee, she gathered her things and headed inside. After peeling off her winter gear and throwing it in the closet, she downed a quick bowl of instant oatmeal before making her way into the bathroom to tackle the first thing on her to-do list.

With a screwdriver in one hand and a pipe wrench in the other, she stood in front of the sink with her hand on her hips. That thing was going to go. Today. Now. She glanced at the sparkling white one she'd unboxed the night before, sitting on the floor.

She had watched the online video ten times and knew exactly what to do. Opening the cabinet below, she grabbed the valve to the water shut-off. Of course, it was stuck. So, she beat it with the wrench until it gave way and turned. Then she got up and pulled off the yellow plastic cover of the clear diamond shaped faucet. Sticking the crossed tip of the Phillips-head screwdriver into the rusty screw centered inside, she twisted. At first, it wouldn't turn either, but finally, after a lot of unladylike grunting and really throwing her back into it, the screw gave way.

Maggie's cry of triumph turned to a scream of terror when water erupted out of the top of the fixture, like a high-pressure fountain.

She threw her hand over it and water shot out between her fingers, soaking her shirt, spraying her in the face and blinding her. "No! *Shit!* Shit!" She let it go, and the fountain resumed its spectacular show, drenching the mirror and ceiling.

"Shit!" Maggie cried again as she covered her head and dropped to her knees.

Ducking into the cabinet, she yanked at the valve. It turned, but the water didn't shut off. Had she broken it? "Shit!" Smacking her head on the underside of the sink, she backed out.

There was at least a half inch of water on her new, beautifully stained wood floor, and worse than that, she didn't know where the shut off was. She hadn't even thought to ask the plumber about it. Grabbing a towel off the rack, she pressed it over the faucet. That stopped the water from shooting up, but it was only a second before it soaked through the towel and began to cascade over the edge of the vanity like a waterfall.

Pressing the towel over the faucet with one hand, she scrolled to find the plumber's number on her phone. She was in the middle of uttering every curse word she knew when a loud bang came from the kitchen.

Her head flew up. Had the other faucets erupted? Or was something about to explode? "Oh, please god no." She heard it again. An ominous clang. Stretching her arm, she tried to peek out the door, but couldn't reach her head far enough without letting go.

Bang! Bang!

"Shit." Whatever it was, it was getting worse. She eyed the faucet—

Bang!

"Fuuuuuck!" Letting go, she dashed into the hall as the water resumed its destruction of her bathroom.

Bang!

She ran into the kitchen, slipping in her wet shoes, and caught herself on a chair before falling over.

Bang!

Spinning around, her wet hair whipped around and stuck to her face like the tentacles of an octopus as she tore it from her eyes.

Bang!

It was coming from the pantry.

She gasped as a river of water made its way out of the bathroom and started flowing into the living room.

Bang!

"Holy shit."

Maggie threw the dining chair out of the way, yanked the pantry door open. Was it the hot water tank? Or the furnace.

She listened, but the banging had stopped.

Her eyes dashed over the hot water heater, wondering if it really was about to explode, when something in the dark corner behind the tank caught her eye, and she jumped back. Not that damn mouse! Had it made the noise? She was about to slam the door when it registered.

Jerking it back open, she gasped. Near the ground, slightly behind the tank, was a yellow lever attached to a pipe. Throwing herself at it, she yanked it as hard as she could. It turned, and she fell backward as her wet hand slipped off the plastic handle. She cracked the back of her head a second time on the table as the rush of water in the bathroom faded.

Jumping up, she raced back to the bathroom, slipping and landing hard on her hip in front of the doorway. Scrambling to her knees, she grabbed at the jamb and peered over the vanity. The water had stopped. Exhaling, she slumped back down, pressing her back against the door and slicking her soaking hair back. "Thank god."

After a couple of breaths, she dragged herself to her feet. She was sopping wet. Thinking she heard laughter, she turned to the living room. No one was there. She touched her forehead. Maybe it was just her inner voice? She felt dangerously close to some form of hysteria.

"*Shit.*" Every inch of the bathroom was wet. She looked up as water dripped from the ceiling. It looked like it was raining *in the house*. Sloshing to the sink, she threw the towel back over the faucet just in case, then reached in her back pocket for her phone. It wasn't there.

"Where's my phone?" she asked, her bedraggled reflection in the mirror.

Sloshing back to the kitchen, she found it on the table. She was about to search for the plumber's number when she realized she needed to get the water off the floor before it got ruined. If it wasn't already. Running to the stairs, she slipped again, falling on her butt with a small splash.

"Damn it!" She thumped the floor, realizing, in her wet clothes, she was making a bigger mess everywhere she went. Getting up, she kicked her shoes off and stripped down to her panties and bra. Then she ran upstairs to the guest room and pulled all the towels out of the closet, and dragged the comforter off the bed. Hurrying back downstairs, she threw them first over the water that had accumulated in the living room, then worked her way back into the bathroom. Drop towels, let them soak, do her best to wring them out in the tub, and do it again.

By the time she was done, she was exhausted and freezing. Sitting back on her heels, she stared at the bathtub full of soaked towels and blankets.

Slowly, she got to her feet, made her way to the hall closet, and grabbed her jacket. Slinking into it, she headed for the kitchen.

Coffee. She needed a coffee. Immediately.

She set the pod in the maker, and as she waited for it to brew, her phone buzzed on the counter.

Hey Mom. Hope you're having a good day. Love you.

Good day? Maggie glanced at her reflection in the window. She looked like a drowned rat, and she'd almost destroyed her house. A strangled sound passed her lips, and she clapped a surprised hand over it.

The next thing she knew, she was laughing so hard her face hurt. Doubling over, she collapsed onto her knees in the middle of the kitchen floor, unable to breathe. Tears filled her eyes as she lifted her head and looked toward the bathroom. Grabbing the edge of the sink she tried to stand, but her legs were like jelly, which only made her laugh harder.

"Oh god," she wheezed, gripping the edge of the counter like it was a life raft. "Oww." Her cheeks and sides ached, but the harder she tried to stop, the worse it got.

By the time Maggie was done laughing like a psychopath, steam was rising from her mug and she was utterly exhausted. Instead of retrieving it, she rolled onto her back, legs splayed in the middle of the floor, in her freezing underwear.

"Too far." She didn't have the energy just yet.

The heat came on, and she pressed her feet to the vent under the sink. Goosebumps rippled across her body, and she pulled her jacket closed as she stared at the ceiling and let the heat warm her.

She knew she had to get up. She knew she had to call someone for help. And she was absolutely certain she would die of embarrassment when that help came, and she had to explain what she'd done.

But for right now, she was just going to lie here, be still, and enjoy the feeling of laughing so hard she could float on air. It had been a *very* long time.

CHAPTER NINE

WILL HAD ALMOST DIED LAUGHING AS WATER SHOT OUT OF THE faucet and Maggie screamed. He'd clung to the door, tears running down his cheeks, while she cursed and screamed some more and sprayed herself in the face. It wasn't until she was under the sink that he even noticed the water running around his feet, outlining them on the floor. Luckily, as she slipped and slid by him like a calf on newborn legs, she'd been too distracted to notice. He should have led her to the shut-off sooner, but it wasn't every day that a beautiful, hilariously wet, sailor-mouthed woman put on a show like that and turned his house into a river. And he knew he had to savor it while he had the chance. So, he'd taken his sweet time. And he was glad. Who knew how long it would be before he laughed like that again? It had been over a hundred years since the last time.

He had almost died a *second* time when he turned around and she was standing in the hall practically naked. Feelings he wasn't sure he'd *ever* had coursed through his body, and he'd almost fallen to his knees right there and worshiped her. The curve of her hips, the way the water beaded at the ends of her hair and dripped down her arms and between her breasts, the plane of her stomach. The triangle of lace below it. He'd never seen anything or anyone more beautiful in his life, and despite knowing he should, he could not look away. As she ran up the stairs on her tiptoes, her body a black silhouette against the bright light streaming through the window, he knew with absolute certainty that he had never wanted anyone more than he wanted the woman occupying his house.

95

Watching her soak up the water in her underclothes was the most erotic thing he had ever witnessed, and he had almost died a *third* time when he looked down and realized he still had the ability to become aroused. It had never once crossed his mind in all the time he'd been dead. It hadn't crossed his mind much in life, either, which only went to prove what a complete imbecile he'd been when he was alive. What man didn't at least take the time to think about *sex*?

She'd closed the show by making him laugh again, as she fell to the floor roaring and giggling and wheezing so hard, he thought she might faint.

As she'd rolled to her back in the middle of the kitchen, hair splayed out in a halo around her head, he'd watched her from the door of the bathroom. As he wiped the happy tears from his eyes, his body had once again filled with desire, and Will found himself wishing he could lie down beside her, terrified that he might, even though he knew he shouldn't.

But she'd covered up, gotten up, and thankfully, his senses returned. He could not stay in the house with her if he started having feelings like that. It wouldn't be right. And he couldn't start having feelings like that because he was dead. What he could have done was shut the water off himself, but he was afraid she'd realize what he'd done, and he was just... His heart still hadn't stopped thumping like it was about to leap out of his chest and take off without him. And he liked that feeling.

SHE'D CALLED two plumbers before settling for a 'Bob the Handyman.'

Will studied him from the doorway. Bob was sitting on the toilet with a toolbox on his lap while Maggie sat on her knees in front of the sink. He looked older than the house itself, and at first, Will had been doubtful he would be any help at all, but the old man was managing. Mostly, he was telling Maggie what to do. He had all the tools and knowhow, just not the energy or the knees to bend down and do the work.

"Alright, now, take this-here tape and wrap it around... No, not that way, you gotta wrap it in the direction you're twisting... Yeah. That's it. Now, thread it onto that one and," he handed her a wrench, and her head disappeared under the sink, "tighten it with this. You don't need to kill it just—" The old man glanced in Will's direction.

It was the third time he'd done that, and it was starting to make Will uncomfortable. He was sure the man couldn't see him, otherwise he'd be screaming his head off and heading for the hills. But if that was true, why did he keep looking that way? Glancing over his shoulder into the living room, Will saw nothing out of place. He turned back.

"Just till it's snug," the old man finished.

Maggie grunted. "There," she said. A second later, she reemerged.

"Okay. Now we test it out," Bob said.

Maggie looked doubtful. "What if—"

"Then I'll holler, and you shut it back off."

Maggie got up, and Will stepped back just before she passed through him. She went to the kitchen, turned the water on, and hurried back.

"Well?" she asked, her brows raised hopefully.

"Well, give 'er a whirl."

Hesitantly, she grabbed the hot water handle and turned it, squeezing her eyes shut as she turned her face away. It reminded him of his sisters when they were little and their mother had made them pluck chickens for dinner. Will smiled at the memory.

There was the soft rush of running water as it tumbled into the sink bowl and down into the drain. Maggie opened one eye, then another, and Will couldn't hold back his laugh as her expression changed from fear to hard-won satisfaction.

Bob glanced at him again, and Will's smile faded. *Why* did he keep doing that?

Maggie's phone buzzed in the pocket of her pants. Turning the water off, she quickly excused herself, explaining it was a client and she had to take the call. He watched her climb the stairs to her 'office,' still not quite sure what she did for a living, but knowing it involved the little television thing she had with the typewriter keys on it. The last people who lived in the house had not had one of those, so he didn't know what to call it. Will leaned back against the door frame, and when he turned, his eyes locked with Bob's.

"Hello, Mr. Morgan," Bob said.

Will felt like a deer in the headlights of a fast-moving truck, and the blood in his head, or whatever it was that was in there, rushed to Will's feet as he clutched the doorjamb. "Y-you can see me?" he whispered hoarsely. And how did Bob know who he was?

"I can." The old man nodded. His hands shook a little, giving his fear away, but all things considered, he didn't seem to be doing too bad for seeing what was presumably his first ghost.

"How?" Will choked, feeling like someone was squeezing his throat.

Bob shrugged. "I seen you before. I suppose that's why I can see ya now."

Seen him before? What did that mean? "You're not afraid?"

"That depends. Do I got somethin' to be afraid of?"

"No."

They stared at each other for a moment. Bob set his toolbox on the floor and got up. "Robert Stahl." He held out his hand, and Will stared for a moment before he shook his head.

"I can't touch—"

"Oh… o'course." Bob sat back down. "You don't remember me?"

Will remembered a family named Stahl. They owned the farm down the road, but not—

"I met ye once before you died."

Will's eyes widened.

"That's how I recognized ya when I saw ya the first time. You look just the same."

"You've seen me *before*?"

The old man shrugged again and began dropping the tools and tape into his box. "A few times. I'm the one that's been putting the paper in your mailbox every now and again. I figured it might help... pass the time."

Will didn't know what to say. It was his first dialogue in seventy years, and to his embarrassment, tears filled his eyes. He blinked them back.

"I always wanted to ask you how it was, you know, bein' dead." Bob's cheeks reddened. "But after you ran off the Wilsons and the Verniers, I was too scairt to come—"

"Sorry about that I—" Maggie bumped into Will, and he reeled as the little prick that usually passed between them became a painful jolt. Maggie stumbled and threw her hand against the doorframe. Pressing her hand to her stomach she doubled over slightly, looking just as shaken as he felt.

"Sorry, I—um." She inhaled deeply.

"Maybe you ought to go sit down, miss?" Bob asked, waiting for Will to clear out of the way before leading her to the kitchen. He held her elbow, and Will had never been more jealous of a hundred-year-old man in his life.

Maggie smiled appreciatively, dropping into a chair as she pulled her hands through her hair. "Call me Maggie, and sorry about that, I got a little dizzy there for a second. Please, have a seat. Can I offer you a coffee?"

Bob glanced at Will, as if asking for permission. Will nodded, feeling odd for even being asked. "Sure. A coffee'd be nice. But only when you're ready."

Maggie got up right away. "I'm fine. I probably just need a cup myself. It's been an eventful morning."

Bob glanced at Will again, and this time his eyes asked a different question.

Did Maggie know he was there?

Will shook his head.

"I can only imagine," Bob said, dragging his eyes back to Maggie, who was busy at the counter.

A minute later, she set a cup of coffee in front of Bob. "Milk or sugar?"

Bob shook his head, and she sat back down.

"I am just so grateful you could come out on short notice," she said as Will stood behind her.

"Well, truth be known, I don't get too many calls these days, but I like the work, 'specially since my Olive passed. It keeps me busy," Bob confessed.

"I'm sorry," Maggie said.

Bob smiled sadly. "It's been a long four years. But I'm getting by."

"Well, actually, I've got a lot of things I need done around here." Maggie's coffee finished brewing, and she retrieved her mug and sat back down. "Small repairs mostly at this point, but I'd like to learn to do them myself." She blew on the top of her mug. "If I paid you your hourly fee, would you be willing to part with a little bit of your time and expertise to teach me a few things?" The grin that spread across Bob's face brought back a memory. And Will knew exactly who Bob Stahl was.

The last time he'd seen him, he was a boy of six or seven, and he'd fallen off his bike in front of the house, spilling a bag of marbles onto the road. Half of them had rolled into the ditch. Will had come out of the barn to find the cause of the awful sound scaring the cows he was trying to milk. He'd been sure the neighbor's dog had been run down by a truck, which would have served it right. The damn animal had broken into his pen and killed two of his hens before he'd been able to scare it off. Instead of the dog, though, he'd found a boy with big teeth and skinned knees crawling through his ditch. He'd yelled at him to quiet down and quit scaring his animals. The boy apologized and shut his mouth. But the sniffles had continued as he resumed the search for his precious marbles. Will had a million things to do that day, namely finish milking the cows, but...

Will looked at Bob, who was nodding vigorously. Yes. It was definitely him.

If he recalled correctly, they'd found every damn marble, and Bob had gone home with *that* very same smile on his face.

"I'd be delighted." Bob took a sip of his coffee.

Then, Will remembered scolding him before he left, for wasting time with games. The small smile that had tugged on his mouth faded into a grimace. He had told Bob he ought to be home helping his father. Will shook his head. What a fool he'd been. The only consolation was that day at least he'd been a fool on his knees helping the boy look.

Maggie and Bob were quiet for a moment.

"How do you like it here?" Bob asked conversationally.

Maggie set her mug down. "To be honest, I love it, but... there are times when I think I bit off a little more than I can chew." She turned and looked through Will toward the bathroom and laughed. "Like this morning, for example. I watch these videos, and they make it look so easy but—"

"Country life suits you then? You don't get scairt bein' out here all alone?" Bob interrupted.

Will was curious to know her answer himself.

"No." She laughed. "Well, maybe the first night started out a little rough but... Actually, I feel less lonely here than I have anywhere in quite a while. And... happier too, I think," Maggie said, staring into her mug.

Bob smiled and winked at Will over her head. Will didn't know what to make of that.

"Glad to hear it. Always nice to meet new folks, and there aren't too many around here, at least not away from the lake. And this place hasn't seen this much... life in a while. It's nice to drive by and see lights on in the windows."

Maggie smiled as Bob drained the last of his coffee.

"Well, I ought to be off."

"How much do I owe you for today?" she asked.

"Thirty dollars ought to do it."

"That's it?" Maggie sounded surprised, but Will couldn't see her face.

"Well, you did do most of the work," Bob reminded her, as she got up from the table.

"I've got cash upstairs. Is that okay?"

"Sure. Money's money as far as I'm concerned."

Will stepped aside as Maggie headed back upstairs. His head was so full of questions he didn't know which to ask first.

Bob spoke up before he could decide. "So, you're looking after her, then?"

Will looked up and heard the floor upstairs creak beneath Maggie's feet. He met Bob's eyes and nodded.

"Nothing more?"

Will understood the question, and why the old man asked. Maggie was beautiful, and he was here, alone with her in the house.

"Nothing more," he promised.

Bob seemed satisfied.

"Why can you see me when no one else can?" Will asked, sitting down in Maggie's chair. "How is this—"

Bob shook his head. "I dunno."

"There has to be a reason," Will insisted.

But Maggie returned before the old man could answer.

She thanked Bob and paid him before following him out. Then

she stood on the porch until he was gone, denying Will the chance to speak with him again.

As Maggie went inside and tested the bathroom faucets again, Will went to his chair and sat down.

He needed to think. Something strange was going on. Stranger than him, and he wanted to know why.

CHAPTER TEN

MAGGIE PULLED INTO THE LAUNDROMAT. THE ONLY THING SHE didn't like about the house was that it hadn't come with a washer and dryer. Worse, there was nowhere to put one even if it had. Snowflakes swirled around her as she lugged the bag over her shoulder and pushed the door open. She was greeted by a blast of hot soapy air. Separating her clothes into washers, she opened a roll of quarters, dumped the soap in, and started each machine.

Huddled in her coat, she sat in one of the chairs that faced the street and watched the snow fall. It was already December eighteenth, only a week until Christmas, and this was the first official snow of the season.

She'd been bringing her computer so she could work while she waited. But she'd forgotten to plug it in last night, and the battery was dead, so she'd left it behind. Picking up a magazine, she flipped through it. It was one of those celebrity types, and after several pages of not recognizing anyone, she set it aside.

Her eyes drifted to the turn-of-the century building across the street. *Lakeside Library est. 1900* was painted in gold leaf on the window.

Maggie checked the washer. She had twenty minutes before the cycle ended.

Grabbing her purse, she decided that was more than enough time to check it out.

Snow swirled down from the gray sky as she waited for the traffic to clear, then crossed the street. Shivering, she climbed the steps and pushed the heavy oak door open wiping her feet on the rug in the vestibule. After passing through a second door, she was greeted by faded yellow carpeting, rows of shelves, and the familiar scent of old books.

She perused a couple of the aisles before getting an idea.

"Do you have any historical books about the town?" she asked the lady knitting behind the checkout counter.

The older woman looked up and smiled. Her name tag said Dorothy. "We do! Some books, and a database with old newspapers and all that sort of thing. It's on the computer over there. Anything in particular you're looking for?"

The words came out before she could stop them. "The Morgans. They owned a farm just out of town and—"

"Ah. So, you're her." The woman nodded.

Maggie frowned. "I'm who?"

"The lady that bought the old Morgan homestead. I'll tell ya, I thought I'd be playing euchre with Jesus up in heaven before anyone bought that old place." She leaned across the counter. "You know they say it's haunted." She raised an inquiring eyebrow.

"Well, I haven't seen anything."

"Nothing?" Dorothy looked fairly disappointed.

"Nope." And that was the truth. She hadn't. Everything she'd experienced she had either felt or heard.

"Darn. I was hoping for a juicy story to tell the gals." She shrugged. "Okay, follow me."

Maggie followed her upstairs to a small room where she pulled two books off the shelf. Dorothy thumbed through the first one and, when she found the pages she was looking for, handed it over to Maggie.

"That's the old homestead there, as it looked in 1920."

The barn looked new. The silo too. It once had a striped top, she noted. There had been a garage between the house and barn and a corral with cows where the east field was now. A dog, a lab maybe, had been sitting under the oak by the driveway. The house looked almost identical, and the weird structure behind the barn that she hadn't been able to figure out looked like some kind of thing to hold corn. The scene made Maggie smile. It was so full of life.

Dorothy dropped another book in her lap. "Um, this here—" She pointed to a photo of a handwritten list with names spelled out in scrolling cursive. "That's the 1910 census, showing the occupants at that address at the time the census was taken."

The first name was the one that caught her eye. William Morgan. W.M. It was on the hammer that she'd been using almost daily for a month. Her heart skipped a beat. She tried to ignore it.

"Are there any photos?"

The woman grabbed the first book back and flipped through several more pages. She stopped on a black-and-white photo of about twenty men, standing in front of one of the buildings in town. "That there is William Morgan, and those are two of his sons. Albert and Louis."

Maggie squinted at the photo and frowned. William didn't look as she expected, which was ridiculous since she had no idea what to expect. She looked back at the census and ran her finger down the names. William, Alice, William, Albert— "Wait, why does it say William twice?"

Dorothy grabbed the book and peered at it through her bifocals. "Oh, that would be his son. See here. Born in 1900. So, there was William senior and William junior."

"Is there a photo of him?" Maggie asked.

Dorothy shook her head. "I don't believe so. At least not one I've seen."

Disappointed, Maggie looked at her watch and realized her time was up. She closed the books.

"Well, thank you for your time. I'd like to borrow these books if I might?"

"You'll need a library card for that. Let's go back downstairs, and I'll get you set up."

Maggie followed Dorothy down the old steps, dashed back

across the street, switched her wash, and hurried back for her books. A shiny new Lakeside Library card was waiting for her on top of the books. "Thank you so much," Maggie said.

Dorothy looked up from her knitting. "I thought of something while you were gone."

Maggie slipped the card into her wallet. "What's that?"

"If you're looking for photos of William junior, you might have luck if you try the computer. The newspapers are on there."

Maggie shook her head. She didn't follow.

"The obituaries. They were cataloged a couple years ago by the kids at the high school." She walked back around the corner of the counter and fired up a rather decrepit looking PC. A minute later, she clicked on a folder and opened a second one. "The names are listed in alphabetical order. Once you find the name, it'll tell you the date. You take that and go in here," she clicked another folder, and a list of icons appeared with dates beneath them, "and look up the closest date. The obit and a picture, if there was one provided, will be there."

Someone else came in, and Dorothy excused herself. Butterflies fluttered in Maggie's stomach as she sat down. Why, she didn't know. Was she hoping her suspicions would be confirmed or denied? Did she want to know who had died in her new house and when?

Scrolling down the list, she found the Morgans. There were a surprising number of them, and four Williams. She picked the first one. Died February 4th, 1919. Going to the 1919 folder, she searched for the February issues of the paper. There were two. When she found the right paper, and the obituary section, she recognized the man immediately as William Senior. He had been born in 1889 and died at the age of forty of a heart attack. He was survived by six children: William, Albert, Louis, Matthew, Claire, and Susanna, and one daughter-in-law, Meredith.

She went back and tried the second William. Died September 23rd, 1946. Wiping her sweaty palm on the top of her thigh, she tugged at her sweater, navigating the mouse to the 1946 folder, and clicked on September. There were four issues. Guessing, she picked the third. He was not there. She opened the fourth paper, scrolled to the obituaries, and there he was, half hidden in shadow under the brim of an Indiana Jones hat.

Even though she could only see half of his face, Maggie knew it was him. The goosebumps on her arms confirmed it. She looked around the quiet library and wondered if he was there with her now.

Her eyes fell back to the screen. The image was black and white and blurry, as if they'd zoomed in on a small corner of a larger picture and cropped it, but what she could see matched what she felt in her mind's eye. Strong, clean-shaven jaw, full lips, piercing eyes she could just barely make out. He was handsome, and his face was kind. At least it felt so to her, but... she looked back at his frowning mouth, and his serious eyes. They did not smile the way she expected. It was him, for certain, but also, *not* him. Maggie bit her lip in confusion, not understanding the statement her brain had made.

She read the caption. He was born in nineteen hundred and was forty-six when he died from a "farming accident." He was survived by a wife, Meredith, and two siblings. There was no mention of children.

She asked Dorothy if they had a printer, and of course they did, but it was out of ink. Maggie took a photo with her phone, thanked Dorothy, gathered her books, and headed back to the laundromat.

Sitting in the uncomfortable plastic chair, bundled in her coat, Maggie stared at the photo of William until her clothes were dry. It was hard to believe she was actually considering the possibility that he was haunting her house, because she knew ghosts weren't real. But—

The dryer buzzed. Sighing, she pulled her warm clothes from the dryer. But if it wasn't him, *what* was she feeling?

Maggie gathered up her clothes and loaded them back in her car. She made a quick run to the grocery to pick up a few last-minute things before Dahlia and Eric arrived tomorrow for their "before Christmas weekend in the country" and headed home.

Home, she thought, as she pulled into the driveway and parked her car in front of the house. That was what it felt like. And it was finally done, just in time for the holidays.

Between her and Bob, she had managed to tie up all the loose ends. The doorbell was fixed; the cabinets had hardware on them. She'd safely replaced the faucet on the kitchen sink, painted all the trim white, and swapped out the old dingy veneered interior doors for pretty, new paneled ones.

It was already pitch black out. Luckily, she'd left the porch light on, so she could see where she was going. The wind blew from the north, and without anything to brace it but the miles of flat dirt fields, it cut through Maggie like an icy blade as she hurried back and forth retrieving baskets of laundry and grocery bags.

Dropping the last bag on the floor, she slammed the door and locked it.

A shiver raced down her spine as she kicked her boots off.

"Damn, it's cold," she said, shaking the snow out of her hair and pulling her coat off. She hung it up, collected her grocery bags, and carried them to the kitchen. Flipping the light on with her elbow, she dropped everything onto the table. The only sounds were the ticking of the clock and the howling wind as it whipped through the trees out back.

She checked her phone and saw her good night text from Eric and a notice for a winter storm warning. For the first time since moving in, Maggie felt a twinge of nervousness about being in the country alone. What if the power went out? What if she got snowed in and stuck without heat?

She tried not to think about it as she put away the groceries, but as the lights flickered and the wind howled, she couldn't help but imagine a power line somewhere hanging on for dear life, ready to snap and plunge her into darkness.

Plugging in her phone, she grabbed the flashlight out of the drawer under the microwave and set it on the counter, just in case. She lit two of the festive holiday scented candles she'd bought in town and put them on the end tables in the living room. Returning to the kitchen, she put on her Christmas Jazz station and connected it to the Bluetooth speaker that was on top of the refrigerator. The saxophone music soothed her nerves, and muffled the wind, as she put the last of the groceries away.

An awful screech brought Maggie to a halt in the middle of the kitchen, and the carton of half and half in her hand fell to the floor. She heard it again, coming from the living room. Peeking around the corner, she listened. Was it an animal or—She heard it again and realized what it was. Nothing more than a branch from the pine tree out front, scraping against one of the windows.

Leaning back against the wall, she pressed a hand over her heart. Damn, that had scared her. And what did she expect?

Shaking her head, she laughed as she picked up the half and half and put it in the fridge. She'd spent half the afternoon hunting for *ghosts*.

Opening one of the bottles of wine she'd bought in anticipation of Dahlia's arrival, she poured herself a glass of chardonnay. Although it had been four months ago, it was still too soon for anything red.

Taking a sip, she smiled. With the music to drown out the wind, and all the blinds closed, she could almost forget there was a blizzard outside.

She surveyed her warm, cozy kitchen. She'd left the old yellow vinyl countertop with metal edging. It was in good condition, and for some reason, she kind of dug the retro vibe. With the dark floors and cabinets, soft gray walls and white trim, the room had a sort of shabby/country/chic vibe going for it. It had never been her style before, but it suited her now.

As she crossed the living room, candlelight flickered over the same gray walls. Her white couch looked a little at odds with the old green chair she'd kept, but she didn't care. The dark accents, coffee table, old bookshelf, end tables, and contrasting white trim, rug, and blinds carried the same theme as the kitchen. Sparse, chic, cozy, with just a hint to the past sprinkled in for good measure.

Maggie eyed the fireplace. She'd been meaning to test it out, and if there was ever a night to sit before a roaring fire, it was this one. Besides, she wanted to make sure it worked before her guests arrived tomorrow.

She set her glass down on the coffee table and went to the coat closet. Biting her lip, she pulled a starter log from the plastic bag on the floor and read the instructions. It seemed straightforward enough. Set the log on the grate. Add dry wood. Light it on fire.

It only took a moment for the starter log to catch, and once it did, the flames spread quickly. Unfortunately, so did the smoke. Maggie coughed and waved it away as the flames grew higher, and some of the smaller pieces of kindling caught on fire. Smoke continued to billow from the opening, and she wondered if maybe there was something stuck in the chimney. A dead raccoon came to mind, and she wanted to kick herself for not thinking of having it cleaned or swept or whatever.

"No. No. No," she moaned, fanning the gray cloud back into the firebox. The air had already grown hazy and now the whole house was going to smell like smoke.

There was only one thing to do. Jumping up, she ran to the kitchen. She had to put it out. Grabbing her largest bowl, she quickly filled it with water and headed back toward the living room.

Maggie skidded to a stop in front of the stairs, and her jaw dropped. The little brass ring mounted on the brick, that she *thought* was a decorative hook, was slowly turning in a clockwise motion. A grinding sound followed from somewhere inside the chimney, and she realized it must have been closed somehow. Motionless, except for the water sloshing back and forth in her bowl, she watched the ring complete the turn, then lay back flat against the brick.

The fire leaped to life, as if recovering from asphyxiation, and the smoke miraculously began to clear from the room.

Quietly, she backed into the kitchen and, even more quietly, set the bowl in the sink. Leaning against the counter, she took a deep, disbelieving breath. Well, if she wanted proof, that was it.

Her house was haunted.

And she knew exactly who it was. His face had been seared into her brain since she'd seen it this afternoon. *William Morgan Jr.* She peeked over her shoulder toward the living room. The question now was, what did she do about it?

Should she address him? Or ignore him? He'd clearly been trying to stay unnoticed, so did that mean he didn't want her to know he was there? Was he afraid? Or was he afraid *she'd* be afraid? Maybe it was both?

Making her way back into the living room, she forced herself not to look at the ring as she walked around the couch. Her heart drummed in her ears as she sat down and stared into the fire. She took a jittery sip of her wine then hid her hands under her thighs to keep them from shaking. Was he watching her at this very moment? Did that scare her?

Maggie caught her reflection in the window. She looked like a terrified kid waiting her turn to go into the principal's office. A small laugh fluttered from her chest. That wouldn't do. What if she frightened him away? She jumped up and grabbed a blanket out of the basket under the front window. Spying the books she'd borrowed sitting on top of her laundry, she grabbed them, sat back on the couch.

Pulling her feet up onto the cushions, she reminded herself that he'd been there the whole time and hadn't tried to kill her yet. So, no, she wasn't scared. If he appeared, she would say hello, and thank him for fixing the fireplace. If he didn't, she would leave him be. That was the plan. At least for now. Maggie dropped the blanket over her knees. Downing half her glass of wine, she rolled her shoulders and opened the first book. The book was titled **Lakeside, From 1900-1950.** She flipped through it, glancing at the photos as she went. It appeared most of the buildings in town had been built in the late 1800s through 1910. Those were considered the 'booming' years. After that, the town had settled into a quiet hub for the farming community that surrounded it and supported a few lakeside mansions built by wealthy automobile tycoons.

The photo of William's father and brothers had been taken at the opening of the new Farm and Country Bank. Upon closer inspection, she realized it was the very building she'd borrowed the book from. The library was in the old bank.

She found the page with the picture of the farm, taking in every detail.

The fields were full of low-lying crops, probably sugar beets or soybeans. The barn looked freshly painted. One of the large doors sat partially open, and she saw something she'd missed before, the front two wheels of a tractor that looked very much like the one that was sitting out behind the barn now. She looked closer and saw a pant leg and a boot. The rest of the man was lost in the shadows. Was that him? Was that...

Maggie turned toward the door and found her photo of the barn on the wall. Slowly, she got up and retrieved it. Bringing it to the fireplace, where the light was the brightest, she sat down on the hearth running her finger over the glass, over the window where she'd always imagined a face looking back.

She squeezed her eyes closed for a moment as the truth settled upon her. That's because someone *was*.

William had been there even then? Opening her eyes, she recognized him clearly now that she knew what he looked like. Yes, of course. He'd probably been here since he died. But that meant... He'd been here seventy-three *years?*

She looked up, almost expecting to see him standing in front of her. No wonder he was afraid to talk to her. What had he been doing here all this time? While she was busy with college, and having children, and getting lost, he'd been *here?* Alone? Wandering around this old house and her beloved decaying barn?

Tears filled her eyes. Now it made sense. This place, everything she felt here, why it spoke to her… It was because *he* was here, and he had been for so long that a part of him was etched onto every blade of grass. She'd sensed it when she came the first time, and she felt it now, his regret, his loneliness, his fear, and longing. Had *he* called her back after all this time? Was that possible?

Maggie wiped her eyes and added a couple more logs to the fire. Draining the rest of her wine, she poured herself another glass. Could it be that it wasn't she and the barn that were meant to cross paths, but she and *him*? It was an oddly comforting thought.

Setting the books on the floor, she curled up under her blanket, watching the fire dance through the wine in her glass. She didn't know why William hadn't gone to where everyone else did when they died, or why he'd chosen to remain here all this time, but she did know one thing. He was not alone anymore. She was there.

"I'm here now. And I'm not going anywhere," she said, hoping he could hear.

Maggie set her glass on the table, and as the storm raged outside, she fell into restful sleep.

MAGGIE OPENED her eyes and blinked. Pushing herself up from the cushions, she shielded her eyes. "What in the—" Turning to the window, she gasped. The world outside was white.

Squinting, she pulled herself to her feet and went to the window. Surrounded by all the snow, the barn almost looked red again. Almost. Maggie had never seen anything so serene.

It was a Christmas miracle. *Or nightmare.* Frowning, she glanced out to where the road should be. It was gone, buried under the thick white blanket.

How were Dahlia and Eric going to get here? She stepped back and noticed the barn photo was back on the wall.

The night before tumbled back into her consciousness, and she stumbled backward, bumping into the end table, before plopping onto it. She *finally* looked at the brass ring. Then at the ashes piled beneath the grate. Had she imagined it? Her eyes fell to her half full glass of wine, then the photo suspiciously back on the wall? Had she done that? *Or did he?*

She pulled her fingers through her hair and took several deep breaths as she headed into the bathroom and closed the door. Leaning against her shiny new sink, she eyed herself in the mirror. *Jesus.* Smoothing her wild hair, she flipped it into a ponytail and brushed her teeth. She couldn't remember the last time she'd taken a shower, something she had to remedy before her guests arrived, *if* they arrived.

But first, coffee.

Pulling the door open, she shuffled to the kitchen, sensing a heaviness in the air. It wasn't the glass and a half of wine she'd had that was weighing on her though. It was everything else. It was suddenly finding herself believing in ghosts. It was thinking there was one haunting her house. It was feeling his presence everywhere, and *liking* it, and not knowing what that meant. She looked over her shoulder. Hell, he might be standing right next to her now. But most of all, it was knowing he had been here for almost two decades alone, and she'd been so caught up in herself, she hadn't even noticed his face in the photo, begging to be seen.

How many times had she sat in the hall back home, staring at it, and looked past him? He'd been right there. *Right* there.

How could she be so blind?

Maggie couldn't imagine being alone for that long. How had he not gone mad? How could he still find it in his heart to comfort her with webs and gentle, reassuring hands on her back—both had to be him—when she had ignored him for almost twenty years?

She'd felt him that day with Dean, maybe even seen him in the shadows. She knew it now. But she'd been so blind then, so naive, and self-centered. The direct opposite of everything she was now. And she had missed him.

Maggie stared at her coffee.

She might not have much going for her at the moment, but she had more than William did, more than a lot of people did. She had Eric and Dee. She had coffee and comfy socks. She looked out over the snow-covered field that stretched for a mile behind the bare oaks and maples. She had the views out these windows, and maybe most importantly, she had the chance, right now, to make her life whatever she wanted, even if she had no idea what that was yet.

Maggie pulled a second mug down from the shelf. Poor William had none of those things.

She wouldn't bother him, but she needed to let him know she knew he was there. He'd been alone long enough. He'd been hiding long enough. She knew what both of those felt like. And she wouldn't make him live through another day of it if he didn't want to. He deserved more.

CHAPTER ELEVEN

WILL PASSED THROUGH THE WALL AND STOOD ON THE PORCH AS Maggie, bundled in her jacket and hat, dragged a dining room chair outside, and set it on the opposite side of her little table. She brought out the rest of her usual things, except the pen, of course. He smiled. She *always* forgot a pen. When she went back inside, he quickly dropped one on the table. A moment later, she reemerged with two piping hot cups of coffee and set them on the table.

His brows came together as he looked out over the road then back at her nestling in her little cocoon of blankets. Once she was settled, she took a sip from her mug.

Was she expecting someone? Bob, maybe? Will squinted against the blinding white landscape. The roads were practically impassable. Surely, she had noticed that?

Setting her mug on the table, she grabbed her journal, and the pen, turned to a blank page and began to write.

At first, he'd peeked over her shoulder, telling himself nobody wrote anything down they didn't really want read, but after a couple days, his conscience had gotten the better of him. As much as he hated to, and despite his desperate curiosity, he'd relegated her notebook to the realm of the bathroom and his bedroom... *her* bedroom. Off limits.

He still wasn't sure exactly what had happened last night.

He'd taken a chance opening the damper, but it was either that or smoke her out of the house. The damn thing had been so rusty and tight it had taken all his strength to turn it, and he'd gotten a little lost in his concentration. When he'd looked to see if she had seen what he'd done, she was still in the kitchen, but later, he'd caught her eyeing the ring, and then she'd pulled the photo off the wall and...

After she'd fallen asleep, he'd sat quietly on the floor beside her and flipped through the books she'd borrowed from the library. The photo of the farm struck him like a blow. He remembered it all of course, but seeing it there in the flesh, he could still hear Meredith ringing the bell for dinner, smell the sweet summer grass and biscuits, hear the dogs barking at that damn rooster that never did figure out he was supposed to wait until sunrise to crow.

He'd seen a picture of his father and Al and Louie in the other volume. What was Maggie doing with those books? Why had she checked them out? Was she just curious about the farm, or had she begun to suspect him?

As the sun found its way through a crack in the clouds, she took another sip of her coffee. The rays turned the hair sticking out from under her hat the color of the red maple leaves at the peak of autumn, and the day spilled like honey into her hazel eyes. Sitting in the empty chair, he counted the dark spokes that radiated out from her pupils like the petals of a sunflower. Twenty-one in her left eye, and twenty-three in her right.

He would get up when her guest arrived. He glanced back at the road buried under six inches of snow. If they arrived. He was doubtful.

Her head dropped back to the page, and he sat quietly, watching her write. Occasionally, she glanced up in his direction, looking... almost disappointed, or stared out over the fields, as if the words she was searching for were hidden between the rows of dirt, then went back to her notebook.

When she was done with her coffee, she stretched and sat up peeking in the mug beside him. The coffee inside had long grown cold. Whoever she'd been expecting hadn't made it. Their loss, Will thought quietly to himself, as she bit her lip and frowned again.

Tearing a piece of paper out of her notebook, she wrote something on it, folded it in half, and slid it under the mug. With what sounded like a disappointed sigh, she got up, gathered her things, and went inside.

Will had promised himself he wouldn't read her diary, but... He touched the paper. This was different. And he was curious. He'd almost wiggled it free of the mug when the door opened and she reemerged with boots on and her purse. Will's brows came together as he jumped to his feet. He really hoped she wasn't going to try to—

She hurried down the steps and got in her car.

"Damn it," he muttered, hurrying after her. The engine roared to life, confirming his fear. She was going to get stuck on the road, and he wouldn't be able to help her. Standing in front of her car, he tried to decide if he should make himself visible or not. He didn't want to scare her, but—She did a U-turn right through him before he could decide. Spinning around, he raked his fingers through his hair as she turned onto the road. "Damn it."

Helplessly, he stood by the mailbox as she slowly made her way down the road. At the intersection she signaled, despite being the only car there, and turned left. She was only a quarter of a mile from the busy highway when he lost sight of her behind a stand of pines. Will exhaled, shaking his head. She shouldn't have gone out, but at least if she got stuck, she wouldn't have far to go for help.

Turning around, his eyes widened in surprise. From the house to where he stood was the clear outline of footprints in the snow. It took a moment to realize they were his.

"What the hell?" he said, looking at his feet. There was snow on his boots. How could he be leaving prints? He looked back up. More importantly, how was he going to get rid of them? Stepping in them all the way back to the porch, he climbed the stairs.

Glancing back at the road one more time, to make sure it was empty, he went over to the table. Hesitantly, he slid the paper out from under the mug. It was crisp and solid between his fingers as he unfolded it. Will's heart skipped a beat when he saw what she'd written, and he gasped.

W.M.

He stared at the paper. Then his eyes went from the mug to the empty chair. "No…"

She'd left it for *him*? The person she'd been waiting for was *him*?

He dropped into the chair she had set out for him, his knees weak with disbelief.

So, she *had* seen him last night? Or… He bit his lip, remembering the books. Maybe she only suspected? Or had she finally noticed him in the photo? Was that why she'd taken it off the wall? He looked back toward the road.

Was she trying to communicate with him? Or was this a test of some kind? Why didn't she just speak? Was she afraid to? A thousand questions tripped over themselves in his mind. Should he reveal himself? What would she say when she realized he'd been watching her all this time? He stared at the cup until ice crystals began to form on the surface. He needed to think, and he always thought best walking the south field, when it was just him and the dirt and the sky.

Refolding the paper, he shoved it in his pocket and started down the steps, then paused.

Looking back at the mug, he made a quick decision. Going back to the table, he lifted the cup to his lips and swallowed the liquid. It had no taste, no temperature, but it disappeared from the cup just the same. Setting it back down, he headed off across the yard, to ponder how he was going to confess his existence to Maggie without running her off.

HE HAD WALKED about five miles back and forth and gotten exactly nowhere when he saw a truck with a plow come down the road followed by a car. He was surprised when they both pulled in the driveway. Will whisked himself back to the house and frowned. That wasn't Maggie's car.

Dahlia got out looking like she always did, as though she had stepped off the pages of a fashion catalog. He smiled, grateful that Maggie had a friend like that in her life. He'd never even come close to having anything like what they shared when he was alive. He had always been so serious in his roles, impersonal. Brother, husband, boss, partner, provider. He'd always been more concerned with feeding his family than feeling for them. Like so many things, it was something he regretted now.

She paid the man in the truck after he cleared a pad on the driveway, then he left. Dahlia opened her trunk, set her little wheeled suitcase on the ground, and made her way, in precariously high-heeled boots, across the drive and up the stairs.

Will slipped through the wall, as a sensation, like walking through a waterfall cascaded over his body. He shook it off and reached the door just as she turned the handle and flipped the lock. Dahlia would freeze to death in those shoes if she had to wait outside until Maggie came back.

Dahlia pushed the door open. "Mags?"

Stepping inside, she stomped her feet on the rug. "Maggie? Hello?" She waited another moment before closing the door.

Shaking her head, she mumbled to herself. "... leaving the goddamn door open? Is she trying to get murdered?" She kicked her boots off, dragged her bag to the steps and set it by the bottom one on her way into the kitchen. Pulling the fridge open like she owned the place, she retrieved a bottle of red wine.

"I'm on vacation," she said to no one, as she poured herself a glass. Sipping her wine, she wandered back into the living room. First, she went to the pictures of Maggie and Eric on the mantle and smiled. Then she inspected his bookshelf, raising her eyebrow on more than one occasion as she grabbed a book and thumbed through it. Finally, she stopped in front of one of the front windows and looked out at the barren field of white across the road. "Damn girl, what in the hell are you doin' out here?" she asked, with one hand hugging her slim waist, like she was cold.

Turning around with a sigh, she shook her head and made her way to the couch. Will's jaw tightened when she found Maggie's diary on the coffee table and opened it. It loosened into a smile when she quickly closed it and tapped the cover with long, red-tipped fingers. "You'll tell me when you're ready, baby."

Will kind of liked that she talked to herself. He wished Maggie would do it a little more.

Dahlia set her wineglass down on the table, went back to her bag, and dragged it upstairs. Will didn't follow. A few minutes later, she returned in an oversized sweater and pants that Maggie referred to as leggings.

Sitting on the couch, she reclaimed her glass and dialed someone on her phone.

"Hey, I made it. Had to bribe a man at a gas station with a snowplow," she laughed. "But I made it."

Will couldn't quite make out the voice on the other end. "She's not here yet. I let myself in."

Pause.

"I don't know, Mama. It's so hard to tell with her these days. I just want her to be happy like she was when we were kids."

Dahlia sipped her wine.

"Yeah, I can't believe I'm saying this, but I liked her better when she wanted to be an astro-whatever and blast off to other planets to look for aliens."

Will's brow went up at that. Maggie wanted to be an astronaut when she was a kid? He remembered the starlight in her eyes the first night she was here. Yes, he absolutely believed that. It would have suited her.

"I'm trying," Dahlia said. "I just can't tell if she's given up, or if she's fighting for her life…"

She swirled the wine in her glass.

"No, the house looks nice, but… there's just something about it that… I don't know. It kinda creeps me out."

Will took the hint and headed for the barn. He was met with the same strange resistance in the wall. He had to push a little harder to get through it.

As he crossed the driveway, he remembered his footprints and realized they'd been plowed away. That was lucky. On his way to the barn, he was careful to concentrate on moving quickly, which caused him to hover, more than step, over the ground. The wall of the barn felt thick, just as the house had, as he passed inside into the darkness.

Twenty minutes later, he heard Maggie's car. He got up off the floor where he'd been sitting with his back against the wall and refolded the paper with his initials on it. Pulling the drawer of his workbench open, he dropped it in for safekeeping, then went to see if Maggie had realized what he'd done.

She was dragging a tree, bound with orange twine, out of the trunk of her car.

"How did you get in?" she asked Dahlia, who stood on the front porch in her socks.

Green needles sprinkled the ground, and the bright, sharp scent of pine filled his nose. It was his favorite smell from Christmas. That and sugar cookies. Maggie smelled like both, and he couldn't resist stepping closer to her just to take it in. Will couldn't remember the last time he'd celebrated the holidays. It would have been before his mother died, and she'd passed when he was sixteen.

"You left the damn door open, that's how," Dahlia scolded. "I swear, if I get a call from these Podunk cops up here saying you've been murdered, I'm gonna bring you back to life and kill you myself."

Maggie paused, looking at the door, then glanced through him toward the barn. "Sorry, I must have... forgotten," she said, dragging the tree onto the porch. Dahlia held the door open as she heaved it over the threshold.

"Don't apologize to me," Dahlia replied. "You're the one that's gonna end up buried in a cornfield."

Will laughed as Maggie set the tree against the wall inside. She reemerged a second later and retrieved a tree stand and a couple of plastic bags. He followed her inside, slipping through the door before she closed it.

He'd stood by the stairs, leaning against the wall with his arms crossed and a smile on his face as Dahlia and Maggie swore at each other and struggled to get the tree up. Finally, he'd taken pity on them and held it in place, so they could get it secured. But once they started talking, and Dahlia dove into the graphic details of her love life, which seemed to be dominated by copious amounts of sex, he suddenly felt like he was eavesdropping. So, he went back out to the porch to wait for Eric. He figured once her son was there, it would be safe to go back in.

By the time his car appeared in the driveway, it had grown dark. But Will didn't mind. He liked watching the snow turn from white to blue and begin to glow like the sky. It was as if the world inverted for a few moments before nightfall, and in them he was weightless.

Eric threw a backpack over his shoulder, and Will followed him back inside.

Maggie had changed, done her hair, and put some music on. He smelled cookies baking in the oven. Not sugar, but something familiar. Gingerbread maybe? He smiled again, god, how long since he'd even thought that word? He'd forgotten it even existed.

Being stuck on the farm, and being there alone, he knew an awful lot about how metal decayed and wood rotted. He could name almost every insect that flew, crawled, or burrowed across his land. He could smell a storm before the clouds even hit the horizon, but gingerbread? Music? Maggie squeezed her boy, and Eric rolled his eyes. Will smiled. Family? Holidays? It had been forever since...

For the second time in a year, tears filled Will's eyes. How could he miss this so much, when he knew he'd never had it to begin with? He remembered Christmas happening, but he wasn't *there* for it. His head was always off in the fields, on the weather, in the cost of seed, or the price of sugar. He was always fixing something, getting ready for the upcoming season. He had wanted to be prepared. And he was for everything *except* what mattered. The tractor was oiled, and the engine repaired a month before the ground thawed, but he'd never remembered Christmas enough in advance to buy his wife a present. She'd raised his siblings, tried her best to love him, and he couldn't even be bothered to buy her a necklace or dress or whatever it was she would have wanted. It filled him with shame. No wonder she'd run off with Al to California. She had been right to leave him.

Maggie, Dahlia, and Eric moved into the kitchen, but suddenly, Will didn't feel like celebrating.

He looked out the window before passing through the wall onto the porch. The world had turned from blue to black, just like his mood, he noted as he headed toward the barn.

A flash of light slashed across the driveway, and he turned as Maggie stepped out onto the porch. Pulling her red sweater around her stomach, she tiptoed in her socks across the rough planks to the table and peered in the mug he'd left for her to find. She picked it up, and her head flew around as her eyes scanned the darkness.

"William?" she called. His name on her lips set his hair on end. But he didn't answer. He wanted to, but... It was too late. Too late for Christmas, too late for meeting a brave, beautiful woman.

"Are you there?"

A part of him begged to answer her, but he silenced it.

"You're welcome to join us if you like."

He turned his back to her and continued walking.

"I know you're here. I feel you everywhere."

He stopped.

"Can you feel me too?"

He turned to face her. The door opened, and Dahlia's unmistakable silhouette appeared in the doorway.

"What in the hell are you doing out here?" she demanded. "It's fucking freezing. And we've got a tree to decorate."

Maggie looked down at the mug in her hands, then out through him to the barn. "Coming." She placed the mug back on the table and followed her friend inside.

CHAPTER TWELVE

MAGGIE PUT HER BOOK DOWN AND LOOKED UP AT THE CHRISTMAS tree. She'd gone to Dahlia's mom's last night for Christmas Eve and spent the night with Dahlia and her siblings. Then after a giant breakfast, she'd gone and spent the day at Dean and Ann's so Eric didn't have to split Christmas between his parents. It had been fun to see Eric play with his little sister. Ann had invited her to stay for dinner and spend the night, but she had declined.

Maggie looked over her shoulder out onto the porch and blushed.

Even though he still hadn't made himself visible to her, she didn't want William to be alone on Christmas, even if it was just for a few hours that evening. The fire crackled in the fireplace as she took a sip of her wine.

She looked back at the window.

Perhaps stupidly, she had gotten him a Christmas present. A wicker rocker to match hers. She'd had to drive the whole hour from the city with her trunk open and tied down, and she'd almost broken her back trying to get it on the porch, but there it was. She'd put a red bow on it, and just to make sure he understood, she'd bought them matching throw blankets, with their initials monogrammed on them. M.D. on hers, W.M. on his. They were carefully folded over the back of each chair.

But it had been four hours now, and he hadn't given her any indication at all that he'd seen it or liked it. It made her a nervous wreck, cycling between feeling stupid and embarrassed, and questioning her sanity. It had seemed like such a good idea before, but now that it was sitting out there... She was a grown woman, for Christ's sake. And she'd spent three hundred and fifty dollars on a Christmas present for a ghost. It was insane, wasn't it?

Her stomach growled, interrupting her unpleasant thoughts.

Pushing the blanket back, she padded into the kitchen in her new Star Wars slippers from Eric. That had been their thing when he was growing up. He and Dean did the sports thing, she and Eric had done the sci-fi movie thing. She pulled a frozen pot pie out of the freezer and turned the oven on.

She hadn't really expected William to appear, but she thought she'd at least feel him, or sense him, or something. But she didn't. Except for a moment when she was setting up his gift on the porch, she'd felt weirdly alone all night.

Maggie bit her lip as she opened the box and put the little pie on a baking tray. Had she somehow offended—

Her head flew up at the sound of rapping on the front door. For a moment, she had the ridiculous urge to hide. After all, who would be out at ten o'clock on Christmas night?

She went to the window by the front door and peeked out. The wind howled, and she noticed the subtle sway of the chairs. Will's knocked against the side of the house, and she let out her breath. For a moment she had thought... hoped... Burying her face in her hands, she shook her head, once again feeling like she'd lost her mind.

The oven beeped as she grabbed her wine off the coffee table and went back to the kitchen to put her dinner in the oven. The door groaned as she pulled it shut. Leaning against the counter, she sighed feeling melancholy. Despite having a very nice holiday something—

She heard it again.

Tap. Tap. Tap.

Setting her glass down on the counter, she quietly went to the window facing the barn, and peeked out. The porch light was just bright enough to make out shadows in the driveway. Her car was the only one in the—

Tap. Tap. Tap.

The hair on the back of her neck stood on end, and she recognized the feeling. He was there. "William," she whispered.

Maggie ran to the door and threw it open. Cold air rushed past her, as she squinted and her gaze swept the porch. Her hand flew to her chest when she finally looked down and saw it sitting squarely on the rug at her feet.

Her head flew up as she searched the darkness again for a shadow or anything at all that resembled a man. But there was no one, just...

Bending down, she picked up the small bouquet.

A stem of bright scarlet berries sat in the center. It was surrounded by spindly twigs of red dogwood, dried shafts of wheat, brown flower pods, and the most beautiful assortment of feathers she'd ever seen. The edges were trimmed in soft pine branches covered in tiny pinecones. The whole thing was tied together with a piece of straw.

A chill raced up and down her spine as she spied the piece of paper tucked in between the stems.

With shaking hands, she pulled it out and unfolded it. In the center were two letters.

M.D.

At the bottom was a name.

"Will," she read aloud. William. Will. "Oh." Maggie gasped, covering her mouth. He'd gotten her a Christmas present too? Tears filled her eyes, and she swiped at them. Did that mean he liked the chair?

A shiver raced down her spine again, and she realized she was still standing in the open door.

"Are you here?" she inquired of the darkness.

He didn't answer.

"Will?"

She didn't know what to do or say next. Maybe he couldn't appear? Did she invite him in? Or would she sound presumptuous? Did he even need an invitation? It was his house, for crying out loud.

"You can come in, if you like."

She waited, but nothing happened.

The wind whipped past her, making her shiver with cold.

"Thank you," she said. Not knowing what else to do besides stand there and freeze to death, she stepped back and began to close the door, then pulled it back open. "Merry Christmas," she added before closing and locking it.

She took her bouquet to the kitchen, unable to take her eyes off it, or the note she still had clutched between her fingers, and sat down at the table.

Running her finger along the silky edge of one of the several brown and white striped feathers, she wondered if they were from a hawk? Or a wild turkey maybe? The two spiky black and white feathers she recognized from the tails of the swallows that inhabited the barn, and there was a single black feather slashed with gold. Oriole maybe? Every item, she realized, was a treasure from the land that surrounded them. She touched the brown pods of lilies, her favorite flower, and wild indigo. It was the most thoughtful gift she had ever received.

Unfolding the paper again, she stared at his name.

"Will," she said as another jolt struck her. He was close, she thought as her fingers brushed over a blue feather and then a salmon pink one. A cardinal maybe? How long had it taken him to find them all? Had he been thinking of her when he had?

The oven beeped, and somehow twenty-five minutes had gone by. Hesitantly, she set her gifts down, glancing over her shoulder every few seconds as she pulled the pan out of the oven and set it on the stove.

Sliding the tiny pie onto a plate, she hurried back to the table, placing a cautionary hand over the stems while she waited for her dinner to cool. It was silly to think it might disappear, but it was also silly to believe in ghosts, wasn't it? And she did that wholeheartedly now.

The hair on her arms stood on end.

Yes. He was *definitely* there.

Keeping her head down, she glanced around. The room remained empty. She wondered again if he *couldn't* be seen, or he just didn't want to be.

Picking up her glass, she took a small sip. Either way, it was okay.

Steam rose from the hole in the crust as she punctured it with her fork.

Silence was okay too.

What mattered was it was Christmas, and they were together. That was enough for now.

MAGGIE YAWNED as she dropped the empty tin in the trash and set her glass and fork in the sink. Leaning against the sink, she smiled at the gift on her feet, and then at the one on the table, all her earlier melancholy gone.

She brushed her teeth and removed her makeup, then climbed the stairs. The second and fourth steps creaked goodnight like they always did, and she smiled again. Setting her bouquet on the nightstand, she plugged her phone in beside it.

Unbuttoning her blouse, Maggie wondered if Will ever followed her upstairs. She slid it off her shoulders, and threw it on the chair, then wiggled out of her jeans, dropping them on top of her blouse, before stepping into her leggings. Her hair crackled with static as she pulled her old U of M sweatshirt over her head. The air was so dry in the winter. Catching her reflection in the mirror, she was suddenly embarrassed again, this time by her frumpy mismatched pajamas. She almost laughed at herself. Was she really worried about what her resident ghost thought of her sleepwear? *Yes.* Her smile faded. Her heart fluttered at the memory of his hooded eyes as they'd stared at her from his photo. As crazy as it sounded, she was. And the reason she was made her insides pulse with something they hadn't felt in a long time.

As she climbed into bed, Maggie realized she'd never once felt Will up there in her room. She'd felt him on the porch, in the barn, in the living room, and just now in the kitchen. She'd even felt him in the trees when she walked by the creek. She pulled the covers up to her chin. But up here, she was alone.

She smiled. Her ghost, it seemed, was a gentleman.

SHE HAD BEEN DREAMING she was flying through the air with the barn swallows, looking down over the fields and the farm, as Will called to her to come down.

"Maggie!" Her shoulders shook. "Maggie! You have to wake up!"

Her eyes flew open as her shoulders shook again.

In the soft orange glow, the shadow of a man hovered over her bed. He squeezed her.

"Will?" she choked, not believing her eyes. Was he really there? Was he—

"You have to get out, there's—"

The light coming from the open doorway flickered and caught

her eye as a hazy cloud rolled across the ceiling. Finally, her brain registered what she was smelling.

"Maggie! You have to hurry—"

It was smoke.

Leaping out of bed, she instinctively snatched her phone as Will's hand slid around her arm and pulled her toward the door. Maggie gasped at the smoke as it billowed up around them. The intensity of the fire from below lit the stairwell, but it was no match for the fire that seeing *him* lit within her. Will's broad shoulders were covered in a white shirt rolled to his elbows. Faded brown work pants covered his long legs and narrow hips. She couldn't see his face, but a shock of brown hair crowned his head. His fingers were thick and strong around her wrist as he pulled and the hair on his forearms shined like the oriel feather in the...

"Oh, no!" Ripping her arm free of his grasp, she launched herself back up the stairs.

"Maggie!" Will's voice was deep and hoarse as he pounded back up the stairs behind her.

Running back into the bedroom, she grabbed her bouquet off the nightstand, just as his hand closed around her arm again.

"Damn it, Maggie! Leave it." He practically dragged her back down the stairs. She held up her arm to shield her eyes as they rounded the stairwell. The tree and bookshelf were ablaze.

"No!" she screamed, as Will tried to pull her toward the door. She needed to get into the kitchen, get water—

His arm closed around her waist, and he lifted her off the ground as she struggled to go the opposite direction.

"No! Let me—"

Throwing the door open, he carried her down the steps as the cold air whipped past them, and set her down in the drive. Maggie watched in horror as the flames inside brightened.

"No!" she screamed, fighting against his arms, trying to go back inside. She had to save the house! She had to—

Will spun her around and caught her face in his hands. His eyes flickered gold as they found hers in the firelight. "Call for help. I'll take care of it. Stay here."

Whether it was the shock of her house burning down, or seeing him face to face for the first time, she forgot how to speak.

"Promise me," he demanded.

Was he really there? Hesitantly, she reached up and touched his cheek. It was cool and smooth beneath her fingers. "How…" she choked, as his hand closed over hers. He felt solid. As real as—

The shattering of glass broke the spell, and they both turned.

"Promise me, Maggie." His voice was rough.

She could only nod. A split-second later, he vanished and the door slammed shut.

Maggie stood in the darkness, staring after him, then down at her aching toes. A crash from inside brought her head up as the tree fell over.

"Will," she gasped. Dropping the bouquet, she dialed 911.

ELEVEN MINUTES. That was all it took for the firetruck to arrive, and when they did, one of the men whisked her into the cab as the others ran for the house.

And now, seven minutes later, it was all over.

Maggie stared at the fire chief. "Do you understand what I'm saying to you?" he asked.

She blinked. No, she didn't. She hadn't been listening. Instead, she'd been imagining the hollowed out remains of her home that had so suddenly been taken from her.

"No, I'm sorry. What…?" Licking her lips, she pulled her hair behind her ears and tried to concentrate on his words.

"I said you're lucky. It didn't spread beyond the living room."

"W-what happened?"

"Looks like the lights on the tree overloaded the old wiring, and the spark from the outlet caught the tree on fire. When we opened the wall, it was full of straw and newspaper."

"Newspaper?" Maggie didn't understand. Why would there be—

"Back when this place was built, they used what they had for insulation. Straw, paper. Then, they plastered over it. It's common in these old houses, as is this old cloth wiring."

He handed her a piece of wire covered in what looked like old rope. "I don't—" She picked at the frayed edge with her fingers.

"It's cotton, believe it or not."

She stared at it for a moment, then got out of the truck, noticing she was still in her wet socks. She couldn't feel her toes. "Can I see it?"

"Yeah. It's safe to go in now. There actually isn't too much damage. Everything will be smokey, but almost everything is salvageable. The plaster helped, and it looks like the water from the tree spilled when it tipped over, saving the floor."

Maggie scooped up her bouquet on the way back to the house, thankful it had not been trampled, then followed the chief inside.

The smoke was clearing through the open windows, and an ominous chill hung in the air as another fireman dragged a hose from the door, and she stepped inside. LED lights on small tripods lit the room, making it look like an alien horror movie.

She gasped at the black stains on the walls and ceiling that radiated out from where her tree and Will's bookshelf had been. The charred remains of the shelf were crumpled in a wet heap, looking like a pile of black bones. Crossing the room, she fell to her knees beside it. Touching one of the book's spines, it crumbled beneath her fingers. The hair on her arms rose beneath her sweatshirt as a hand pressed against her shoulder. She thought it was the chief until she turned around and saw him standing by the door.

"Will," she whispered sadly. Her heart broke for the loss of his books. He gave her a quick squeeze, then let go.

Wiping her eyes, she got up. Everything was covered in ash.

Dragging her hand across the back of the couch, she smeared the soot across the leather.

There was a hole in the wall beside the door, and one in the wall that backed up to the steps.

"What are these holes from?"

"We opened them up. To see how pervasive the insulation and wiring are. We checked the kitchen and upstairs too. The house is full of it."

"What does that mean?"

"It means you can't live here until it's replaced."

Replaced? How? "How are they going to get the old wires out and then new—"

"Sometimes they can fish it through. But with all of this," he reached into the gap beneath the picture of her beloved barn and Will, and pulled out a handful of decaying straw, "it's all gotta be ripped out."

"Ripped out?"

"All the walls have to come down. Ceilings too. Everything's gotta be taken down to the studs and redone."

Maggie swayed, and Will's invisible hand closed over her arm again, steadying her.

"All the flammable debris has to be removed," the chief continued. "Everything has to be re-insulated and rewired. I won't lie to you. It's a big job."

"But—"

"Do you have somewhere to go? Family maybe?"

Maggie shook her head then pressed her fingers to her forehead. Wait, yes, she did. "But they are down in the city. Can I just stay here tonight, and tomorrow—"

"Nope. Sorry. It's considered condemned until it passes inspection by a county certified electrician."

"Condemned?" Maggie whispered.

"Unlivable. Power's gotta stay off."

"But—"

"I'm sorry."

Maggie's knees buckled, and Will caught her briefly against his chest until she found her feet again. Her hand shook as she steadied herself against the couch. "But—"

"You can grab a few things right now if you want. But you gotta go."

"Go?" She couldn't leave Will alone here with this. "I can't leave. I can't—"

"It's okay, Maggie," he whispered.

She turned in the direction of his voice. "No, I—" she shook her head, not wanting to leave Will now that she'd finally found him. "It's the middle of the night... Where am I supposed to..."

"I'm sorry, Ms. Dubois. We can't leave until you do."

Will squeezed her arm. "Go, Maggie." His breath on her ear sent a shiver down her spine as she stared at the bouquet in her hand. "I'll be okay."

She exhaled. "O-Okay."

And then he was gone.

"We'll give you a couple minutes to get your things together."

Back-up Maggie came online, and she nodded like she knew she was supposed to. Going upstairs she changed her socks and pulled her overnight bag out of the closet. She threw her recently discarded clothes from the night before inside and grabbed a handful of underclothes from the drawer, and stuffed them in too, followed by her phone charger and laptop from the other room, then headed back downstairs. Going into the kitchen, she grabbed her purse, which was slung over one of the dining room chairs. She felt around for her keys as she pulled her photos of Eric off the mantle and picked up her journal as she made her way to the door. The chief waited by the door as she slipped her feet into her boots.

At the last minute, she grabbed the photo of her beloved barn off the wall and quietly whispered to Will, "I'll be back in a little while."

The firetruck followed her all the way to the hotel, then turned left at the intersection as she pulled into the parking lot. She was a completely different person than she had been the last time she was there. For one thing, she was homeless. The night receptionist checked her in and she went up to her room. Maggie stood by the window, in the dark until the last of the volunteer firemen cleared out of the station that was only a block or so past the light. Then she slipped downstairs and got back in her car.

There wasn't a single car on the road as Maggie drove home. Pulling into the driveway, she half expected to see Will standing there, waiting for her. But it was empty, and the house and barn were just shadows in the periphery of the headlights.

Getting out, she headed toward the house, then stopped. Turning around, she stared at the barn for a moment, overcome by an intense déjà vu, then headed toward it.

Wedging herself against the narrow opening, she shoved the doors apart.

The screech of the rusty wheels was deafening in the quiet as she stepped into the darkness

"Will?"

She couldn't see anything, but she could hear him shuffling in the shadows.

"I'm so sorry," she offered when he didn't answer right away.

"It's just a house." His deep voice sent a shiver down her spine as it echoed through the void, but he remained out of sight.

"I can't stay. Not until it's fixed." Then she remembered he was there and had heard everything. "Will you be okay?"

He didn't answer.

"Will—

"Are you coming back?" he asked.

It was her turn to pause. It was barely the fiftieth word they'd spoken to each other, but the question felt loaded. She caught movement out of the corner of her eye.

"Yes," she said slowly.

"Why?" His voice came from behind her.

It was a good question. She turned, remembering every detail of his body. His broad shoulders, the way his hair fell over his eyes as they bore into hers, the feel of his rough hands on her arm, and his arm around her waist as his heart thudded against her back. And he deserved an honest answer. "Because my heart is telling me to."

"I'll be fine." His voice had moved away.

Maggie hovered between thinking she was crazy, and wishing he was human instead of...

Ghosts are not real one part of her interrupted, while another, that sounded like her mother countered with a whisper, *anything is possible.*

Maggie had read a book once in college that claimed the human mind was elastic, like a rubber band, and there was no end to how far it could be stretched. She hadn't believed it at the time, but as she listened to Will's breath in the darkness and considered the very real possibility that she was attracted to him, she hoped it was true. Otherwise... The band that had tethered her to reality had been severed the moment she'd dragged a chair onto her front porch for a phantom.

"I don't want to go," she offered. She was talking to a ghost. A ghost she wished desperately would touch her again. A jolt raced through her veins at the thought.

Instead of saying *I don't want you to go either,* he said rather coldly, "You have to."

Frowning, she asked, "Can you come with me?"

"No. I am bound to the land."

"What—"

He sighed, sounding almost bored. "If I try to leave, I end up back here. In the barn."

"Oh." Maggie stared out the door as the telltale blue of dawn filled the crack. The night was fading, and the rapport between them with it. Was it because of her confession about following her heart? Or her inability to forget the feel of his palm against her cheek. Or was he angry about his house? Tears filled her eyes.

"Thank you for saving me," she said, feeling like an idiot. "And I'm so sorry again about the house. I should never have bought that tree. I-I knew it was too dry, but it was the last one they had, and I wanted to make the weekend special for my friend and my son." Instead, she'd practically burned his house down.

Tears spilled down her cheeks when he didn't answer and she swiped at them, then hugged herself as the cold settled around her. Had he left?

"Will?"

The barn was silent.

"Well, I'd better go," she said as a sob crawled up her throat.

She tried to swallow it, and her hurt feelings, as she fled the barn. The doors screeched as she pulled them shut.

The sky lifted a heavy lid, and the pale blue eye of day dawned in the east, as she stumbled to her car. Two steps away from the door, her legs buckled. Will was not there to catch her, confirming her theory that he had gone. Knowing she was alone, her sob finally broke free as cold gravel bit into her palms and she fell to her knees. Tears froze on her cheeks and chin as she sobbed, feeling irrationally abandoned by her ghost. Where had he gone? Didn't he know she was as devastated as he was? Didn't he know she needed him? And replace every wall? Were they kidding? Was that even possible without the whole house collapsing? What if they got into it and said she had to tear it down? Maggie's shoulders shook with the effort of trying to rein her spiraling emotions in, but it was no use. The wind howled through the barn, its song sad as loneliness and despair swept through her, like it always did, threatening to consume her. Squeezing her stomach and rocking over her knees, she cried until her fingers were frozen and ached with cold.

Not wanting to add frostbite to her list of woes, she dragged herself to her feet. Sniffling, she brushed off her wet knees and got into her car. As she pulled out of the driveway, she looked back at the barn and was just able to make out Will's silhouette in the window. Fresh tears filled her eyes. He hadn't left after all. What he'd done was worse. He'd watched her cry and hadn't tried to comfort her.

CHAPTER THIRTEEN

JANUARY WAS NEVER A GOOD MONTH FOR WILL, BUT THIS ONE WAS by far the worst in recent memory. He stood in the corner, watching as the drywall crew began to gather up their tools.

For the last three and a half weeks, the house had been overrun with workers. He didn't like strangers in his house, and he especially didn't like the way they talked about Maggie when she wasn't there. It put him on edge every time she came up from Dahlia's to check on their progress. He'd practically ground his teeth right out of his mouth as one of the electricians, who'd only an hour before declared to his coworkers that he'd like 'a piece of that ass,' stood next to her, smiling, and pointing out the magnificent work they'd done.

Will pressed his lips together. When had men grown so vulgar and crass? Or had they always been that way and he never noticed?

He eyed one of the workers, a blond kid with bloodshot eyes who said he'd like to "fuck her brains out" while eating his lunch that day. There was something not quite right about him. But there was something not quite right about the rest of them too, because they had either agreed with him, or said something *worse*. The married one had volunteered to 'put her out of her misery,' whatever that meant, and the others had laughed again.

Will followed the married guy and the foreman as they carried unused buckets of drywall mud out to their truck.

He was glad they were leaving. They did alright work, but they were assholes. All of them. And Maggie deserved a lot more respect than that. A *lot* more.

It had just been so hard for her to find anyone to do the work. She hadn't had the luxury of being choosy, especially if she wanted the work completed anytime soon.

He'd stood beside her as she sat on the porch, making frustrated call after frustrated call. No one wanted to start before the New Year, and almost everyone else was booked until May.

The only companies she'd been able to find were ones from the city, and there was a reason they were not busy. The demolition crew had looked like a bunch of tattooed murderers, the electrician was a cocky bastard he'd found going through the *drawers* in her bedroom before scaring him off, the insulation guy was okay, but now she had to deal with these guys... How did single women survive? How had they not decided to abandon men all together?

Hopefully, the painters and carpenter were better.

Will moved off the steps as the blond kid dragged an industrial vacuum inside and plugged it in.

The whole thing had been hard on her financially and emotionally. He'd seen the tears in her eyes as the estimates came rolling in. Seven thousand to remove the plaster, lathe, and debris. Eighteen thousand to rewire the house. Eleven thousand to drywall. Eight thousand to paint.

Every time they'd made their exorbitant demands, Will had held his breath, thinking she'd finally decide it wasn't worth it, scrap the whole thing, and move back to the city to be closer to her son. Instead, she wiped her eyes, bit her lip, and signed the checks. And now, thankfully, they were in the home stretch. At least, he hoped so.

The drywall guys were done now, and the painters were coming on Monday. Apparently, it only took two days to paint an entire house these days. Maggie had scheduled the carpenter to install the base and trim on Wednesday and Thursday, and on Friday she was moving back in. He couldn't wait. And he was terrified. Something had changed between them the night of the fire, and he wasn't sure he had the self-control to... He sighed and dragged his face over his hands. He would. They would just be friends.

The foreman told the blond kid to finish vacuuming and reminded him to lock the door when he was done. Then he and two of the guys hopped in the first truck and drove off.

Will went out to the barn to get away from the horrible sound. Going to the workbench, he opened the drawer. Pulling Maggie's note out, he slumped to the ground, pressing his back against the old trough, and unfolded it again, as the fox scurried out from behind it and fled. He'd done it so many times the paper had grown soft and one of the seams had torn. Just like him, he thought with a sad smile.

The night of the fire had completely overwhelmed him. Not the damage to the house, he couldn't have cared less about that, but the damage to him when he'd touched Maggie, held her body to his as he pulled her from the house, felt her hot, smooth skin beneath his calloused fingers, smelled her minty breath as she stared into his eyes and pressed her frozen fingers to his cheek. It was the first time he'd experienced either hot or cold since he had died, and it felt almost as wonderful as she did beneath his hands. He'd almost kissed her, and even now the thought of it sent lightning through him, just like she had, when she'd stood in the dark of the barn, her body begging his to come to her. The ache of stopping himself had been so sharp, he had almost cried out.

When she broke down in the driveway, it was like a knife twisting in his heart. He *wanted* to go to her, to comfort her, but... he was afraid to touch her. Because he knew if he did... Will's breath quickened and his hands shook at the memory. If he'd gone out there, he wouldn't have been able to stop himself. He would have done what he still wanted to, now, which was cross a line he couldn't step back over. And he couldn't taint her with what he'd become, even if she wanted him to.

So, unable to go to her, and unable to turn away, he'd stood by the window of the barn as the most beautiful woman he'd ever met, inside, or out, sat in the snow and cried. He watched her sob like an idiot. And an idiot he was for falling in love with a woman he could never have, for listening to her heart break and doing nothing to ease her suffering. But there were already enough assholes in the world, he'd told himself. He had nothing to offer her, and he never would, and he couldn't take advantage of her trust and her heart like that.

Eventually, she'd gotten up and left. Will dropped his head into his hands. But not before meeting her eyes through the window of her car. If he hadn't already been dead, the expression on her face would have killed him outright. She knew he'd been watching her.

Realizing too late, he couldn't let her leave thinking he didn't care, he'd gone after her, shouting and waving his arms. But if she saw him, she hadn't stopped. Every time she'd been back since, he'd wanted to explain, but when the time came, words eluded him. What could he say that wasn't either a confession of his feelings or an outright lie?

Will got up, folded the paper, and put it back in the drawer. Turning toward the door, he realized the vacuuming sound had stopped, and it was silent. Thank god. That machine was almost as awful as the music they blared through their tiny radio with incredibly loud speakers all day. Passing through the barn wall, he noticed it had once again become easy.

As soon as he was outside, he noticed Maggie's car parked next to the truck. His brows came together. He hadn't heard her arrive. Why was she here? He looked toward the house. She wasn't supposed to come until—

She was on the porch. Her back was pressed up against the wall of the house and the blond kid's hand was splayed across the hip of her jeans, the other in her hair as he leaned in and... Will stilled as the boy bent his head toward hers and her hands slid from his chest to his arms. Will's jaw dropped in shock. "Maggie?" His voice was barely a whisper. That boy was half her age. How could she—

Turning her head away, she cried out, her eyes wild with fear, as the boy's mouth found the side of her neck. She cried out again, struggling beneath his weight, as fire tore through Will's vision. That *boy* was hurting her. He was—

"Hey!" Will yelled, breaking into a run. "Get away from her!"

The kid's head flew around as Will took the stairs two at a time and threw his hands up, but it was too late. Will had seen his white fingertips squeezing Maggie, holding her in place, while he assaulted her. Dragging her behind him, Will tried to figure out how to protect her against someone he could not touch. She clung to the back of his shirt, pressing her head against his back, as her warm shallow breath burned his skin beneath the fabric.

"Who the hell are you?" the kid asked, looking thoroughly confused.

"Go inside and lock the door," Will said over his shoulder. She released his shirt, and a second later, the door slammed.

Will turned back to her attacker, wishing he had a baseball bat. "Get out of here," he growled.

The kid didn't move.

Will whisked himself across the two angry steps that separated them and bent down until the sour smell of whiskey filled the air between them, and he could see his reflection in the kid's wide eyes. "I said, get out of here," Will said slowly, finding it difficult to enunciate the words through his rage. "And if I ever see you here again, I will fucking kill you," he seethed, pulling a phrase from Dahlia's extensive playbook. And by god, he would too.

The kid finally found his legs, stumbling backward before making a run for it. Leaving the vacuum, he ripped down the steps, slipping across the packed snow, and jumped in the truck. The tires skidded as he backed out of the driveway and gunned it down the road.

Will turned and hurried through the door, which had suddenly become very solid again.

"Maggie?" he called, pressing his palm against the wall, and dragging himself toward the kitchen.

She didn't answer, but he saw that the bathroom door was closed. He knocked on it. "Magg—"

Before he could get her name out, she'd flung the door open and rushed into his arms.

He stumbled backward, reeling both from her momentum and the feel of her body pressed against his once again. His arms betrayed him, just like he knew they would and rather than pushing her away, they closed around her instead. One rubbing her back as the other stroked her hair. He still didn't understand how he could touch her when he passed through everyone else. "Shh," he whispered against the top of her head while she shivered and cried. Her hair was like silk against his lips, and the heat from her body filled him from the inside out until he was sure he glowed like a sunrise. She, on the other hand, was a lightning storm in his arms. The pricks against his skin where her fingers pressed into the small of his back made him ache with pleasure. "Maggie. Shh. It's okay. You're okay now."

Eventually, she stopped shaking and stepped back. Her eyes were wide and red and full of tears. She looked like she was dying as she shook her head and whispered helplessly. "What are you doing to me?"

Her words were a blow to his gut.

Will put another step between them. He shouldn't have touched her again.

"I'm sorry," he choked.

She opened her mouth to speak, but he turned and fled before she got the words out.

CHAPTER FOURTEEN

MAGGIE WAS ALMOST DONE UNLOADING HER NEW TRUCK. WELL, IT was new to her, anyway. In reality, it was thirty years old and ugly as sin. Painted brown with a white stripe down the middle and a worn-out bench seat inside, even she, with an eye that was known to find beauty in almost everything, was at a loss. But she'd had to sell her car to cover the expense of the repairs, and like so many things lately, she'd not had the time to be choosy.

Climbing the steps, she pushed the door open and dropped the last of her purchases on the floor. The house looked almost exactly as it had before, with a few exceptions. Where Will's bookshelf had been was a newer, larger one she'd had custom made, and where there had once been a tub, there was now a tile shower and a closet with a stacked washer and dryer. Also, the base that lined each of the walls was slightly taller and a little more decorative. Otherwise, everything looked the same. It smelled different, though, newer, and there was still a hint of smoke in the air. Probably from all the linens she had yet to wash.

She wondered if Will was happy with the way it turned out, or if he missed the old smell and ancient plaster walls. He had yet to make an appearance, and she wondered if he was still upset with her.

Kicking her shoes off, she headed upstairs to gather the first load of laundry.

As soon as she'd said the words, she knew he'd misunderstood what she meant. And then he'd vanished before she had a chance to explain. She would have gone after him, but how did one chase something invisible? So, she'd apologized to the empty room, and then went out in the barn and did it again, clarifying that what he was doing to her, what he made her feel was *good*. But when after an hour, he hadn't responded, she'd left.

Maggie dumped the stack of sheets into the washer, then found the bag with the laundry soap and dryer sheets. As soon as she'd started the cycle, she went back to the living room and uncovered a heavy cardboard box that was buried under her purchases. Shoving it across the floor with her feet to the bookshelf, she hoped it would prove how truly sorry she was and convince Will that she wanted him there.

Pulling her hair back and securing it with an elastic, she bent down and opened the box. The smell of old books was in sharp contrast with the fresh paint. She hadn't been able to remember all the titles that he had before, but she recalled a few, and during her month at Dahlia's, she'd made several trips to local used bookstores, looking for the exact editions he'd had to refill the new bookcase she was having made for him. It helped pass the time, and looking for books she thought he'd like made her miss him less.

First, she shelved a book of poetry by Robert Frost, and another by Walt Whitman. On the next shelf, she put the same old copies of *A Field Guide to North American Wildflowers*, *Encyclopedia of Insects A-Z*, and *Great Lakes Wildlife* next to each other. She set a compilation of stories by H. G. Wells on the next shelf. Those were the only ones she specifically remembered. For the rest, she'd had to improvise. He'd said he couldn't leave, so she'd bought several photo books. One on national parks, another on the deep ocean. A third on the evolution of skyscrapers. She'd also got a visual guide to the night sky, and a book titled *Michigan Lighthouses*. On a whim, she'd purchased him several more books of poetry. She didn't know if he liked it or not. Most men she knew didn't, but as she kept stumbling across her favorite poets in college, she'd been inspired to add them to the collection. Then she'd picked up every major series that had been made into a blockbuster movie in the last fifty years. As she organized the books, she realized she didn't even know if he liked to read or had ever read the books on his old shelf, but... When she'd fantasized about coming home, the image of the two of them sitting across from each other on the couch before a roaring fire, reading, or discussing poetry, had filled her with such joy, she couldn't help herself. Grabbing the last three books from the box, she sighed. But neither of those things would happen if she couldn't convince him that her question had been rhetorical and what she'd meant was...

Maggie placed the last Tolkien book on the shelf, wiped her hands on her jeans, and stood up.

How had he done it? How had he revived her hunger for life with a single touch when he wasn't even alive? How did a man who died half a century ago take her breath away with a single look, and make her question everything, *everything* she knew about love? It was madness. It was magic. And she craved both almost as much as she craved him, whether he felt the same way or not.

She shook her head. She'd spent the last month missing a man who'd left her alone to cry in the snow, and she didn't even care. *That* was what she meant, by what was he doing to her. She wished she could tell him. But... She looked out the window. He wasn't there. Why wasn't he there?

After switching out the laundry, she went back to the bags, trying to distract herself from the gnawing feeling in her belly. She put the new white rugs on the bathroom floor, and the cream-colored throw pillows decorated with old-lithograph style drawings of wildflowers on the new leather couch. Running her finger over the patterns—lilies, indigo, chicory—the gnawing turned to worry as she looked up at the bouquet Will had given her, in the vase, on the mantle.

The green pine branches had browned and hardened, and they suddenly felt like a sign, an answer to the question she'd been avoiding all morning. Her heart thump nervously as she went to the window. She hadn't sensed him once since that day. And she'd been telling herself that he was just avoiding her, but what if he was…

"No," she said before the thought could finish itself.

Then why don't you feel him? Her reflection in the window asked.

Maggie took a shaky breath. He was there. He just didn't want to talk to her.

Then why are you so scared?

Pressing her fingers to her temples, she hurried to the door, shoving her feet into her boots. Fresh air. She just needed a little air, and—throwing the door open, it thwacked against the closet then bounced closed as she hurried down the steps—a walk to clear her head. It was cold, but most of the snow had melted, and the sun was shining. Squinting in the brightness she headed out to the barn first, reminding herself as soon as the weather warmed, she was going to paint, and trying to ignore the butterflies flitting against her ribs telling her that Will wasn't there, either.

She walked to the edge of the east field, then back past the silo. Her pace quickened as she went around the back of the barn and past the tractor. He wasn't there either.

Clouds billowed from her mouth as she hurried the length of her little thicket of woods heading west along the stream until she reached its narrowest point at the far end of her property, just before it opened into the small pond. Fear exploded in her stomach as she hopped over a sheet of old shingles protruding from the ice. Will wasn't there either, and she was running out of places to look. Had he truly gone? "Will?" she called. Had he crossed over without saying goodbye?

A tree branch snapped in her face, stinging her lip as she stumbled through the trees and brush into the back field. She could barely see through her tears, and it was becoming difficult to breathe around the lump in her throat, and the panic soaking into her brain. The dirt rows were frozen solid with little rivers of ice in the valleys between the mounds. "Will?" she choked, sliding in her untied boots as she scanned the horizon. Her field merged seamlessly with the one behind it, making it impossible to tell where her property ended as she headed out into the middle of it. He didn't answer.

"Will?" she cried, knowing if he wasn't there, she was out of places to look. "Will!" She ran, stumbling across the rows.

Had she imagined him? Had she imagined all of it? A wild fear replaced the panic.

"Will!" she screamed, gasping for air as she ran. "Will!"

Her toe hit a rock and she fell, slamming her knee into the hard black soil. Pressing her palms to the frozen earth she jumped back up swiping at her tears. "Will!" she wailed into the still afternoon. He couldn't be gone! "W—"

"I'm here, Maggie."

His voice brought her to such an abrupt stop, she fell backward. Scrambling to her feet, she felt the air in front of her. "Will?"

He didn't answer.

Had she imagined it? Her head whipped around. Where was he? "Will?" She turned back the other way, pulling the hair out of her eyes.

"I'm here." His voice was low, and his breath tickled her ear.

Maggie spun around again choking on her own breath, as lightning spread through her body. She squeezed her eyes shut. Thank god. He was still there.

She stumbled backward. "Oh… I just—" The words got tangled in her head as she realized several things at once. He *hadn't* gone into the light. Which meant he *had* been avoiding her Which meant… What did that mean? "I thought… I-I'm home," she stuttered.

"I know."

His confession hit her like a slap. Maggie blinked back tears as she stood alone, paralyzed by humiliation. She was such a fool. He clearly did not care about her as much as she cared about him. "I'm sorry I bothered you," she managed without crying.

Before he could say anything, if he even wanted to, she ran back over the undulating ground, knee throbbing, heart throbbing harder, toward the house.

PUSHING THE DOOR OPEN, then slamming it again behind her, Maggie sagged against it and let out a frustrated, angry cry. Sliding to the floor beside the remaining bags, she swiped at her tears, realizing even though he was real, she'd still lost her mind because she'd developed romantic feelings for him.

"What am I doing?" she whispered, pulling her hands through her hair, as she stared at the back of her new two-thousand-dollar couch.

Why had she come back here? Was it because she wanted to be here, or was it because she wanted *him*? She desperately wanted to say it was for her. That she was there because she loved the space and the quiet, the land and the stars, and it was healing her. But her tears, and the emptiness she felt now at his rejection, were seriously throwing that into question. If she loved this place so much, what did it matter if Will was here or not? "Jesus." Had she really done it *again?* Distracted herself with someone else so she didn't have to face *herself?* With her elbows resting on her knees, she thumped the heels of her hands against her forehead. "What is wrong with me?" She'd just spent more money repairing this house than it had cost to buy the whole damn farm, and she'd done it because she wanted to be near him. And now he didn't even want to—

"I didn't mean to hurt your feelings," Will said.

Her eyes flew open at the sound of his voice. But when she looked up, she was still alone. Knowing that he could appear, but chose not to, stung.

She buried her head in her hands. It was her own fault for letting herself think there could ever be something between them.

"I mean it, Maggie. I don't want to hurt you. I just can't be what you want—"

"Don't." If he finished that sentence, her heart would turn to dust in her chest. "I'm fine. I just…" Getting to her feet, she avoided looking in his direction. "I thought you'd gone without saying goodbye. That's all."

"I wouldn't do that."

Facing the closet, she pulled her muddy boots off. "Oh."

"I'm… glad you're home," he offered from behind her, and damn it, she still ached for him to touch her. A bolt of electricity shot down her spine as she wiped her eyes and tried to put her game-face on.

"Th-thanks." She turned around.

"What is this?" His voice was further away, by the bookshelf, as she tried to harden her heart against the sound of it.

"I couldn't remember most of the titles of the ones you had before, so I-I got you some new books."

Will laughed. His voice was deep and smooth, sending another shock wave through her. "I told you, Maggie, I don't care if I never see any of those books again."

She pulled her hands through her hair and hesitantly stepped closer to his voice.

"But I thought—" Shoving her hands in the back pocket of her jeans, she stared at the floor.

"They are all I had to read since the Verniers left. Which was… What year is it?"

"Two thousand and nineteen."

He laughed again. "Fifty years ago. I know every word in every one of those books by heart. I couldn't care less if I never saw them again."

"Oh…" She hadn't thought of that.

"It was a very kind gesture, though."

Gesture? Yes, she had been a fool. Either that, or he was still

154

upset about what she'd said. "Listen, about the other day when I said..."

"Forget about it."

"No, I—"

He cut her off. "And I see you got me quite a few new volumes as well." The friendly, conversational tone in his voice confused her, as did his dismissal of her apology.

"Um... yeah. I put the non-fiction and poetry on top, and the more notable fiction of the last fifty years on the bottom."

"Oliver?" Will asked, reading the spine of one of the books.

"She's a wonderful poet. I think—I thought you would like her work."

"*Geology of Michigan?*"

"I thought you might find it interesting."

"*Breakthroughs in Neuroscience?*"

"Actually, that one is for me." She pulled it off the shelf. It was quickly beginning to look like she should read that sooner rather than later.

"What is it about?"

"Um, how the brain works, processes information... malfunctions."

"Malfunctions?"

Maggie walked around his voice and set the book on the stairs.

"There's nothing wrong with your brain, Maggie," Will said to her back.

She huffed before turning back around. "I'm talking to someone I can't see." *You fell in love with someone you don't even know.*

"I just think it's better this way, that's all."

"So, you can spy on me?" She regretted the question as soon as she asked it, and her tone.

"I never—"

She held up her hand. "I know. I'm sorry. I should not have said that."

"Besides, I thought you said you could feel me?" His voice was close to her ear.

Goosebumps rippled across her shoulders, and she remembered exactly what his eyes looked like in the firelight of her burning house.

"I can." Maybe he was right. Maybe it was better she couldn't see him.

"I know." His voice was far away again. It sounded like it was coming from his chair.

"How do you know? Do you…"

"I can see it," he said.

Maggie frowned. "See it?"

"Sparks jump from your body to… mine." Just as he said it, it happened. Will laughed again. "Exactly."

Maggie stared at the empty chair.

"Is it okay if I stay and read while you work?" he asked, snuffing out the cozy fireplace scene she'd been rehearsing for the last month.

"Yeah. Of course."

"Thank you."

He said it like he was a guest.

"It's your house too."

There was a pause before he answered. "Roommates, it is then," he said, driving the final nail in the coffin of her fantasy.

When he didn't say anything more, she went into the bathroom and switched the wash. After that, she got back to work setting up her home for the second time.

BY THE TIME it was dark outside, there was an open book in front of Will's chair on the coffee table, and all her linens were clean and folded and put away. She'd also rewashed all her dishes and cups and emptied all the bags. Putting some music on softly in the kitchen, Maggie pulled her recipe book down off the shelf. If there was ever a time for comfort food it was today, and there was nothing more comforting than her mom's chicken and dumplings. As she chopped vegetables, she tried not to think about Will in the other room. But every time he laughed, her mom's voice whispered, *welcome home sweetie.*

While the soup simmered, Maggie poured herself a glass of wine and stood at the sink, staring out the window into the darkness, drinking it. Will was still reading, because every couple of minutes, she heard the crinkle of turning pages. *This is okay*, she told herself. Maybe it was better than okay. Maybe it was *exactly* what she needed. A friend, and nothing more to distract her from becoming… whoever she was meant to be.

"Do you eat?" she asked out loud.

"I can ingest," he answered from the other room. "But I don't get hungry, and food doesn't taste like anything, so I don't. But I can smell."

Maggie wiped her hand on a towel and glanced around the corner, then smiled sadly to herself. He'd started a fire in the fireplace after all. He just hadn't invited her.

Shaking her head, she made her way into the living room. "How is that possible?" she asked, staring at the flames, remembering the exact shape of his lips, wondering why she seemed to intent on making herself miserable today.

Will snorted. "I don't even know how *I'm* possible. So, your guess is as good as mine."

She remembered the curve of his jaw and the way his brows came together over his hooded eyes as they searched hers—

"Don't worry, Maggie. I'll watch it."

Blinking, she glanced at his chair. "What?"

"I'll watch the fire."

"Oh." She paused, pushing the memory away. "Did you believe in ghosts before you were one?"

"Nope. Did you believe in ghosts before you met one?"

She smiled for the first time all day, and the tension between them broke. "Nope." At least they had that in common.

Will turned another page, and she went back to the kitchen to finish making her dinner.

After two bowls of soup, Maggie switched out the laundry yet again and took the basket of dry, fluffy kitchen towels into the living room to fold. The fire had died, leaving only glowing coals in the hearth, so she switched on a lamp.

The book on the table closed as soon as she sat down. "Would you like me to add more wood?" Will asked. "I'm about to head out, so I was going to let it go out, but if you'd like—"

Maggie suppressed her hurt feeling again and looked at her phone. It was only eight-thirty, but the truth was, she was exhausted. "No, that's okay. I'm pretty tired." She glanced out the black window and shivered. "What do you do out there in the dark?"

"The same things I do during the day."

"Which are?"

"Observe, mostly. A whole new world comes to life after the sun sets, and it's just as beautiful as the one lit by day."

Maggie shivered again, not sure if it was because she was imagining the cold or feeling him.

"Maybe even more so."

"What do you mean?"

"During the day, it is easy to imagine that this earth, the land, the cities, the people, is all there is. It's easy to think we understand the universe and our own existence. But when night falls, and the curtain is pulled back…"

Maggie paused her folding.

"I spent a long time trying to make sense of what I've become. I tried so hard to make it fit into the world I knew when I was alive. But no matter which way I turned it, it just wouldn't go. Why me? Why be able to smell, but not taste? Why can I touch you and not anyone else?"

"You can't touch other people?"

"No. I pass through them the same as I do other things. Actually, I bumped into you once, early on... when you were fixing—"

"I remember now."

"Anyway, it scared me that I didn't fit anymore. I felt separated from everything I ever knew and would have loved if I'd just taken the time. I was lonely, and if I'm being honest, angry. But then one night, I was just laying out in the back ten. It was late spring, the corn was just sprouting, and I was staring up at the sky. There were a million stars, and I realized that..."

Maggie stared at her hands, listening, having completely forgotten about her laundry.

"The earth is a small place, and there is so much more out there that we can't imagine. I am still real. I am still a part of this universe, the same as you or anyone else is. I am just a different part. And uncommon *here*. I am just..."

"A piece of glass among the stones," Maggie supplied.

Will was silent for a moment. "What?"

Maggie blushed and resumed folding. "It's a line from a poem. I got you her book. It's on the shelf up there. The skinny one with the orange spine, if you want to read it sometime."

They were quiet as Maggie finished folding the stack of towels. She loaded them back into the basket and got up.

"Well, I'm going to put these away, then head up to bed."

"Good night, Maggie."

"Good night, Will."

After putting the towels away, she went into the bathroom to brush her teeth and complete her nightly routine. Dahlia balked at the fact that the bathroom was downstairs, but it didn't bother Maggie in the least.

She was about to head up the stairs when she heard Will's voice at the front door. "I'll see you in the morning." There was a pause. "I'm glad you're home," he said again.

Maggie leaned against the wall and peeked around the side, despite the fact there was no one to see, and smiled. "I am too."

She climbed the stairs to her room, and without turning on the light, pulled the covers back and crawled into bed. The day hadn't gone exactly as she planned, but it had gone. She had her house back, and she had Will. And again, it was enough.

THE NEXT THREE days went by in a blur. Will's genuine affection for her quickly revealed itself as he followed her around as she did her chores, or sat and chatted with her while she cooked. While not what she'd initially imagined, or hoped for, it was intimate and wonderful, and again she wondered if maybe it was for the best that he'd insisted on 'roommateship.' He seemed to intuitively know a lot about her, but she knew almost nothing about him. So, she peppered him with questions, which he didn't seem to mind. He filled in the blanks as she hung shelving in the new upstairs closet. They walked the property twice, sometimes three times a day. They were having unseasonably warm weather for February, and each day, as the ground melted, it changed, transforming into a slightly different place than it had been before. Will was much more sensitive to the differences than she was, but she was a quick study, and her eyes grew sharp as they wandered and talked.

His mother had died in childbirth when he was seventeen. His father had said he could never remarry, but the kids needed a mother, so he'd enlisted Will to get them one instead. Meredith was the oldest of three daughters, and her father was an abusive alcoholic, so she'd jumped at Will's proposal. She raised his three youngest siblings—Suzie took most of her time— while he worked the farm with his father and brother, Al. After his father died, it was just him and his brother. At nineteen years old, Will was responsible for six people and trying to run a three-hundred-acre farm. He 'put his nose to the grindstone,' and didn't look up until he was dead. Somewhere in there, his wife had left him and run off with his brother.

Maggie stepped over a fallen tree and her feet squished in the mud.

"Thankfully, all my younger siblings were gone. Grown and married off."

Maggie shook her head. "Your wife left you for your brother, and you were just thankful for her timing?"

Will was quiet a moment, and Maggie wished she could see his face, so she could tell what he was thinking. "I wasn't at the time. But now that I've had seventy years to think it over... She was right to go. I never loved her the way I should have, the way Al did, and she was a good woman."

"If you could go back and do it again, do you think you could?"

"Could what?"

"Love her the way you should have?"

Will was silent for a long while after that, and she almost wondered if he'd gone. Finally, he answered. "It seems to me that some people just naturally know what love is, while others need to be taught. It took dying for me to figure it out. But that's only half of it."

"What's the other half?"

"Finding the right person."

Maggie stepped over another log, noticing the flat white fungus that clung to the side of the black bark, like little steps.

Will continued, "I cared for Meredith, but I never loved her the way a husband should love a wife. And I know now, I never could have. She knew it too, I suspect, which is why she left with Al."

"Have you ever met anyone—" Maggie stopped. She shouldn't have asked that. Their friendship was still too new and—

"I did once."

Maggie was unprepared for the jealousy that filled her heart. "What happened?" she asked, unable to stop herself.

She slipped in a slick patch of mud beside the steep creek bank. Will caught her just before she landed on her butt. Lightning raced through her body as he righted her. He let go immediately.

His voice was far ahead when he spoke next. "By then, it was too late."

Maggie wanted to know more, but she sensed a shift in his mood and felt one in hers too. Maybe they needed a little break. Slowing down, she took in her house and the barn from her place in the trees. It was serene, beautiful. A truck drove by on the road, and the driver waved. She waved back.

She thought about her house in the city, where she and Dean had raised Eric. Her small, but perfectly manicured lawn, their big craftsman style house, her office, and her fancy work clothes. Eric's basketball and baseball games, her six week standing hair appointments, and Friday mani/pedi. Drinks with the girls and Pilates.

She didn't miss any of it except Eric, but there had been some good days there. Years, actually. The more she thought about it, the better she remembered, and instead of feeling lost or robbed of the person she'd intended to be, she felt… grateful. Grateful that she'd had a beautiful home to raise her family, grateful to have met a wonderful father for her son. Grateful that she'd built a successful business and had the luxury of getting her hair done. It might have all been a step off the path of where she'd wanted to go, but… Maggie looked back at her new home, then down at her muddy boots and smiled. Somehow, life knew better than she did. It hadn't taken her where she wanted to go when she was twenty; instead, it had taken her to where she needed to be at thirty-eight.

It had brought her here.

She continued walking as the sun warmed her cheeks, and the balmy breeze tugged at her hair.

As soon as she'd taken that first step, albeit a drunken one, and attempted to regain control of her life, look at what she'd discovered. This place. A whole world she never dreamed was possible, on twenty acres of land, out in the middle of nowhere.

Will was much of the reason she was back. There was no denying it. How could he not be? He was more miraculous than anything she'd ever dreamed of finding out in space, but there was more to her return than that, because she had *chosen*, as her mother had urged her to, to come back. It was not the easy thing, or even the sanest one. It definitely wasn't cheap. But it was deliberate.

Maggie crossed the yard and climbed the back steps. She smiled at the clawfoot tub that sat on the small deck. Once it was spring, she was going to run hot water out to it and turn it into a little outdoor soaking tub.

She pushed the door open and pulled off her hat. Sun streamed in the kitchen window, illuminating the house. Will was part of the reason she was back, but not all of it. This was too. The fire had tried to take away her control, send her away from her home. But instead of letting it push her, she'd taken it right back and stayed. And now look. It was even better than before.

Glancing at her phone, she realized it was Monday, and she hadn't even opened her computer. She'd taken on a few extra clients during her time in the city, hoping to offset some of the cost of the repairs, and now she had several projects that required her attention, and a few looming deadlines.

She put her coat and boots away, and she was making a cup of coffee when Eric's daily text came through.

Aced my midterm. Babysitting Sophia for Dad and Ann. Love you.

Maggie climbed the stairs and texted him back.

So proud of you. Have fun. Love you too.

A strange tapping noise drew Maggie's attention away from her work. Reaching for her mug she went to take a sip of her coffee and realized it was empty. Then she noticed the window above her desk was black and covered in droplets of water. She squinted into the darkness. Was it *raining*?

She glanced at the clock in the corner of her screen. Apparently, seven hours had passed without her realizing it. That sometimes happened when she got in the zone, but it had been a while since her head had been clear enough to focus like that. She heard the strange tapping again.

No, not a tap. It was more of a…

Drip.

Drip.

Maggie got up and followed the sound across the landing into her bedroom.

Drip.

Drip.

Drip.

She turned on the light. It only took a second to locate the source of the noise.

The drywall on the ceiling, where it transitioned from flat to slope, was cracked. A dark halo, like a gray bruise, surrounded a three-foot patch of freshly painted white around it.

Drip.

Leaking from several places along the crack, drops of water splashed onto the wood floor.

Maggie gasped. Her new drywall! Her new paint. Oh god, her eighteen *thousand* dollars' worth of electrical work. Would the water ruin it?

Then she remembered the shingles she'd seen by the creek. Were those from *her* roof?

"Shit."

She ran downstairs, pulled her coat and boots on, and grabbed a flashlight. Standing back from the house, she shined the light up toward the roof. The beam barely reached, and the rain stung her eyes, but she saw it. Sure enough, a sheet of shingles was missing, and there were huge gaps in the wood slats beneath.

"Damn it." The rain was literally pouring in.

Throwing her arm up over her brow, she raced around the house toward the trees. The rain was blinding, and the whipping wind chilled her to the bone. It only took a moment to find the place where she'd seen the shingles and pull them out of the slushy creek. The sheet was intact, except for one corner which had been torn off.

It flapped in the wind as she ran to the barn.

"Will! Will! I need your help!"

She shoved the door open, but he didn't answer.

Wiping the water from her face, she called, "Will?"

He wasn't there, and she didn't have time to look for him. Running to the workbench, she grabbed his hammer. The spot where the shingles were missing wasn't all that high up. Pulling drawers open until she found nails, she grabbed a handful and shoved them in her pocket. Maybe she could reach it from the ladder? She had to at least try.

Maggie grabbed the extension ladder that Bob had given her, explaining he was too old to climb it anymore, and dragged it to the side of the house. She stretched it out and locked it, like he'd instructed. Shoving the handle of the hammer down her pants, while leaving the head hooked over the band of her jeans, she grabbed the sheet of shingles. Then, as carefully as she could on the slippery rungs, Maggie began to climb.

When she got to the top, she threw the sheet onto the roof and pressed it down with her hand, so it didn't blow away. But she'd misjudged the distance. It was too far to reattach from the ladder. She was going to have to climb onto the roof.

And that wasn't a good idea, but—turning slightly, she scanned the darkness—there was no one else.

Gripping the edge of the roof, she called for Will one more time, but he didn't answer. She pulled the flashlight out of her pocket and shined it up as rain ran from the peak of the roof into the wide gaps in the exposed decking. The thought of all of that water running through the walls broke her heart. Her poor house. She *had* to do something. She owed it to Will after practically burning it down.

"The faster you get it done, the faster you can get down," she whispered. It wasn't much of a pep talk, but it was all she could muster.

Clenching the small flashlight in her teeth, she climbed up on the roof. Thankfully, once she was up, she didn't have far to go. Wicking the water out of her eyes, she crawled the three or so feet to the gap. The roof was steeper than it looked from the ground though, she thought as she sat back on her knees, just far enough to work.

With shaking arms, she lifted the sheet of shingles above the exposed section and shoved the missing piece back into position under it, scraping her knuckles against the rough edge as she went. Her jaw ached from holding the flashlight, and she was soaked to the bone. Wrestling the hammer out of her pants, it almost slid out of her wet hand as she dug into her pocket for a nail.

She lifted the upper sheet again, exposing the top of the loose piece, and propping it up with her arm, did her best to nail it down. The first missed the board beneath completely, but the other two were true, and the sheet was once again secure. The whole thing had taken less than five minutes.

Pressing her palms against the roof, she sighed in relief. Setting the hammer between her legs, she pulled the flashlight from her mouth. Maggie shined the light on the edges, checking to make sure there were no gaps. It fit perfectly. She'd done it! Had she not been up on a damn roof, in the dark, in the rain, she might have taken a moment to be proud of herself. But she was on the roof, and she still had to get down. She let the hammer slide off the roof and swayed with vertigo as it disappeared over the edge. Panic blossomed in her chest when she didn't see the ladder. "It's there," she said, briefly squeezing her eyes shut. She just couldn't see it.

Pocketing the flashlight, she slowly began crawling backward toward it, as lightning split the sky. Flattening herself to the roof, she groaned. A thunderstorm in February? She pressed her forehead to the rough shingles. "Are you kidding me?" Taking a deep breath and trying to stay low, she started backward again. If she didn't get down quickly, she'd probably be electrocuted.

She was almost there when a huge gust of wind raced down from the ridge of the roof and shoved her hard in the chest. Instinctively, she threw herself flat again as adrenaline replaced the blood in her veins. A second later, she heard a horrific crash and realized the ladder had fallen.

Maggie pressed her face to the gritty shingles, afraid to even lift her head. The shaking that had started in her arms rapidly extended to the rest of her body.

"Will!" she screamed into the wind.

If she fell off the roof, she would die. If she fell off the roof, Eric would be left without a mother, and she'd miss his college graduation and his wedding, assuming he ever married. A tear rolled down her cheek. If she fell, she'd never hug his sweet little babies. And what about all the Christmases she'd miss? First steps and birthdays? And how could she leave Dahlia? They'd promised to grow old together, to always be there for each other. They'd made plans to be nursing home roomies. The thought of Dahlia as an old woman, alone in an empty room was almost as unbearable as... Her lips brushed the rough shingles. "I want to be a grandma," she sobbed. And she wanted to see another sunrise and sunset, and she wanted to hear her son laugh like he had on Mackinac, and call her *mo-om,* and she wanted... Maggie squeezed her eyes shut, realizing she had way too much to live for to die now.

"Will!" Rain mixed with tears on her cheeks and dripped off her nose, joining the rivulets of water that rushed down the roof and plummeted twenty-five feet to the ground below.

"Will," she cried pitifully.

CHAPTER FIFTEEN

WILL LIFTED HIS HEAD AND LOOKED BACK TOWARD THE HOUSE. HE couldn't be sure, but he thought he heard something fall. Metal maybe—

He began walking back, noticing as with the snow, his feet were leaving tracks in the dirt again. If he were in a less pensive mood, it would have made him smile. Lightning split the sky, and he looked up, shaking his head. He couldn't remember the last time there'd been a thunderstorm this time of year. It had been at least thirty years.

Crossing the edge of the field into the trees, he hoped it wasn't another one of the tin panels flying off the roof of the barn. Maggie had already spent so much money on the house. If the barn fell apart now—

He stopped, and every hair on his body stood on end as he listened.

The millions of collective drops of rain onto the earth around him were a dull roar in his ears, but he thought he'd heard—

"Will!"

"Maggie?" he choked, as all the reasons she might scream for help raced through his mind at once, before stopping on the drunk drywall guy. Had he returned? Had he—

Spiriting himself back to the house, Will landed on the porch and spun around. She was not there. He went inside. "Maggie!" She wasn't there, either. His panic felt as thick as the wall as he struggled back through it onto the front porch. Pulling at his hair, he spun around again. "Damn it." *Where* was she? "Mag—" He noticed the barn door ajar.

A second later, he was inside. "Maggie?" His voice echoed off the cavernous walls. "Where are you?"

"Will!" Her voice was faint.

He hurried back outside.

"Maggie!" he shouted, blinking the water out of his eyes. Where in the hell was she?

"Will!" Her voice was louder, and she was sobbing.

He scanned the darkness. She was not on the porch, not in her car. Not by the road. He spun around, looking toward the silo. Not there either. He turned again and squinted behind the barn. The trees? Had one fallen on her? He ran toward the back of the house. "Maggie, where—"

"Will!"

He skidded to a stop in the middle of the driveway and followed the sound of her voice up. He almost fell over backward when he saw her huddled on the very steep roof. The *roof?*

Launching himself skyward, he flung himself over her, crushing her against the shingles, as she cried out. But he couldn't tell if it was in relief or pain. "Jesus Christ, Maggie." His words wobbled over his fear like water in a brook as his lips brushed her wet hair. Lightning illuminated the side of her face as he ran his hand frantically across her skull, down her back. What was she doing up here? Was she hurt? She yelped again, wiggling beneath him, and he realized he was smothering her. She whimpered as he pushed himself up on his elbows, rolling his body off hers.

"What in the hell are you doing up here?" he demanded.

She scooted closer until they were touching again. "I was fixing the roof. The ladder fell."

Propping himself higher, he finally noticed the ladder on the ground below. He sighed. "I'll be right back."

Maggie's arm snaked behind her, and she sunk her nails into his hip. "No! Please don't—" she cried, the terror returning to her voice, as he tried to ignore how good her fingers felt.

"I have to get the ladder. You'll be fine." He squeezed her shoulder. "Don't move."

She released him. "Hurry."

A moment later, he was on the ground, dragging the ladder back to the house and onto its legs. Too frantic to contemplate why it felt so light in his hands, he shoved it up toward the roof. But every time he tried to lock it, it slid back down. Then he saw why. The locking mechanism was sheared off. "Damn it!" he shoved the ladder to the side, and it crashed back to the ground a second time.

He went back up to where Maggie lay sprawled and crouched down beside her, pressing a steadying hand to the back of her jacket. "The ladder is broken," he said as calmly as he could. "You need to..." He blinked in the rain, surveying the roof. Damn it. He didn't know what she needed to do. If he was alive, he'd run to the neighbors and borrow a ladder or call the fire department... But he wasn't. He thumped the roof. "Shit!"

"W-Will?"

"It's okay." Squeezing his eyes shut, he forced himself to take a deep breath, then opened them and surveyed the situation again. If she could make her way toward the front of the house, maybe she could hop down onto the roof of the porch. If she could do that, she could hang over the side and catch the railing. It wasn't a great plan, but it was better than nothing. "You have to move toward the front of the house."

"I can't."

"Maggie, you can't stay up here all night, and I-I can't get you down. But I can help you."

"I can't," she insisted.

She had to. He sat down beside her, then leaned over and wrapped his arm around her. "Of course you can," he said gently. "You're the bravest woman I know."

She shook her head. "N-no. I'm—"

"Yes, you are. You go into haunted barns alone. You buy abandoned farmhouses and move out into the middle of nowhere by yourself." She huffed beneath his arm as he leaned closer to her ear and whispered. "You aren't afraid of ghosts." Lightning shot from her to him as the scent of her skin flooded his senses. He leaned back. "This is nothing." He patted her back, praying that was true. "Come on. You can do it. It's not far."

"Okay."

He waited while she gathered herself together. Then, propping herself up on shaky arms, she dragged her knees under her. "Oh god." Her hair hung around her head in stringy ropes that waved in the wind.

"That's it. Okay, just go slow."

She slid her knee to the side, and a moment later, her hand followed. Her arm shook as she dragged her other knee toward the first. "O-oh god." He couldn't see her face, but her hand moved to the side again. Thunder boomed and her shoulder jerked. He put a hand on it.

"It's just thunder. That's it. Okay. Again."

She was in the middle of her third attempt when a wall of wind rolled over the roof. It caught her like a sail and pushed her back. She screamed as her toes dug into the shingles and she began to slide on the slick soles of her sneakers.

"Will!"

He fell on top of her again, afraid his arms wouldn't have the strength to hold on to her if she went over the edge. His heart thudded painfully in his chest as she groaned under his weight. Her fingertips were white as they pressed into the roof, and the knuckles on her left hand were bleeding.

Will looked over his shoulder. That was close. They were about a foot away from the edge, and they had about four more feet to go until they were over the porch. The wind blasted over them again. The storm seemed to be worsening.

"We have to keep going, Maggie," he said in her ear.

She shook her head.

Trying his best to ignore both the warmth of her body beneath his, and his fear of her plummeting from the roof to her death, he carefully lifted himself off her again. When he was sure she wasn't going to slide anywhere, he created a cage around her body with his. Putting a firm hand on her waist, he nudged her on. "Come on. You can do it. Just a little further."

Instead of getting back to her knees, she army crawled on her belly and elbows, sideways. "Don't let go," she begged, trembling beneath him.

"I won't." He pressed his hand against her side reassuringly.

After what felt like an eternity, they made it over the porch. It was still a ways down, about nine feet, and god only knew, if when she landed on it, she'd fall right through or not. But they had no choice. It was either that or stay on the roof until the storm blew over and someone drove by. It could be days.

He pulled her sopping hair back off her face so he could see her as she pressed her head to the roof. "Okay." His hand found her cheek, and it burned against his palm. "So, the good news is, if you fall now, you won't die."

The corner of her mouth twitched as she glanced at him out of the corner of her eye. A spark flashed between them, hitting him square in the chest.

"Great. What's the b-bad news?" she stuttered.

He smiled reassuringly. "You're gonna have to take a little... leap of faith."

"A wh-what?"

"You have to slide down to the edge, hang your legs over the side and drop onto the roof of the porch."

"What?" she cried.

"It's not that far. I'll help you as best I can, but I'm not sure... I don't know if I can catch you or not, so you need to be prepared to fall. But the roof is almost flat. You will not roll off."

"Super." Maggie squeezed her eyes shut, inhaled deeply, then nodded. "Okay." Slowly, she scooted down to the edge. As soon as her toes went over the side, she froze. "Oh god."

"You can do it."

She lifted her head and looked over her shoulder. "I don't see it."

"It's there. Trust me. Now keep going, get your legs over the side. When you are ready, I'll go down and try to guide you."

"I am a fucking idiot," Maggie breathed.

He was inclined to agree, but now was not the time. "We will discuss that once we get you down. Are you ready?"

She nodded again and did as he asked. What felt like an eternity later, Maggie was hanging from the roof, legs dangling. Will stood beneath her and reached for her legs. "Okay. Get as far off as you can... Now jump."

With a strangled cry, she pushed herself off. He caught her, and they tumbled to the roof in a heap. Miraculously, it held. "Are you okay?" he asked, rolling her on her back.

Her terrified expression dissolved into a grin, then into raucous laughter interspersed with sobs of relief, as she lay half beneath him, clutching her stomach and wheezing.

The thumping in his chest sped up again as he stared at his hand on her hip. He pulled it away.

"Oh my god," she breathed, raking her hands through her hair, shoving it back out of her face. "Ow. That hurt," was all she managed before being overwhelmed again by uncontrollable giggling, that rendered him breathless, as her ribs bounced against his side. It reminded him of the day in the kitchen, after she'd flooded the bathroom. Same soaked hair, same droplets of water clinging to her eyelashes, same smile. Half little girl, half beautiful woman. The only difference was...

Unable to stop himself, Will brushed her cheek with his thumb. Maggie's smile faded as he pressed his palm to her cheek, then slid it down, gently cupping her jaw in his hand. A quiet moan fell from her mouth and her pulse raced beneath his fingers as he pressed them softly against her neck. God, that was a beautiful sound. Lightning erupted from her body, strike after strike, like a summer storm, flashing and sparking, burning him down with every bolt as the lesser storm continued overhead. Her eyes locked on his and with a tight gasp, he released her, and sat back panting as she scrambled onto her elbows and then up to sitting. Her chest heaved as breath rushed from her mouth in quick clouds that were instantly carried off by the wind. She licked her lips.

"Will?" The question in her eyes was clear, but his answer was not. If he were alive, it would be. But he wasn't. And he could not—

"We're almost there," he said hoarsely. "You have to do the same thing one more time. I'll guide your feet to the rail, and you'll be down."

The way she was looking at him made Will think he never should have touched her. *And wish you had never stopped.*

He squeezed his eyes shut. What was she doing to him?

They opened again as she continued to stare.

Was that what she meant the other night when she'd said the same thing?

Finally, she nodded, her wide, unblinking eyes glued to his, and he was so lost he couldn't even remember what he'd said or what she was agreeing with. "One more time."

He blinked. Right. "Come on." His voice was thick with something he didn't want to dwell on, as she broke the stare and rolled back onto her stomach.

A moment later, Maggie was out of the rain and safely back on the porch.

"Thank god," she sighed. She took a step toward the door and threw her arms out as her knees buckled.

"Woah." Will caught her arm as she crumpled to the floor, then crouched down beside her, putting a hand on her back. "You made it. You're okay now. That's just nerves." He squeezed her arm, but she didn't move. "Let's get you inside and warmed up."

She looked from him out into the untamed night, her eyes filled with the same intensity as the wind. Lightning struck the rod on the top of the barn, and a split-second later a clap of thunder shattered the air, and they both ducked.

She grabbed at his arm. "It's just as b-beautiful as I…" The chatter of her teeth prevented the rest of the sentence from being spoken, but her eyes softened briefly, as they did when she saw something magical. Yes, it was beautiful, but now was not the time to admire it.

His hand closed gently over her arm. "Let me help you up."

Shakily, she got back to her feet, then gasped as she stumbled against him. "W-who is that?"

Will followed her eyes to the empty chair, rocking in the wind. "Where?"

"Th-that woman."

The hair on Will's arms stood on end, as Maggie stared at the chair, but he saw nothing. Was there possibly *another* ghost? Or was it just her overloaded senses?

"It's nothing. Come on. You're shivering." She leaned on his arm as he turned the knob and pushed the door open. With his hand on the small of her back, he urged her inside, then closed the door and leaned against it with a sigh of relief. They'd made it.

Her hand bounced as she tried to catch the zipper of her wet coat between her fingers. Her chest was still heaving.

"Come here," he said.

She took a step toward him. Brushing her fingers away gently, he met her eyes and caught the zipper. Feeling like he was having a heart attack, he pulled it down slowly, unable to unimagine he wasn't undressing her. *Don't kiss her.* He swallowed hard past the tightness in his throat. "Let's get you out of—" His voice trailed off as he slid the jacket off her shoulders. *Please, don't kiss her. Please don't—*

The red stain on the front of her shirt that ran down onto her jeans caught his eye, bringing his amorous thoughts to a grinding halt.

Maggie looked down and gasped in surprise. "Oh." Slowly, she lifted her shirt. Amid the red scrapes that covered most of her stomach was a single deep red line. "Oh my…" she stumbled back against the wall. "That's a little worse than I was expecting."

Will caught her arm and pressed his fingers to her stomach, eliciting a shiver and a weak spark. "What happened?"

"When I was sliding off the top roof."

Will squeezed his eyes shut. It must have been a popped nail. "You need to go to the hospital."

"No, I'm sure it's… fine. I just need to sit down a minute."

No, it was not fine. "Maggie." In fact, he knew exactly how not fine it could be. He looked in the direction of the tractor that sat exactly where he'd left it a week before it killed him.

"I'll just splash some hydrogen peroxide on it and—"

"Where is your phone?"

"What for?"

"You need an ambulance."

"I'm fine. I got a tetanus shot last year." She pushed past him, stumbling into the bathroom. "Or maybe it was two years ago?" She tried to pull her shirt over her head and moaned in pain.

The fact she'd been inoculated was slightly reassuring, but still. "Maggie, you are not fine. Where is your phone?"

She dropped her arms as she sat down on the toilet. "Upstairs?"

Will raced upstairs, returning almost immediately. "It's not there. Did you take it outside with you?"

She shook her head, clutching her wound. Blood seeped between her fingers. "I don't remember."

If she didn't have her phone, how was he supposed to call for help?

"Can you drive?" he asked.

"What?"

"Can you drive? Can you make it to town?"

"I-I think so."

Grabbing her keys out of her bag, he shoved them into her hand as he dragged her to her feet. "Go, now!"

"But—"

"Go, Maggie!"

Throwing the front door open, he dragged her back out onto the porch. She stumbled and fell out of his grasp. Pressing her palms into the decking, she leaned back, leaving a bloody handprint on the floor in front of her. "I'm okay. Just give me a..." she swayed on her knees. Shock. She was in shock. And she definitely could not drive.

"Damn it!" Will pulled his hands through his hair. He paced the porch once again, not knowing what to do. Did he look for her phone? Did he take her back inside? Or did he stand on the edge of the south field and scream for help?

With strength he didn't know he had, he scooped her up and carried her back inside.

"No!" She struggled, clinging to his neck as he tried to lay her on the couch.

"What?" He set her on her feet.

"Not my new couch! My shirt is—"

He rolled his eyes. "Who cares—"

"Help me," she said, tugging at the hem of her shirt.

Caught in the whirlwind of a horror story-turned-fantasy, his fingers immediately found the edges of her shirt. Before he could tell himself no, his hands slid up her slick sides, over her ribs, then the goosebumps on her arms as he pulled the shirt over her head.

And there she was again. Maggie—his breath forgot which direction to go as he stared—in all her glory. Adorned in black lace. He was *definitely* going to have a heart attack.

Yanking the shirt from his hands, she balled it up and pressed it to her stomach as she dropped onto the couch with a groan. "The peroxide and first aid kit are on the counter in the bathroom."

He blinked. *What?*

She looked up. "Will?"

The spell he was under cracked, but did not break. "Don't move." He got the bandages, a stack of towels, and the disinfectant.

"Lay down," he said, shoving a towel under either side of her stomach. Maggie groaned as she pulled her feet up onto the cushions, then again as Will poured the peroxide on her wound. Once it was clean, he dabbed it dry with a towel. Thankfully, it didn't look too deep. More blood appeared. Quickly, he peeled several butterfly bandages. Wiping as he went, Will did his best to close the seven-inch gash that went from just under her breast to... He unbuttoned her pants, and she moaned quietly.

He winced. "Sorry."

The cut intersected a scar that ran horizontally across her waist. It looked like someone had tried to gut her. He met her eyes. "Jesus, Maggie." Who had done this to her?

She opened her eyes briefly. "What?"

"What happened—"

Following his eyes, she smiled slightly before closing hers again. "Tummy tuck."

A what? "A what?"

"Nothing."

His eyes went from her old injury back to her new one as blood seeped from between the bandages. It was lessening, though. At least, he thought so. He pressed the towel over them. "Can you hold this while I go look for your phone?" he asked.

"Sure," she said quietly. "But don't call 911."

Will hurried back outside, searching the ground as quickly as he could. It wasn't too dark for him to see. It just wasn't there. He pulled his wet hair out of his eyes. It had to be... He caught a glimpse of something in the grass and ran to it. His hammer. He looked up. That meant—

He spirited himself to the barn. Her phone was on the edge of his workbench. Snatching it, he raced back to the house. It wasn't until it smacked the siding and flew out of his hand that he remembered it had to go through the door. Retrieving it, he pulled the door open and closed it quickly behind him.

"Maggie." He shoved the phone in her hands, knowing his fingers wouldn't work on the buttons. Something about whatever he was and electronics didn't mix. Her eyes fluttered, but remained closed.

"Maggie. Call Bob."

Her eyes opened, and her brows came together. "What?"

"Call him now. Or I'm calling the police," he lied.

"But he's my handy—"

"I know who he is. Do it. Now."

With her thumb, she navigated the phone to Bob's number and dialed. Activating the speaker, she laid it on her chest. "What do you want me to say?" she asked as it rang.

"That you got hurt, and I need him to come."

"Hello?" Bob's sleepy voice answered on the third ring

Maggie stared at Will. "*You* need...?"

"Do it."

"Bob?" she asked, as her eyes probed his.

"Yes?" the old man answered.

Will nodded encouragingly. He would explain everything later. "Do it. It's okay."

"Um, it's Maggie... Dubois," she winced, trying to sit up. She grabbed the phone. "I've had a bit of an accident, and my friend... um..." She met Will's eyes again, and he nodded again. "My friend Will would appreciate it if you'd come by..."

"Just in case you need to go to the hospital," he whispered.

"Just in case I need to go to the hospital," she repeated. "But if it's too much trouble—"

Bob cut her off. "I'll be there in twenty minutes. You be okay for that long?"

"Yes. I think so."

"Alright, sit tight. Tell William I'll be there shortly." The line went dead.

Maggie hung up and stared at Will in disbelief. "He *knows*?"

Will nodded, guiltily. "Lay back down." Exhaling, Maggie fell back into the cushions as Will sat beside her. "He knew before you did, actually."

"What? *How?*"

"I don't know. I think it's because he knew me before, when I was alive." Will pulled the towel away. To his relief, the bleeding had slowed. He poured a little more peroxide on it.

"He did?" Maggie asked.

"Yeah."

Holding her arm out to him, she said, "Help me upstairs before I ruin my couch—"

He shook his head.

"... or scandalize Bob?" Her brow went up as his eyes fell to her lace-covered breasts.

She had a point there. But he didn't want to touch her. Especially unclothed. Well, he *did,* but...

"Please?"

With a deep sigh, he slid his arm under her back, hooking his other arm under her legs, and picked her up. Maggie snapped and crackled gently in his arms as she leaned into him as she wrapped her arms around his neck. Will swallowed a groan of pleasure as he inhaled her intoxicating mixture of wildflowers, wind, and soap. God, how was this happening? The whole night. It was like he was human again.

"I wish I knew you when you were alive." Her eyes were closed, her voice quiet as he made his way around the couch.

"Yeah?" His lips brushed her cheek as he looked down. She was so beautiful he almost dropped her. *Steady Will.*

"Yeah," she said, snuggling closer, her breath fluttering against his neck as he carried her up the stairs. He saw the water damage immediately. It was bad, but not bad enough to kill herself over.

"Why is that?" He set her on the end of the bed, grabbing her sleeping shirt off the chair. Slowly, he pulled it over her wet head, and gently threaded her arms through.

"Maybe then we would have had a chance."

Her eyes were full of pain, but he couldn't tell if it was physical or emotional. A little of both, he suspected. Swallowing hard, he extracted her hair from under the collar of her shirt and laid it over her back.

"Can you stand up?"

She nodded, and he pulled her back to her feet. As she held onto his arms, he reached for the zipper of her jeans, hesitating until she nodded. The sound almost undid him. Crouching down, face-to-face with her seductive underclothes, and sliding his hands over her bare hips *did* undo him, and he tried not to faint, as he pushed the wet fabric down over her smooth, very touchable legs. Pressing her hands to his shoulders, she lifted one foot, then the other, and stepped out of her pants. His eyes paused again on the minuscule triangle of fabric between her legs that left *nothing* for his poor imagination to do, before gently taking her hips and pressing her down onto the bed. "Okay… s-sit down."

Exhaling heavily, she sat. "Damn, that hurts."

"Are you okay?" he asked, grabbing her leggings and wishing to god she would stop wearing black lace.

She laughed. It was quickly followed by a grimace and a groan. "Oh, ouch. Well, I *did* almost fall off the roof of my house."

Will huffed a laugh as she stepped her feet into her dry pants. He pulled them up to her knees. Taking her hands, he said, "One more time. One, two… Ready?"

She nodded.

He pulled her back to her feet, and slowly pulled her pants up, trying to convince himself he was taking his time because he didn't want to hurt her. Her fingers closed over his arm, then slid around his neck, as he settled the waist band low on her hips. Maggie pressed her head to his chest, and with all his heart, Will wished he could pull her into his arms and keep her there for all eternity.

"Holy shit, I'm tired," she breathed.

Instead, he let her go. "Lay down."

He helped her back down, and she collapsed against the pillows with another groan. Lifting her legs into bed, he checked her stomach again. It was still bleeding a little. He ran downstairs to get a clean towel, then hurried back up and pressed it over her belly.

"Why don't you want me to see you anymore?" she asked, sounding sleepy.

He pulled her shirt down and tucked her in.

"I don't want to… complicate things."

"You make them breathtakingly clear, actually."

He wanted to ask what she meant, but didn't. "Get some rest."

"Don't go," she said, grabbing his hand.

"You know I can't leave."

"No, I mean… Stay *here*." She tapped the bed. "With me tonight."

"I don't think that's a good idea. Besides, Bob will be here any minute. He will sit—"

"I want you, Will." The words cut him like a knife, and he knew exactly what she meant.

"Maggie…" He wanted her too, but damn it, he couldn't! *They* couldn't.

"How about just until Bob comes then? Eric left some clothes in the other bedroom." Her eyes closed.

Will frowned and sat down beside her.

"What?"

"Wear whatever you want."

"What?" He pressed the back of his hand to her forehead. What on earth was she talking about? Was she hallucinating?

She opened her eyes. "You're soaking wet. Go change."

He looked down at his shirt clinging to his chest and gasped. Running his fingers through his wet hair, he gasped again. Will jumped up from the bed. There was a wet spot where he'd been sitting. "What in the hell?"

He hurried down the stairs into the bathroom and stared at his reflection in the mirror. He was sopping wet! How was this possible? He didn't get wet, or cold, or... anything. But he could feel it now. The cool water against his skin. A shiver rolled across his shoulders as he slowly unbuttoned his shirt, peeled it off, and hung it over the shower door.

In a daze, he went back upstairs into the guest room. First the footprints, then the walls, and now... this? He found one of Eric's T-shirts and pulled it over his head. Something was changing. After all this time, something was happening to him and... He crossed the landing and went back into Maggie's bedroom. And he was sure it had everything to do with her.

"What are you doing to *me*, Maggie?" he asked as he lay down beside her.

She did not answer.

Will watched the rise and fall of her chest beneath the blankets until he heard Bob's truck. Then quietly, he made his way downstairs to let the old man in.

Just in case the bleeding began again or... anything happened. He wanted someone there that was... real.

CHAPTER SIXTEEN

MAGGIE CHECKED HER INJURY IN THE MIRROR. THE PLANE OF HER stomach was still covered in tiny scabs, but the redness was gone, and the gash on her stomach was closed and scabbed over too. Bob had taken her to the walk-in clinic the next morning, where the nurse told her she'd done a good job taping herself up, and the doctor wrote her a prescription for antibiotic just in case. Heading into the kitchen, she pulled the second cup of coffee out from under the machine.

It had been almost a week, but she still couldn't wrap her mind around the fact that Bob knew about Will. She didn't know why, she'd just assumed she was the only one who could sense him, but it turned out Bob had seen him clear as day the first time he'd come over.

Maggie didn't know what they'd talked about, but that night when he'd stayed, every time she woke up, she heard their voices downstairs. It was a comforting sound.

Maggie pulled her outerwear on and grabbed the coffees off the end table before heading out.

"Will! Coffee!" She shouted, scaring the chickadees off the railing of the porch.

He was in the barn. She didn't know what he did out there at night, but maybe it was better than imagining him wandering the house while she slept.

Ever since her little mishap, he'd made himself visible again. And while harder in some ways, it was better in others. So much of what a person said was spoken with their expressions. His words told her what he thought, but his face showed her how he felt. And if their first precious week together of seeing him every day had told her anything, it was that his head and his heart were not on the same page. Despite what he'd said, he did feel *something* for her. She could see it in his eyes. And it made her heart race.

Maggie set the mugs down and called for him again.

Between her injury, the fifteen thousand dollars it was going to cost to replace the roof, and the fact that it had been cloudy and overcast for the last several days, Maggie had been sleeping in.

The day had already dawned gray as she snuggled under her blanket. A thick, white bank of clouds covered the sky like wool.

Will passed through the barn wall and crossed the driveway toward her, as her lips tipped up in a smile. He said it felt like walking through a waterfall.

She knew it was pointless to think of him as anything but a friend, but watching him walk toward her shoulders back, body lean from his years of manual labor, muscular arms exposed above hands which were thrust in his pockets... Goddamn, he was handsome. Not a body builder type, the way Dean had been, but all man. One hundred percent, strong, capable man.

Grabbing the rail, he climbed the stairs and Maggie tried to ignore her jealousy of the piece of wood beneath his palm.

He sat down in his chair. "How did you sleep?" he asked.

"Too long, again."

"January and February are the hardest out here."

"They definitely seem to be the most expensive."

Will laughed. "My grandad bought the whole damn farm with three hundred acres for less than the new roof will cost." He shook his head. "Are you sure they are charging a fair price? It seems like extortion to me."

"I've worked with contractors before, for my job. They might have padded the quotes, because they knew I was desperate, but they've been close enough. Everything is more expensive than it was in 1940."

"The last family that lived here moved out in eighty-two, I think. So, that's the last time I had a real good sense of the world."

"So, you haunted them too? Like you do me?"

Will gave her a strange look, and she regretted her phrasing. "No. Not like I do you. I didn't let them see me. But I was here."

"So, you just listened to them talk, eavesdropped?"

"Sometimes, but not often. Most of what I learned came from television. Mrs. Vernier had it on all day long."

Maggie sipped her coffee.

"I'm sorry everything is costing so much money. Believe it or not, I've been trying to keep it up but..."

Maggie smiled. "I know. I noticed it the first day, when I came to look at the house. It's half the reason I think I went ahead and bought it."

"Still."

She sighed. "It's just money. I picked up a few more clients. It should be fine."

"And you sold your car."

She shrugged. "It's just a car."

"What did Dahlia think of that?"

Maggie laughed. "She thinks I've lost my mind, and I want to tell her, to explain, but she's... She's not as open-minded as I am. She's very... practical and down to earth."

The other thing was, Dahlia knew Maggie too well. The moment Maggie even mentioned Will's name, Dee would know how she really felt about him. And then she'd probably have her committed for her own safety and 'lose' the key to her comfortably padded room.

Will took a sip of his coffee.

"It still doesn't taste like anything?" she asked.

He set his mug down. "No."

He'd confided that strange things had been happening to him

lately. After her harrowing night on the roof, when he'd changed into Eric's shirt and pants, he confessed to falling asleep at the kitchen table around dawn while Bob made himself a coffee. He said Bob woke him up a moment later, and he was back in his old clothes, and Eric's were crumpled beneath him in the chair. How he'd managed to get wet in the first place was a mystery, as was his super-ghost strength that night, first with the ladder and after with her. He had no explanation for any of it.

Yesterday, she had asked him if he thought maybe it was a sign that he was ready to move on. His expression matched her own alarm over that thought. They had both become quiet and pensive afterward and she hadn't brought it up again.

Will regaled her with stories of his childhood, the farm as it was in its heyday, complete with cows and chickens. The east and west fields used to be corrals for the animals. The back field used to encompass all the land past the next farm to the tree line over two miles away. "That all used to be mine." He sounded wistful as he spoke.

"We could try to buy some of it back?" Maggie suggested.

Will took another sip from his mug and rocked in his chair. "No. I don't want all that dirt anymore." He stared out past the barn. "It's funny how people change." He laughed. "Some people anyway. If I would have lived, I probably would have been the same man I was on the day I died for the rest of my life. In a way, I'm glad I died. It helped me to see things I just couldn't when I was alive."

Maggie smiled. "I've been thinking about that a lot, too. Not dying, but change. When I started out, I expected to be something different than what I became."

"What did you expect?"

She laughed. "I wanted to be a scientist. I wanted to discover. I craved adventure and the unknown. I wanted to find life on other planets, and study it, if we ever found any."

Will was silent.

"And up until recently, I felt like life robbed me of that dream. But…"

"But what?"

"The truth is, if I could go back and do it all over again right now, I can't figure out what part I'd change, because I know if I'd done anything differently, I wouldn't have Eric. I probably wouldn't have Dee. I wouldn't be here. I wouldn't know you." Goosebumps rippled across her body under the blanket.

Will's eyes met hers, and they were sharp with pain and longing. She knew he felt it too.

She looked away. While it was easier to read him when she could see him, it was becoming harder to control the quickening of her pulse, and the throbbing everywhere else when he looked at her like that. She'd dreamed of him several times now, once he was sleeping beside her in bed, as she lay on her side, her back to him reading a book. She hadn't even turned to confirm it was him. She'd just known it was, and it had been one of the most serene moments of her life. But in most of the others, they'd been making love. For the last two days, every time her mind was allowed to wander, that's where it went. To his hands on her body, his mouth on hers, the pleasure that ripped through her when they came together. She'd been waking in the middle of the night, so overwhelmed with desire, she'd been forced to satisfy herself before she could even think of falling back asleep. And, of course, his face was the one she imagined when—

She knew he was a ghost, and the situation was not ideal. But she also knew he could touch her, which meant—

Her phone buzzed on the table. She looked. It was Connor.

Will drained his mug and stood abruptly. "I'm going to head back out to the barn. Come find me later if you want."

Maggie quickly stamped out her wandering thoughts and picked up her phone.

"Hey!"

"How's farm life treating you?"

She hadn't talked to him since before Christmas, but she was sure he didn't want to hear the laundry list of things that had gone wrong over the last six weeks.

"I'm hanging in there."

"Have you found yourself yet?"

She watched Will's retreating form as he crossed the driveway. "I definitely found something."

Connor laughed. "I'm glad to hear it. Hey, um, the reason I called is…" He hesitated. "Hear me out, okay?"

Maggie frowned. "Okay."

"The singles club is doing another weekend in Lakeside, for Valentine's Day. This Friday and Saturday. And I was wondering if you'd be interested in joining me…"

His tone was joking, but she sensed the seriousness of his question. He was asking her out on a date. It had been six months since they'd met and he told her he wasn't ready for a relationship. Perhaps that had been long enough for him to mend?

She didn't know what to say. He was incredibly handsome, and kind, and probably a generous lover, but… she looked at the barn.

"I would love to, but I already have plans for this weekend." She didn't know why she was lying. "My best friend is coming up for a girls' thing." Dahlia was going to Chicago with her newest boy toy. "We are doing a chocolate and wine tasting." Dahlia hated chocolate.

"Oh. Okay. I figured you might have plans already." He sounded disappointed. "I guess I'll be flying solo once again." He laughed. "Which I suppose is expected at a singles event."

Maggie laughed. "I'm sorry."

"No worries. Who knows, maybe I'll meet an interesting woman who likes to get drunk and buy boats."

Maggie laughed again. "You're hilarious."

"It's good to hear your voice, Maggie. You sound happy."

"It's good to hear from you too. If you get desperate, or

cornered, give me a call, and I'll see if I can slip away for an hour and save you."

"I will."

Hanging up, she stared at her phone.

With a sigh, she got up and headed inside. She made a bowl of oatmeal and another cup of coffee. Her conversation with Connor had left her feeling restless. Was she being stupid to turn him down? He was a good man. Kind, funny. He'd proved all that the day they met. She knew why she had of course, but was that stupid as well? If Will were… alive, everything would be different. But he wasn't.

Swapping her slippers for boots, she hugged her sweater around her middle, hunching against the wind, and hurried to the barn.

Will was stacking boards in the corner. Her heart leaped at the sight of him. It did *not* do that for Connor. How could Will look and feel so real? It defied the laws of nature, didn't it? And things that defied nature didn't exist. That was physics 101. Which meant that someone somewhere was missing a fairly large piece of the bigger picture. He had to be right in his theory. There had to be a lot more out there than people thought. At least she knew she wasn't crazy. Bob proved she wasn't. He'd stopped by twice since the night of her accident, and he and Will chatted about the crops and the weather like old friends.

Leaning against the door, she asked "What is it like to be dead?"

He turned, and there it was again. That look. It stole her breath away. "What do you mean?"

"What is it like? I know you can't taste, or feel the weather, but in your body, in your mind, do you still feel… things?"

Wills brows came together. "Things like what?"

"I don't know. Fear, anger… desire?" The last word came out a whisper.

He studied her a moment, then laughed. The birds above fluttered in their nests as the sound echoed. "Anger, sometimes. But desire? You mean physical desire?" He laughed again, like it was the most ridiculous question he'd ever been asked and looked away.

"I don't even have a real body, Maggie. What would I desire with?" He threw the plank he'd been holding against the others, and it clattered to the ground.

"I'm sorry."

"No, you're not." He met her eyes. "And no, I don't."

"I didn't mean—"

"I know exactly what you meant. I can see it in your eyes."

"I'm sorry, Will."

"What do you want me to say, Maggie? Huh?"

She didn't understand his sudden hostility. Yes, he'd insisted he only wanted to be friends. But that was before she could *see* him. Did he really think she hadn't noticed the way he looked at her? "I don't know. I—"

"My 'desire' has been dead as long as I have been."

That was a lie. "That's not true."

"Yes, it is."

"No, it's—"

"Yes, it is!" he roared, storming over to her, and throwing his hand up. For a moment, she thought he might hit her, but he was just pointing his finger toward the door. "Now get the fuck out of here!"

Maggie's eyes filled with tears as she backed toward it. Her cheeks burned with humiliation as Will gasped. His expression softened as his eyes filled with regret. "Wait!"

She slipped out the cracked door and rushed back toward the house, swiping at her eyes with the back of her hand. It wasn't true. He was lying.

"Maggie, wait! I'm sorry I yelled."

She spun around at the foot of the steps as he closed the gap between them. He was lying, and she was going to call his bluff.

He stopped in front of her. "I didn't mean—"

Maggie's hand snaked up around the back of his neck as she pulled his mouth hungrily to hers. Underestimating her strength, they tumbled backward as their lips collided. Will caught her around the waist and braced their fall with his other hand as she landed on the gravel. Sharp stones pricked at her backside and shoulders. He groaned as he squeezed her and she pressed herself into him. Grabbing his face with her other hand, she deepened the kiss. Fireworks exploded in her chest as their bodies came together. He moaned again as his tongue brushed her teeth. He pushed them apart and tasted her. A shudder ran down her spine as her hand slid from his face to his chest, to his hip. Never had she wanted anyone more. And he *clearly* wanted her too. She knew it!

"Make love to me, Will, plea—"

The stones jabbed at her once more, as she fell back into the dirt. When she looked up, he was standing over her, his face a mask of anger.

"What's the m—"

"Don't ever do that again," he seethed.

Maggie sat up, almost crazy with need for him. In almost forty years, she had never felt anything like it. "I know you want to. And I want you."

"You know nothing about me!"

She got to her feet. Why was he so angry? "I know everything that matters!"

"Don't ever touch me again, Maggie. I mean it."

"Why not?"

"Because I don't want you to!"

Again, his words stung like a slap. Actually, a slap would have hurt less. A soft sob fell from her mouth. How many times she was going to let him do that to her? Hurt her like that?

She shook her head. "You haven't learned anything, have you?"

"I've made my peace with what I am. You need to too."

She smiled sadly. "Resignation and peace aren't the same thing, Will." She climbed the steps and looked back. "I see the conflict in your eyes every time you look at me. You are not at peace with *anything*. Maybe that's why you're still here. Because you don't know how to be honest with yourself."

Climbing the stairs of the porch, she went inside. His rejection hurt, but—she squared her shoulders—now she knew for sure where she stood with Will. He didn't want her, and she had to respect his decision.

She poured herself a glass of water and sat at the kitchen table, opened her phone, and scrolled to Dahlia's number. She wished she could call her, but there was no way to explain what she felt without sounding insane.

She scrolled back up and saw Connor's name at the top of her calls, and stared at it. Will didn't want her, and the faster she got over that, the better off she'd be. "Fuck it," she muttered, pressing her thumb to the screen.

He answered on the third ring. "Hey, what's up?"

"Good news. Girls' weekend got canceled."

"Oh no, what happened?"

"A guy." She wouldn't say which one. She wouldn't say he was a ghost, and he'd ghosted her.

Connor laughed. "Of course, what else? So, we're on?"

Maggie took a deep breath. "Yep. Let me know when you're up, I'll meet you there."

"It's a date," he said.

"It's a date," she repeated.

CHAPTER SEVENTEEN

WILL KNEW MAGGIE WAS ANGRY AND UPSET, BUT DAMN IT, SO WAS he. After she'd blindsided him with that kiss, he couldn't go anywhere near her. Even her scent in a room after she'd walked away drove him mad. He slammed his fist into the trunk of the oak that appeared in front of him.

Was he capable of desire? What the *hell* kind of question was that? He pulled his hair back off his forehead in frustration. Of course, he fucking was. And he'd never wanted anyone more than he wanted Maggie! But he couldn't risk it. What if they came together and... Will shook his head, and took a swing at a helpless sapling. What if he killed her? What if, whatever he was, spread to her? What if—

It had been four days, and he'd spent all of them storming back and forth across the fields, going in circles in his head. Wanting things to go back to the way they were before, but not wanting them to go back. He touched his lips, remembering the velvety smoothness of hers. Wishing so badly he was alive again, and knowing it was impossible. Then wishing he were just dead, so he could be free of his misery. And to top it all off—he raised his head and looked in the direction of the lake and Lakeside—she was out with *Connor*.

He'd seen her leave the house, dressed up in a pair of leather pants that left absolutely nothing to the imagination and a pair of heels he was almost certain she must have gotten from Dahlia. She'd styled her hair in soft waves around her head, and her eyes had looked almost green, lined in black, and her lips were the color of ripe tomatoes. He'd heard Dahlia call the shade "Come Fuck Me" when she'd gifted it to Maggie over Christmas. "Goddamn it."

Will swiped at another poor tree and then turned back out onto the open field and started walking along the west edge.

She'd spent the evening with Connor yesterday, too. And why wouldn't she? She was a beautiful, single woman who deserved to find happiness and companionship. As far as he could tell, Connor was a nice guy. A little soft, maybe, but decent. So why was he so damn angry?

Will stared out over the land. Everything was gray and black, as if someone, God maybe, had smote the land along with him. Will was angry because *he* wanted her. He was angry because he'd literally had her in his hands, and he'd—

He kicked the dirt and bellowed.

She was right. He was not at peace. He'd merely resigned himself to his existence and mistaken it for something it wasn't. His feelings for her proved it. There was no peace in his life. There never had been. There had just been work, then anger, then resignation, and now regret. For all of it. How could he stay here now with her here? How was he going to survive seeing her every day and not...

He looked up at the sky, addressing God for the first time in his life. "You goddamned son of a bitch! Why did you bring her here?"

God didn't answer.

WILL WALKED until headlights flashed across his eyes. He hadn't even noticed the sky growing dark. He walked back toward the house and saw Maggie get out of her car. Again, he felt the pull to go to her, to try to explain, but... What would that help? Nothing.

Another car pulled into the driveway, and Will recognized it. "Connor," he whispered, crossing the driveway.

The other man got out, straightened his sports coat, and whispered to himself under his breath. "You can do this. You can do this. It's time."

Will frowned. *Do what?*

He knew he shouldn't, but he followed him into the house when Maggie opened the door. The top she was wearing was white and silky, looking more like a chemise than a shirt, and he could see the outline of her bra through it. She looked both indecent and wildly beautiful. There was an open bottle of champagne on the coffee table, and she had lit a fire in the fireplace.

Will tried to breathe, but it was like someone had poured concrete down his throat.

"The house looks great," Connor said, taking his coat off and sliding out of his shoes. Maggie took his coat and hung it in the closet as Connor stared at her backside, and Will tried not to do the same.

He wanted to leave, but he couldn't. The concrete migrated to his feet, rooting to the spot.

"Come on, let me give you a tour," she said. The nervousness in her voice was obvious. Or was it anticipation? He couldn't tell.

"Why don't we have a drink first?"

Will looked from Maggie to Connor. They were both nervous. That made him nervous. What was going on?

You know.

Dear god, he hoped not. "Shit."

Maggie glanced in his direction. "Oh, okay, sure."

They sat down, and their glasses clinked together. "Cheers," Connor said.

"Cheers." Maggie smiled and swallowed half the glass.

That was *definitely* not good.

"You look beautiful tonight," Connor said, and Will wanted to punch him in the face.

"Thank you. So do you." Maggie tucked her hair behind her ear shyly. "It's been a while since I've dressed up. It's been a while for... a lot of things."

Will ground his teeth together and clenched his fists at his side, lest he punch a hole through the new drywall.

"If you'll excuse me for a minute." Maggie got up and went into the kitchen. Will followed her.

She spun around. "I know you're here," she whispered.

He just stared.

"I want you to leave."

He didn't answer.

"Do you hear me, Will?"

He wanted to throttle her. She didn't know what she was doing. She—

"Will."

"I hear you," he growled.

"Get out."

"You're making a mistake, Mag—"

"No, *you* did. Now get out." She turned and left.

Will stood there a moment, knowing she was right, but that was no reason to—He rounded the corner, and his jaw almost dropped out of his mouth.

Maggie was straddling Connor on the couch. His head was pressed against the back, and she was kissing him. Instead of pushing her away like he had, Connor groaned and pulled her closer. One hand slid under the back of her shirt, while the other moved over her hip, pushing her down against his lap. "My god, Maggie. You are so beautiful," he said. Reaching under her hair, he pressed her mouth harder against his, and she moaned softly into his mouth.

Will watched helplessly, feeling like he might be sick as his wildest fantasy play out in front of him. Everything, every detail was just as he'd imagined. Everything except the man. She was kissing the wrong man.

Connor lifted the corners of her shirt, and Maggie helped him slide it over her head. Her bra was composed of thin white lace and he could see straight through it. Connor buried his head between her breasts.

Will finally regained control of his body and turned away, afraid the scream welling up in his chest would bring the house down on them. He had to get out of there. The wall was like gelatin as he clawed his way through it. For a moment, he thought he was stuck, and panic rushed up around him, but then he came out the other side, chest heaving like he'd run a marathon. He glanced back over his shoulder and immediately wished he hadn't.

Maggie's bra was gone, and Connor was exploring her nakedness, touching her breasts, running his hands up and down her bare back.

The scream pressed against Will's clenched teeth and throbbed behind his eyeballs.

With their lips still locked, Connor lifted her off the couch.

Maggie wrapped her legs around his hips as they stumbled around the couch toward the stairwell.

Unable to bear it anymore, Will ran.

He ran to the farthest corner of the darkest field and dropped to his knees. Grasping at the dirt, he shoved handfuls in his mouth to muffle the cries that tore from the hole in his heart where Maggie belonged.

He loved her. He loved her more than life or death, and she was —Connor's hands on her body flashed through his mind, and his screams became wails as the land that killed him fell from his blackened mouth.

CHAPTER EIGHTEEN

IT HAPPENED SOMEWHERE BETWEEN WHEN SHE'D UNBUTTONED HIS shirt, and when their naked torsos came together, that Maggie knew she couldn't go through with it. A part of her wanted the release, but she could tell, in the way Connor touched her, in his gentleness, that what he felt for her was more than causal sex. The truth was, sex meant more to her too.

"I'm so sorry," she said, sitting beside him on the edge of the bed covering her chest.

He dropped his shirt over her shoulders. "It's okay."

"No. I shouldn't have started it if... I thought I could do it. I just..."

"You don't owe me an explanation, Maggie."

But she wanted to explain, to be honest with him. "I meant what I said. You are incredibly handsome and kind." She put a gentle hand on his knee and squeezed.

"It's okay. You're not ready. I, of all people, understand that. I can wait."

But she was ready. Just not for him. "Connor..." She didn't know how to explain. "You'd be waiting a *very* long time."

"Oh."

"Believe me, if I thought we could both wake up tomorrow and be okay with being fuck-buddies—"

"I want more than that."

"I know you do. That's why I had to stop. I don't want to hurt you the way your wife did. I want to restore your faith in love, not destroy it."

He put an arm around her shoulders, and she leaned against him.

A moment later, he released her. "Do you mind if I crash on the couch? I drank half that bottle of champagne while you were in the kitchen, and I'm not in any kind of condition to—"

Maggie laughed and got up. "So, you were nervous too?"

Connor blushed a little in the darkness. "Yeah. It's been a while and—"

Maggie held up her hand. "Please, you're preaching to the choir here. And of course, you can stay. You can sleep in the guest room." She reached for his hand and pulled him to his feet. "Do you need a toothbrush? I have an extra one downstairs."

"Yeah, that would be great."

Connor followed her down the steps, and as he brushed his teeth, she gathered up her clothes and banked the fire.

They went upstairs together.

As Maggie lay in the dark, listening to Connor snore softly in the other room, she knew she'd done the right thing, at least in the end, anyway. Will was right. She had almost made a terrible mistake. She had almost used Connor as a diversion, as an object, to soothe her broken heart, and she did not want to be whatever kind of person that would have made her.

When Maggie woke the next morning, Connor was gone. He'd left a note, thanking her for the evening, and signed off with *I hope you find whatever your heart is looking for. I hope I do too. Connor*

Maggie smiled and flipped her hair into a messy bun. On the face of it, the night before had been a disaster. But in her heart, there was peace. She went downstairs and brushed her teeth. While her coffee was brewing, she poured the remainder of the flat champagne down the sink. The sun was just coming up, and there wasn't a cloud in the sky. Light shot through the east windows, setting the refrigerator and the bookshelf in the other room aglow.

She made Will a cup of coffee, hoping he'd show up and she could apologize. He hadn't shown himself since the day she'd kissed him, and he hadn't spoken a word to her before last night in the kitchen. But if they were going to live here together... They had to make amends.

She set the coffees down on the end table, then bundled up and let herself onto the porch. As soon as she was out the door, she heard it. A terrible crashing sound coming from the barn.

Quickly, she set the mugs on the table, spilling the hot coffee and scalding her hands. Maggie wiped them on her sweater and ran in her slippered feet across the driveway. She pulled the door open and gasped at the mess.

"Will?" She hurried inside and ducked as a metal bar flew past her, shattering the little window that faced the road. The window she'd once looked in. The swallows chirped and fluttered nervously up in the eaves as Will scooped up an old bucket and threw it against the wall. All the drawers were pulled out of the workbench, and there were nails and screws and bolts everywhere. The milk cans were knocked over, and the door at the back of the barn had been ripped off its hinges.

"What are you doing!" she screamed.

Will spun around, and she swore she saw fire in his eyes. "What am I doing?" he demanded, storming over to her. Huge clouds of dust erupted from his feet, and they churned like ash in the air as they rose through the seams of light piercing the darkness. "What am *I* doing?"

Maggie backed up as he threw whatever was in his hand to the ground. "Why are you so angry?" She had an idea, but what right did he have after he'd rejected her? What did he want her to do?

He only stopped when he was a breath away from her. "Don't you *ever* bring a man to my house again," he seethed.

Anger rose in her throat as she glanced between his eyes. How dare he stomp on her heart like it was nothing and then treat her like a damn child afterward? "Your house? *Your* house? Really?" The venom in her voice made it wobble.

The muscle in his jaw twitched, but he didn't answer her.

"It's mine! It's my fucking house! I've poured every *ounce* of my soul into it. I have given up *everything*—" Her voice broke. Why was she even arguing with him? "It's fucking mine!" she screamed before wheeling around and storming out the door.

The sunlight was blinding as she swiped at her angry tears. "Jerk," she snapped, stomping back toward the house. The gravel bit through her slippers, jabbing at her feet. How dare he destroy her beloved barn? *Fuck him.*

Stomping up the steps, she grabbed the edge of her little table and slammed it over. The mugs spilled and broke as the glass tabletop shattered into tiny pieces.

The door knob cracked against the closet door as she threw it open. *His* house? Maggie crossed the room, shoving over the end tables and the decorations she's placed on them. *His house?* She grabbed the edge of the bookshelf. He thought he could destroy her barn? "Fine." She pulled as hard as she could. The windows shook as it crashed to the floor, spilling books everywhere.

"I'll destroy *his* fucking house," she hissed, storming into the kitchen.

Throwing the cabinet open, she grabbed the first thing she saw, a bowl, and threw it against the wall. It dented her brand-new drywall before shattering into a million pieces. God, that felt good. She grabbed another.

Smash!

And another.

Then she moved to the plates. Grabbing the edge like a frisbee, she threw it through the window on the back door.

"Maggie—"

She grabbed the next one and flung it in the direction of his head.

"Stop."

She grabbed another. "Leave me alone!"

"Maggie, stop it!" he demanded.

She had no intention of doing anything he asked her after what he'd done. "Leave me al—" She slammed the dish against the edge of the counter as she turned. The rest of the word got stuck in her throat as a searing pain shot down her arm. Her eyes widened in surprise at the rush of warmth across her palm, and the red pool rapidly accumulating on the floor beside her. Will gasped. *Jesus.* Was all that *hers*? Slowly, she lifted her arm and rolled her bloody palm skyward, as a long sliver of the plate came into view. She gasped. It was sticking out of her arm. "Oh, shit." With her other hand, she quickly extracted the dagger shaped shard—

"Maggie, no!"

But it was too late. She watched in amazement as the blood squirted from her arm like a fountain. It reminded her of the bathroom sink. But red. She swung around, and it splattered against the window, tinting the light, and spraying the cabinets. It was only seconds before she felt lightheaded. A warm, gentle mist covered her face, and she turned her head away. The tang of blood was sharp in the air.

"Maggie, you have to call 911." Will was holding her phone out. She went to reach for it, but as soon as she let go of the counter, the world turned sideways.

"Maggie!"

There was a loud crack, like a tree being split in half, and her lips felt like lead as she spoke. The words were long and drawn out, like an old film reel that had lost power. "Maybe we will haunt this place… together now." It was a beautiful thought. She could almost see it. The farm in the summertime. The wildflowers. The daisies and the lilies. The stubborn chicory. She in a sundress and one of those floppy straw hats, and Will—

"Maggie!"

… Will, looking just as he always did, handsome in his white shirt, rolled up to his elbows.

Maggie felt Will's hand on hers.

She smiled. Yes. They would walk hand in hand along the creek, watch the storms roll by and the corn grow, and sit together as the day drew to a close, and the sun disappeared. She'd lean her head against his shoulder, feel the thumping of his heart beneath her ear, and they would gaze up in wonder as the first stars appeared and the sky turned…

"Mag—"

Dark.

CHAPTER NINETEEN

WILL SEARCHED THE ROOM FOR SOMETHING TO TIE OFF HER ARM with. How could there be nothing here? It was a damn kitchen. He looked down at his belt and pulled it off, praying it wouldn't disappear as soon as he got it around her arm. He cinched it as tight as he could, and the spraying slowed to a trickle. He wrapped the belt around her arm several times and looped the end through it and pulled. It looked painful, but it was better than bleeding to death. Cradling her head against his arm, he grabbed her phone and her hand, pressing her fingers to the keys. 021002. Eric's birthday. Then he pressed her limp finger against the button with the little phone on it and then dialed the numbers.

A second later, someone answered. "Nine-one-one, what is your emergency?"

"I need help! I need—"

"Is anyone there?"

"I need—"

"Hello?"

"Goddamn it!" He almost threw the phone. She couldn't hear him.

"Tap if you can hear me," the dispatcher said.

Hope blossomed in his chest. He banged the phone on the floor.

"Tap again if you need help."

Tap, tap, tap.

"You are on a cell phone, so it is going to take some time to locate—is this Margaret Dubois?"

Tap, tap, tap.

"Are you in your car?"

Will held the phone still.

"Are you at home?"

Tap, tap, tap.

"Is your address 5557 Morgan Line in Lakesi—"

Tap, tap—

"Alright. I've already sent out the call. Hold tight, Ms. Dubois, and stay on the line. Help is on the way."

Will pushed her hair back, the blood on his hands turning it into an even deeper shade of auburn. He pushed it back over his arm. "I'm sorry. I'm so sorry. Hang on—" He pressed his forehead to hers. She smelled like coffee and sunflowers dipped in the sharp, dangerous tang of wet, rusted metal. "Don't die. Please don't—"

"Maggie?"

Will's head flew up.

"Maggie?" Dahlia's voice sounded frightened, as she called again from somewhere near the front door. A second later, Will heard her say, "Stay out here and call the police."

Will looked down at Maggie's head rolled back over his arm. Should he stay or should he go?

"Maggie?" Dahlia's voice had moved closer. He didn't want to, but... Will gently placed Maggie's head on the ground and disappeared as Dahlia rounded the corner.

"Oh my god! Maggie!" Dahlia screamed, dropping to her knees. "Eric!" she cried. "Call an ambulance."

Will's heart broke as Maggie's son ran into the room. No son should watch their mother die. He knew from experience. The bouquet of lilies Eric was holding fell out of his hand, and as they hit the floor, their sweet musky scent mixed with Maggie's blood, making Will want to vomit.

"Mom!" Eric slipped in the pool of blood and fell to the ground beside her. "Mom?" He shook her shoulder. Maggie's eyes fluttered open for a second and closed again. "Mom!"

"Maggie, baby. Stay with me." Dahlia touched Maggie's blood splattered cheek. "Oh my god—"

Maggie made a sound, and Dahlia jerked her hand back. "Shit." She looked up and gasped at the red spots on the ceiling as she tried to blink back her tears. "Jesus—" She looked at Eric. "Wh-what do we do?"

Dahlia leaned back over Maggie, her hands hovering over her body. "What do we—should I not move her?"

"Hello? Hello?"

They both turned and looked down at Maggie's phone.

Dahlia hit the speaker button. "Hello! Help! We need help! Who is—"

"I'm a 911 dispatcher, ma'am. Are you a family member?"

"Yes," Dahlia answered.

"Can you explain to me what has happened?"

Dahlia looked around the room. "Oh my god. There is blood everywhere. I-I think someone tried to kill—" She stopped as her eyes settled on Will's belt around Maggie's arm.

"Is she breathing?" the dispatcher asked.

Dahlia leaned forward. "I don't know! I don't think—" She met Eric's eyes over Maggie's body. "You need to send someone now!"

"They're on their way Ms…"

"Johnson. Dahlia, Johnson. What do we—there is so much fucking blood."

"Don't move her. Just wait. Help should be there any minute."

Will heard the sirens. A few seconds later, they were followed by the screech of tires on gravel. A man dressed in jeans and a construction T-shirt rushed in.

"Jesus Christ," he said, as Dahlia moved back, and he took Maggie's pulse. "What in the hell happened?" He looked at Eric.

"She was like this when we got here. She-she's my mom. She… Is she gonna die?"

"Did you do this?" The man pointed to the tourniquet Will had made with his belt.

Eric shook his head.

"Okay, my name is Liam. I need you to go stand over there." Eric got up, the knees of his pants soaked in blood, and stood beside Dahlia who stood next to Will by the door. The wind whistled through the broken window.

Liam confirmed for the dispatcher that he was on the scene, and the dispatcher ended the call. He pressed an ear toward Maggie's mouth. Then he sat back, shaking his head.

Dahlia made a gasping sound and clutched Eric's hand. "Oh, Jesus. No… No, no… come on baby…"

Pulling his phone out of his pocket, Liam held it up to her mouth as Will heard the wail of another siren. Maggie's breath barely misted the screen.

"Oh, thank you, Jesus," Dahlia whispered, squeezing Eric's hand.

"Is she going to—" Eric began again, as another man ran in, in full fire get-up.

He stopped short. "Holy shit. What the *fuck* happened in here?"

He looked at Dahlia and Eric, and they just shook their heads.

"I dunno," Liam said. "But she's still with us, barely. What's the ETA on—"

"I saw the lights on my way in. They'll be here in under two."

The fireman picked up her phone as two more men in similar dress entered the room. Will recognized the fire chief. "Who called it in?" he asked, as he crouched down and touched Will's worn leather belt that was still tied around Maggie's arm. He looked at Dahlia and Eric.

"I-I called," Eric stuttered, "But they already knew."

"Nine-one-one was already on the line when we got here."

"Did you pick up her phone?" the chief asked Eric.

He shook his head.

The chief held up Maggie's phone. Will's bloody handprint was clearly visible on the back. Will sucked in a sharp breath and looked down at his hands, soaked with Maggie's blood. He wiped the blood onto his pants, then pulled his hands through his hair, trying not to cry out. Oh god, what had he done?

The paramedics came in with their bags and gear.

"Call the PD. This is a crime scene until further notice," the fire chief informed them, as they stabilized Maggie's neck and took her pulse. "No one touches anything." He looked at Dahlia and Eric. "I'm going to need to know exactly what you touched, where you—"

"What happened here?" one of the paramedics asked, lifting Maggie's shirt, revealing her scraped belly, and healing cut.

"I don't know!" Dahlia cried. "I don't fucking know what's—"

"Shh, Aunt Dee," Eric said, pulling her into a hug. "She'll be okay. She'll be—"

Someone brought in a stretcher, and on the count of three, Liam, the paramedics, and the chief lifted Maggie onto it. One of the men strapped her down. Her skin was so pale, Will could see her veins running like roads on a map beneath it.

"She'll be okay," Eric repeated while Dahlia cried.

Will couldn't swallow. He was overcome by the terrible fear that his guilt would make him visible. If Maggie died, it was his fault. If Eric lost his mother, it was because... He looked at Dahlia and Eric, both horror-stricken and crying.

For the second time in two days, Will ran to escape.

Peering from behind the corner of the barn, Will watched in disbelief as half the fire department and the local police swarmed the property. The paramedics carried Maggie out on a stretcher, and he went to her as they hurried her to the ambulance. "Fight, Maggie. Don't die. Think of Eric. He needs you. I need..." He squeezed her hand just before they loaded her into the back and slammed the doors. Eric and Dahlia ran to her car.

Will followed the ambulance to the road.

Dahlia and Eric spun out a moment later. The blaring wail from its speaker matched the cry in his heart as he stood by the mailbox and watched them disappear in a cloud of dust.

"Hey! You guys gotta see this," one of the firemen called from the barn.

Will turned.

Maggie was right. He hadn't learned his lesson.

The fireman shouted again. "Someone was here. And they were pissed. If the vic dies, I think we're looking at murder."

Murder? Will had not learned to love what was in front of him when he had the chance.

And now she was gone.

CHAPTER TWENTY

MAGGIE BLINKED. SHE FROWNED AND BLINKED AGAIN, WONDERING if she was still dreaming because—

"Dean?"

He looked up from his phone, and his brows went up in relief as he set it on the table beside her bed and took her hand.

"Hey, sunshine," he said with a soft smile. "How are you feeling?"

Maggie's frown deepened as she looked around the room. A hospital room? Why was she... She looked down at the bandage on her arm and it all came back. Will and the barn, and her own anger and the accident.

"I'm fine. What are you doing here?"

"I sent Eric back to campus. He was here all night, and he has an exam this afternoon at two-thirty. Once we knew you were going to be okay, I figured..."

All night? She looked at the window and the blue sky beyond it. How long had she been out? "Of course."

"Dee was here too. I told her we'd stay so she could run home and get a change of clothes."

"We?"

"Ann and Sophia are down in the cafeteria getting some lunch. Dee should be back anytime."

"How long have I been here?"

"They brought you in yesterday afternoon."

Maggie stared at her arm. She remembered nothing after putting her arm over the sink.

Dean leaned forward; his blue eyes full of concern. "What in the hell happened, Maggie?"

There was no way she could explain and avoid being committed. "I don't know."

Dean's eyes searched hers. "The police think they were looking for something."

"They?"

"Whoever vandalized your house and the barn. When Dee and Eric found you, there was blood and broken dishes, and everything was overturned—"

Maggie swayed. "Eric and Dee? Why were they there?"

"They'd decided to surprise you for Valentine's Day."

"Oh god."

"You don't remember anything?"

Maggie shook her head.

"You would have been dead by the time they got there, but someone… The police think one of the thieves put a tourniquet over your arm to stop the bleeding before they left, because you wouldn't have lasted five minutes otherwise. Do you remember that?"

She shook her head.

"They used an old leather belt."

As soon as he said it, Maggie knew whose it was. Will must have done it.

"The police have it, and some bloody prints on your phone. The police chief wants you to call him as soon as you're able." Dean pointed to a card on the table.

Fear ripped through Maggie. What if they found out about Will? Could they? If they had his fingerprints, would they turn up on some kind of database? Or had he died before they would have records like that?

"Earth to Maggie."

She blinked. "I'm sorry. I just—" She rubbed her forehead with her uninjured arm. The tube from the IV that was stuck in the back of her hand moved with her.

"Does it hurt at all?" Dean asked.

Maggie looked at her arm. "No. What-what happened exactly?"

"You were impaled with something. They think a piece of one of the dishes they found. It nearly severed your radial artery."

"Oh…"

"You don't remember?"

She remembered the dish, and the blood spraying the window, but nothing after that.

"The doctor said you were really, *really* lucky."

Maggie leaned her head back against the pillow and closed her eyes. Luck had nothing to do with it.

SHE OPENED her eyes and Ann and Sophia were there with Dean, and so was Dee. They all turned.

"How are you doing, baby?" Dahlia asked, sitting on the bed.

Maggie tried to sit up, and a sharp pain sliced through her arm.

"Here." Dahlia pushed the button on a remote control that was hung off the side of her bed, and the mattress brought her up to sitting.

Maggie smiled at Ann. "Hi. Hey, Sophie." The little girl waved.

"We were just getting ready to take off," Dean said.

Maggie nodded. "Thanks for coming. All of you."

Ann smiled and squeezed her leg. "We're just glad you're okay."

A moment later, they were gone, and Maggie was staring into the very determined face of her best friend.

"What?"

"What in the fuck happened yesterday?"

Maggie sighed. Lying to Dean was one thing, lying to Dahlia was… next to impossible. She closed her eyes. "Can we not do this right now? I just—I've had a rough couple of days."

"Yeah, I can see that."

There was a long silence, and Maggie peeked at Dahlia.

"Are you in danger now?" her friend asked, eyes full of concern.

Danger? "What do you mean?"

"Whoever trashed your house, are they gonna come looking for you? One of them patched you up. Why did they do that? Do you know them? Did they threaten—"

"No. I'm fine, Dee. Just tired."

Dahlia exhaled heavily. "Alright, well, I'm here now. Brought some work. So, you just rest."

"Thank you."

"Make no mistake, you will tell me what happened."

"I will."

"Okay, go to sleep."

Maggie drifted off again.

It felt like only moments later that Maggie was discharged into Dahlia's care, and they were on their way to her condo. Maggie had spent one more night in the hospital, but except for the hour when Eric was there, had slept until this morning. She had met briefly with the police chief before they left the hospital and spent the majority of her fifteen-minute interview shaking her head and saying, "I don't know." She avoided Dahlia's eyes as she perjured herself.

"You want to stop and get a coffee?"

"I'd prefer something stronger."

"It's ten-thirty a.m., and you're on pain meds. The strongest you're gonna get is dark roast."

Maggie nodded. "Fine."

They got in line at the drive thru, and Maggie looked at her best friend. Dahlia rarely had a hair out of place. She was always calm and always together. Except for now. Now she looked exhausted and on the verge of tears.

"I'm sorry, Dee," Maggie whispered.

Dahlia swiped at her moist eyes with the back of her fingers. "Are you gonna tell me what happened now?" Her car inched forward.

"Yeah. But…"

Dahlia turned and looked at her. "But what?"

"I'm afraid you won't believe me."

"Why is that?"

"Because… I can hardly believe it myself."

"Alright. Let's just enjoy our coffee and get you home. Once we're all settled in, we'll sit down, and you will explain to me exactly what the fuck is going on."

"Yeah."

They ordered their coffee, and Dahlia was unusually quiet on the forty-five-minute ride, giving Maggie plenty of time to think about how she wanted to explain Will. Unfortunately, as they pulled into Dahlia's parking spot, she had not come up with a way that didn't make her sound like she'd lost her mind.

They rode the elevator up to Dahlia's loft. If there was an opposite to Maggie's old farmhouse, this was it. Everything was new, smooth, and modern. Dahlia entered the key code and pushed the metal door open. The room was bright and wide open. The walls were white and covered in expensive local art. It overlooked Woodward, one of the main thoroughfares that ended at a small park in downtown Detroit. Maggie could see some of the larger buildings by the river if she pressed her head to the wall of windows that faced the road.

Dahlia had brought her a pair of yoga pants and a zip up sweater to wear home, and as she curled up on the couch, her friend made a quick call to the diner at the corner for some soup and a club sandwich.

Dropping her phone onto the table, Dahlia sat down on the opposite end of the couch, pulling half the chenille blanket that Maggie was using over her slim legs. With a deep sigh, she nodded. "I'm ready if you are."

Maggie took a deep breath and dove in. "Okay, so you know how I told you the farm was 'special'?"

Twenty minutes later she came up for air, and as she expected, Dahlia's expression was half disbelief, half terrified certainty that Maggie was certifiably insane. Her mouth opened and closed several times, but no words issued forth. It wasn't a good sign when Dahlia was speechless. It usually meant she was composing a scathing and curse-laden reply.

But Maggie was saved by the ringing of Dahlia's phone. Her eyes did not stray from Maggie's as she answered. "Dahlia Johnson. Yes… Oh. Right. Sorry. I'll be there in a minute."

Still staring, she got up and slipped her phone into her back pocket. Her eyes narrowed. "I'm gonna go get our lunch. You don't move till I get back. Got it?"

Maggie nodded.

Ten minutes later, Dahlia returned, and a minute after that, she thrust a cup of soup under Maggie's nose. Then she sat back down in her spot and set the sandwich on the glass coffee table, and resumed her hawk-like stare.

Maggie took a sip of the steaming soup as Dahlia's eyes bore into hers.

"*What?*" Maggie asked, exasperated. She set her soup on the table.

"I'm trying to figure out whether you're lying to me, or if you really believe—"

"I knew you wouldn't believe me! That's why I didn't tell you before."

"How can I believe you when you're telling me you bought a haunted farm and fell in love with a fucking ghost?"

"I didn't say I was in love—"

Dahlia gave her *the* look. "You kissed him, Maggie. I can hear it in your voice. I can see it in your eyes when you talk about him. It. Your ghost." She shook her head. "Fuck. I can't believe I'm even—"

"Dee—"

"Ghosts are not real, Maggie. Neither are superheroes or... leprechauns. This... this is the real world. Do you not understand that anymore?" There was genuine fear in her eyes as she spoke.

Maggie didn't know what to say. She wasn't lying, and she wasn't wrong. Maybe leprechauns were real, or maybe Will was something else, not a ghost, but—

Dahlia shook her head again. "I knew something was wrong. I could feel it. I should have—"

"I need you to believe me, Dee."

"How am I supposed to do that?"

"Because you know me." Maggie met her eyes. "And because I've never lied to you."

Dahlia broke the stare first.

"Will is the one that saved me. It's his belt they found around my arm."

"Fuck."

"And it's got to be his prints on the phone."

"Fuck."

"And the reason the place was torn apart is because... He was upset. And then I got upset." Maggie sighed. "It was me who broke the dishes and overturned the house. Because I was angry. And my arm... It was just an accident."

"Fuck."

"That's why I lied to Dean and the police. How could I explain?"

"Why was he upset?"

"What?"

"Will, or whatever his name is. Why was he—"

"Because I had a guest over."

Dahlia's brow went up at that.

"His name is Connor."

"The doctor from the singles thing?"

"Yes. Nothing happened. Well, something happened but—" Maggie stopped, not wanting to go into the details. "Will didn't like... strangers in the house," she finished lamely.

Dahlia gave her *the* look again. "That isn't true, and you know it."

"Fine. He didn't want *men* in the house. But I don't understand why he was angry. He made it clear how he felt. He told me to leave him alone, but then... He made me feel like I betrayed him. I still feel like I did."

"If what you are telling me is true, and that is a big if, what are you going to do?"

Maggie picked her soup back up and stared at the noodles. She'd been wondering the same thing since she woke up. "He clearly doesn't want me there anymore. But I can't... I can't sell the house, either."

"Why not?"

"It's his home, Dee. And he can't leave. I can't sell it."

"Well, you don't have to make a decision now. You can stay with me for as long as you like." Dahlia picked up a half of her sandwich and took a bite.

"You believe me?" Maggie asked hopefully.

"I believe you enough to guarantee you will never step foot in that house again alone."

"He wouldn't hurt me."

Dahlia scoffed. "If what you're telling me is true, sweetie, he already has."

Maggie stared at her noodles more.

CHAPTER TWENTY-ONE

IT HAD BEEN A WEEK SINCE THEY CARTED MAGGIE AWAY, AND WILL still hadn't gotten word.

He'd almost made himself visible to the deputy that had returned the following day as part of the ongoing investigation, to ask if she'd made it, but he was afraid the man would call a priest and try to have him exorcized. And he could *not* go to hell without knowing she was okay.

He stared at the stain on the floor that had turned brown and cracked.

All he knew was that she wasn't back, in human or ghost form, and being there without her was torture.

He picked up another piece of porcelain and dropped it into the trash. The sound it made as it crashed into the other pieces brought it all back. The jealousy in his heart, the betrayal and anger in her eyes. That damn plate breaking at just the right time and angle, the smell of blood. Her last words…

Maybe we'll both haunt this place. He prayed that didn't happen. She deserved heaven or wherever the good souls went.

It seemed like each piece he picked up was heavier than the last, but he kept at it, until he couldn't move anymore, until the memory was as sharp as the edge of the dish that had cut her. Then, he went to his chair, that smelled like her, and sat paralyzed as it played over and over until his strength returned. Once it did, he got up and started again.

He dropped another deadly piece of porcelain into the bag.

He was glad he had straightened up the barn first. He wouldn't be able to move any of those things now. Since Maggie had gone, his strength had deteriorated. No more moving ladders or carrying injured, beautiful women up a flight of stairs. The walls had grown thinner again too.

It confirmed his theory that it was she who had temporarily changed him.

He dropped another shard into the trash.

It had been seven days, and they had felt longer than the seventy previous years combined.

He couldn't get himself to believe she had died.

But if she was alive, why hadn't she come back?

Why hadn't she at least let him know she was okay?

Unless…

Will heard tires on the gravel outside, and his heart practically leaped out of his chest, as he jumped from the chair.

Bob's truck pulled to a stop in the middle of the drive as he passed through the wall onto the porch.

Will raced to the door as the old man got out.

"Is she okay?" he asked.

Bob's hand flew to his chest as his head whipped around. "Oh, Christ, William."

Will realized he could have given the old man a heart attack. "Sorry. I need to know. Is she—"

"She's okay."

"Thank god." His knees wobbled with relief as he followed the old man up the stairs.

"Do you mind?" Bob asked, stopping in front of the door.

Will went inside and unlocked it.

The old man pushed the door open and stepped inside.

"Where is she? When will she be home?"

Bob looked at the overturned tables and bookshelf. Will had been unable to move those, so they'd remained where Maggie had left them.

Bob pulled the old ball cap from his bald head and scratched his neck.

"Um... She's at her friend's house. And..." His eyes became sad as they met his. "I'm sorry, son, but she's not coming back."

Will stumbled backward, his second-to worst fear confirmed. "I scared her."

Bob eyed him nervously. Will had scared him too. "She asked me if I'd just clean up the, um... blood, so she could have somebody come and straighten up the place."

"To sell?"

"No. I don't think so." Bob walked into the kitchen, and his eyes widened. They went to the ceiling, and the dried blood that had splattered across it. "Jesus." He crossed himself.

"Then how do you know she's not coming back?"

Bob met his eyes again. "Because I asked her, and she said so. She said as soon as the house was clean, her ex-husband and son are going to come up and get her things, and she is going to—"

Will fell against the wall, covering his head with his hands. "No." She had to come back. He needed to apologize. He needed to—

"I'm sorry," Bob said again. He stared at the mess for another moment before asking, "Do you know where the broom is?"

Will nodded toward the pantry.

The old man hobbled to the door and retrieved the broom and dustpan.

Slowly, he began scooping up what would have taken Will another week to collect and dumped it in the trash. It was painful to watch, and Will's shame resurfaced.

"It was an accident, Bob."

The old man didn't say anything.

"I got angry, and I shouldn't have. I yelled at her, but I didn't..."

Bob continued to sweep.

"It was an accident," Will repeated helplessly.

Once the broken dishes were up, Bob turned to the stove and

pulled a dish towel off the bar. He searched the cabinets until he found a pot. Holding it under the faucet, he filled it with water.

Very carefully, the old man got to his knees and began scrubbing the floor.

Will, using every ounce of strength he had left, dragged a second towel from the stove. "Can you tear this in half?"

Bob looked at the towel in Will's outstretched hand. He shook his head. "This might be easier." He pulled a folded hanky out of his back pocket, dunked it in the water, and squeezed it out with his old, gnarled hands before dropping it in front of Will.

"What exactly happened, son?" Bob asked.

Will did his best to explain, as they scrubbed Maggie's blood off the floor. The metallic sweetness gagged him as the water in the pot turned a sickening shade of brown.

BOB SAT IN THE CHAIR, looking up at the ceiling. "How am I gonna get up there?"

"I'll do it," Will said.

"How?"

He had no idea, but he would. "Can you just leave an open bucket of paint?"

"I'll see if she's got some in the closet as soon as I can get up."

They sat in silence for a moment. They had cleaned everything except the ceiling.

"I *need* to talk to her. I have to at least try to apologize."

"It's not my place—"

"You're all I have. I can't call her. I can't leave here and go to her."

"I don't—"

"I know I don't deserve a second chance. Hell, I didn't even deserve my first one, but I am begging you. Please. Just call her for me. Just tell her I'm sorry, and I just want to see her to apologize."

Bob didn't look convinced, but he pulled his phone out of his jacket pocket and dialed.

"Hi there... Yeah, I'm at the house... No, no, everything is fine... Um, well, the thing is..." Bob glanced at Will from under his bushy white eyebrows. "William is here, and he's askin'... Rather, he wanted me to tell you he's sorry and... He's inquirin' if you'd consider comin' up, just once more, to accept his apology in person?"

There was a long pause, and Bob had the phone pressed so hard against his ear that Will couldn't hear her answer.

"I understand. And of course, that is up to you." He looked at Will and shook his head apologetically.

Will leaped up from the chair and pulled his hair, wishing he could rip it out.

"I know you're not asking for my advice, but can I offer it anyway, as a man who's learned a little bit over a lot of years?"

Will looked up.

"Your life is made up of a lot of moments, Maggie. But only a handful of 'em are gonna end up truly defining it. I got a real strong feeling this is one of those moments for you." He looked at Will. "For both of you. So... you know, think it through all the way before deciding what you want to do."

Bob was silent for another moment.

"Well, I think sometimes you've got to ask yourself whaddaya got to lose? If it ain't much..."

He paused, listening.

"Well, that I don't know. But I will say this. I think when it comes down to it, most folks is afraid of being hurt. But to my way of thinking, a body that's never been hurt has probably never done much livin', either. Same goes for your soul, I'd wager. And if that's true, what's worse? Not hurtin' or not livin'?"

Will sat down, in awe of the old handyman turned philosopher.

"Okay," Bob said a moment later. "I understand. You gotta do what's right for you."

Will's heart sank a second time. "Damn it," he whispered, wishing the table felt more solid so he could hit it harder.

Bob set his phone down.

Will dropped his head into his hands. It was over then. "What did she say?" he asked.

"She said she'll come."

Will's eyes flew up, and hope rushed over his soul like water. "What? Really?"

Bob nodded. "But, son, you better plead a damn good case, or you're gonna lose her."

Will nodded. He'd already decided. He'd do whatever she asked.

Bob got up and winced as he straightened his back. "I'm sure it ain't easy being dead, but getting old is no walk in the park, either." He found the primer and ceiling paint for Will and left both on the table.

As he headed for the door, Will remembered something.

"Before you go, I've got something I want you to have. It's in the barn, though, and I don't think I can carry it out here."

Bob raised an eyebrow. "There's no need to—"

"It's just a little something."

Will directed him through the door, which was still cracked and letting in snow, to the workbench.

He pointed to a jar sitting against the wall.

Bob picked it up and poured the handful of marbles into his hand. He rolled them around in his palm and smiled. "God, how I used to love that sound." He glanced at Will with misty eyes. "So, you do remember?"

Will nodded. "Yeah. I do now. I'm sorry I yelled at you."

Bob dropped the marbles in his pocket and set the jar back on the bench. "All's I remember is you helping me." He walked to the door and paused. His silhouette bent in the shape of old age. "You were a good man, William."

Will shook his head. No, he wasn't. That's why he'd been punished.

"You're the same now."

Will huffed. He wished that were true, but washing Maggie's blood off the floor indicated otherwise.

"Maybe that's why I can see you, and others can't."

"What do you mean?"

Bob shrugged. "Because I knew who to look for."

A moment later, Will heard the turning over of an engine and the retreat of tires on gravel.

He went out to the middle of the driveway, halfway between the house and barn, in the exact spot where Maggie had lain down and looked up at the sky.

He stared at the dirt until he was sure he could make out the imprint of her body as she held her hand up, trying to catch a cloud. The air was still and cold. The sun had disappeared behind a blanket of gray, and the universe, the earth, the very air around him seemed to pause. Time stopped, and he with it. And he knew it would not move forward again until Maggie returned and set it back in motion.

CHAPTER TWENTY-TWO

"I don't know why you want to go back," Dahlia said, watching her in the bathroom mirror.

Maggie winced as she tried and failed to pull a brush through the mass of tangles her hair had become.

"Oh, stop. Let me do it." Dahlia grabbed it out of her hand and pushed her down onto the toilet seat. "Sit."

Maggie sat and turned her back to Dahlia. "I know you don't. And I can't explain it to you, either. I just… need to go back."

"And do what? He's dead. What is there to do?"

"Something."

"Like what?"

Maggie thought about it as Dahlia worked the tangles. "I don't know yet," she admitted. But the way they'd left things… At the very least, she needed the closure of confronting him.

The more she thought about Will, about what he was and why he was there, the more she began to wonder. Either he was the result of some massive cosmic glitch or… he was there for a reason. The scientist in her balked at the idea of some lesson wielding force manipulating wayward souls, but it also demanded that she take all the facts as she knew them and accept the simplest theory that satisfied them all. As Ockham said, pluralities should not be posited without necessity. In other words, don't overcomplicate what can be explained simply.

There was a reason. And the answer was there, at the farm. That was why he could not leave. Clearly, he had not figured out what it was yet. And it seemed he could not pass on to wherever he was meant to go until he did. So, what could it be?

She thought about her conversation with Bob. He'd forced her to see the choice she was making. And he was right. She was afraid to face Will again because he'd hurt her, because he'd rejected her, and she didn't want him to do it again. She wanted his love, but she was afraid to ask for it again.

Dahlia ran a gentle hand over Maggie's hair. "There."

Maggie met her own eyes in the mirror. Maybe that was where she'd gone wrong. Maybe love wasn't something you could ask for?

"What are you thinking about?"

Maggie wasn't sure how long Dahlia had been standing there watching her. She blushed. "Love."

Dahlia's brow went up. "So, you *do* love him."

"I'm thinking love is something different than I thought it was."

Dahlia nodded. "Gran always said, you can't accept love without knowing what it is. And you can't give love unless you have a heart that's already full of it."

Maggie smiled. That was why Dahlia was such a good friend, because she was full of love. And that was why Maggie's love for Eric was so strong, because it was the only part of her that was filled with love, and the well it sprang from would never run dry, because there was nothing on Earth that could ever drain it.

Dahlia smiled in the mirror. "I was like seven at the time, so of course I had no idea what she was talking about. I said so, and she told me to think of our hearts as fragile cups."

Maggie waited.

"Remember the tea set I had when we were kids? With the strawberries on them?"

"I only remember two plates and one cup that we used to fight over."

Dahlia laughed. "That's because we broke the rest of them, which is maybe the point Gran was trying to make. Those were the cups I pictured, fancy little pink and red teacups sitting in our chests. She said we're all born with one, and the only way to keep them safe is to keep them filled with love. When we are kids, our parents look after them. They keep them safe and full. Their love protects us." Dahlia smiled at the memory.

Maggie could easily imagine Gran saying that and smiled too.

"But as we grow, that responsibility becomes our own. And if we don't learn to love our little china cups in the same way our parents did, unconditionally, patiently, forgivingly, and keep them full, they become vulnerable. They start to chip. They crack. And pretty soon, they're so riddled with holes that no amount of love from anyone can fill them, no matter how much is poured in."

Maggie thought about that. After her mother had died, she'd felt so empty. After Eric left, she'd felt the same way. In the beginning, she'd been alone at the farm. The isolation had given her the space she needed to heal. And it felt good. But once she met Will, instead of staying the path, she'd done what she always did, exactly what she'd done to Dean she realized. She looked to someone else to find the love she so desperately needed, and she tried to make him give it to her. Was that why he turned her away? Because he had nothing to give, either? What a sad pair that made them, if that was true.

"Do you understand what I'm saying?"

"Kind of." Maggie thought of Connor. He was a man on the mend. She could feel it as soon as she saw him. He had found a way to fix his cup, and he was ready. She was not.

"First, we gotta remember we have a cup. Then, we've got to care about ourselves enough to fix it when it cracks, which it inevitably does, because life fucking sucks sometimes."

Dahlia gave her shoulder a squeeze, and Maggie smiled sadly. If she had a cup, it was a pile of rubble now.

"After that, we got to remember what it's made to hold and fill it up, because what kind of cheap-ass fool shows up on anyone's doorstep empty handed, right?"

Maggie laughed.

Dahlia flashed her a smile. "Once you do that, you're ready to go. You're not freeloading anymore. You have something to *give*. And once you start giving…" She smoothed Maggie's hair beneath her palm. "You're going to find yourself in possession of a very solid cup with a little extra room in it. And when *that* happens, you will be ready and capable of accepting the love of others."

Maggie knew Gran was right. So was Bob. So was Dahlia.

"Do you understand me now?" Dahlia asked, putting her hands on her hips.

Maggie nodded.

"Life is BYODL, girl," Dahlia said seriously.

"BYODL?"

"Bring your own damn love, or you're gonna be the only one sitting in the corner not having any fun."

Maggie laughed again.

"Is that Gran's advice too?"

"No. That's mine."

"When did you become so wise?"

"Apparently, while you were losing your damn mind."

"Dee…"

"And I'm not wise. It just makes sense. If everybody shows up with an empty bottle, it's just a room full of sad people in need of a recycling bin. If everyone shows up with a full one, it's a party. I prefer to party."

"Me too," Maggie agreed.

"Then fix your fucking cup."

"I'm trying."

"Try harder."

She didn't know how, but one thing was for sure: she owed Will an apology. She should not have forced herself or her needs on him like that. "That's why I need to talk to Will." She should have helped him figure out why he was stuck… She should be helping him to move on, even though that thought made it hard to breathe.

"Have you not been listening—"

"Dee, Gran was right about everything. That's why I need to go back."

"For him or you?"

"He is part of my journey. I am sure of it. And I am part of his." Otherwise, her ending up back there didn't make any sense.

"Maggie—"

"Just maybe not in the way I'd hoped."

"What does that mean?"

"It means I have to go back."

"There is no way in hell I'm letting you go back up there alone."

"I know. That's why I *asked* you to go with me." Maggie paused. "I want you to meet him, Dee. He's an extraordinary man."

"Hmph."

"Are you ready?"

Dalia lifted a brow. "To meet a ghost?"

"To trust me."

"You know I do."

Maggie got up and went into the living room. She pulled on Dahlia's sweater and zipped it up with her left hand.

"Not sure I'm ready for the ghost thing, though," Dahlia said, grabbing her keys off the hook.

Maggie smiled. "Trust me, he's not ready for you, either."

Dahlia laughed and pulled the door open. "Now, *that*, I believe."

CHAPTER TWENTY-THREE

WILL PAUSED HIS NERVOUS ROCKING AND SAT UP IN THE CHAIR. Was that a car he heard? He waited. But the sound didn't come closer. It must have been a truck on the highway. Disappointed, he slumped back in the chair and resumed his back-and-forth motion.

Bob had come this morning, saying Maggie would be here by noon, and Will had been a nervous wreck ever since.

He already knew he'd been wrong to turn her away, and Bob was right. This was his last chance to make things right with Maggie. Will ran his fingers over her initials, sewn into the blanket hanging over the arm of her chair. He'd rehearsed his apology so many times, he knew every word by heart, and he was ready except for...

The chair stopped.

For the first time since he died, Will was dreaming again. The first time was the night after Maggie had been taken to the hospital. He had awoken in terror, standing in the middle of the driveway in the dark, and it had taken the dawn, as dreary and pathetic as the light had been, to drive the madness away. He'd dreamed of her many times since, and every time was worse than the last. Every time, the emptiness that followed lasted longer.

Will stared at the horizon. The sun had climbed the sky already, and there was a bank of clouds pressed against the lake. The longer he stared, the more they looked like snow-covered mountains rising up across the water. According to Maggie's geology book, the land there had seen many things over its long history. Buried under the soil were remnants of ancient seas and, perhaps, ranges that looked very much like the scene before him. They had taken millions of years to form and fade. He wondered if he would haunt this land long enough to witness changes on that scale. The thought left him feeling more hollow than usual.

He didn't know why he should start dreaming now. He didn't know why it was always the same.

They started out so beautifully. The love in Maggie's eyes shining like the noon-day sun on a field of sunflowers. Then, she closed them, and their lips met. Instead of pushing her away, like he had before, he drew her in, as Connor had done. Every touch that he'd witnessed through the window became his, as Will traced the shape of her body with his palms. It was *he* who tasted her lips and the soft skin of her neck, felt coarse lace against the stubble on his cheek as he inhaled lilies and vanilla, and her heart pounded against his mouth. It was *he* who slid his fingers over the smooth black leather of her pants as he carried her up the stairs. It was *him* she undressed and pressed her hips into and moaned for.

A chickadee landed on the rail of the porch and began to call for its mate. Will stared at it.

But in the midst of their lovemaking, the dreams changed. She stilled beneath him, and when he opened his eyes... hers stared back at him, unblinking and drained of color. He tried to wake her as her skin turned gray, then black, and began to crack. He tried to hold on to her, but she turned to dust beneath his fingers as he collapsed into her lily-scented ashes, and they erupted from his bed in a cloud. Crying out, he grasped at her in horror, but there was nothing left. She was gone. The wind whipped through the room and stole even her smell while Will stood alone at the open window watching her disappear like a wisp of smoke into the night sky, wanting to follow her, but knowing he could not. The agony in his soul, as he screamed for her, set the house on fire. It spread quickly through the grass to the barn, then the fields beyond. Everything burned. Everything but him. It burned until there was nothing left but darkness and his madness.

"Chick-a-dee-dee-dee!"

Will blinked, and the little bird came back into focus. Its glossy black eyes studied him. Its head tilted from side to side, as if it were trying to figure out what strange creature it had discovered. The chickadee fluffed its wings and shivered, the way birds did when it was cold out, and Will spotted an almost imperceptible cloud of moisture escaping its tiny beak as it called again. It must be cold this morning.

"Chick-a-dee-dee–dee!" it called as it fluttered off.

The dream scared Will. Almost as much as—

He heard another sound, and a moment later, a black spot appeared on the road. As it got closer, he recognized Dahlia's car.

He pushed the dream away. He'd already decided. He would do whatever Maggie asked. *Anything*, if she would only come back.

Standing up, he held his breath and waited as the car came to a stop in the driveway. Maggie emerged first, pulling herself up using the door, and her left arm. Her hair swirled around her head, a dizzying shade that danced between rust and the deep, lush brown of *Typha latifolia*, the cattails that lined the pond. She pulled it down and twisted it behind her head, as several strands broke free and reached for him.

Dahlia's door opened, and she got out, scanning the horizon over the top of her car, as Will made his way down the steps. "How do you know if he's here?" she asked.

Lightning arched off Maggie as he approached her, and its sting felt like heaven. So did her smile. That was a good sign.

"He's here," she said.

Will stopped and looked around. Who were they talking about?

"Where?" Dahlia glanced nervously over her shoulder. "How do you know?"

Maggie turned and looked right through him. "Because I can feel him."

Another jolt struck Will in the side, and his eyes widened. Had Maggie told Dahlia about him? He didn't know if that was a good thing or a bad thing.

"Why can't I see him?"

"Will?" Maggie asked.

He closed his eyes and took a deep breath. Whatever she wanted. "Because I didn't want to scare you," he said, as Dahlia gasped and met his eyes.

"Jesus f—"

"Dahlia, this is Will. Will, this is my best friend, Dahlia."

Will nodded. "It's a pleasure."

Dahlia stood there with her mouth hanging open, as her normally warm, toned skin paled a shade.

He turned back to Maggie. "How is your arm?"

"Just a little damage to a couple of tendons. I'll live… thanks to you," she smiled and pulled something from her pocket. "I think this belongs to you."

Will stared at his belt for a moment. Hesitantly, he reached out to touch it. His fingers passed through it, just as he expected they would.

Maggie's eyes flew to his, wide with worry, and he jerked his hand back. "What's happening to you?" she cried.

"It's okay. I've just gone back to the way I was."

"The way you were?"

"Before you."

Her eyes were saucers. "W-what does that mean?"

He shrugged. "I don't know."

Maggie stared at him until Dahlia cleared her throat. They both turned. Her color had returned, and her look of utter disbelief had faded. A little.

"It's fucking cold out here. Are we going inside or—"

"I'd like to talk to Maggie for a few moments, alone, if I could," Will said.

Dahlia walked around the car, shaking her head. "Nope. Not

happening." She stood beside Maggie with her arms crossed, reminding him of the porcupine that lived in the hollowed-out elm at the east end of the property. Tough and prickly on the outside, but once you got past that…

"Dee…" Maggie began.

Dahlia shook her head. "I said—"

"Go inside. We'll sit on the porch. You can get a coffee and watch us from the window."

Dahlia looked from her to Will and back again. "Fine." She met Will's eyes. "But if you lay a finger on her, I will have a priest here in less than thirty minutes to exorcize you back to—"

"Dahlia!" Maggie grabbed her friend's arm.

"You have my word," Will said. "I won't—" He glanced at Maggie. "I won't touch her."

Dahlia stared him down for a few more seconds before heading for the house. He and Maggie followed more slowly.

They made their way to the porch, and Maggie noticed her blanket as well as his in his chair. "Cold?" she asked.

He shook his head. "No. I just…" A fluttering filled his stomach, reminding him of the snow-white linden moths that chased the full moon as it reflected off the creek in late spring. "I missed you," he confessed.

She took her blanket and folded one leg under her as she sat. "I missed you too, Will." There was a heaviness in her voice, and he knew he'd better get to his apology quickly.

He sat down on the edge of his seat. "Thank you for coming."

"Bob can be very persuasive."

Will nodded in agreement.

"He was also right. It was cowardly of me to—"

He cut her off. "No. It was me who was the coward, and I am so, so very sorry." The words came out in a rush.

Maggie smiled sadly. "I know you are."

"And I will do anything to make it up to you, Maggie. Anything."

She met his eyes, and he felt it again. A weight. Her sadness. It both scared him and drove him on. "I was wrong to push you away. And I lied to you when I said my desire was gone. It's not. It is here. Stronger than it ever was when I was alive and... I desire you." The moths took flight again in his belly. In all his life, he had never uttered words like that to anyone. It was strangely liberating and completely terrifying at the same time. He forged on. "I am so ashamed of the mess I made in the barn, the words I spoke to you in anger, and the way I treated you after you slept with Connor. I had no right to—"

Maggie stopped him. "Maybe you shouldn't have gotten angry, but you were right to push me away."

His brows came together. That was not what he was expecting her to say. And now that she had, he did not like the sound of it at all.

"And I know you lied. I could feel it then, I can feel it now. But it's okay, I understand that too."

She understood? What did she understand?

"And I didn't sleep with Connor, Will," she said quietly. "I wanted to, but my heart was... elsewhere. And in the end, I just couldn't do it."

Will tried and failed to process that last bit of information. So, his jealousy had been over nothing? Well, not nothing. He'd seen plenty, but she hadn't gone through with it? He searched her eyes and knew where elsewhere was. *Him.* The same expression had been on her face when she'd gone to the barn to find him the next morning. But he'd been so busy wallowing in his own self-pity that he hadn't even bothered to notice.

"I'm sorry, Maggie."

"I didn't come back for an apology."

He was almost afraid to ask. "Why did you come back then?"

"Closure."

The breath fled his lungs, and if he weren't already dead, he would have suffocated under the weight of her words. "Maggie, please. I'll do anything you ask. I'll *be* anything you want. Just come back. Stay."

He had hoped his words would soothe her, assure her, bring a smile to her face. Instead, they had the opposite effect, and her eyes filled with tears. "That's not how it works, Will."

"How what works?"

"This. Us. Love."

He was losing her. He could feel it. Like in his dream when she disappeared beneath him. "Oh, really?" His voice was shrill with panic, and the words tumbled out of his mouth before he could stop them. "This has happened to you before? This exact situation? You know how this works?"

She smiled her first genuine smile. "No. But I know how life works. And I finally know what I need, and—"

Will didn't want to hear the rest. "I can't bear to be here without you, Maggie. And I cannot leave this place." The madness from his dream circled him like a hawk eyeing its prey. "I know it's incredibly unfair of me to ask, but I'm begging you. Please don't go."

She met his eyes; her smile gone. "I won't."

"You won't?"

"If you agree to my condition."

"Anything," he said without hesitation.

She held up her hand. "You might want to hear—"

"Anything," he repeated vehemently.

"I was hoping you'd say that." It sounded like the truth, but felt like a lie. "Then, I'll stay."

He almost fell out of his chair. "You will?"

"Yes."

He fell before her in relief. A weird buzzing sound filled his ears as he reached for her hands, forgetting his promise to Dahlia. They were warm and solid beneath his. "I love you, Maggie. God... I have loved you for so long. And then when I saw you again, sitting by the road, screaming at my corn... I fell *in* love with you."

Again, his words had the opposite effect they should have. More tears filled her eyes.

"You don't believe me?" he asked softly.

"I believe you want to."

"I will make you happy. I promise."

That seemed to pain her more, and he didn't understand what he was saying wrong.

A tear spilled down her cheek. "Don't make promises you can't keep."

He brushed it away with his thumb. "I will keep it, I—"

"Happiness comes from *within*, Will. So does love."

He didn't understand.

More tears spilled down her cheeks.

"What's wrong?" he asked, as his worry rushed back in and crashed against him like an angry wave.

"Nothing."

If nothing was wrong, why was she so sad? "It will be alright. I know you're scared, but I'm here and I—"

She looked away.

Will stared at her profile as her hair whipped between them. Was she lying? Was this some kind of— "Maggie, what's wrong? Do you not want to stay? Is that it?"

She shook her head.

"Are you afraid of hurting me? Do you want—"

She shook her head again and squeezed his hands, like she was afraid he'd disappear, whispering something unintelligible.

"What?" he asked, leaning closer.

"I want *you* to go. To move... on."

He stared at her.

"That is my condition."

He didn't understand.

"And you agreed."

"No—"

"Yes. You did."

He fell back. She had tricked him? All of this had been a ploy to get him to… The buzzing grew loud in his ears again, and he turned toward the barn and the sound.

"You don't belong here, Will. I knew it from the start, but you were so wonderful, and I was so…" She covered a sob.

Anger sparked in his chest. If she wanted him gone, why was she crying?

"You need to move on."

"No." He didn't want to move on. For the first time in decades, he wanted to stay right where he fucking was.

"So, I'm going to stay. And together we are—" Her voice broke. "We are going to fix… this."

He backed against the railing. "Why? Why would you—how could you—"

She stood up. "We have to, Will."

"Why?"

"Because I want a chance!"

"A chance for what?"

"To love you and *be* loved by you," she cried.

"That's what I'm offering—"

She crossed the distance between them. "You cannot give me something you don't possess, Will. And I can't, either."

"What are you saying?"

"I'm saying we are broken. I am saying—"

"Then we will fix each other."

"You are dead. And you can't fix me. I have to fix myself! Don't you see?"

No, he didn't. But he was afraid to say it. "Fine!" he shouted. "What do you want me to do? I'll do it."

A moment later, the door popped open, and Dahlia stuck her head out. "Everything okay out here? Because I don't like the tone I'm hearing from inside."

Maggie turned to her friend. "We are fine."

They were anything but that, but Will held his tongue as Dahlia closed the door.

"We have to find out why you are here and correct whatever mistake you made."

Will shook his head in disbelief. "I don't understand, Maggie. I thought..."

"Everything you thought is true. I care about you. And there is a part of me that wants you to stay, but—"

"I will."

"And then what?"

"What do you mean?"

"What if I have another accident, or I get sick and die? What will you do then?"

"Maggie."

"I am going to grow old, and you are not. How do you think that will make either of us feel?"

Will shook his head again. He had not thought about that, but he didn't care.

"You were here, walking these fields before I was born, and you'll be here long after I die. Is that what you want?"

His dream resurfaced. Is that what it was trying to tell him? He could barely stand the thought. "No, but—"

Maggie took his hands in hers. "One day, one way or another, we are going to find ourselves facing this exact situation. One of us having to leave, and the other one being left behind. If I go, you stay here... forever. But if you go..."

"What?"

"I can meet you there in a few years."

Will stared. Meet him? Did she mean when she died? He shook his head. It was a beautiful thought, but unfortunately, they were not heading to the same place.

"I don't want you to go, Will. But I am more afraid of what will happen to you if you don't."

That was because she didn't know where he was going, he thought darkly.

She pulled him back to his chair, and he sat.

Dahlia opened the door and carried out two coffees. "I don't know if you drink—" She eyed Will. "But it's cold as shit out here, so I thought—"

"Thank you, Dahlia," Will said as she placed the cup beside him.

She went back inside, as Maggie took her mug and pressed it between her palms, as he'd watched her do so many times.

"And what about you?" Will asked. "What are you going to do once I'm gone? Be with Connor?" He regretted the jealousy in his voice, but could not hide it.

Maggie looked up from her mug. Tears spilled from her eyes. "No. The only person I need to be with isn't out there." She swiped her hand toward the horizon. "She's in here." She pressed a hand to her chest. "That is my journey. That is what I need to fix before I am whole."

"There's nothing wrong with you. You're wonderful, Maggie. The most incredible woman I've ever known."

She looked out over the fields. "There *is* something wrong with me, Will. Because when I look in the mirror, I see a stranger. Because when I am alone, I feel like *nothing* inside." She twisted her hands together in her lap. "When I got pregnant with Eric, life got all tangled up in my head. I would not trade motherhood for anything, but I was so young then. When Dean asked me to marry him, I said yes, when I should have said no, and suddenly I was living a life I didn't recognize, making decisions that were not what I truly wanted, and somehow, I lost myself. For a while, my mom kept me afloat. She was my anchor, but then she died, and... I don't know what happened. I had this gaping hole in my chest that I didn't know how to fill and instead of learning to doing what I needed to, to heal, I spent the next fifteen years clinging to Dean, demanding *he* do it. And he tried. So hard. But he failed. For the same reason you would."

She sniffled.

"When he and I parted, that damn hole was still there. And again, instead of doing what I should have, I clung to my motherhood, to Eric, afraid to face the empty space where *I* was supposed to be. And then Eric went off to school, I found myself standing in the driveway, in the same *fucking* position again, alone with a hollowed-out stranger I didn't know."

Will touched his mug, expecting his hand to go through it. It didn't. Maggie had returned his strength to him. He picked it up and inhaled the scent. At least he could still do that.

"How can a stranger be a good mother to my son?" Maggie glanced over her shoulder through the window at Dahlia. "How can emptiness be a good friend?" She met his eyes. "How can *nothing* truly love you?"

Will sighed.

"I don't want you to go because I'm looking for a lover, Will. I've already found him."

The beginning of his dreams surfaced. The good parts, when she was solid and whole in his arms.

"I am desperately seeking the *woman* who can love him back." Maggie's voice wavered. "And I don't think she can reveal herself to me until I have something to offer her. And I won't, until I stop hiding behind other people, including my son. Including you."

The chickadee came back. A moment later, its mate fluttered to the rail of the stairs. They stared at him, as if to say hello before taking off into the sky together.

"So, you'll stay if I go?" he asked.

"Yes."

"What if I can't? What if it takes years? What if we never figure it out?"

"We will. And I promise to stay until we do."

How could she be so certain?

"But you have to promise me that when we do figure it out, you *will* go."

He'd been there seventy years already. Surely, if there was a way to move on, he would have found it by now. Maybe the deal she was making with him wasn't so bad. "And in the meantime?"

"In the meantime, we get to know each other as friends."

"Friends?"

"Roommates. Like before."

Will laughed bitterly as she used his words against him. That was the last way he thought about her now, and she knew it. But at least she was staying. Maybe there was time to convince—

"And we try to be grateful for this gift we've been given."

Gift? Was that what she thought this was? He shook his head. Did Maggie really think he'd been relegated to roam this land for eternity because of something *good* he had done? He almost laughed. No, decent people went to *heaven* when they died, like his brothers and sisters, like his parents. If he was going anywhere after this—a chill raced down his spine—it wouldn't be anywhere good.

Maggie watched him carefully over her mug.

But if it meant they would be together, even for a while longer, it was worth it. She was worth it. He'd do whatever she asked.

"Okay," he heard himself say.

"Okay?" she repeated.

"Yes. I accept your deal, with a condition of my own."

"What is that?"

Will looked over his shoulder at Dahlia, who had been sitting on the couch the whole time, eyeing him with distrust. "You have to tell her you're staying. Because if I do, she'll probably try to kill me all over again."

Maggie laughed. "You, sir, drive a hard bargain."

His mouth bowed up in a small smile. "Do you accept?"

Maggie pulled her blanket aside and got up. "I accept. You may want to cover your ears."

Will looked at Dahlia again. Her brows were drawn into a frown as her brown eyes bore into his. "I think I'm going to go for a walk."

Maggie nodded. "That might be a good idea."

CHAPTER TWENTY-FOUR

"You are not staying here with him!" Dahlia shouted.

"I am not your child, Dee! I am a grown woman."

"Then start acting like one!"

They stood nose to nose in front of the couch.

"I'm not doing what you think I am. He needs to move on, and I think I know what he—"

"What if he can't? What if he doesn't want to? What if he lies?"

"I know he can, and he won't. He promised."

Dahlia rolled her eyes. "And then what, Maggie? After he's gone?"

"*Then* we'll finally see what I'm made of." Maggie sighed heavily and plopped back on the couch. Dahlia stood, arms crossed over her.

They had been yelling at each other for thirty minutes, and Maggie had a headache. She understood Dahlia's concern, especially in light of recent events and the fact that her situation with Will was... unusual. But what Dee was failing to realize was that the choice wasn't hers.

Several emotions rushed across Dahlia's eyes like fast-moving clouds. Maggie was hopeful for a moment, but it was shattered when her friend shook her head. "Nope. I don't buy it. I just—"

"May I speak with Dahlia alone?" Will asked.

Maggie's head spun around. Will stood just inside the door.

"Oh, no. No way," Dahlia said, as Maggie turned back to her friend.

Dahlia waved a finger between her and Will. "I'm a lawyer," she continued. "I've seen some shit. And I watch a lot of TV. I know how this ends. If I go anywhere alone with you, they'll find my body stuffed in an old refrigerator—"

"Dee!" Maggie gasped.

"I assure you, the only refrigerator is in there." Will pointed toward the kitchen. "And you are *much* too tall to fit in it." He crossed his arms.

Maggie almost laughed as Dahlia's brow went up in surprise.

"I promise not to murder you," Will said solemnly.

Dahlia shook her head. "Nope."

"Please?" Will tried. "We both want what is best for Maggie."

Dahlia's eyes softened. "Fine." She turned to Maggie. "Go... upstairs."

"Actually, I'd prefer if you met me out in the barn?"

Dahlia studied the two of them for a moment. Then, sighing, she grabbed her coat off the back of the chair. "Oh lord, don't let him kill me," she mumbled, as she turned and followed him.

Will laughed as he walked through the door.

Dahlia opened it and glanced over her shoulder at Maggie. "If I'm not back in five minutes... you can have all my shoes." She started to pull it closed behind her, then pushed it back open. "Except for my *Allesandro* stilettos. You know, with the blue sole and the diamonds on the bottom? I want to be buried in those bitches."

The door closed behind her, and Maggie leaned back on the couch for a moment, wondering what Will wanted to discuss with Dahlia that he didn't want her to hear. And why the barn?

She got up to inspect the kitchen while she waited for them to return. To her surprise, it looked like nothing had ever happened. She went to the sink and looked out the sparkling clean window before looking down at the floor where her blood had pooled. There was nothing but shining wood. Her accident felt like a dream... At least until she opened the cabinet and found it almost empty.

Pulling a glass off the shelf, she poured herself some water. The clock above the refrigerator ticked, moving time but also making it seem like none had passed. She tried to imagine herself there, without Will. It scared her. It made her want to cry.

"I am doing the right thing."

It didn't feel like it, but...

"I am." For *both* of them.

A minute later, Maggie heard the turn of the knob. She hurried into the living room. Dahlia stood by the door, her eyes wide and soft like Gran's, and Maggie knew exactly what that meant. Whatever Will had said had changed her mind. Her friend looked suddenly like she might cry.

"Dee?"

Dahlia closed the distance between them and pulled Maggie into her arms. "You know I love you, right? And I'm just trying to protect—"

Maggie squeezed her, feeling the full little china cup inside her friend overflow. "I know."

Dahlia pulled back. "Okay then. You do... whatever it is you gotta do. But I want you to call me if you need anything. Anything at all."

"I will. You can stay the night if you want. There's no need to rush—"

She looked over her shoulder toward the barn and huffed. "No need? Your house is fucking *haunted*, Maggie. I'm going the fuck home."

Maggie smiled. "I understand."

"You sure you're going to be okay?" Dahlia asked.

Maggie nodded, not sure of anything.

Dahlia laughed. "Liar."

Maggie smiled. "I promise I'll call you if I'm not."

Dahlia sighed dramatically. "I knew it." She turned toward the kitchen, and Maggie followed.

"Knew what?"

"I knew you were trouble the minute I met you. You walking up to me with those big hazel eyes, asking me to be your friend. I should have said no."

Maggie laughed as Dahlia slung her purse over her shoulder.

"First, I had to deal with your astro-whatever business and worry about you dying in space, and now it's ghosts. Fuck my life."

She followed Dahlia to the door. "I like to keep things interesting."

"No. Schnoodles are interesting. Savory ice cream is interesting. This—" Dalia's hand circled her head like a lasso, "this is fucking crazy. That's what this is."

Maggie pulled the door open. Will was leaning against the barn door, watching them. He was smiling. She committed the image of him, right there like that to memory. She supposed it was a little crazy.

"Keep your phone on at all times," Dahlia said.

Maggie nodded and hugged her.

Dahlia was halfway down the steps when Maggie called out. "Hey!"

Dahlia turned.

"What in the hell is a schnoodle?"

"It's a schnauzer and a poodle mixed together. They're fucking adorable."

A moment later, her best friend was gone. Maggie looked toward the barn, but Will had vanished too.

That was okay. She went back inside and closed the door. The last couple of days had been a roller coaster and the next few, assuming she was actually able to help Will move on, were going to be a scary ride. She looked at the couch. But she wasn't going to worry about any of that right now. Right *now*, she was going to take a nap.

Maggie pulled a blanket from the basket and dropped onto the couch. Tucking a pillow under her head, she closed her eyes as the pressure escaped her body and she sank into the cushions. Damn, she was tired.

A FLICKERING SHADOW beyond her eyelids drew her back to consciousness. She stretched, pressing her feet against the arm of the couch as she blinked in the bright firelight. She glanced out the dark window. Then her eyes settled on Will, who was sitting in his chair, leaning over a book on the coffee table.

"Hey," she said, yawning. Her arm ached as she pressed her hand over her mouth. She was long overdue for a pain pill.

"Hey," he said, looking up with a smile that made her melt.

Sitting up, she asked, "What are you reading about?"

"Your brain book."

"What do you think?"

Will smiled. "Clearly, there is more to us than what we appear to be on the surface."

She smiled back. "Clearly."

His eyes grew serious. "So, how is this going to work?"

"How is what going to work?"

"Getting me... gone?"

Maggie's stomach growled, and she realized she hadn't eaten lunch or... She picked up her phone. It was past dinnertime. "Well, first, we see if there is anything edible left in the fridge." She highly doubted it. "And then we get to know each other better."

"And what will that do?"

"I don't know. But we need to start somewhere. And the only clue we have is that you are bound to *this* land. There has to be a reason. Something you did, or something *here*, has called you back from... wherever it is we go when we die. We just have to find it."

A cloud passed over Will's eyes when she said that.

"What?"

"Nothing."

"In order for this to work, you have to be honest with me."

"I know. I'm trying."

"The good news is, there are only twenty acres here to search, if it's an actual thing we are looking for."

"The bad news?"

Maggie got off the couch and crouched beside him. He was handsome by any standard, but he was earth-shatteringly handsome by hers. She wondered what he'd smelled like as a man. As a ghost, his scent was closer to the fresh, cool, ionized air that followed a thunderstorm. "I think what we are looking for is in here." She tapped his chest. "Not out there."

She got up and left him to mull that over.

Maggie had only pulled the refrigerator door halfway open before she slammed it closed it again. "Oh god—" The smell was disturbingly foul.

Will appeared. "What?"

She sighed. "It smells like a ripe Camembert and a dead possum had a baby in there."

Will tilted his head to the side. "A ripe what?"

Maggie sighed again. "It's a kind of French cheese."

"That smells like a dead animal?"

"Yep."

Will stuck his head through the pantry door. *That's a sight you don't see every day,* Maggie thought, staring at his body sans head. He pulled it back out. "You have a can of soup in there. Why don't you have that, and I'll deal with the possum after you've gone to bed?"

Opening the can was much more difficult than it should have been, and she had to pour it into a mug, since she'd broken all her bowls. Once it was hot, she sat at the table. Will sat across from her, his shirtsleeves rolled up on his forearms the way they always were, as he rested his elbows on his knees. His eyes were soft and full of wanting.

"I am glad you're back," he said, touching the back of her hand as it rested on the table.

She stared at it a moment, then pulled it away and picked up her spoon. "I missed you too." It was the understatement of the century.

Pursing her lips together, she blew on her soup. She ached for his touch, but it would only make things more difficult when it was time for him to go. And it was already going to be nearly impossible.

So, she tried to focus on the task at hand instead. They had to figure out what had triggered his... ghostliness. And the logical place to start was—

"How did you die?"

He sat back, looking as nervous as she felt.

"Do you want to start with something else?"

"No. I just—" he gave her an apologetic smile. "I'm not used to all of this."

"All of what?"

"Talking about myself. Talking period."

It finally dawned on Maggie. "When was the last time you had a meaningful conversation with another person? Talked to anyone?"

"Well, Bob and I spoke—"

"No, I mean before that. Before I came here."

She was not prepared for the devilish grin that spread across his face. It set her heart pumping in her chest. "Talked or haunted?"

Her brow went up, and she could not stop herself from smiling back. He must have given his mother the same look when he was a boy and up to mischief. And haunted? That couldn't be good.

"There were a couple of families here for a while. The ones that bought the farm after I died, and another family tried to make a go of it in the late 1970s."

"And what happened to them?"

"They left."

"Why?"

His grin spread into a wicked smile, and she nearly fainted. "Because the place was haunted."

He'd scared them away? "You didn't."

Will shrugged. "They were ruining my house, and..."

"And?"

"And I haven't always been the... pleasant man you know."

"What does that mean?"

"It means I was still angry, and they had put ugly linoleum over my beautiful floors."

"You haunted them out of your house?"

"Yep. Creaky chains, the whole nine yards."

Maggie couldn't help but laugh despite how positively terror stricken those poor people must have been.

"I feel bad now, but at that time..."

"Why were you angry?"

Will shrugged. "Because I was dead, because the girls had sold the farm, because there were strangers living in my house, and I couldn't leave. Pick one."

Maggie sobered and remembered her original question. "So, your last real conversation before me and Bob was..."

Will rubbed his chin. "Probably sometime during the week before I died. I recall a neighbor, Bob's father, actually. But you know, we talked about the weather and—"

His confession sucked the air from her lungs. She stared. Will hadn't had a conversation with another human being for *seventy* years?

Her face must have reflected her disbelief because Will stopped whatever he'd been saying, and his forehead creased in a frown. "What?"

"Before I got here, you hadn't had a single conversation with anyone since 1946?"

He didn't answer right away, and she watched as his brows lifted in surprise. "Hm. Nope. I guess not." He scratched the back of his neck. "I never even thought about it."

"Oh my god." She couldn't even imagine it. "How could you not?"

"Well, at first, nobody could see or hear me. At least, my sister couldn't. So, I stopped trying to communicate. But later, I realized if I concentrated, I could move things." Will ran his fingers over the grain in the table, and Maggie tried to bury her jealousy. "So, I—"

Lightning pricked her hand closest to him, and the corner of his mouth twitched as he met her eyes. He'd felt it too. It happened again, sending her heart into overdrive, and Will rewarded her with a look that could melt iron.

She groaned inwardly. "Shit."

His smile widened, and his eyes crinkled at the corners as they bore into hers.

Maggie looked down at her soup, her cheeks on fire, and tried absolutely *not* to think about his hands or the tingling in her body. "You?" she encouraged, twisting her hands in her lap

"Eventually, I figured out how to do it, become visible, be heard. But by then, I wasn't interested in talking anymore. I just wanted them gone."

Well, no wonder he was stuck here. How could he find the peace he needed to move on when he'd spent the last seventy years in what was essentially solitary confinement? She couldn't believe he hadn't gone mad.

"Maggie?"

"You were going to tell me how you died. Your obituary said 'farming accident.'"

"You saw my obituary?"

She nodded. It pained her much more to think about now.

The tension in his jaw returned. "It was my tractor."

She blanched. A tractor accident? That did not sound good.

"I was out in the back ten, well, it was more like a hundred and ten at that time, harvesting corn. There had been a lot of rain that fall, and it was hot. Hotter than I ever remembered it. I was afraid of everything rotting on the stalks, so I was in a hurry to get it off the fields and into the crib—"

"The what?"

"That long narrow thing out back, with the roof. We used to use it to dry corn."

"Oh." She had wondered what that was for.

"There are some rocky spots at the southeast end of the field, where the neighbors' farmhouse now sits. I was going down a row, and a rock jammed the corn picker. It wasn't all that uncommon, but it was the third time that day, and I was frustrated. I should have turned off the tractor, but I was stupid when I was alive, and I was in a hurry, so I left it running and hopped off."

The bitterness in his voice was not lost on Maggie, but she remained silent.

"I went to get the rock out, and long story short, I got caught in the gathering chains. Ripped my glove clean off and tore up the side of my hand pretty good before I got it out."

Maggie paused with her spoon in midair. "That doesn't sound so bad."

"It wasn't. It hurt like hell, but... I knew people who'd lost limbs to those sons of bitches. One guy got so tangled, he bled out and died right there in the dirt. His kid came out that evening looking for him when he didn't come home for supper, and there he was, mangled all to hell."

She blanched.

Will continued. "I didn't even lose a finger. I wrapped my hand, finally grew enough brains to turn the tractor off, got the rock out, and got back to work. I worked from dawn till dusk for the next several days—"

"Were you alone then, on the farm?"

"Yeah. Had been since Suzie married her husband Stuart. All of my other siblings had long since been gone and married."

"And you were forty-six?"

He looked down at his chest, and she noticed he was wearing his belt again. "I still am, depending on how you look at it."

"So, you were running the farm on your own? What about your brothers?"

"Well, Al was with—"

"I remember, but what about the others? Louis and Matthew?"

His expression darkened. "They were dead."

Maggie's eyes flew to his. "Dead?"

"Louie died in France."

France? She didn't understand "What was he—"

"The war, Maggie."

She covered her mouth. Of course. World War II. He'd lived through that. Both World Wars, actually.

"And Matthew?"

His expression grew darker. "He joined the Army Air Force, went MIA somewhere over Metz, France, and they never found his body."

"Why weren't... didn't you go—"

"Because I was too worried about the damn farm." He shoved the edge of the table, and it rocked, sloshing Maggie's soup in her mug. The regret in his voice was palpable.

"You had a choice?"

Will huffed bitterly. "Yeah, I had a choice."

"But your brothers didn't?"

"No, we all did, but... They decided to go."

"How did that work?" she asked, setting her spoon down and taking a sip from her mug instead.

"The draft was in forty. But there was this thing called a farm deferment. You could get it depending on how many animals you raised and whether or not you could feed them all."

"I don't understand."

"Well, you can't win a war if your soldiers are starving. The government needed us. So basically, if you had a certain number of animals, eight milk cows, ten hogs, two-hundred and fifty chickens

I think it was, or whatever, *and* you produced all the grain to feed them, you were a valuable asset to the war, and they'd give you a pass. At the time, we had twenty-five or so cows, which was plenty to get us all exempt, but they... They hated the fields. Both of them. It pissed me off. Our father and grandfather worked so hard for the land we owned. My father killed himself working it, and they couldn't wait to get as far away from it as possible. So, they went, and I stayed to protect the family legacy."

"That makes sense," Maggie said. "You had to, or you'd lose the land."

Will jumped up from his seat and began to pace the kitchen. "It doesn't make *any* sense, Maggie."

She sat back in her chair as he went back and forth between the stove and the refrigerator. Why was he so upset? "Well, yeah, it does. How else would you have saved the farm?"

"Who cares about the goddamn farm!" He dragged his fingers through his hair and came to a halt in the middle of the room. "You know who cared? *I* did. I cared more about this fucking farm than my own brothers!"

The curse sounded especially cruel coming from his lips. But she was sure that wasn't true.

"Legacy? My father's children were his legacy. Not the damn corn," he muttered, as he went to the sink and stared out the window. "I should have made them stay. Or... gone with them."

"Would the military have let you serve together?"

"No. Not *with* them. But at least I would have been there."

"They still would have died, Will."

"At least we would have been buried together."

"And what good would that have done?"

He continued to stare out the window. He didn't seem to have an answer for that.

"Were they married?" she asked. "Did they have kids?"

"Yeah, they both were married. Only Louie had kids. Two girls."

"What happened to them?"

"Matt's wife Abigail remarried and moved away. Penny stayed with the girls. They lived just down the road."

"Who supported them?"

There was a long pause. "I did. Penny and my sister Suzanna, who also lost her husband, got death benefits, but it just wasn't enough. After I died... they couldn't run the farm themselves." He shook his head. "They ended up leasing the land for a year before selling it off. So, my staying back it was all for nothing anyway. I should have just died in France."

That was a little harsh. And also, untrue. "No, it wasn't. You saved the farm, and the farm took care of your family once you were gone."

"They sold it. For almost nothing."

"Yeah, but maybe they got the money they needed to support themselves."

"But Matty and Louie—"

"How old were they when they got drafted?"

"Matty was thirty-three, Louie was thirty-six."

Maggie's brows went up in surprise. She'd assumed they were really young based on Will's protectiveness. "They were grown men?"

It was Will's turn to look surprised. "Well, of course they were."

"Then why do you feel so responsible for them?"

"Because they were my brothers, Maggie!"

She set her spoon down in her mug. "No, that's not how—" She remembered something. "When did your dad die again?"

"When I was nineteen."

"How old were your siblings?"

Will rubbed his eyes. "Um, Al was seventeen, Claire was sixteen, Louie was fifteen, Matty was twelve, and Suzy was two or three."

Maggie stared at him as the pieces came together. "So, you

became a father of five children and inherited a farm when you were nineteen years old?"

He dropped back into his chair. "Yeah, I guess so." He sounded a little surprised by his own answer.

"You guess? You don't remember?"

"Yes, I do. I just—" Will's shoulders slumped, and he rested his elbows back on his knees as he stared at the floor.

She leaned over and squeezed his arm. "You were not responsible for your brothers. At least not when they died, Will. They were grown men by then."

"No. I should have made them stay."

"Made them?" Maggie asked softly. "How?"

Will didn't answer.

"You were not their father, Will, even though you probably spent most of your life feeling that way."

He jerked his arm away. "I was what they had, and I failed them, and their families."

"No. That's not how—"

"Can we be done for now?"

She wanted to keep at it, but the truth was, she wasn't sure how much more of his past she could listen to without crying. "Can we at least finish the story of how you died?"

Will's anger dissipated, and he sighed. "It was about a week before I started feeling bad. My hand wasn't healing, but I thought..." He shrugged. "I was putting in fifteen, sixteen-hour days, running the tractor, taking care of the animals. I just thought I was tired, worn out."

He pressed his lips together for a moment, lost in thought. "I lasted another five or six days, I think. The end is a little fuzzy. I felt terrible. I had a fever. My entire body ached. The last thing I remember was feeling dizzy, and so I went to sit down for just a minute and... Poof. The next thing I know, I was like this."

"So, you died from a scratch on your hand?"

"Kind of. It took a while to figure it out, but what I got from the girls, in the bits and pieces I heard when they were here, was that I got an infection. That is what killed me." Will shook his head. "Like I said. I was stupid."

"No, you weren't."

"Yes, I was."

Maggie let it go and drained the last sip of soup. Will was still staring at the table, lost in thought.

She tried to imagine what his life had been like. The pressure, the demand for him to be what he became. When he was nineteen, he was a father to five siblings and a business owner. When she was nineteen, she was skipping school and taking road trips with her boyfriend, and getting herself pregnant. She shook her head. At nineteen, she hadn't even been able to take care of *herself*.

His head came up. His eyes were sad, and she wished she could take his pain away. He really had spent his whole life working. He'd never relaxed, like she did so often with Dahlia. He'd never had *fun*, like she'd had as a young person, or as a mother playing with her son at the beach. It broke her heart.

"Let's do something fun," she said.

"What?"

"Let's do something fun," she repeated.

"Like what?"

"I don't know." She glanced out the window. It was pitch black. And he couldn't eat or drink. "What's the last movie you saw?"

"When I was alive?"

"Whenever."

He thought for a moment. "I don't know. I only went to the theater once when I was alive... took my sister Claire. I haven't watched television in thirty years."

Maggie had an idea. "Do you like science fiction?"

Will shrugged.

"Space?"

"Yes."

"Okay, let me grab my laptop. I'll meet you on the couch."

CHAPTER TWENTY-FIVE

THE THIRD MOVIE ENDED, AND WILL LOOKED DOWN AT MAGGIE AS the theme song played. She was fast asleep with her head resting on his lap. He gently brushed her hair back off her face as she snored softly. He smiled, wondering if this was what their life would be like if he were alive. Conversations over dinner, cozy evenings curled up on the couch. It didn't seem like much, but to him it was everything and summed up all he'd missed. The *good* parts of life.

As credits ended, the room fell silent. Light hovered on the horizon through the side window, and by the looks of the spotty clouds, he knew it would be a brilliant sunrise. He looked at the little clock in the corner of her computer. It was after six in the morning.

Closing his eyes, he rested his hand on her shoulder. He almost felt real again, and it felt so damn good. If he had just one wish, it would be to stay like this forever. Stay in this feeling of complete satisfaction for all eternity. He couldn't remember ever experiencing anything like it when he was alive.

Talking to Maggie the night before had been such a strange experience. Her look of disbelief when he'd told her how long it had been since he'd spoken to another person had given him pause. It was like he said. At first, he thought he couldn't, and for a while, he didn't want to. By the time he was ready... there was no one left to talk to. So, he hadn't given it much thought. But now that he had, well, that was a long time for a person, alive or dead, to be left with their own thoughts. A *very* long time.

Her reaction to the events in his life caught him off guard too. She had not responded the way he thought she would. When he confessed to not enlisting with his brothers, she'd said it made sense. When he'd admitted that he should have tried harder to make them stay, she'd insisted it wasn't his place to do so. When he'd told her how stupid he'd been, she'd looked at him like he was crazy and said...

No, you're not.

Of course he was! Otherwise, he wouldn't be here. He'd be with Louie and Matt, and the rest of his siblings, wherever they'd gone.

Will looked back at the window, trying to decide if he should wake Maggie up to see the sunrise or not. Then he remembered the fridge and his promise. Reluctantly, he removed himself from beneath her, gently set her head on a pillow, and went into the kitchen.

Hopefully, whatever it was that smelled so bad was light.

FIFTEEN MINUTES LATER, the container of spoiled leftovers was gone. It was backbreaking work to carry it all the way to the edge of the west field, but he was glad to be able to do some small things for Maggie after all she'd done for him. Even if she was trying to get rid of him.

It stung less every time he thought it, because he could feel how much she didn't *want* him to go. She was just trying to be helpful. As misguided as it was, it was also one of the most selfless things anyone had ever done for him, besides his parents maybe.

Will walked between the muddy rows, back toward the house, remembering when he and Al and Louie were boys, taking their shoes off and racing down the rows like racehorses on a track. They were careful to stay in the ruts, because their father would clock them upside the head if they crushed even one of his seedlings. His mother would sit on the back porch, snapping beans or peeling potatoes with Claire at her feet, and cheer for the winner. Will smiled. It was usually him, since he was the biggest. But every once in a while, he'd let the others win. They'd hoot and holler like it was Christmas morning, and he'd act upset. He remembered once, after he'd let Louie win, the boys had tackled him in the yard, declaring his new name to be 'Slow-Poke Will.' Afterward, he'd climb the stairs to the porch, and his mother had called him over to her chair where she was peeling carrots into an old towel on her lap. Taking his face in her rough hands, she'd smiled, and he was surrounded by the sweet damp smell of things just plucked from the earth. "You are a great many things, my boy, but nothing amazes me more than your heart. It will earn you great love one day. I promise." A chill raced down Will's spine as he thought of Maggie, wishing his mother could have kept her promise. Then she had kissed his nose, something he hated at the time and missed fiercely now, before sending him off to help his father.

He'd completely forgotten about that. And why he should recall it now was a mystery, unless...

A chickadee called to its mate from somewhere in the branches, and a second later, the mate answered.

He looked toward the house where Maggie lay sleeping. It was a black shadow against the watery sky. His mother had seen something in him back then, and he felt the same thing from Maggie too last night. He wanted nothing more than to believe both of them, but he couldn't. He tried to imagine what his mother would have said if she'd found out he let her boys go off to war. To his surprise, the first words that came to mind were the same ones Maggie had spoken last night. *They were grown men, and you were not their father.*

Will reached the edge of the field and went up the stairs onto the porch. The bathtub now occupied the place where his mother had once sat. He passed through the door, noticing it was firmer again, and went to the couch. Maggie was gone. He smelled coffee, and his eyes were drawn to the window. She was in her chair on the front porch, waiting for the sunrise. He leaned his head toward the glass and saw she was writing. He hesitated, thinking she might need space. But when he saw the steaming cup on his side of the table, he passed through the wall and sat down beside her.

She looked up. "Sorry I bailed on you."

"Bailed?"

She smiled. "Fell asleep."

Was she kidding? That was his favorite part of the whole night. "That's okay."

"What did you think?" She raised her eyebrows and took a sip of her coffee.

"Of the movies?"

"Yeah."

"Good."

She frowned. "Just good?"

"Well, I always thought of space as a more peaceful place. The part about the dad being the villain was an interesting twist, although that means the princess was Luke's sister and…"

"What?"

"Well, she kissed him before. On the mouth."

Maggie threw her head back and laughed. "Yes, she did."

Beams of light shot from her through him, filling his dark places. He smiled. "Last time I checked, that was not… um… recommended?"

"It's still not."

His gaze went from her to the barn, where he heard the same low buzzing sound before. It seemed louder now. What in the hell was that?

Maggie followed his eyes. "What is it?"

"Do you hear that?"

She listened for a moment and shook her head. "Hear what?"

He didn't know quite how to describe it. It was a mix between a hive of bees and a low hum. "That buzzing sound."

She listened again as he got up and went to the steps. It sounded like it was coming from everywhere, but when he closed his eyes… It tugged at him, the way Maggie did… sort of. And it was coming from the barn.

"I don't hear anything."

He went down the steps. This was the third time he'd heard it.

"Will?"

Maggie touched his arm. He glanced down at her socks before meeting her frightened eyes, and the buzzing stopped.

"What's the matter?" she asked.

He looked toward the barn, then back at her and shook his head. "I don't know. I thought… I thought I heard something."

"Was there a white light or anything?"

He laughed before realizing she was serious. "No. It sounded like…" He couldn't imagine what it could be, but it was odd that she hadn't heard it. "It's probably a loose wire, or one of the light bulbs in the barn is going out."

He led her back to the porch, and they resumed their seats. But Will sensed her nervousness as she sipped her coffee.

"What's the matter?" he asked.

"Nothing," she lied. "Um, the roofers are coming today so…"

"I'll stay out of the way."

"No haunting," a small smile played on the corner of her mouth. Her eyes widened, and she gasped. "The cat!" she exclaimed.

"The what?"

"That was you." Her eyes narrowed with her accusation.

Will had forgotten that. To his horror, he blushed. "Yeah. Sorry, I—"

Her smile returned. "And the webs, of course…"

He nodded.

"And that first day after I called Dee, when I couldn't breathe?"

He nodded again.

"Why?" The question felt heavy for only being a single word long.

"Because I—" He knew why, but knowing and saying were two different things. For twenty years, he'd thought about her. He remembered every detail of her brief visit. Every expression, every flower she'd held in her hand. The way she saw the world fascinated him. He'd been so envious of her freedom, and her obvious joy in... nothing.

He'd always imagined her living some gloriously happy life, and for some reason, the thought had brought him a lot of comfort over the years. To know that while there would always be fools like him who squandered their lives, there would be people like her, captivated by the moment, taking it all in, as he'd seen her do.

The truth was, *she* had inspired him to look first. And once he did, the world changed. It became something new. He became something new, and for the first time since his death, he didn't feel alone. He walked the land through the seasons, imagining it through her eyes, and he saw so many beautiful things.

When he saw her on the road, her joy replaced with sorrow and pain, he almost didn't recognize her. When he realized she could no longer see what was in front of her... It broke his heart.

"I remembered you from before, Maggie."

"I know."

"No, how you were. Different... happy."

"That was before my mom died."

"It pained me to see that you weren't anymore."

"But I was just a stranger. I mean, surely other people have poked their heads around here."

"But none of them left me what you did."

"Which was what, exactly?"

Will took a deep breath. He might as well tell her now.

"It is well with my soul
Not salvation, hell no
But this
These walls

The voices within it
This body
This place
The dark
And the light that cuts it..."

Will glanced at her, and she was staring at him with her mouth hanging open. He continued.

"My longings
My joy
And regret
Tangled up in the breathtaking impossibility of being here at all
When I take time to be still
My soul rejoices
And heaven descends
Into..."

"Ordinary living," Maggie finished.

Will nodded.

"You found my notebook, my poems."

"You left it here. I found it in the barn after you'd gone."

"I can't believe it..."

"Believe it. I've spent the last two decades believing that poem was for me, about us in that moment. I read your diary over and over. And it changed my life, Maggie. Long after you were gone."

She didn't say anything.

"I've known you a long time."

"Who I *used* to be," she said, lost in thought. "What happened to my notebook?"

"It got damaged in a storm we had about three years ago. A tornado went through, just to the south, and took several panels off the roof, blew rain every which-way through the barn. I thought the whole thing was going to come apart."

Maggie was quiet.

"That woman you used to be, she's still there. She is still *here*."

"How do you know?"

Will shrugged. "I see her in you. Or you in her."

She shook her head. "No. I don't think—"

"You came back, Maggie. And I know it sounds crazy, but I think *she* is the one that brought you back."

"I think we can both agree that crazy flew out the window the day you became undead," Maggie said. "And finding this place again was just an accident."

Will smiled at her. "Are you sure?" Because he was not.

CHAPTER TWENTY-SIX

MAGGIE ROCKED IN HER CHAIR. WILL SEEMED SO CERTAIN THAT THE carefree woman she'd once been was still buried in her somewhere. But it didn't feel that way.

"She is here, Maggie," he insisted.

She smiled sadly. "Then why can't I see her?"

Will studied her. "Maybe she's a little like me."

"Like you?"

"Hard to find, if you don't know where to look."

She sipped her coffee. *Maybe.*

"I've seen her," Will said, and her eyebrows went up.

"You have?"

"Yeah."

"Where?"

"Laying out in the middle of the driveway trying to catch clouds. Sitting in that very chair waiting to greet the sun. Laughing like a lunatic on the kitchen floor after trying to fix a bathroom sink."

Maggie's cheeks burned in the cool air. He had been there? "I forgot about that."

"I didn't."

She stared into her mug. Maybe Will was right. Maybe she just wasn't looking in the right places. Maybe she wasn't looking at all.

She met Will's eyes, and lightning shot through her as the corners of his mouth turned up in a smile.

It was kind of hard lately to see anything past the miracle in front of her.

"I know you think… I have to go before you can find her," Will said, as if reading her mind. "But I don't. She's already here."

"Then why can't I find her?" Maggie asked again.

"I told you. Because you don't know where to look." Will looked toward the horizon. "Lucky for you, I do."

"You do?"

He got up and held out his hand. "Yeah, but you're going to need muck boots, and we need to hurry."

"Muck what?" She set her coffee down, and a jolt pricked at her hand as she dropped her fingers into his palm.

His cool hand closed around hers "Galoshes, something waterproof—"

"Rain boots?"

"Yes, and hurry."

She ran into the house and pulled her rain boots on. Will led her through the kitchen and out the back door, and the next thing she knew, she was stumbling through the west field trying not to fall.

"Come on," Will called, several steps ahead of her.

Maggie picked up her pace as the wind pressed against her face, throwing her hair out behind her. "I am!"

"No, you're not." His hazel eyes crinkled at the corners with laughter as he looked over his shoulder and reached for her hand. Tears stung her eyes, and she felt *it*. The… thrill of being alive that used to course through her veins like blood. Will grinned at her, as if reading her mind, and she could almost see it, the lightning that sparked between their fingertips, as their hands came home again.

His glance fell behind her, and a frown briefly crossed his face as he yanked on her arm. "Faster."

Faster? Maggie pulled her hand away and broke into a run. Her eyes watered in the wind, as she tripped over the rows of dirt, but she put everything she had into her legs and just… ran.

The sky had turned an arctic blue, and it pulsed in time with her heart as it pounded against her ribs. She felt like she could run forever. For some reason, the sensation made her laugh. She remembered Eric when he was little, running around the yard or the house, screaming and giggling. Was this what he'd felt all those times?

Maggie pressed on, and was just about to overtake Will, when her toe hit a clod of dirt and sent her flying into him. They both tumbled to the ground, and Maggie's palms hit the dirt with a squishy smack.

She jumped up as mud soaked the knees of her jeans and looked at her black hands. She didn't have anything to wipe them on.

"Your jeans."

She hesitated for a moment before doing what she was told. She glanced at Will and noticed the wet spots on his knees as well. "Sorry."

He stared down at his dirty hands and pants for a moment, before glancing behind her toward the house.

"Are you okay?" she asked.

He wiped his hands on his thighs. "Yeah. Come on."

He led her to the edge of the field, where the creek turned to the north and went under the road. She waded across, at the bend, while he stood on the other side walking back and forth, looking toward the house at something she couldn't see.

When she made it across, he grabbed her arm and dragged her down into the leaf litter, beside the creek, until she was lying on her belly. She propped herself up on her elbows. "What are we—"

"Look." Will nodded toward the horizon.

She looked up and gasped. From where they were laying, the quietly bubbling creek stretched out in an almost straight line toward the lake. It was framed by leafless trees on either side. Maggie held her breath as the sky began to change. An orange glow appeared on the horizon, directly over the creek, lighting it on fire. Then, the clouds stole the show, reflecting in the water, every shade between rose and violet, turning the rippling current into a sparkling path that reflected the sky. The trees were transformed into cathedral arches, and Maggie had never been anywhere holier.

Will's hand closed over hers, and he squeezed. "There she is," he whispered as she met his eyes.

A moment later, the sun burst from the creek, drawing her attention away.

Squinting against its brightness, she could almost hear it sizzle as it ascended from the cool depths into the riotous sky.

Remembering she needed to breathe, she inhaled and exhaled again, as her breath momentarily clouded her vision. The colors changed so fast. Every time her eyes moved, they shifted, brightening and darkening, merging into one another, transforming imperceptibly into a completely new shade. Her brain could only name a handful of the thousands of colors that exploded, rushing up the creek, filling her eyes. Blush, salmon, marigold, honey, sherbet, orchid, plum...

As the sun climbed higher, the colors quickly faded. The clouds turned slate, and the sky blued, and a second later, it was morning.

"That was—" Maggie turned, and the look in Will's eyes stole the rest of her words away.

He touched the side of her face, and it sent a shock wave crashing through her body. "Beautiful," he whispered.

Slowly, she shook her head. "Will—" A second later, she was lying on her back, staring up at his face. She pressed her hands into his chest. "Don't make this harder."

He brushed her hair back into the leaves. "It's going to be hard no matter what, Maggie. Don't deny me the only thing I want in the time I have left."

Another wave washed over her as his hand found her cheek again and turned her head to face him. Another broke as he leaned closer. And another, as she slid her arms around his neck, pulling him on top of her. And another as—

His lips found hers, and the colors erupted again, but this time from inside. Every nerve in her body leaned into his touch, and she gasped at the pleasure it brought. A small part of her wondered how it could be happening, how he could feel so real, and not even be there, but the rest of her believed fully—

His tongue gently slipped between her teeth, and the muscles in her back contracted, pushing her into him, needing more. He delivered, sweeping into her mouth, eliciting a sound from her throat that was half cry half groan.

"Here she is," he whispered against her lips, as his hand slid under the back of her coat and found the hollow of her spine. The cold air was sharp against her skin as his fingers followed its curve over the strap of her bra until he reached her shoulder blades. The cry came again as waves of pleasure welled up from somewhere in him and surged through her. She kept thinking they would stop, that *she* would stop, but they didn't. They just kept coming. Harder. Stronger. *Faster*.

Maggie returned his kiss, his touches, unable to do otherwise as Will's palm spread against her back, and his arm tightened around her until there wasn't a single gap between them. The sensations that tore through her left her gasping, even with their clothes between them. It was as if he'd found a way into her brain and was making love to her from the inside out. A familiar tingling welled up in her belly and spread lower, as his lips went from hers to her jaw before tracing kisses down the side of her neck.

"Maggie—" He moaned. He felt it too. She could hear it in his voice.

Her breath came quicker at the thought, and the feeling pulsed between her legs as he pressed his hips into hers. "Oh god," she whispered, as he brought her to the brink of ecstasy. She was close. She was so close—

Will's head flew up, breaking the contact between them, and he turned toward the house. Fear pricked at the back of her neck and tangled with the pleasure spreading through her body. "What is it?" she choked.

When he met her eyes again, his were wild. He stared at her as if he'd never seen her before as her body hovered between joy and terror.

"What—"

"Nothing," he growled as his calloused hands tangled in her hair and pulled. Sparks stung her lips as his mouth closed hungrily over hers and he pressed his hips into her. "Maggie," he groaned. Hearing her on his breath again was all it took to send her spiraling over the edge.

"Maggie."

The waves crashed again.

"Oh, my sweet Maggie."

Maggie closed her eyes unable to quiet the cry that flew from her mouth as the universe contracted to the size of their intertwined bodies, then exploded, filling every corner of the cosmos with the energy that blazed between them.

"Maggie," he cried out as she clung to him and it contracted and burst around them again.

THE WIND RUSTLED the handful of leaves still clinging to the branches overhead, as her insides quieted. Will's eyes were closed, but his chest still heaved beneath her ear. She placed a tentative hand on it feeling and listening to his heart thump simultaneously.

His eyes opened, and his expression made her insides quicken again. "You are incredible, Maggie Dubois," he whispered, brushing the hair off her face. "Every day you take my breath away. How do you do it?"

She stared at him, feeling exactly the same way, trying to process what had just happened. Had they just had—she didn't even know what to call it. It was so much more than sex, yet—"What was that? How did you do—"

He shook his head. "I-I have no idea."

"Did you feel it—"

"Yes. I—" Will's head shot up and his entire body stilled. Even his breath paused as he looked behind her. Maggie pushed herself back on her elbows as fear replaced the satisfaction in his eyes. She turned and followed his gaze. The house and outlying buildings sat quietly in the early morning sun, as fear pricked at her like tiny needles. "What is it?" she asked.

Shaking his head, Will got to his knees and backed away from her.

Maggie sat up as he continued to stare at the house...

And the barn.

Dread wrapped its icy fingers around her and squeezed. *Oh, no.* "The buzzing sound?"

He nodded.

"It's not a broken light."

He shook his head, getting to his feet. "No. And it's getting louder."

"What do you think it is?" she asked, as he pulled her up.

"I don't know."

But he *thought* he did. She could tell by the way his lips pressed themselves into a worried seam. And she did too. It had something to do with his crossing over.

The thought that he might disappear at any moment, and she'd never see him again sent adrenaline cascading into her bloodstream.

She reached for his hand. "Do you want to check it out?"

He shook his head and looked at her, his eyes softening into a smile. "No. It's gone now, anyway."

She looked toward the house. Was it calling him back? Why now? Was it because of her? Because she said she wanted him to go? Had she opened some kind of... portal to the other side?

Will squeezed her hand. "Hey."

She met his eyes; hers filled with worry. If it was, letting him go was still the right thing to do. She knew it. But now... Now she wasn't sure if she could go through with it.

He picked at the leaves in her hair. "I know you think I have to leave in order to 'fix' yourself..." As his arm slid around her waist, he pulled her close and whispered. "But, Maggie, you aren't broken." His breath tickled her ear. "And neither am I. Not anymore."

Goosebumps rippled across her skin.

"Come on, I have so much more to show you." He took her hand in his, and she followed him through the trees, as her mind waged war with itself in the quiet morning.

CHAPTER TWENTY-SEVEN

As a week turned into a month, Will showed Maggie everything. The chipmunks napping away the remains of the winter in the den he'd discovered under one of the fallen bricks from the silo. The old tree where *Dryocopus pileatus*, the giant Pileated Woodpecker carved out its home. They watched as the first wildflowers of the season, bloodroot, marsh marigolds, crocus, and the pitcher-shaped *Symplocarpus foetidus,* commonly called skunk cabbage, poked their tiny green heads from the earth and climbed skyward. He showed her the tilted elm with the sloped trunk that was perfect for sitting and whiling away hot summer afternoons. They celebrated the return of the robins and their sweet melody with a picnic dinner on the porch and a bottle of wine that smelled divine, but he could not taste.

She had questions about the farm and farm life. Did they grow their own food? Of course. Why was there a hole in the side of the barn? There used to be a chicken pen there, and the hen boxes were inside. What was a hen box? Where the chickens lay. What about those boards there, why were they replaced? There used to be a brick shed attached at the back, where his father kept his tools. Why was the house built at such an odd angle? His mother loved the light, and his father loved her enough to build a cock-eyed house. That thought had brought tears to her eyes, and his, as he realized just how much his dad had loved his mom, and how heartbroken he must have been when she died.

Will turned to find Maggie staring at him from her seat on the porch. A soft smile played on the corners of her mouth. The change in her over the last several weeks was remarkable. Her suffering was slowly being replaced by something else, and it had softened her face and relaxed her shoulders. It was almost as if she were growing young again before his eyes, and he knew, even if she didn't, that whatever she'd been looking for had been found. "What are you thinking about?" she asked, as the air around them began to vibrate.

"You."

That had changed too. The sound in his ears had become as frequent as Maggie's laugh. At first, when he'd noticed the pull it had on him, it had scared him. It scared her too, he could tell, because they had both thought the same thing. It was there to take him away.

The day in the woods, when they had watched the sunrise over the creek, it had screamed in his ears as her body went supernova and pleasure rippled across her face. It was one of the most beautiful, terrifying moments of his death, watching the sparks burst from her skin and feeling the screeching pull toward the barn.

But since then, it had changed. It had grown gentler to his ears and more consistent. Instead of a harsh buzz, it was more of a soft hum, a whispery song, and it no longer frightened him. The pull was still there when he closed his eyes, but instead of feeling like it was dragging him toward the barn, he now felt as if it was leading him there.

"What about me?"

"That you are incredibly beautiful."

She laughed, and the song sang a little louder. He glanced at the barn.

Maggie's eyes followed his. "Is it doing it again?" Every time she asked, her voice sounded sadder, and it pained him that it still worried her when it was beginning to bring him so much joy.

"Yes." It brought him joy because it now reminded him of *her*. Every time he thought about her, it played.

"Is it louder?"

It had become the anthem of their days together; the record turning in the background while they strolled together through the muddy fields, or talked the night away on the couch, or sat, like they were now, on the porch, listening to the rain. He shook his head. "No." Just sweeter, softer, more beautiful.

"Is it still pulling at you?"

"Yes." It was. And every day, the pull was stronger.

"Do you want to—" She'd been asking him that a lot. But she never finished the sentence.

Yes, he did. That feeling was growing stronger too. He *wanted* to follow it. He avoided Maggie's eyes. It was getting harder for him to lie. He shook his head.

She exhaled heavily, and he glanced at her as she pulled the blanket up to her neck and stared out into the dreary day.

Will was certain now he could convince Maggie he didn't need to leave, but now, ironically, he wasn't sure he wanted to stay. Or more accurately, he wasn't sure if he *should.*

He had noticed something strange. The happier he felt in any given moment, the stronger it pulled, the clearer the tune became. And he was happy. Finally, after a lifetime and an even longer deathtime, he'd found peace and joy. And every day, he was finding more. Now, because of Maggie, it was singing to him constantly, drawing him in, begging him to come. And the fact that it had been the loudest when he'd touched her, and brought her to joy, made him think that somehow... He needed to go for her. Or maybe closer to the truth was, he needed to go if he *loved* her.

And he did. Because he had *finally* remembered what it felt like to love and be loved.

At first, her inquiries into his past had angered and embarrassed him. But the more she demanded to know, and the more he was forced to recall... the more surprising the memories became.

Talking to Maggie about his mother and his siblings, his life, and his death, had brought back that piece of him that had been missing for so long. Between the memories he'd forgotten of his family, and her insistence that he'd committed no crime worse than ninety percent of the rest of humanity, she'd convince him that...

Will looked at the tractor, remembering not with bitterness, but with understanding.

At the time of his own death, the death of his brothers was still heavy on his soul. It was more than a year later, but he still missed them every day. He couldn't bear to visit Penny and the girls because, when he saw Louie's smiling eyes staring back at him, it broke his heart all over again. He remembered the nightmares of them being shot, of their mangled bodies among the wreckage of burning machines. How many times had he bolted up in the middle of the night in a cold sweat, feeling like he couldn't breathe?

Sometimes he would dream of green fields lit by moonlight and filled with laughter, and those hurt even more, because in those dreams his brothers were still alive, and when he awoke, he felt like they'd been stolen from him all over again.

Will stared at the dilapidated barn. It had been red and new and beautiful when they were boys that still played in corn.

When he'd awakened in his new state, the first question he'd asked himself was why weren't they together? He had immediately assumed he was being punished for not stopping them. And once that seed had been planted in his mind... every mistake he'd ever made was drawn to it like metal to a magnet. And his solitude left him with plenty of time to recall *all* of them. Every failure, every angry word, every missed opportunity. Eventually there were so many... the man he had actually *been* was overcome, buried, replaced by a monster who had squandered the only thing that really mattered. Precious *life*. And where did monsters belong? They belonged in the dark, in cages, in Hell. Will had convinced himself that was where he was headed after Fate, or God, or whoever had brought him here was done with him.

He ran his fingers over his initials on the blanket that hung over the side of his chair. For seventy years, those initials had brought him shame. But the truth was, he had been a good man. He had been a man who loved and was worthy of love. He had just... forgotten somehow. He'd made plenty of mistakes, like not being present in his life, like not seeing what was right in front of him. But they were only that. Mistakes. Accidents. There had been no intention behind them. Nothing worth punishing.

That day Maggie kissed him, he'd pushed her away, thinking she had no idea who he really was, thinking if she did, she would not be looking at him the way she had. He had felt unworthy of her love, but now he knew *he* was the one who had been blind. She had seen him for who he really was. He had not.

Maggie had told him he couldn't give something he didn't have, and she'd been right. He had felt helpless and heartbroken when Louie and Matty went off to war. When they died, blaming himself and being angry had been easier than dealing with the pain of having loved and lost them. And as soon as he'd started down that road, love for himself or anyone else had slipped out of his grasp.

Until now.

He glanced at Maggie, sitting in her chair with her journal.

This was the second time she'd saved him from himself.

The first time was when she sat, looking very much like she did now, on the floor of the barn. He had been alone and miserable for so long at that point. But she'd brought light into his darkness. Through her words she had spoken to him, she helped him to see. It was her that made him realize that punishment or not, he didn't want to waste another second being an ungrateful fool. If death was all he had left, he wanted to embrace it, the way she embraced life.

Maggie smiled to herself, and his heart thumped with joy.

When all hope had been lost, she had brought it back to him.

Chewing her lip as she did when she was searching for a word she couldn't find, she paused. Then her hand began to scribble again and her scrunched brows parted as a smile lit up her face. *There she is.*

And she was doing it again. Taking his fear, his suffering, and turning it into something beautiful.

The tune thrummed through his chest.

She was right.

Something benevolent had brought him back. He didn't know how, exactly, or why, but it had not been to punish him. If it had, he would not be feeling the way he did now. And he knew something else. It was not the same entity that had trapped him here and wouldn't let him leave.

That creature was something totally separate.

He looked at Maggie, then gasped when he saw it in the window behind her. It stared at him with his mother's eyes and his father's shock of brown hair. Will's mouth fell open. "No." Could it be?

That terrible creature was *him*?

The song swelled around him as the hair on his arms stood on end and leaned toward the barn.

"Will?"

Maggie rubbed her arms as if they were covered in goosebumps beneath her jacket, as he met her gaze. Could she feel it too?

"Will? Are you okay?"

This had *always* been a gift? From the very start?

Yes.

Finally, he remembered. The pull. He'd felt it before. Not *exactly* how it was now, but close. Right after he'd woken up. How had he forgotten?

"Yes?" he whispered distractedly.

He'd always been able to leave?

Yes.

The truth slammed into his chest, and he braced his hand against the side of the chair. "Oh…" He had just been too afraid of what lay on the other side to go.

"Will? Are you okay?"

"I'm fine." Was he?

"Are you sure?"

Turning, he watched the rain drip from the eave onto the ground. He stared at the barn as the memory came into focus.

That was where he'd died. On the bench in the corner of the barn. He'd gone out to feed the animals. Every muscle in his body ached. He'd been dizzy. He fed the hogs and, feeling hot, sat down to catch his breath. The air in the barn had been cool and dark. He'd rested his head against the wall, intending only to close his eyes for a minute. Turned out to be a long minute.

The bench was still there, buried under a pile of old shovels and hoes. He hadn't so much as touched it in all the years he'd been dead because the only time he ever got near it, there had been an ominous pressure in his chest, and it had frightened him. He recognized it as the same pull he felt now. With the self-loathing gone, it no longer felt sinister or hostile.

Will scratched his head in disbelief. The way out had always been there, right in front of him, but his fear had clouded it, hid it in a fog of uneasiness.

"I'm cold. I think I'm going to head inside. Do you want to join me?"

"In a minute."

She gave him a long, penetrating look before gathering her things and heading inside.

Did that mean he didn't belong here?

He looked at Maggie's vacated chair.

Was that why it was pulling him? Was it trying to tell him it was time to go?

But how could that be true when he'd only just found happiness?

How could that be true when *she* was so—

Will gasped. He'd been so focused on himself; he hadn't even noticed until now. The music became louder when *she* was happy too.

The scream that day in the woods, their *combined* love that made it happen, not his alone.

Will stared.

She was drawing him to it too? Did that make sense? Did that mean she really *did* want him to go? Or needed him to, even though it contradicted every look she'd given him over the last month.

His earlier thought returned, making more sense. That was why he felt like he needed to go. Because each time *either* of them was happy, it pulled him away. Why would it do that unless he was supposed to go?

He remembered what Maggie had said when she'd returned. She would continue to age, just as she had been, while he stayed the same. He tried to imagine if their roles were reversed. How would he feel, becoming an old man like Bob, while she... He didn't even have to finish the thought to know.

Will looked down at his hands. He concentrated for a moment and drew his fingers through the coffee mug beside him without so much as a ripple.

He felt like a man, especially when he was with her, but the truth he kept forgetting was that he wasn't anymore. Maybe that's what the pull was telling both of them. She might love him, and he her, but maybe what *she* needed was someone to grow old with. And she would never have that if he remained.

She'd said they had to fix themselves, and maybe there was some truth to that, since she couldn't make him forgive himself for the life he lived any more than he could make her love the woman she'd always been. But she was wrong about having to do it alone. People were not meant to be alone. If he'd learned anything, it was that. She'd just gotten lost in her grief, the same way he had, and had forgotten to take care of herself. She hadn't been lost. All she needed was time to get reacquainted with who she'd always been. And she had. He heard it in her voice every time she laughed. He saw the peacefulness in her eyes every time she smiled. She was no longer empty, no longer nothing. More importantly, he was sure now she would be fine if he were gone.

And if that was true—whether it was Connor, or someone else, she had the chance to find real love again, the kind that could follow her anywhere and didn't have to stop at the end of the driveway. He had bound himself to this place for seventy years, and while it had turned out to be the best decision he'd ever made, he could not do that to her. She was still alive. She had a son and friends, and the world was so much bigger than the twenty acres on which they stood. He could not rob her of that.

Will got up and walked to the stairs. The rain had slowed to a light drizzle, and he listened. Between the drops, the barn hummed a happy tune, reminding him of one his mother used to sing when she washed dishes.

He crossed the driveway, then pushed his way into the barn. The walls had turned to Jell-O again since Maggie's return. The sound echoed off the walls in the semi-darkness. The swallows were roused from their rest and chirped restlessly as they disappeared out the gable window.

He crossed the damp dirt, and it grew louder. His heart thumped in time to the strange beat as he approached the pile in the corner where the bench lay hidden and began to pull the shovels away. A weird sort of anticipation welled up inside him as the leg and half of the seat came into view. Hesitantly, he touched it. His eyes widened. It was warm like a summer afternoon, just like the day Maggie came into his life. Whatever was on the other side felt like her. It was good. It was *wonderful*.

Maggie had said she wanted a chance. He knew what she meant. She meant there. On the other side, where they would be equal in whatever form it was, they found themselves in.

Was that really how it worked? Could she find him—

"What are you doing?"

Will jerked his hand back and spun around.

Maggie stood behind him, sopping wet, looking utterly terrified. He hadn't heard her come in.

"I-I was just looking for—" He glanced back at the bench. The urge to touch it again was almost overwhelming. He shoved his hands in his pockets, trying to ignore it. "I was just looking for something I thought was back—"

She cut him off before he could finish his lie or wonder why he didn't want her to know the truth. Her eyes bore into his, and he knew she knew. "Don't go," she begged.

"What? Where?"

Her breath stuttered from her mouth as tears filled her eyes and overflowed. She tried and failed to smile. "I know, Will." Her voice was barely a whisper and filled with so much sadness he almost couldn't breathe.

"Know what?" he choked.

Her chest shook as she tried to inhale again. Then she shrugged helplessly, looking like she'd rather die than say the words out loud. "You found it. The way out."

He opened his mouth, but the words wouldn't come.

"I can see it in your eyes." She glanced at the bench. "You found it and... you're going to go, aren't you?" Her shoulders trembled as she sucked in a shallow breath and swiped at her eyes. "I-I thought you might have already left."

"I would never leave without—"

Her hand flew to her mouth as one of the most painful sounds he'd ever heard fell from her lips, and he realized what he'd just confessed. Tears stung his eyes. He said he wouldn't leave *without*. Without saying goodbye. "Maggie."

"I know what I said before. But I lied, Will." Pressing the back of her hand to her cheeks, she wiped her eyes, sniffling. "I don't want you to go." She pressed her hand over her mouth again to hide the sob that followed. "Don't go, Will. Don't go. Please?" she begged. "I can't—" She swiped desperately at her eyes again.

"Hey." He pulled her into his arms and the song that had been humming quietly while she confessed swirled through the rafters.

Her chest fluttered against his as she tried to breathe, and tears spilled down her cheeks, and she buried her head against him. "I don't want you to leave me!" she cried helplessly. "I just found you." He could barely hear her above the beautiful sound that enveloped them.

Tears filled his own eyes as he pressed her cheek to his chest and smoothed her hair. "Shh. I'm not going anywhere," he said, knowing it was a lie. The pull was almost unbearable, and his body ached to go. Squeezing her, he held on for dear life. Had he lost his mind? What was he thinking? He *loved* her. And what if she was wrong? What if this was it? He closed his eyes, and a tear slid down his cheek. *Damn it.*

He was thinking he *still* wanted to go. Another tear fell.

Maggie was saying something. "Just…" She fought with the words and her breath, as silent sobs wracked her shoulders.

"Shh." He ran a hand across her arms, then pulled her back so he could cup her face in his hands. When he met her eyes, the song swelled again. The barn practically shook with the melody, and half of him wanted to cover his ears while the other half wished he could just fall into it.

"Shh." He swiped at her tears with his thumbs.

Her eyes were red, and he almost couldn't bear the pain he saw in them. Or the love.

"I know you're… going to go, Will…" she shrugged, almost as if in apology. And he wondered why she was sorry when *he* was the one leaving.

His facade cracked, and he pressed his forehead to hers. "Shh." He couldn't deny it. A cry exploded from his mouth and his grief tore him to shreds, as he ran his hands over her cheeks and through her hair, wanting to remember every detail of the way she felt beneath his palms. His lungs forgot how to breathe. His hands shook as they cradled her face. "I'm so sorry." Was all he could say before there was no more air.

Maggie placed her hand gently over his shaking ones, smiling through her tears. "Hey, it's okay." Her voice broke, but there was something in it that reminded him of his mother, when he'd been a boy and woke up in the dark terrified. "It's okay. It's going to be okay," she said softly.

The music was so loud, so deep and so beautiful, as he buried his head against her neck. How was it going to be okay? How could anything ever be okay again if he left her? "I'm sorry. I just—I can feel it now. I know it's where I belong—"

She pulled him back into her arms as her face fell. "I know. I know. And its—" A wail filled the space between her words. "I-it's okay. It's okay. It will be okay." The words rushed out of her mouth, and he wondered if she was talking to herself or him. Another cry erupted from her throat and she pressed her lips to his chest, the vibration of her voice mixing with the song that was already humming through it, until they were one in the same.

She wasn't okay at all. And neither was he. But he had to go.

"Maggie..."

"Just... just stay one more night? Please? I just need..." Between her tears and sniffles and gasps for air, she could barely speak. She wiped her nose on her sleeve, stumbling over the words. "Just *one* more? I'm not ready—"

The song billowed around them as he shoved her. "Then we have to get out of here. Right. Now."

Dragging her away from the bench, he prayed he had the strength to make it to the door without turning around.

CHAPTER TWENTY-EIGHT

MAGGIE THREW THE DOOR OPEN AND GASPED AS THE COOL AIR HIT her wet cheeks. Will stumbled out behind her. Her legs crumpled beneath her and he caught her around the waist as she fell.

"I've got you," he said, turning her like a rag doll and pressing her head to his gasping chest.

She grabbed at him and cried out angrily, knowing she should have let him go and hating herself for asking him to stay. As soon as she'd said it, she knew she'd made a mistake. "I'm sorry! *Damn it.*" she cried. "I should have let you go! I should—"

"It's okay, Maggie."

No, it wasn't. She was being selfish. She was doing what she always did. "Damn it!" she yelled, pressing her forehead to his shoulder. She sucked in air, but for some reason, it didn't feel like it was filling her lungs.

Will pushed her back. "Hey—"

"It just happened so fast," she panted. "I wasn't—I wasn't ready."

He took her face in his hands again and found her eyes. It started to rain again. "Neither was I."

"Yes, you were!"

"How could I ever *want* to leave you?" The pain in his voice made her wonder who he was asking. He looked back toward the barn. "Come on, let's get you inside." He reached for her hand.

"I'm sorry, Will," she said, taking it and following him back to the house.

It only took getting to the stairs before the emptiness that always accompanied her sadness started flowing in. But just as she was about to float away, she pulled herself back down. She was not going to do that anymore. She was not going to let that emptiness take his place in her heart. She couldn't, otherwise…

He walked through the door, and she pushed it open. Otherwise, it would be like he never existed.

Will's tears were gone, and he'd regained his composure. "Let's get you in some dry clothes, okay? Maybe make some tea?"

Maggie fought the numbness that promised to take her pain away. It made no sense. She'd begged Will to stay, and now all she wanted to do was peel away from him and hide. What was the matter with her?

"Maggie?"

"I'm sorry."

"Stop saying that."

"But I am. I don't know why…" She shook her head.

"You don't?" His expression hardened along with his voice.

Her eyes locked on his. "Wh-what?"

"Finish that sentence."

She didn't understand.

"You don't know why what?"

She was going to say she didn't know why she'd asked him to stay. But she did. It was because she loved him. Fresh tears filled her eyes, and the urge to withdraw doubled and lodged itself in her throat.

"I love you too, Maggie," he snapped. "That's why you asked me to stay. And that's why I did. And *that* is why this hurts—" His voice was rough as it broke. "That is why this hurts so damn much." He shook his head. "Do not apologize for the way you feel about me. Ever. It has been the greatest gift and honor of my life. Do you understand?"

She nodded slowly.

"Okay. Now go upstairs and get some dry clothes on. We have one more night. Let's not waste it."

She wiped her eyes.

"Okay?" He tucked her wet hair behind her ear.

She nodded. He was right. They had one more night. She climbed the first step, then turned. "You promise you'll still be here when I come back down?"

"I promise."

She ran up to her room, threw her wet clothes off, and pulled a pair of leggings out of her dresser. She pulled a sweater over her head and ran back downstairs. Will was in the kitchen, staring out the window. His reflection wavered like ripples on the surface of the water. She smiled sadly. He really was a ghost. It was so easy to forget sometimes.

She crossed the room in her bare feet and stood beside him. It was still raining, and the overall gloom matched her mood, as the world slowly began its descent into night.

"What does it feel like?" she asked quietly, looking up at him. She was going to miss that. Looking up and seeing him standing there beside her. It seemed like a funny thing to miss, but maybe not.

He continued to stare out the window. "What?"

"Whatever it is in the barn. Does it feel… safe?" Tears filled her eyes again as she tried to keep her voice steady. "Or scary…"

"It feels… good."

"It does?"

"I'm not afraid, Maggie." He turned to look at her.

But *she* was. She was afraid that maybe he hadn't been ready, and she'd forced it on him, and now he was just trying to spare her.

"Can you describe it to me? What it feels like?" she asked again.

"Make yourself a cup of tea and come sit with me on the couch, and I'll tell you."

She brewed a coffee instead. If this was their last night, she wanted to be awake for it. Then she lit the fire that she'd set in the grate that morning and pulled the blanket out of the basket and sat down beside him. Will draped his arm over her shoulders as she tucked herself against his chest. How could he be dead when she could hear his heartbeat?

He took her hand and intertwined their fingers. "Do you feel this?"

A tingling spread through her chest, lighting her insides on fire while illuminating the deepest, darkest corner of her heart.

Will laughed. "Yes. You do."

She smiled. "Yeah. I do."

"It feels like this, times a hundred. Maybe a thousand."

Was he just trying to make her feel better? "How can that be?"

"I don't know." He rubbed his thumb over her hand. "But that's how I know it's right. That's how I know... I need to go."

"Did you see anything? Like a glimpse of what's on the other side?"

"No." He paused. "But I hear it."

"The buzzing sound?"

"It sounds more like music now that I'm... ready to listen."

Ready to listen? She knew it. This was her fault. "I shouldn't have pushed you like I did!" she cried. "I thought if I helped you move on, I'd prove to myself that... I don't know. That I was okay on my own. But I don't need you to go to know that now. I don't—"

He squeezed her hand. "Shh. You did the right thing, Maggie."

"No. This is my fault. I—"

"No, it's not."

"Then, why now? After all this time? Why is it coming for you *now*? After I said I wanted..." Now that it was actually happening, she couldn't bring herself to say it.

He pushed her back so he could see her face. "I told you. The reason it is calling me now is because I am ready to hear it. I wasn't before."

She shook her head. "I don't understand."

"I've always been able to pass over. I was just too afraid to go."

"What? Why?"

"I thought I was being punished, so I assumed whatever brought me here was making me stay. But it wasn't. My existence here, it was a gift, and my fear of where I was headed after this kept me from…"

"You thought you were going to Hell?" Maggie had not even considered that a possibility. Hell didn't exist, did it? But then again, where was Will headed, if not to heaven?

"I just didn't understand what I'd been given. But thanks to you, I didn't waste it all."

"I left you here for twenty years."

"You didn't know I was here."

She turned and glanced at the picture on the wall. Now that she knew, it was clearly him.

"And you didn't leave me. You were here with me, in my heart and in my head every day that you were away. Just as we've been these last few weeks. We walked the fields together. You spoke to me, encouraged me." He pulled her back under his arm. "You made me look up when my head was down. And I saw it all, this time around."

"I don't—"

"And after all of that…" Will's voice was hoarse. "You came back to me, Maggie."

She wiped her eyes. She'd come back too late.

He coughed, clearing his throat. "Then you practically destroyed my house," he said. "Flood, fire…"

She laughed.

"But you rebuilt my heart, so—"

She sniffled and laughed again.

"And now I am filled with a peacefulness that only comes with knowing you have no regrets. I loved my family, I loved my brothers, and maybe I missed out on my own life, but… Somehow, that brought me here, to you. So, how could I regret that?"

"But all that time…" Maggie couldn't imagine.

"Yeah, all that time."

"So, you really are ready to go then?" She reached for her coffee and took a sip.

"I'm not ready to leave you. But I think there's a reason why the living and the dead don't normally coexist."

Maggie had never thought about it. Honestly, she hadn't even believed in anything before meeting Will, God, ghosts, or otherwise. "A reason? Like what?"

"It's hard to be grateful for what you have when you are constantly being reminded of what you don't."

Like the fact that he would look just as he did now if he stayed. Locked in his handsome face, his strong body, while hers bent and wrinkled, and decayed.

"What's better? Eating the apple or living long enough to watch the tree grow from a seed?"

She didn't know. "They both seem pretty special."

"They are. But it doesn't feel that way when you can only have one, when you can't share the joys in your life with the people you care the most about."

Maybe he was right.

"This place, Earth, or real life, or whatever you call it, this is for the living. This place is meant to be tasted and explored. Everything here should be free to roam. No consciousness should be bound to any one place, no matter how beautiful it is, or how stupid they are. Yes, life is risky and fleeting, but that's what makes it exciting. Life is the journey. Where I am headed... I think that's the destination."

"What do you think it will be like?"

"Lots of cumulus clouds, and fat little babies with wings."

Maggie punched his stomach lightly and laughed. "I'm serious."

He shrugged around her. "To be honest, it feels a lot like being here with you, only... magnified."

"Magnified?"

"Yeah. I don't know how to explain it. When I let it take me, it kind of feels like *you* that's pulling me in. Like *you* want me to go as much as I want to."

She thought about that. Maybe heaven worked differently than Earth did. Maybe some part of her was already there waiting for him. It was a happy thought. "I'd probably go too. I think. If I felt like you were calling me."

He laced their fingers together again. "Thank you for saying that. Even if you don't believe it."

Maybe she did. She needed something to get her through the next day.

He gave her hand a reassuring squeeze. "Maybe heaven is different for everyone. Maybe it takes our greatest joys in life, whatever they are, and enhances them somehow."

"You mean like, collects all the love we've been given and saves it for us, to live over and over?"

Will was quiet for a moment. "Yeah."

It was a happy thought. "Did you sense your family at all?"

"No. I didn't."

The only thought that was making this bearable was that she would find him again when her turn came. But what if it didn't work that way? What if—

Maggie pushed the thought away. She didn't want to spend the whole night crying.

"Tell me stories about when you were little," she said, changing the subject.

Will's laugh rumbled against her ear. "Well, there was this one time Al…"

MAGGIE BLINKED AND STRETCHED. She'd had the most beautiful dream about a field of wildflowers. Eric had been a little boy, and she was chasing him through the spindly green stems of Queen

Anne's Lace. He'd screamed with laughter as her fingers brushed his sides, and he wiggled away. She hadn't needed to look behind her to know Will was there. She just knew. He was always there, tugging at her, humming through her bones. He had been leaning against the tree behind her, watching them play.

He brushed the hair off her cheek as she rolled back and smiled. A second later it faded as her eyes flew to the window and the lightening sky beyond it, and her dream sank like a stone in a sea of dread.

It was morning.

"I didn't want to sleep!" she cried, scrambling to sit up. Will pressed her head back onto the pillow on his lap.

"Shh, Maggie, just relax."

"No!" Panic churned in her stomach, making her insides lurch, and she thought she might throw up. "Why did you let me—"

"You were tired."

"I'll have the rest of my life to fucking sleep, Will!" She pushed herself up to sit. Raking her hands through her hair, she swore as tears stung her eyes. "Shit." How hard was it just to stay awake?

"You look so peaceful when you sleep."

She tried to blink them back. "I wanted—"

"And I wanted a little bit of time with you that didn't feel so…"

Maggie swallowed past the knot in her throat. "Sad?"

"We've already said everything we need to."

He was right. They had talked most of the night away, but still. "Why does it not feel like enough?"

"When it comes to love, is there ever enough?"

She wiped her eyes. "I suppose not." The sky was brightening frighteningly fast. She bit her lip. "When—when are you going to go?"

"When you are ready."

Sniffling, she tilted her head back, begging the tears back into her eyeballs. It didn't work. "You're going to be waiting a while, then," she said, meeting his eyes as they cascaded down her cheeks.

Will's voice was pained as he took her hands in his. "I need to know you're going to be okay, Maggie. I can't do this if you're not."

She knew that. And, damn it, she *was* trying. "I know." She squeezed his hand back. Yesterday she had failed. But today... today she would do better. Today, she *would* be brave and do what was right for Will. And she would not run from it, or him, or *herself* after he was gone, no matter how much she wanted to. *He* was the one stepping into the unknown, after all. Not her. And she didn't want him to do it halfway or leave any part of him behind. Wherever he went, she wanted him to be whole. *She* wanted to be whole too. "I'm fine. This is the hardest part. After you go..." It was déjà vu all over again. First her mom, then Dean and Eric. All of it was the same. *Except* her. Maggie took a deep breath and squared her shoulders. "I'll be fine..." Still, her voice broke on the last word, and more tears came.

Will wiped her eyes. "You're not very convincing."

She laughed through her tears and met his blurry eyes. "I will be fine. I promise," she said with more confidence than she felt.

Did you hear that? she asked herself. She was going to do more than survive this. She was going to go on living until it killed her. So, when she did die, *she'd* be whole too, and have earned her place in heaven beside Will.

"Would you like to have breakfast first?" he asked, stroking her cheek.

The thought of eating made her want to vomit, even coffee turned her stomach. Her hand closed over his as she shook her head. She looked back at the window. The rain clouds had fled overnight, and the ones that remained were high in the atmosphere, already changing colors. Maggie met Will's eyes. It was all happening too fast. But then... She wondered what would have happened if they'd been able to meet when they were alive? Would they have fallen in love? Would she have been a farmer's wife? Or he a designer's husband, living in the suburbs? Two whole lifetimes together flew through her mind, and she knew even then, it wouldn't be long enough. Why did life have to be like that? The happier you were, the faster things went by. The sadder you were, and time slowed, almost to a stop.

"I think we should just get it over with," she said.

"Yeah?" Tears filled his eyes, but he looked relieved, and Maggie knew he was struggling just as much as she was.

"Yeah. It's not going to get any easier if we wait."

"No. It's not."

She wiped her eyes and got up. "Let me just put my shoes on and—" The pressure in her head forced more tears from her eyes as she went to the closet. Her hands shook as she reached for her muddy boots. Every walk they had taken together rolled through her mind. The shape of the land. Their laughter. The way his eyes sparkled when she shivered and whispered, 'Oh, Will... It's beautiful,' at yet another miracle of nature that he'd pointed out. Those were hers to keep.

Will stood by the window, looking out as she slid them on. Sunlight poured through it, casting his flickering shadow across the bookshelf. At least there was that. A sunny morning.

She stood up and tried to breathe, but it was quickly becoming impossible.

"Ready?" she heard herself ask. They needed to do this before she passed out.

"Yes."

"Okay." Her throat ached from the strain of silencing all the sounds that wanted to pour out of it as she reached for his hand and pulled the door open. The sun was blinding, and her legs wobbled as she stepped out onto the porch. Cool, crisp air brushed past her as she held up her free arm to block the sunlight. She squeezed her eyes shut for a moment. *You can do this, Maggie,* she whispered silently to herself. Then tightening her grip on Will's hand, she tried not to think about how long it might be before she held it again as they headed down the stairs and slowly made their way across the drive. The morning was still and quiet, except for her sniffles.

Maggie swiped at the tears that refused to stop with the sleeve of her sweater. Even the robins seemed to know it was not a day for singing. The gravel crunched beneath her feet.

"Do you hear it?" she asked, straining her ears. "The barn's song?"

"Yes."

"Does it still sound good?"

"Yes."

They reached the door. "Let me go in and move the stuff out of the way," Maggie said.

"I can do it."

"I know, but I can do it faster, and I don't want to drag this out anymore—"

Will nodded and released her hand.

Maggie pulled the door open. The squeak of the wheel shattered the quiet, and the birds shifted in their nests as bits of dust and straw fell through the beams of light that pierced the darkness.

Making her way to the back corner, she moved the rakes and shovels, disturbing the generations of spiders that had taken up residency there. Carefully, she inspected the flowerpots and crates that were piled on the bench for bugs before moving them to the floor.

The bench was long and narrow, and looked like it had once belonged to a picnic table. The wood was gray with age. A dark stain at the end of one of the boards was its only defining feature. She wiped it down with her sleeve. It was hard to believe that a nondescript piece of outdoor furniture was Will's portal to the afterlife.

Hesitantly, she pressed her hand to it and listened, wishing she could feel or hear even a hint of what Will did. But she felt nothing but splintery wood beneath her fingertips. Wherever it was taking him, she was not invited.

Standing back, she stared at the place where he had died alone except for the animals, hoping, *praying* that she was already there, waiting for him on the other side.

Then she wondered where she would die. *When.* There was a place, somewhere, at this very moment, waiting for her to arrive. It was a strange thought, but it didn't frighten her as it once might have. She hoped, when the time came, she was as ready as Will was now. Perhaps something would sing to her? A sweet melody like Will's, calling her home? Turning toward the door, she took a deep breath.

It was time to say goodbye.

The sun had gained the horizon outside, and it shot through the barn in horizontal beams. She walked through them, wishing she could hide in the darkness in between, and keep Will waiting on the other side of the door forever. But that wouldn't be fair. He *wanted* to go. And she wanted him to be happy. As happy as she…

The wind whistled through the gaps in the boards and the tin roof hummed, dragging Maggie to a stop. She inhaled sharply, pausing in the darkness between the light, and *remembered.* The elusive woman she'd been searching for—Maggie looked up into the rafters—she was here. A shiver raced down her spine as she turned, and the feelings and memories rushed back into her consciousness. "Oh…" She was *everywhere.* Maggie breathed her in as fresh tears filled her eyes. Looking down at her hands, she stared in amazement. Then she looked up.

Will was right. She had been looking in all the wrong places. But she remembered now the right places where *she* dwelled. It was here, on the edge of the unknown, between fear and action, when Maggie was suspended between light and darkness, past and future, life and death, surrounded by the belief that *anything* was possible, magic was *everywhere,* and love was indestructible, that she'd left herself.

There she is.

Maggie turned back to Will's bench and stared at it in wonder. Her sadness was still unbearable, but her fear… that was gone. It had been replaced with hope, with a certainty that everything would be okay. Fresh tears filled her eyes.

Turning back to the door, she took one step, then two more, until all that stood between her and heartbreak were the weathered pine boards of the barn that had started it all. The wood was cool against her forehead as she leaned against it. She took one deep breath, then two more. "I am Margret Anne Dubois," she whispered as her fingers closed over the rough edge of the door and her nails dug into the soft grain. She took one more deep breath, knowing it would be a while before her next one, and pulled the door open. "And I am not afraid," she whispered.

Then she stepped back into the light.

Will turned from watching the sunrise as she stepped back outside, a new woman. Or rather, an *old* one. Through her tears, she smiled. Surrounded by the glowing dawn, he was like a painting. It reminded her of a Van Gogh she'd seen. Beautiful—she hiccupped a laugh—and a little blurry.

Emotions, one after another, rolled across his face like a summer storm, coursing through her like music as the barn behind her began to hum again. And then she heard it.

The song.

Her mouth fell open as his brown hair flashed sepia in the sunlight, and goosebumps erupted across her body. His piercing eyes, that smiled when he laughed, crinkled at the corners. Her smile widened as she traced the bridge of his nose to his lips, remembering them cool and soft against hers, as the wispy tune serenaded her and sent another shiver down her spine before vanishing.

He crossed the distance between them, and swiping at her tears, she committed to memory the slope of his shoulders, the muscles in his forearms, which were always exposed under his rolled-up sleeves, his hips, his long legs, and the pair of old leather work boots she had never seen him without. A part of her wished she could go with him, but... It was not her journey. Not yet. Lines from a poem she'd once read echoed in her head. They were as true for her as they were for him.

He stopped just in front of her. "What are you thinking about?"

"A poem." Her voice wobbled as she wiped her eyes again.

His smile squeezed her heart. "Which one?"

"By Whitman.

'Not I, not any one... else can travel that road for you,
You must... travel it for yourself.

It-It is not far," she stuttered, gasping for air and the rest of the words.

He wiped her tears and finished the verse with her.

"... it is within reach."

Will's arms closed around her. "God, I will miss you," he whispered against her hair. "And I'm so glad our roads crossed, even if it was only for a little while."

She flung her arms around his neck. "I'll miss you t—"

His lips closed over hers, and for once, instead of rushing by, time stood blessedly still. His hands bunched into fists in her hair as his mouth moved over hers, sending shock waves through her body. Tiny needles pricked her everywhere as the universe pulsed around them, and he groaned. "I love it when you do that." His calloused hand brushed her cheek. "I love the way you love me, Maggie." Will's voice broke against her lips.

Her nails dug into his back as she held him. Her tongue slid between his teeth, and she tasted him. Cool and minerally, like a stone. He groaned again and pulled harder on her hair.

She wished they could stay like that forever, to feel the love in her heart flowing out of her into him, and back again, as it was now. How could Fate bring them all this way, only to rip them apart now? It seemed so cruel.

His tongue flicked against hers, sending another jolt down her spine. But it was too late for all of that now. Will was ready to move on. And she'd promised to let him go. So, she did the only thing she could. She kissed him back while she had *now* and poured every ounce of love she could spare into it. It had to be enough to last him until it was her turn to join him.

It was Will who finally pulled away. "I love you, Maggie. More than I ever thought possible."

"I-I—" The hand of goodbye closed around her throat and squeezed the air out of her lungs.

"And I'll be waiting." His voice was rough.

The pressure in her head returned as the tears slid down her cheeks. She wanted to answer him, but the words were trapped in her throat.

He wiped her eyes and smiled. "But no rush."

She laughed.

"*You must habit yourself to the dazzle of the light and of every moment of your life,*" he said, quoting another section of the same Whitman poem. "I want you to live a long, full, *happy* life."

She nodded, not trusting her voice. She would. She knew that now.

"Stay out here," Will said, his voice barely a whisper, as his hands moved over her cheeks and hair. "I don't know if I can do it —" His voice broke again. "…if you're there."

She nodded again, part of her wishing she were actually dying rather than just feeling like it, so then they could be together. So, *then* she would be able to speak, and tell him how much she loved him instead of suffocating on the seconds until he was gone. But the other part of her knew her road had not ended yet. She had more to do here. More to be.

He cupped her face in his hands. "Who knows? Maybe it won't even work, and… I'll be right—"

She shook her head. No. She did not need false hope now.

"Sorry, I—"

Taking his head in her shaking hands, she kissed his lips, then stared helplessly into his eyes through her tears, hoping he could see everything she couldn't say.

He pressed his forehead to hers. "Promise me you won't go on the roof again?"

Another small laugh slipped out of her mouth.

Her thumb throbbed as she drew it over his mouth. She nodded as he pressed her palm to his mouth and kissed it. "And only artificial Christmas trees from now on."

Squeezing her eyes shut, she nodded again.

"I'm going to go now."

His words closed around her heart, crushing her insides, and she wanted to scream, beg him not to go. But she nodded again.

"I love you," he whispered, and his voice sounded just like it had on that first day.

Now was her last chance. Her last chance to tell him.

"I... l-love you... t-too," she stuttered. They didn't even sound like words. Inhaling, she tried again. "I love—"

Maggie's arms collapsed as she stumbled forward.

Her eyes flew open and darted around wildly until they found him. Her last glance of Will's broad shoulders as he passed through the barn dragged her to her knees. Gravel bit into her palms as she hit the ground, forcing the air from her lungs. Stuffing a fist into her mouth, she pressed her head to the ground, trying to keep the scream inside until she was sure he was gone. It pounded against her eyes, the screeching pressure feeling like it was about to crack the sutured bones of her skull apart.

Tremors wracked her body as she tried to breathe, and she wanted so badly to peel away from the moment, to escape the pain, but she didn't. Because she was not that woman anymore. Pressing her palms to the dirt, she lifted her head off the ground, letting the fresh air and her sadness fill her. Part of love was loss, and part of loss was the terrible, soul-crushing grief that was blazing through her now. The shrieking inside welled up again as an icy wind blasted past her. Maggie's head snapped up, and she stumbled to her feet. Was that it? Did that mean he was gone? She took a step toward the barn then stopped. What if he was still there?

What if he isn't?

Both made her want to scream. Spinning around, she ran for the house, as the wail she'd been holding back clawed its way up her throat and ripped the quiet morning in half.

Maggie gripped the railing, throwing herself onto the porch. Her knees gave way, and she fell into the floor, gasping for air. Scrambling on hands and knees, she reached for the knob, twisting frantically. The door opened, and she crawled in and slammed it shut as another scream freed itself from her throat. Pressing her hands to her mouth, she tried to silence it, not because she wanted to stop it, but just because it was so painful to hear.

But as soon as that one was gone, another took its place.

And another, because that was what a body did when it was in pain. It screamed until it couldn't, then wailed until it couldn't, then cried until it could not anymore.

EVENTUALLY, her voice stilled, and the tears stopped. The pain and sadness were still there, sharp as pieces of glass in her mind, but her body was weaker, and her throat had grown too tired to cry. She didn't have the energy to get up, and she had nowhere to be, so she stayed where she was, lying on the rug by the door watching motes of dust drift through the sunlight that streamed through the window, as the day pretended that nothing out of the ordinary had happened.

The buzzing of her phone on the coffee table drew her around, and she finally sat up, blinking, wondering if perhaps she'd fallen asleep. She got to her feet, despite the weight of the empty house, and went to get it.

She sat on the couch, where only an hour before, she had slept in Will's embrace. She picked up her phone. It was a text from Eric.

Happy Thursday, Mom!

She stared at the first word. *Happy?* Looking up, she stared into the fireplace. The clock ticked quietly in the kitchen. Happiness. Joy. Did she still know what those words meant?

She looked out the window toward the barn. Will was gone. In her heart, she knew it. She didn't know how, but she just did. Her eyes fell to the photo on the wall beside it, and instead of breaking more, her heart overflowed. Did she know what happiness meant? Unbelievably, yes. Yes, she did.

She had her memories, and she had her beloved barn, and the rest of her life to make into whatever she wanted. She had Eric and Dahlia, and she had the hope of seeing Will again someday.

Sniffling, she texted Eric back. **I love you. Happy Thursday.** She would be okay. She *was* okay.

She dialed Dahlia next. Her friend picked up on the second ring. "Hey, baby. What's up?"

Maggie's heart swelled again at the comforting sound of her best friend's voice.

Her own voice got lost again for a moment, and her tears returned. She swiped at them, trying to steady her breath.

"Maggie? Are you al—"

"He's gone," she whispered.

"What? Are you okay?" Dahlia's voice was sharp with worry.

Maggie took a deep breath and cleared her throat. "Will is... He's gone, Dee."

"Oh..." There was a pause. "I'm on my way."

"No." Maggie shook her head. "I don't—"

"I said I'm on my way."

"I need a little time by myself."

"No, you—"

"But will you come up after work tomorrow? Plan to stay the weekend? I think by then I'll be ready for a little cheering up."

Dahlia was silent on the other end of the line.

"They opened a new restaurant in town. It's on the water. We'll go," Maggie insisted.

"Are you sure?" Dahlia didn't seem convinced at all.

But Maggie was. She needed to mourn for a little while on her own. Be with herself, and her sadness, and whatever else welled up within her before she could lean on Dahlia's comfort. "Yes. I'm sure."

"Okay. Hey, I need you to do me a favor," Dahlia said. "I need you to get a screwdriver."

Maggie frowned. A screwdriver? She wanted to ask what for, but Dahlia continued before she could.

"He told me it's the second one from the bottom. The one that creaks. He said you'd know. You're gonna have to wedge the screwdriver under the step and pop it up. He left something for you…"

CHAPTER TWENTY-NINE

WILL WIPED HIS EYES AS THEY ADJUSTED TO THE DARK. THE SONG no longer sounded like it was coming from the barn. Now it sounded like... He pressed his hand to his chest. It sounded like it was coming from him.

He looked back toward the door, knowing Maggie was just on the other side.

He'd *almost* backed out. He'd almost told her to grab a book of matches and burn the whole damn barn to the ground. But then—he stopped in the middle of the floor and closed his eyes—the pull... It knew what buttons to push, and every tug felt like *her. Her hand on his arm, her hair beneath his palm. The rush of her breath against his lips.*

He went to the bench, seeing it fully for the first time in ages. She had dusted it off, and it was ready for him. Did he just needed to touch it? Or sit on it? His heart banged against his ribs as he took a seat. *Her smile. The way she holds a cup of coffee in her hands.* So, this was it? It was finally over? It seemed impossible. He had been there for so long. Two lifetimes, really. The pulling sensation lessened slightly, but the joy remained as he leaned back against the wall and laid his palms on the wood. *Her face when she sees something magical. The reflection of the stars in her eyes...* Will closed his eyes and took a deep breath. *The smooth skin of her back beneath his fingertips. Her silhouette bent over a sheet of paper. The light that erupts from her body when she thinks of him.* His insides began to hum with a strange vibration, in time to the music, as a feeling somewhere between ecstasy and homecoming enveloped him like a cocoon. He sank into it. *Her lying beside him. The spokes in her eyes as she holds his face in her hands and smiles.*

"Erhem."

Will's eyes flew open.

Bob stood before him, looking embarrassed, as the music died to the whisper of the wind through old boards.

"I just wanted to, um, say goodbye."

Will smiled. The old man had turned out to be an unexpectedly good friend in the short amount of time they'd known each other. "Thank you for coming."

"For what it's worth, I got a real good feeling about where you're going."

Will nodded. "Thank you."

"And you deserve every minute of happiness you find when you get there." Bob winked.

Will frowned, not sure what to make of the gesture. He sure hoped so.

"A part of me wishes I could go with you, but... another part of me is okay with where my journey has led me." Bob grinned. "More than okay really."

Instead of jealousy, Will felt glad for him, that he and Maggie had each other. "Take care of her for me?" he asked.

Bob laughed. "Who? Maggie? Have you seen her lately? What that woman can't do, I'll tell ya. We both know she can take care of herself just fine."

Will smiled. That was true.

The old man gave him a look he couldn't quite decipher. "But... just the same. I'll make sure she's looked after." He winked again.

Will smiled. "It's been a pleasure knowing you, Bob. In life, and death."

"In life and death," Bob repeated, shaking his head with a chuckle, and scratching the back of his neck. "Well, you take care now."

"You too."

The old man hobbled back into the darkness and disappeared.

Will closed his eyes again listening to the wind, and waiting for the song and the ecstasy to return.

Only they didn't. There was no pull to the bench anymore either. He opened his eyes. Why was the music gone? He pressed his hand to his chest, trying to focus on the vibrations, but they had faded into a familiar thump beneath his ribs. His heartbeat? No, that wasn't the sound he wanted to hear.

Taking a deep breath, he rolled his shoulders, closing his eyes again. "Maggie... Maggie," he repeated under his breath. But the more he thought about her, the way her hair stuck out from under her hat, and the fire in her eyes when she was angry, the harder it became to keep his ass on that damn bench. Rubbing his temple, he exhaled, and readjusted his position. "No... no, no. Come on!"

His knee bounced as he waited, five then ten minutes. Or maybe it was seconds. Either way, it felt like an eternity. But the only thing he felt was mounting frustration and an intense desire to flee the barn, wrap her in his arms, and never let go.

"Come on!" he bellowed, flinging his eyes open.

The birds took flight in the rafters, and a few escaped through the open at the crest of the barn. Had Fate changed its mind? Or had he done something wrong? Had Bob interrupted the process? "Damn it!" It *had* to work. He pressed his finger into his eyelids. He couldn't put Maggie or himself through this hell twice.

He sat, not knowing what to do. Should he wait longer? Or—

A low whistle filled his ears, and the hair on his arms stood on end. It slid up an octave, then back down and was joined by another. For a moment, he thought it was the song. But then he realized it was only the wind... A chickadee landed on the windowsill, watching him from outside. Or was it? The notes changed, sank into a soul-steadying ohm, as the hair on his arms rippled. *Great love,* his mother's voice echoed in his head. He closed his eyes and saw Maggie as a young woman, sitting in the dirt in the sunlight, smiling *at him*. The pull returned, *finally,* only… His eyes flew open, and he jumped up, heart thumping. Now it was going the wrong way. Instead of toward the bench, it was pulling him… "Maggie?" It was urging him *outside*. Toward the house. Toward *her*.

"Maggie?" He called again as the ohm deepened and filled the barn and the rest of the sparrows took flight and disappeared.

Will looked down at the bench. Had the whole thing been a test? He turned toward the door. Had he passed it? His breath caught. Or was this what failure felt like? A shiver raced down his spine as Maggie tugged at him again. Or maybe it was just his own desire. He looked at the bench and felt nothing. Whatever had drawn him there before was gone.

His breath quickened as he leaned down and pressed his palms to it. "If you want me to go, you'd better do it now, or I'm going back," he shouted over his shoulder.

Still nothing happened.

"I mean it. I will not leave her again," he warned, pushing back and spinning around. The chickadee in the window fluttered off as the song in the barn faded.

"Last chance!" he yelled, as it swelled in his heart, blossoming like wildflowers after a storm. The pull became an irresistible longing to touch her, as his eyes settled on the door—*"Maggie"*—and he was filled with a feeling of joy and homecoming twice as powerful as the one that had led him into the barn. It was all the proof he needed.

Will broke into a run.

A second later, there was a crack, and his vision went dark as something slammed into his face and he fell on his back. Blinking away stars, he sat up and touched his nose. It hurt like hell. When he pulled his fingers away, they were wet.

He licked his lip and tasted blood. "What in the—"

Jumping to his feet, he pressed his hands to the wall he'd tried to walk through. It was solid and rough beneath his palms.

"What in the hell?" he mumbled, feeling his way along it to the door.

He didn't even remember Maggie closing it. Gripping the side, he pulled. It rolled open easily in his hands, without so much as a squeak, and he blinked in the blinding sunlight. "Maggie?" Will shielded his eyes. Where did she go?

Even though it had only been minutes, the thought of holding her again made him breathless.

"Maggie!" he cried, stumbling like a newborn foal across the driveway. He stopped in front of an SUV he didn't recognize. Had Bob traded in his old truck?

Maggie.

Will took the steps in one leap. "Maggie!" he cried in relief. He was so happy he could cry. He *knew* it wasn't over between them. Maybe it was not ideal, but they would figure it out. And they would do it together. And when she did eventually die, he would go too then. Maybe that's what today was about. Just a glance at what lay ahead, and proof that it wasn't his time... yet.

He threw the door open. "Mag—"

A man leaped out of his old green chair, and Will froze. *Connor?* What was he doing here? Will looked back outside. That was *his* car? Had Maggie asked him to come? When—

"Who are you?" Connor asked, looking worried. He held up his hand to someone in the kitchen and shook his head, warning them back.

Will's heart nearly did a backflip as he crossed the room. "Maggie?"

He turned the corner to find Dahlia standing in the middle of the kitchen. She'd cut her hair, and it was styled like a boy. "Dahlia?" What was she doing here? He looked back at Connor. What was going on? When had everyone arrived?

She dropped the glass she was holding, and it shattered at her feet. "Will?"

The scent of lemons and sugar filled the air.

Something strange was going on, but right now, he just needed to find Maggie. "Where is she, Dahlia?"

Dahlia pointed out the kitchen door. "She's out by the road picking—"

Wildflowers. Of course she was. The glass ground beneath his feet as he rushed to the door.

"Wait!" Dahlia called. He turned, and she held out a towel. "Your face."

Will touched his bloody lip, then took the towel, and raked it across his nose and mouth. The pressure brought tears to his eyes. He looked up at Dahlia.

She nodded. "Better. Go."

He raced out the door and jumped off the steps, blinded again by the sun as he stumbled across the yard. He spotted her immediately and a roost of butterflies took flight in his belly. She was in the ditch, between the west field and the road, picking flowers. She wore a red and black plaid shirt, a pair of blue jeans cut indecently short that showed off her long, tanned legs, and the same muck boots she'd worn when they watched the sunrise over the creek.

Will broke into a flat-out run. "Maggie!"

Stumbling through the grass and the dirt, he raced along the rows, leaping over the dried yellow leaves. "Maggie. Maggie!"

As if in slow motion, she turned.

Will's chest burned as he ran, and his cheeks ached from the grin plastered on his face. "Maggie!"

Her fingers gripped the corner of her sunglasses, and she pushed them on top of her head, in the exact same fluid motion she had all those years ago, as he would get to watch her do, for at least a while longer, and the song in his heart exploded. It was the same tune the barn had sung, the same sweet anthem that followed him whenever he was with her. And it urged him on, begging him to run faster.

Laughing like a lunatic, he leaped over the last row. "It didn't work!" he said breathlessly. "I don't know why but—"

Her terrified expression brought him to a stop at the edge of the field, where the black dirt gave way to shimmery shafts of wild grass, and long stems of goldenrod.

Her lips parted as the purple asters and Queen Anne's Lace she'd collected fell from her hands. The skin beneath her sunburned nose and cheeks paled. Will stared, not understanding her distress. Why was she looking at him like that? "Maggie?" Why was she looking at him like she didn't know who he was? For a terrifying moment, he wondered if he'd imagined it all. Their friendship, her love, everything that had happened between—

"Will?" Her voice was a barely a whisper.

He exhaled in relief. She remembered him. It wasn't a dream. "It didn't work!" He smiled, feeling deliriously happy for the first time in his life. He took a step toward her and shrugged. "I don't know why—"

She stumbled back and held her hand up between them, warning him back. Tears filled her eyes. "Will?" she repeated, her voice filled with disbelief.

His smile faded. Why wasn't she happy to see him? He searched her eyes. Was she in shock? To be fair, he felt a little overwhelmed himself. "What's wrong?" He tried to make a joke. "You look like you've seen a ghost."

Instead of making her laugh, it brought more tears to her eyes. "Have I?"

He took another step, and so did she, back toward the road. He paused again, not understanding anything he was reading in her face. Fear. Sadness. Something wasn't right. Why would she be afraid of him?

Then he noticed her hair. It was longer. *Longer?* And lighter. Instead of cattails, it reminded him of the deep shimmery caramel-colored June beetles that appeared in early summer. The soybeans he'd leaped over finally registered in his brain.

He turned around and stared at the field, dried and yellow. *Soybeans?* But they hadn't even planted yet. He spun back around.

"What in the hell is going on?" he demanded.

Maggie looked like she was going to faint. "Wh-where have you been?"

Will looked over his shoulder toward the barn and threw his arms up. "What do you mean where have I been? You just saw me fifteen minutes ago."

"Two years," she interrupted.

Will's heart paused in his chest, and he swayed. He must have heard her wrong. Two years? No. "I'm sorry, what?" It had only been a few minutes. Hadn't it?

"You've been gone almost two..." The suffering in her voice was sharp as it faded away.

His eyes went back to her hair, and then to the ready-to-harvest crop, and his stomach knotted. He turned, inspecting the landscape he knew by heart, and the knot twisted. Some things were the same, but others... The woodpecker tree was gone. And the scraggly brush that had crowded the creek was suspiciously missing too. Will turned and looked at the house. And those shutters hadn't been there this morning, had they? His mouth went dry.

He turned back to Maggie.

"But I just... We just said goodbye," he said, helplessly.

She shook her head.

"Two years?"

She nodded.

He pulled his fingers through his hair. He'd been gone two *years*? But... gone *where*?

She licked her lips. "Well, almost. A year and a half really, I guess. But it's felt like... forever."

"What month is it?"

"September."

"September?" It didn't make any sense.

"September twenty-thir..." she gasped. "Oh my god."

"What?"

"Today is the day you died." Tears filled her eyes.

He stared at her. "It is?"

She nodded again. "What are you?" The fear was back in her voice.

"What do you mean?" He took another step, and she backed up the opposite side of the ditch and onto the gravel road, out of his reach.

Will turned and looked back toward the house. The monarchs in his chest stilled. *Connor.* "Oh god." He was too late. He found Maggie's eyes and searched them again. Was that why she was crying? "You're with Connor—" All the air was sucked from his lungs, and he couldn't get the rest out.

She shook her head. "No."

Breath seeped back into them. "You're not?"

She shook her head again.

"Then, what is he doing—"

The corner of her mouth lifted briefly. "He and Dahlia... They're together."

Will's brows went up as he pressed a hand over his heart. *Thank god.* "Oh. That's—"

"Come here," she demanded in a wobbly voice.

Will squeezed his eyes shut in relief. *Finally.*

He crossed the ditch, snatching a bunch of daisies as he went. His smile faded as she backed up into the middle of the road. "What are you doing?" he asked, stopping at the edge of the gravel.

"Come here."

He shook his head. "You know I can't."

"Just try."

Will rolled his eyes. "Maggie, I'll just end up back in the—"

"Please!" Her voice was harsh. "J-just try, Will!"

He sighed. "Okay. Fine."

Lifting his foot, he reached for the gravel with the toe of his boot.

His mouth fell open as it landed on the gritty road.

He stared down in disbelief as his heart sang again and the

butterflies resumed their flapping inside his chest. "What in the *hell?*"

Maggie's muffled sobs joined the symphony in his head as he lifted his other foot and placed it beside the first.

"*What...?*" he choked.

Will stared at his feet. Then he looked at Maggie who looked like she might faint. "But..." He couldn't go on the road. He turned around. He couldn't leave the land. "How..."

"Come here." The fear in her voice was replaced with hope.

Will finally understood the question she was asking. He looked back at his feet, and stared at the answer. *He was human again.*

"Will?"

His head snapped up.

"Will?" she choked.

He closed the distance between them in four determined steps.

"Are you—"

Yes, he was.

Their mouths collided as he dragged her into his arms, and he tasted her for the first time. Lemons, and sugar, salt. Tears stung his eyes, and he squeezed them shut, as the barn's song swelled, and her name rolled through his head like an unforgettable refrain. After all those years, he'd finally made it. If heaven existed, this was it. Life, her. She dug her fingers into his neck and swept her tongue between his teeth, and his legs buckled.

Will fell to his knees, clinging to her as she ran her shaking fingers over his hair.

"Will? Will?" she repeated over and over.

He pressed his face to her stomach, wiping his wet cheeks on her shirt. *He was human again?* He squeezed her, feeling like he might faint. *He'd been given a second chance?*

Maggie fell to the ground in front of him, and her arms snaked around his neck. Anchoring her fingers in his hair, he groaned as she found his lips again. He could feel her hunger, and he wanted nothing more than to be devoured. Shoving him back, she climbed on top of him, deepening the kiss as she straddled him in the middle of the road. He was about to laugh, but looking up into her smiling, tear-stained face as she leaned back and tucked her hair behind her ear, then at her body riding his, he lost his damn mind instead. Dragging her mouth back to his, he wrapped her hair around his fingers, as his other hand found her thigh and followed it up under her short pants and panties, to her hip and around her backside. Her skin was smooth against his palm. Moaning, she leaned into him in all the right places, and his body answered her, never feeling more whole. *Dear god*, he loved this woman. He kissed her until his lungs screamed for air, then pushed her back, gasping. He also needed to get her somewhere decent immediately. "I am not... making love to you in the middle... of the road."

"Why not?" she laughed. She meant it as a joke, but the look in her eyes begged the same thing her lipstick from Dahlia had.

The wind blew, swirling her hair, whispering in his ear, *there she is.*

His body pulsed as she leaned down and touched his face. He caught a peek down her blouse... Jesus, yes, there she was, and they needed to get inside *now*, before she turned him into a liar.

He pushed her back and leaped to his feet, dragged her to hers. Laughing, she cupped his face in her hands and shook her head. "How?"

He shook his head, not quite able to catch his breath. "I don't know." He sucked in air. "And I don't care," he added, pulling her down the road.

She dug her heels in. "Wait!"

He turned.

Her smile faded, and fear flashed across her eyes. "You're really here? I'm not dreaming?"

"Do you dream of me often?" he demanded, needing suddenly to know if she did.

Tears filled her eyes again, and her voice broke as she answered him. "All the time."

He kissed her hard on the mouth. "I love you. Come on."

Grabbing her arm again, he prayed they made it upstairs before he became too impatient.

"What's the big hurry—"

Turning, he scooped her up and tossed her over his shoulder like a bag of grain. "You're too slow," he growled, as he stalked down the driveway.

Squealing, she pressed her hands into his back. "Will! Put me down!"

Her behind wiggled on his shoulder, and he stifled a groan. That was definitely *not* happening.

Stomping up the steps, he threw the door open. Dahlia and Connor turned from where they'd been watching from the window. As they passed, Maggie laughed and said, "Connor, this is Will—"

He thumped up the stairs.

"Will, Connor!" she yelled.

Will kicked the bedroom door open. "Nice to meet you," he hollered before slamming it shut. Maggie laughed again, a gloriously happy sound he'd never tire of, as he set her down in the middle of the room and then... His mind went blank, and he froze.

It had been close to a *century* since he'd been intimate with anyone, and he and Meredith had never shared anything more than... necessary relations. *Twice.* "Jesus," he said under his breath, realizing he'd never made love before.

Fear flared in Maggie's eyes. "What's the matter?"

"No," he reassured her. "It's not that, it's just I haven't—I don't know—" *I'm practically a virgin?* He could *not* say that.

Her eyes went from his to his pants, where his desire was quite obvious. "I do."

Pulling her shirt over her head, she went to him. He barely had time to appreciate her rather enticing underclothes before her mouth was on his again. Her fingers fumbled with the buttons of his shirt, as the most delightful sounds issued from her throat. When she finally got it undone, her palms pressed against his chest, and she groaned against his lips as she pushed it back off his shoulders. His hand slid around her waist, and he felt the dip in her back, the one he'd discovered that day in the woods, and followed it up to her bra. He hesitated, not knowing how to unclip it, as her hand reached behind her and unclasped it for him. He slid the thin strap of lace down her arms before discarding it as she dragged him to the bed. As they fell into the bed, his dream came back, the good parts, and he remembered how to love her. She rolled him on his back, trailing kisses across his chest.

The rest of their clothes vanished, and the universe retracted until all that remained were her lips and whatever part of his body they were on. His eyes closed as she touched him. *Oh god.* He heard a low moaning sound, then realized it was him. *He* was moaning. And he couldn't stop. *Oh god.* Dragging her lips back to his, Will's hands slid over her skin, exploring every dip and swell she possessed. When his breath ran out, he pushed her back and stared up at her breathtaking body. The gentle slope of her shoulders, the mind-altering curve of her breasts, the plane of her stomach and the scars that crossed it, one horizontal and thin, the other vertical and still red.

Her pull became a roaring current, and his body hummed as she drew him in. And *then* he understood.

The song had felt like Maggie because it *was* her. She'd been the destination all along. That was why it was so irresistible. That was why he couldn't deny it, because it was *her* bringing him *here* all along.

Will pulled her back down, and her hair fell around them as she met his eyes. He pushed it back over her shoulders, drew his hand around the back of her neck, and touched her cheek. "I love you," he whispered. "I've never wanted anyone like I want you, Maggie. And not just this—all of you."

She put her lips next to his ear, and a shiver raced down his spine. "Love me, Will."

So, he did.

CHAPTER THIRTY

MAGGIE BRUSHED HER FINGERS OVER THE GOLDEN HAIRS ON HIS chest and shook her head. After all this time, he was back? And he was *human*? She tried not to think about it, but it seemed too good to be true.

Will cocked his head so he could see hers. "What?"

She pushed the thought away. "What happened to your face?"

Laughing, he touched his nose. "I ran into a wall."

Hiding her smile, she asked. "Does it hurt?"

He chuckled again and shook his head. "No."

Or maybe it was just the right amount of good to be true. She propped herself up on her elbow, loving everything about her life in that moment. The joy in her heart, the warmth of his side against her chest, his scent as it mingled with hers.

"I wondered what you'd smell like."

He stared at her for a moment before a look of pure horror crossed his face. "Dear god, I didn't even think—" He tried to push her away, but she snuggled back down and threw her naked leg over his.

"I wasn't complaining, Will."

"I'm sorry—"

Maggie propped herself up again and frowned. "You wanted to make love to me. Don't ever apologize for that. As a matter of fact, I'd like to do it all over again as soon as possible, if you're not too tired."

Will laughed and pushed her hair back. "Women in this time

certainly are different than they were when I was alive... the first time," he added for clarity.

She knew what he meant. "Or maybe we just have more freedom to say what's always been on our minds."

"I'm almost afraid to ask, but... what do I smell like?"

Maggie leaned over and pressed her nose to his throat. "Like a dusty field, like sweat, cut grass, and fresh cut planks of cedar." Pressing her hand lightly to his chest, he inhaled sharply as she ran her tongue from his collarbone along the side of his neck to his ear. "And you taste like salt..." She kissed the sharp corner of his jaw. "And clay..." She kissed his lips, taking the bottom one between her teeth and pulling. "And sunshine."

"Well," he said against her mouth. "That doesn't sound so bad."

She smiled. "It's not."

He took her wrist and, in one fluid motion, had her pinned on the bed beneath him. He bent down to kiss her, but was interrupted by a ferocious growl from his belly. Maggie laughed. "You must be *very* hungry."

He nuzzled her neck as his hands swept down her side, covering it in goosebumps. "It can wait."

"Are you sure?" she asked rather breathlessly.

"You said as soon as possible, did you not?" His lips tickled her neck, then her sternum.

Her heart thumped against her ribs as a shiver went down her spine as he moved lower. She buried her hand in his hair. "I—Oh, god, Will."

He smiled up at her. "No. Not a god. Not even a ghost. Just a man. Who is mightily and madly in love with you, I might add."

She pressed his mouth back to its task, and her back arched in pleasure.

A man was all she needed, she thought, as Will loved her body and brought her to pleasure again.

WILL RESTED his head on her stomach, and she ran her fingers through his hair as her heartbeat decelerated back to its normal pace. So, this was what it felt like to live out her wildest dreams? A smile tilted the corners of her mouth. It was like she'd died and gone to...

"Are you sad you didn't end up in heaven?" she asked.

Will turned his head and pressed his lips to her stomach. "How do you know I didn't?" he asked, lifting himself onto his arms and leaning over her.

"I'm serious."

"So am I. How could heaven be better than this right here, right now?"

"Does that mean that I'm in heaven too?"

"I think our souls are just rejoicing."

He was quoting her poem again. "So, heaven has come to us?"

Will fell onto the bed beside her and propped himself up on his elbow. "I believe it did."

It was a beautiful thought. "Oh! I got your gift. The one you hid beneath the stairs." She squeezed his hand. "Thank you."

Will was quiet.

"I thought when you said my notebook was destroyed, it was gone."

"It almost was, but I had the time on my hands." He laughed. "So, I carefully separated the pages and dried them out."

"And then you filled in all the blank ones with your own..."

"Heart."

"Yes. I felt you in every page. I could almost imagine I was standing beside you as you sketched and wrote. Your poems were lovely." They had curbed her loneliness, but not filled it. Tears filled her eyes. "I missed you so much."

"I know the feeling well." His stomach growled *again*, and his hand bounced on her stomach as she laughed.

"You really need to eat something."

He kissed her and then rolled onto his back. His stomach gurgled again in apparent agreement. "I think you're right."

Maggie got up and put her underclothes back on. Slipping her shirt over her head, she deemed it long enough to slip downstairs in. If she had her way, neither of them would be wearing pants or anything else for the rest of the week. "I'll go grab something and be right back."

The stairs creaked as she crept down, and she smiled as she always did when her foot hit the second step. Smoothing her hair, she peeked around the corner into the living room, hoping she didn't look as thoroughly loved as she felt. "Dahlia?"

Her friend wasn't there. Maggie tip-toed into the kitchen. That was empty too. But there was a note on the table.

The place started to feel a little crowded... and loud. Decided to head home early. Call me when you get a chance. I have questions. Love you babe. Dee

Pressing a hand to her blushing cheek, Maggie smiled and set the note back on the table. She went to the stairwell. "They left," she shouted. "It's safe to come down."

Will appeared at the top of the stairs in just his pants, and Maggie fell against the wall. Had she just made love to *that* magnificent man?

He met her at the base of the stairs and said, "Whatever you are thinking, I like it." His stomach growled again.

She wrapped her arms around his waist and kissed him. "I'm thinking you better hurry up and eat before you die of hunger." Her hand flew to her mouth as she realized what she'd just said. "Oh—I…"

He smiled and put a gentle hand on her shoulder. "Relax."

She shook her head. No, she didn't want to jinx whatever was happening. "I shouldn't have said that."

"Afraid you're tempting fate?"

She met his eyes. "I'm afraid of a lot right now."

When Will didn't ask for clarification, she knew he was wondering the same things she was. What if this was just a brief stopover on his way out? What if this was just a chance to say goodbye? Or worse yet, what if it was just a beautiful dream, and when she woke, he was gone again?

For months after he'd gone, she had dreamed of him. Beautiful, peaceful, happy dreams, only to have him stolen from her each morning. It had been excruciating to experience the loss over and over. She had almost left. But the only thing worse than being reminded of him in every little thing was not being reminded at all. The few nights away from the farm, visiting Dahlia, for Eric's ball games, and Dean's fortieth birthday party made it so easy to feel like none of it had happened, that Will was just a fantasy, and he'd never really existed. And while that might have appealed to her before... She was not that woman anymore. The memory of Will was worth the pain. The experience of knowing him was worth the loss. *She still loved the gift she'd been given, even though it had been taken away*. It had taken a while, but she'd finally found the gratitude she should have had all along, and she had moved on. She really had. But now that he was back...

Will's stomach rumbled. "Don't look at me like that."

Maggie blinked. "Like what?"

"Like I might disappear any second."

She pressed her head to his chest. "How do you know you won't?"

"I don't, but I won't waste whatever time we have being afraid."

He had a point. She sighed, and he reached for the top button of her shirt and popped it open. Maggie's insides lit up. "What should we do then?"

"First..." He nuzzled her neck as his fingers worked the next button, exposing her bra. "… I want to write a thank you letter to whoever makes your underclothes."

She laughed as her shirt fell open.

Will's rough hands caught on the lace of her panties as he picked her up and set her on the counter. "Then I want to make love to you…" He kissed her lips, sliding his fingers up her sides and over her breasts. "… until I know your body like I know this land. And *then*—"

His stomach gurgled pitifully, and his shoulders sagged as she giggled.

Pushing him back, she slipped to the ground. "Eat. Please."

"But I don't want—"

"Put your stomach out of its misery, Will. Besides," she winked at him, "You'll need your strength if you plan to satisfy this woman."

He burst out laughing, and Maggie's heart overflowed.

Wrapping his arms around her, he nuzzled her hair. "God, I'm glad I survived long enough to hear women talk like that." His hands slid beneath her shirt again.

Her grin widened as she pushed them down. "No, you don't."

"Fine." Releasing her, he turned toward the refrigerator. "What have you got to eat around here?"

Maggie went to the door and pulled it open. She had plenty of food, but what would he be in the mood for after a seventy-year fast? "What do you feel like? There is some chicken in here. We were going to grill—"

"Oh my god," Will said.

Maggie spun around. He was staring out the window.

At the *barn*.

Her fear surged as she clung to the refrigerator door. "What?"

Will turned, smiling. "You painted the barn?"

She righted herself and pressed a hand over her wildly pounding heart as the door of the fridge swung shut. "Oh. Yeah, I did."

"Are you okay?"

Blood thudded in her ears. No. "Yes." She thought it was calling him back.

"Maggie?"

"I just thought you meant…"

He looked at the barn and back at her. His smile faded. "Oh. I… I'm sorry. I didn't mean to scare you."

"No. It's okay. I'm just a little…" She couldn't find the right word. Nervous? Terrified? Deliriously happy and afraid it was all going to be ripped out from under her any moment now?

"Me too."

She went to stand beside him, and he tucked her against him as he looked back over the yard. "I painted it by hand, actually. Rented a cherry picker. You cannot imagine how many gallons of paint that thing absorbed."

"And… you rebuilt the coop too?"

She nodded. She'd also rebuilt the toolshed out back and had concrete poured in the barn. "Yeah. There have been quite a few changes since you've been gone. Bob helped out quite a bit before… He passed away last fall."

"He was a good man."

"Yes, he was."

"I'm glad he came to see me off before I left."

She frowned. "Bob didn't come that day."

Will gave her an odd look. Then squeezed his eyes shut. "Where I was headed…" he muttered, opening them. "*He* came to see me before *he* crossed over."

"He did?"

"I think… Somehow, he knew I was coming back."

Maggie smiled. "Did he seem happy?"

He was silent for a moment. "I think he was."

"I'm glad."

He turned and grabbed an apple out of the bowl on the table. "Come on. I want to see what you've done."

"But what about food?"

"This will do." He took a bite. "I want to know everything. What did I miss while I was gone?" he said, heading for the stairs.

What did he miss? Quite a lot, actually.

"Bring my pants down?" she called after him.

"Not a chance." He shouted from her bedroom, making her laugh.

Grinning, Maggie went to the closet and pulled on her boots.

A few moments later, they were on the porch, he with no shirt, her with no pants, walking down the steps.

"So, tell me everything," he said.

"I quit my job in the city. My heart just wasn't in it anymore."

Will laced his fingers through hers. "What have you been doing, then?"

"I took up photography again. I don't know if you noticed, but the guest room is a dark room now. There's a gallery in Lakeside that sells my photos. And I host events in the barn now. Mostly weddings." As they neared it, she grabbed his arm. "You don't hear anything, do you?"

Will shook his head, swallowing another bite of his apple. "Nope. Not a peep. So, weddings, huh?"

Now that he was back, she wondered what he'd think about all the changes she'd made. "I know that's where you died, but... It's also what gave you to me, and it's brought so much joy to my life. I..." What if he didn't like having people around the way she did, or sharing the land? "I just wanted to share that with..." Or using his mausoleum to host weddings? *Jesus*, what had she been thinking? "We can stop. I can cancel everything if you don't want to—"

Will dragged her to a stop. "I love it, Maggie. Sharing our magic, filling the barn with love." Pushing her hair back, he smiled. "Maybe that's what brought me back?"

Maybe it was. She thought of Will's song. The one she thought she heard that day too. "It still sings. People love it."

"I know, I heard it."

Holding on extra tight to his hand, just in case, she slid the door all the way open. He gasped as she flipped on the overhead strings of lights. She'd left his bench where it was. And the milk jugs. The contractor looked at her like she was crazy when she told him to pour the floor around them. "Your workbench is part of the bar. And we fill the old trough with ice and drinks."

"Oh my god. It was so dark, and I was in such a hurry, I didn't even notice before."

"I couldn't evict the swallows after reading your poem about them, so we keep the tables under a tarp and power wash the floors before events."

Will shook his head. "It's gorgeous, Maggie. Truly." He turned to her. "Have *you* ever thought about getting married in here?"

Her breath caught in her throat. Was he asking if she'd met anyone since he'd gone? If so, the answer was no. But if he was asking if she'd want to marry *him*... "Do *you* want to get married?"

He touched her cheek. "I couldn't care less if we are married. Either way, I will choose you every day for as long as I live." He tucked her hair back behind her ear. "But I would love to see you beneath these lights, walking toward me... in a white dress..." He pulled her against him and his lips found her ear. "... or nothing at all."

Maggie's insides sparked as he kissed her neck.

"The latter can be arranged immediately," she said breathlessly, sliding the door closed.

Buttoning her shirt, Maggie dragged her hand through her mussed hair and pulled Will to his feet. Shaking his head, he gave her a sideways smile. "Well, that was a first."

"Really? You mean you never... did the deed out here?"

Wrapping his arms around her, he shook his head and kissed her. "Nope."

That made her smile. "But you're a farmer."

His eyes crinkled. "What exactly do you think farmers do all day, Ms. Dubois?"

She winked at him and pressed her palm to his chest. "I only care what *this* farmer does, and I hope it's more of what we just—"

He cut her off with a kiss as his hand reached around her backside and squeezed.

Laughing, she broke away and pulled the door back open, letting the sunlight back in.

"So that's it?" he asked, reaching for her hand, returning to their earlier conversation. "That's all I missed?"

Was it? "Oh. No. I wrote a book of poetry too." Then she remembered that wasn't quite true. "Shit."

Will tilted his head. "What?"

She'd always imagined she'd have his blessing for the things she done, but she *had* done them assuming he'd never know. "Well, *we* did."

"We did what?"

Maggie stared at her boots, not sure how to explain. Would he be angry? "I-I did it early on…" When the pain was still fresh. When she couldn't close her eyes without seeing his face or walk the land without hearing his voice beside her. She searched his eyes. Would he feel betrayed? "… as a way to cope. I-I didn't think you'd mind. I didn't use *all* of your writings. The ones that were addressed to me, or felt private I kept for myself," she rushed, "but the others —They were so beautiful and they spoke to me, comforted me, brought me so much joy when I was down. I didn't want them or the way they made me feel, or-or what we shared here to disappear after I was gone. I thought—"

"It's okay, Maggie." Will's eyes were soft and full of love. "I'm not upset."

She let out the breath she was holding. "You're not?"

He shook his head. "What did you call it?" he asked.

Smiling shyly, she bit her nail. "*The Second Step.*"

He pressed a chaste kiss to her lips and laughed. "It's perfect."

"It's also a New York Times Best Seller."

"Really?"

"Yeah, they keep calling me to do The Today Show. That's a news program, but..." Time had helped her move on, but her *longing* for him had remained as strong as it was on the day he left, and the ache in her heart was sharp enough to draw tears every time someone smiled and said '*So, tell me about W.M.*' She had only done one interview, and it had been disastrous, rendering her a blubbering mess.

"But what?"

Tears flooded her eyes. "I've been happy, Will. I really have. But still..." Sniffling, she swiped at them and shrugged as they rolled down her cheeks. "When I thought about you, when people asked me about you... This is what happened. I wasn't even sad, really." She huffed a sad laugh. "Not *all* the time, anyway." She sniffled and shrugged again. "I just missed you s-s-*so* much."

Will wrapped his arms around her, and she fell against him, reminding herself there was no longer a reason to cry. He was here. "I didn't want to cry on national TV," she confessed.

He smoothed her hair against her head. "I was only gone ten minutes, and it was unbearable. I can't imagine..." His voice was soft. "I'm sorry I made you wait so long." Then his laugh rumbled beneath her ear. "But boy, am I glad to be back."

She squeezed him. "Me too."

"I'm not dreaming, am I?" he asked, stealing her earlier line.

She smiled against his shirt then leaned back. "Do you dream of me often?" she asked, stealing his.

He wiped her tears away with his thumb. "Every day for the last... twenty years. First as a friend, and now... in every way that a man can love a woman."

She stared into his eyes, knowing they'd go crazy if they tried to understand what was happening. It was better to just enjoy it. "If you are, then we *both* are. Come on." Grabbing his hand, she led him back outside. The past was gone, and the future hadn't arrived yet. All they had was *now*, and she wasn't going to waste it. Rolling the door closed, she smiled. "There is a full garden out back, behind the barn. Turns out I love weeding."

Will laughed, and his voice steadied her resolve.

"And I have my herbs here, as you can see."

She showed him her herb garden, the coop, and the chickens. "I have seven. The two white ones are my best layers. It only costs me about twelve dollars an egg."

Will laughed again at that.

They went past the barn to the silo. "I left the vines. They are so pretty in the summer when they bloom. And Dean came up and helped Eric and I repair the fallen bricks. Except for the one that the chipmunks live under, of course. They had *eleven* pups this year."

Will intertwined their fingers as they walked around it. "Dean comes up?"

She couldn't tell if he sounded jealous or not. "Yeah. He has become a part of my life. *Again.* We are really good friends now, actually."

"Yeah?" He didn't sound too upset.

"I guess it makes sense. We have so much history, and Eric, of course. Only Dahlia knows me better, and… It's been good for me to have someone to share that part of my life with again. He's always reminding me of good things I'd forgotten. Or maybe never appreciated in the first place."

"Like you did for me?"

She laughed. "Yeah, maybe." She turned to him. "They're coming up next weekend, actually. I told him and Ann to bring Sophie so they could pick pumpkins. Eric is coming with his girlfriend too. But if you'd rather not have visitors—"

Will interrupted her. "I would love to meet them. *All* of them. I am glad that Dean is still in your life, and has been a good friend."

She smiled. "Me too."

She followed his gaze to the tractor, out from its hiding place behind the barn. "I moved it so it could be seen from the road, and I had it repainted. It doesn't work anymore, but... I thought it was pretty, and they use it for wedding photos..." Once again, her stomach dropped. "Oh god," she said as it sunk into her love-riddled brain that she'd restored Will's murder weapon, and just confessed to using it as a wedding prop.

"What is it?"

While this place had brought *her* so much joy, his experience had been quite different. And then she'd gone and changed everything while he was away. She pulled him to a stop. "Does any of this upset you? Be honest with me. Or do you want to leave?"

Will frowned, as if not understanding the question.

"Should we go? Get as far away from here as possible?"

"Why would we do that?"

"You died here, Will. And all those years here, alone... Surely, you want to get as far away—"

"You brought me, and this place, back to life, Maggie. Quite literally, it appears in my case."

"But—"

He kissed her, then pulled her into his arms and set his chin on top of her head. His heart thumped comfortingly against her ear. "I'm not saying I'd mind a vacation every now and again. Maybe a weekend trip to Lakeside. I hear they have fantastic singles events —" she buried her head against his chest and laughed. "But this... what you've done here? My god. Have you ever seen a more magical place?"

She turned her head. The sun had dipped toward the horizon, bathing the fields, house, and the barn in a sherbet haze. Waves of dry leaves fell from the branches of the oak and rolled across the drive, as the chickadees sang, and the chickens clucked in their pen. No, she hadn't. That's why she stayed.

"This is home, Maggie. Right here, with you, in this life you've created."

She smiled up at him, then at the barn towering behind them.

She had been right. They'd healed each other. And look at them now.

Will wrapped his arms around her waist. He pulled her into a gentle hug, and her heart, once empty, overflowed. Pressing her face to his shirt, she breathed him in. That was why they'd been given a second chance. Because they had both learned how to and love themselves. And that had allowed them to *truly* love each other. And *that* had been powerful enough to bring him back, if it had ever let him go in the first place.

He pushed her back, his eyes crinkling at the corners, as they stared into hers. "There she is," he whispered, touching her cheek.

"Here she is," she agreed, smiling, as the fearless, adventurous *whole* woman who had stumbled that place all those years ago pulsed through her veins. "She's been here, waiting for you since the day you left."

He took her hand and pulled. "Come on, let's go home."

Squinting into the sun, she fell into step beside him. In his poems, Will had called her a goddess. But as they walked arm in arm back toward the house, Maggie knew she was just a woman. A woman who had chosen to *live* her life instead of simply survive it.

And that was enough for her.

ACKNOWLEDGMENTS

I'd like to thank my FB groups: Moms Who Write, Romance Writers Support League, Trauma Fiction, you all are the best, I couldn't have done it without you! My proofreaders with their eagle-eyes who combed the book for my mistakes; Kayla M., Ronnie H., Lindsay B., Aliza K., Amber W., Corrie T. ,Natalie Dale M.D. and her wonderful book A Writer's Guide to Medicine, your expertise is always appreciated.

My formatter and PA, Laura Martinez, you are my peace of mind.

Thank you to my amazing cover designer, Esther van Bokhorst-Beentjes at Meraki Cover Design. You captured the essence of my entire story in a single image, and it is breathtaking. Words cannot express my gratitude for your skill as a designer, your encouragement, and your friendship (We *are* friends now, right?).

Thanks to my editor Whitney Morsillo at Whitney's Book Works for your keen eye and understanding of commas. Lol.

A big thank you to my husband, for your encouragement and doing the dishes so I have time to write.

Last but not least, I want to thank my kids for not getting sick for the two weeks it took to write this book. Once again, *we* did it. Space Needle (round two) woohoo!

ALSO BY J.N. SMITH

Song Series

Barn Song

One ghost is all it takes to mend Maggie's heart. A single impossible choice is all it will take to break it again.

When Maggie Dubois's son leaves for college, she is left alone in a house too big for one person on a collision course with a midlife crisis. A slight detour leads her to a singles' retreat in Michigan's gorgeous lake country, and impending doom is averted. Sort of.

Instead of finding love, Maggie gets drunk and buys an abandoned, foreclosed farm. When she uproots her life and moves there, she discovers it is haunted by a farmer named William Morgan, whose spirit cannot leave the land that killed him.

Has she purchased a nightmare, or the beginning of a dream come true?

Available Now

War Song

One minute thirty-four-year-old Army Air Force pilot Matthew Morgan is plummeting to his death over eastern France, the next he wakes in a field, back home in the States. *His* field, to be exact.

Elegant eighty-four-year-old spinster and French expat, Camille Lamaire goes into the kitchen to make a cup of tea. When she returns, there is a dripping pilot falling over the chair in her living room, babbling in broken French about a war that ended seventy years ago.

As he and Camille search for answers to the questions of why he has returned home, the extraordinary happens. Something neither is expecting, and both want more than anything.

Available Now

Field Song

Nineteen-year-old Claire Morgan, born in 1906, wakes up in a field in a soiled party dress and snagged stockings with no memory of how she got there.

Twenty-two-year-old Daige Johnson is a modern-day major league football player relegated to the bench for a bruised shoulder and his third concussion.

While recuperating at his cabin in the bleak Michigan countryside, their paths collide and they become unlikely companions on the search for the truth about Claire's existence.

Available Now

The Veil Series

Book 1: **DETROIT**

Between her first cup of coffee and her daily dose of Xanax, Jane receives a cryptic warning from a trusted friend.

Get out of the city. Now!

Narrowly escaping with her children, she watches in horror as Detroit, along with dozens of cities across the globe, becomes trapped behind "Veils".

As Jane navigates the modern-day dystopia, she meets Army veteran Matt Patterson. Together they fight for her children's survival, and a future neither expected.

Available Now

Book 2: **ATLANTA**

Social influencer Katie Newman and tow-truck driver JJ Dayton have nothing in common until a mysterious 'Veil' surrounds the city of Atlanta and they find themselves amid chaos, in possession of a school bus full of orphaned children.

As the days turn to weeks and unspeakable tragedies unfold, they must band together to survive, or risk losing the only thing they have left. Each other.

Available Now

The Keepers of Samsara Series

Josephine and the Lighthouse Keeper

Josephine washes ashore during a horrific storm, injured and alone, with only a whisper of name for a past. She doesn't know where she came from, or where she was going.

Awaiting rescue, she makes herself at home in a small cottage nestled beside a candy-cane striped lighthouse perched on the edge of the sea.

As the storm rages on and the days of isolation grow, she is drawn into an enchanting world of monsters and magic, where anything can happen and nothing is too good to be true, including Josh, the ghost of the lighthouse keeper who used to live there. Or is he?

Available Now

Kiss of the Siren

Joshua Cahill is living his dream life until a chance encounter with Josephine Walsh. As soon as he touches her, he knows two things. One, he has crossed a line, and two, he never wants to stop.

Torn between his own guilty conscience, the rules of society, and a woman he cannot forget, Josh must decide what he truly wants.

Doing the right thing will cost him her.

Doing the other will cost him everything else.

Now Available

A Light in the Lantern Room

It was all a lie. Everything.

As Josephine learns the truth of her harrowing ordeal, she must come to terms with the coward she was, the Self she's lost, Josh's betrayal, the broken woman she has become, and decide once and for all; does she believe in magic or not?

Now Available

Standalones

The Bend

Tristan wakes up in a ditch on the side of a country road. Injured and in need of medical attention, he stumbles to the nearest farmhouse, looking for help. Instead, he finds Anna Boyd, the skittish ghost with a hole in her chest, who steals his heart the minute she tucks her hair behind her ear and says "Don't be afraid."

But the longer it takes for help to arrive, the more he wonders if he should be.

Now Available

About J.N. Smith

J.N. Smith is a scientist, turned mother of two amazing kids, turned writer. She enjoys reading and writing stories that bring people of all walks of life together. Her hobbies include watching her kids play on the shores of the Great Lakes and running. She lives with her husband, kids, and three chickens, in rural Michigan.

Connect with J.N. Smith Today!

Hi there! Did you enjoy reading A Light in the Lantern Room? Want to be the first to know about new books, sales, giveaways, and other exclusive fun stuff? Make sure to join my **newsletter**!

I'm always posting book news and reviews, pictures of Lake Huron, bugs (LOL), and sneak peeks of upcoming projects on my social media too. So, let's chat!

Want to join my ARC team? Fill out this **form** and someone from the team will be in touch!

Find all important links about me at https://linktr.ee/authorjnsmith